AKBAR

AKBAR

Shazi Zaman

SPEAKING
TIGER

in association with

राजकमल प्रकाशन

SPEAKING TIGER BOOKS LLP
125A, Ground Floor, Shahpur Jat, near Asiad Village,
New Delhi 110049

First published in Hindi by Rajkamal Prakashan in 2016
This English edition published by Speaking Tiger in 2021

ISBN: 978-93-5447-062-2
eISBN: 978-93-5447-063-9

10 9 8 7 6 5 4 3 2 1

Typeset in Adobe Jenson Pro by SÜRYA, New Delhi
Printed at Shree Maitrey Printech Pvt. Ltd., Noida

In memory of Amin Saheb,
my teacher at St. Stephen's College

Contents

Cast

Royalty

Changez Khan: Mongol ancestor of the Mughal emperors and creator of the largest continuous land empire history has known.

Amir Timur: Turk ruler to whom the Mughal emperors traced their ancestry; creator of a vast empire which he ruled from Samarqand in the thirteenth century. Married into the family of Changez Khan for prestige and called himself Gurkan, the son-in-law.

Zahiruddin Muhammad Babur: Gained and lost the prestigious throne of Samarqand thrice and was forced to flee and find a base, first in Kabul and then Hindustan. Defeated the Afghan ruler Ibrahim Lodhi in the first Battle of Panipat in 1526; founded the Mughal dynasty in Hindustan that was to last till 1858. He died within four years of the Battle of Panipat and left a shaky kingdom for his son Nasiruddin Muhammad Humayun. He was called 'Firdaus Makani'—dweller of paradise—after death.

Nasiruddin Muhammad Humayun: Inherited the kingdom from his father Babur but lost it to Afghan ruler Sher Shah. Battled his brothers' recalcitrance and spent some time in exile in Persia before regaining the throne of Hindustan. He soon fell to his death, resulting in the kingship falling to his teenage son Akbar. He was called 'Jannat Ashiyani'—dweller of paradise—after his death.

Abul Muzaffar Jalaluddin Muhammad Akbar: Became the ruler of Hindustan at the age of fourteen and ruled for about half a century (1556–1605). In this period, he took on numerous opponents and won every contest in the battlefield, but found his personal battle with the forces of faith the toughest. He was called 'Arsh Ashiyani'—dweller of the skies—after his death. He drew his lineage from Amir Timur's third son, Miran Shah, and Changez Khan's second son, Chaghatai, and was thus a Turko-Mongol.

Nuruddin Muhammad Jahangir: Eldest son and heir of Akbar, who had a strained relationship with his father and rebelled against him towards the end of the former's reign. Married the daughter of Raja Bhagwant Das of Amber who bore him the son Khusrau (who too rebelled). Married Jodhbai, the princess of Jodhpur. The son from this marriage was Khurram, who succeeded him as Shah Jahan, the emperor of Hindustan.

Khurram: Son of Jahangir, he succeeded his father as Shah Jahan. A favourite of his grandfather Jalaluddin Muhammad Akbar.

Khusrau: Son of Jahangir and nephew of Raja Man Singh and son-in-law to a powerful noble Mirza Aziz Koka. His rebellion was crushed and he was later put to death.

Hamida Banu Begum: An independent-minded girl who initially resisted marrying Emperor Humayun but finally gave in. Mother of Jalaluddin Muhammad Akbar. Lived till the year 1604 CE. She enjoyed the title of 'Maryam Makani'—the one with the station of Mary.

Maryam Zamani: Daughter of Raja Bharmal of Amber who was married to Akbar. This was the Emperor's first marriage among the Rajputs. Her original name is not clearly known but she was bestowed the title 'Maryam Zamani'—Mary of the age.

Shah Begum: Princess of Amber, daughter of Raja Bhagwant Das. She was Prince Salim's (Emperor Jahangir's) first wife and it is believed that both Islamic and Hindu rituals were performed at their marriage. She was given the title 'Shah Begum' when she gave birth to Khusrau. She committed suicide when Khusrau rebelled against his father.

Mani Bai: Daughter of Mota Raja Udai Singh of Jodhpur, she was married to Prince Salim. At this wedding, Emperor Akbar and Prince Salim themselves carried her palanquin. She was bestowed the title of 'Taj Bibi' and was also called Jodhbai because she belonged to Jodhpur. She bore Salim the son who later ruled as Shah Jahan.

Mirza Hakim: The younger stepbrother of Emperor Akbar, he was the son of Emperor Humayun and Mah Chuchak Begum. He enjoyed near autonomous rule in Kabul and also posed a challenge to Emperor Akbar, even becoming a rallying point for rebels within the empire. Finally, a military campaign brought him to his knees.

Hindal: Stepbrother to Emperor Humayun. Son of Emperor Babur and Dildar Begum. Lost his life fighting for Humayun against Mirza Kamran.

Kamran: Emperor Humayun's rebellious stepbrother. Son of Emperor Babur and Gulrukh Begum. Finally, Humayun had him blinded. After that, he was sent to Mecca.

Askari: Emperor Humayun's rebellious brother. Son of Emperor Babur and Gulrukh Begum. He too was sent into exile by Humayun.

Murad: The second son of Emperor Akbar, also called 'Pahadi' because he was born in the Sikri hills. He died at the age of thirty towards the end of Akbar's reign.

Daniyal: Youngest son of Emperor Akbar who died of excessive drinking in the Deccan at the age of thirty-three. He predeceased Akbar. He was married to the daughter of Abdur Rahim Khan-i-Khanan.

Bibi Mubarka: Emperor Babur's Afghan wife.

Maham Begum: Emperor Babur's wife, mother of Humayun.

Dildar Begum: Emperor Babur's wife, Hindal's mother.

Gulrukh Begum: Emperor Babur's wife, mother of Mirza Kamran.

Gulbarg Bibi: Wife of Emperor Humayun.

Bakhshi Banu Begum: Stepsister of Emperor Akbar, wife of Mirza Sharfuddin.

Ruqayya Begum: Daughter of Hindal, wife of Emperor Akbar.

Salima Sultan Begum: Daughter of Emperor Humayun's sister. She was Bairam Khan's wife. Akbar married her after the death of Bairam Khan.

Mah Chuchak Begum: Wife of Emperor Humayun and mother of Mirza Hakim.

Haji Begum: Akbar's stepmother, wife of Emperor Humayun.

Fatima: The lady who was instrumental in convincing Akbar to seek more matrimonial alliances in Delhi and Agra. This perhaps was the cause of a crisis.

Sakina Banu Begum: Akbar's stepsister, daughter of Emperor Humayun and Mah Chuchak Begum. Real sister to the rebellious Mirza Hakim.

Mirza Abul Qasim: He was Kamran's son. It seems that Bairam Khan had contemplated raising him to the throne. He died in the Gwalior Fort.

Khwaja Muazzam: The stepbrother of Akbar's mother Hamida Banu Begum. Guilty of many follies, he finally ended his life under arrest in the Gwalior Fort.

Nobles, Loyalists, and Attendants

Bairam Khan: He served three generations of Mughal rulers from Babur to Akbar. He attained the highest office of Vakil and the exalted title of Khan-i-Khanan under Akbar but was ousted when the Emperor decided to take up the reins of government himself. He was killed in Gujarat on his way to Mecca and was survived by a son, Abdur Rahim Khan-i-Khanan, who earned fame as a poet, courtier, and administrator.

Abdur Rahim Khan-i-Khanan: Son of Bairam Khan who was brought up by Akbar after he was orphaned. Distinguished himself as a poet, a general, and an administrator. He rose high in the imperial hierarchy and first got the title of Mirza Khan and then Khan-i-Khanan which had once been his father's.

Munim Khan: A loyalist of Emperor Humayun who served Akbar with distinction in the battlefield—especially in the campaign in the east—and outside. He was suspicious of Bairam Khan and thus stayed in Kabul until Bairam Khan was unseated. He was awarded the title Khan-i-Khanan and the office of Vakil that was taken away from Bairam Khan.

Maham Anga: A powerful personality of the early days of Akbar's rule who was instrumental in the downfall of Bairam Khan. Her faction lost power when her son Adham Khan Koka was killed on the orders of Emperor Akbar. She had nursed Akbar even when he had been separated from his parents in the difficult years of exile.

Shamsuddin Muhammad Atka Khan: Rose from the position of an ordinary soldier to that of a powerful noble. His wife Jiji Anga was Akbar's foster mother and for this reason was called 'Anga' while Shamsuddin Muhammad was called 'Atka'—foster father—

enjoying a high position in the court. He was killed by Adham Khan. His son Mirza Aziz Koka became a powerful noble.

Mirza Aziz Koka: Was the 'Koka'—foster brother—of Emperor Akbar and very dear to him and, for this reason, given a very long rope. He initially disagreed with Akbar's religious views and left Hindustan for Mecca without permission of the Emperor but later returned. He was a very powerful and high-ranking noble of the Mughal empire.

Raja Bharmal: Ruler of Amber, he was quick to see an opportunity in seeking a political and matrimonial alliance with the Mughals. His daughter was married to Emperor Akbar. The heir to the Mughal throne, Jahangir, was born of this marriage. Bharmal himself served the Mughal empire as a senior *mansabdar.*

Raja Bhagwant Das: Son of Raja Bharmal of Amber, a high-ranking noble of the Mughal empire. His daughter was married to the heir to the Mughal throne, Jahangir.

Raja Man Singh: Son of Raja Bhagwant Das of Amber and a high-ranking general, administrator and courtier of the Mughal empire. His father's sister was married to Emperor Akbar. He was so dear to Akbar that he called him 'farzand', i.e. son or protege. He sided with Akbar's grandson Khusrau over Prince Salim in the struggle for succession.

Raja Birbal: Then known as Birbar, he was a poet, a close courtier, and a companion of Emperor Akbar. He lost his life in the campaign against the Yusufzais of Afghanistan, which caused immense grief to the Emperor.

Raja Todar Mal: A Khatri from Lahore, he was a very high-ranking courtier and minister of the Mughal empire and was especially famous for his revenue administration.

Sheikh Mubarak: A free thinker who found merit in all faiths. Provided intellectual support to Akbar's quest to break free of the control of the ulema. Among his sons, Abul Fazl and Faizi attained fame and became part of Emperor Akbar's close circle.

Abul Faiz Faizi: Brother of Abul Fazl, an excellent poet—given the title 'Malik-us-Shora', i.e. poet laureate—and translator and a close courtier. He pursued Emperor Akbar's agenda and challenged the clergy.

Tardi Beg: He had been in the service of Emperor Humayun. Under Akbar, when he was the governor of Agra and Delhi, his inability to hold Delhi against Hemu plunged the shaky Mughal power into a serious crisis. Bairam Khan had him killed on this ground without permission from Emperor Akbar.

Mota Raja Udai Singh: Ruler of Jodhpur; his daughter was married to Prince Salim.

Ram Das Kachhwaha: He came from a humble background but rose high. He was always in attendance of the Emperor. He sided with Prince Salim when Akbar was on his deathbed.

Pithal: Prithviraj Rathore, a warrior and poet of Bikaner who was Akbar's close courtier.

Prithideep: The Rajput noble who was assaulted by Akbar on that crucial day of May 1578.

Jaimal: Son of Rupsi, who was brother of Raja Bharmal of Amber.

Rana Prasad: Ruler of Umarkot in Sind who gave refuge to Humayun and his wife and followers when they were fugitives; Jalaluddin Muhammad Akbar was born here.

Jiji Anga: She had breastfed Akbar, hence called 'Anga', and was very dear to him. Her husband Shamsuddin Muhammad Atka Khan and son Mirza Aziz Koka rose high in the Mughal nobility.

Adham Khan Koka: The ambitious, powerful, and unruly son of Maham Anga who got Shamsuddin Muhammad Atka Khan killed. Akbar immediately ordered his execution.

Qulij Khan: A high-ranking noble of the empire who served the dynasty through several generations. He had an orthodox bent of mind and took a strong stand against the Jesuit priests when he was the governor of Lahore.

Qutbuddin Muhammad Khan: Brother of Shamsuddin Muhammad Atka Khan; he was a senior noble of Akbar's court but refused to join Din-i-Ilahi, the order established by the Emperor.

Shahbaz Khan: A devout Muslim and a prominent noble who refused to join the Din-i-Ilahi.

Zain Khan Koka: Foster brother of Akbar and a prominent noble. His mother Picha Jan Anga had breastfed Akbar.

Saif Khan Koka: Elder brother of Zain Khan Koka, son of Picha Jan Anga, he was very dear to Akbar. Lost his life in the Gujarat campaign.

Mirza Sharfuddin: He was married to Akbar's stepsister and was a senior noble but rebelled against the Emperor. His slave made an attempt on Akbar's life in Delhi.

Pir Muhammad Khan: Bairam Khan's 'vakil'—representative. Bairam Khan sacked him and ordered him to go on Haj. He was sent after Bairam Khan after the latter was sacked.

Hakim Ali Gilani: One of the royal physicians, he was an expert of the Unani system of medicine and treated Akbar unsuccessfully in his last days.

Maulana Chand: The astrologer who was kept in readiness near the place of confinement of Hamida Banu Begum to record the exact time of Akbar's birth. He drew the first horoscope of the Emperor.

Jotik Rai: A prominent astrologer of Akbar's time. His advice was sought to ascertain the effect of a comet that was causing concern to Akbar and many others.

Opponents and Rebels

Sher Shah: The Afghan king who defeated and overthrew Humayun. Known for his administrative and strategic acumen. Enjoyed a short reign. His death in an accident at Kalinjar made it easier for Humayun to stage a comeback.

Islam Shah: Son of Sher Shah. Also known by the name of Salim Shah.

Hemu: Also known by the name Basant Rai. He forced the Mughals to flee Delhi. He sat on the throne of Delhi for a very short while and took the name 'Vikramaditya'. He was defeated by the Mughal army in the Second Battle of Panipat, taken prisoner and killed by Bairam Khan.

Muhammad Hussain Mirza: Descendant of Amir Timur, related to Akbar. He was defeated and killed when Akbar personally marched from Sikri to Ahmedabad in nine days and took him by surprise.

Ibrahim Hussain Mirza: Brother of Muhammad Hussain Mirza. He was married to Gulrukh Begum, the daughter of Akbar's uncle, Mirza Kamran. He also rebelled against Akbar and was defeated in Gujarat. He later died of injuries in Punjab.

Ikhtiyar-ul-Mulk Gujarati: The Abyssinian associate of Muhammad Hussain Mirza.

Ali Quli Khan: A powerful Uzbek noble who was very close to Humayun. He defeated Hemu and earned the title 'Khan-i-Zaman' in Akbar's reign. He later rebelled and was finally defeated and killed in a campaign that was personally led by Akbar.

Bahadur Khan: Brother of Ali Quli Khan-i-Zaman. He too had been close to Emperor Humayun. He too was killed for rebelling against Emperor Akbar.

Rana Sanga: Ruler of Mewar who led a Rajput–Afghan confederacy against Babur in the Battle of Khanua and lost.

Maharana Pratap Singh: Fiercely independent ruler of Mewar who did not submit to Akbar. The Battle of Haldighati was fought between him and Raja Man Singh. He fled the battlefield and could never be captured.

Jaimal: The governor of Chittor Fort, who was killed by Akbar during the siege. Akbar installed his statue at the gate of Agra Fort.

Patta: Chittor's brave warrior who was killed in the battle. His statue was also installed at the gate of Agra Fort by Akbar.

Daud Khan Karrani: Self-styled Afghan king who resisted Mughal rule. Akbar made him an offer of direct combat which he refused. Fled Patna when Emperor Akbar launched his attack but later met his end at the hands of the Mughal forces. His head was dispatched to the Emperor.

Bir Singh Bundela: The Orchha chief who killed Sheikh Abul Fazl at the behest of Prince Salim. The Prince feared that Abul Fazl could poison Akbar's ears against him and affect his chances of acceding to the throne.

Distant Allies and Rivals

Shah Tahmasp: An emperor of the Safavid dynasty of Persia who believed in guiding his subjects in religious and worldly matters. Shah Tahmasp gave refuge and help to Emperor Humayun but also forced him to accept the Shiite faith. The Safavids had declared Shiism as the state religion.

Shah Abbas: A Safavid emperor who unleashed terror against the Nuqtawi sect that believed that the age of Islam would end in the year 990 of the Hijri calendar, that is around 1582 CE, and under their messiah, the Nuqtawi religion would reach its pinnacle. Shah Abbas was Akbar's contemporary.

Shaibani Khan: He rebuilt the Uzbek empire and was ruler of the Uzbek confederacy. Babur had to give his sister in marriage to Shaibani Khan after a defeat. Shaibani Khan was killed in a battle with Shah Ismail of Persia. The victorious soldiers of the Shah ate Shaibani Khan's flesh.

Abdullah Khan Uzbek: Ruler of Transoxiana who was a clear threat to the Mughal empire. After he captured Balkh and Badakhshan, Emperor Akbar moved his capital to Punjab to keep a close watch over the situation. He drew his lineage from Jochi, the eldest son of Changez Khan.

Sultan Murad III: Ottoman emperor and Akbar's contemporary. Ruled from 1574 to 1595 CE. Hejaz, including the holy cities of Mecca and Medina, was part of the Ottoman empire. He expressed displeasure at the activities of the Mughal emperor's relatives in the holy city of Mecca.

Sharif Abu Nomay II: He was the ruler of Mecca and was under the Ottoman emperor. Ruled from 1524 to 1584 CE. Mecca saw peace and prosperity under him.

Phillip II: The Spanish Habsburg monarch who in 1580 became the king of Portugal and its overseas territories. He took interest in Jesuit activities at the Mughal court. It seems Akbar wanted to make a pact with him against the Ottoman Turks. However, nothing came of it.

Men of Religion

Pope Gregory XIII: He was keen to convert Akbar to Christianity and wrote a letter to persuade him.

Ibn-i-Arabi: Born many centuries before Akbar, he is known for his pantheistic thoughts. He believed that all creation is a manifestation of the divine light and different religions are thus the same. He is believed to have been a major influence on Emperor Akbar.

Sheikh Abd-un-Nabi: Held the high office of Sadr-us-Sudur which dealt with matters of religion and land grants to men of religion. His opinions were deemed final in matters of faith. However, his overbearing attitude along with Akbar's own desire to exercise supremacy over forces of religion led to his downfall. First exiled to Mecca, he was later found murdered in the custody of Abul Fazl.

Makhdum-ul-Mulk Abdullah Sultanpuri: A high-ranking cleric of the Mughal empire. He was held in high esteem by the Afghan and the Mughal emperors till he paid a price for disagreeing with Emperor Akbar. He was also exiled to Mecca along with Sheikh Abd-un-Nabi.

Mir Sadr-i-Jahan: Was a compliant Sadr-us-Sudur and a member of the Din-i-Ilahi. He also enjoyed Prince Salim's confidence.

Sheikh Qutbuddin: He challenged the Jesuit priests to an ordeal by fire to test whose Book and faith were true but the Jesuits did not agree to it. Akbar did not like him.

Mullah Muhammad Yezdi: He declared that it is a religious duty to rebel against Emperor Akbar.

Qazi Yaqub: He declared that the scourge of God is being visited upon Akbar in the shape of rebellion.

Shah Tayyab: A cleric who bitterly opposed Akbar.

Sayyid Muhammad: He belonged to Jaunpur and in 1495 CE declared himself the Mahdi—the promised messiah, the guide who would strengthen religion, the path shown by whom Muslims would follow. Inviting the wrath of the ulema, he was forced by Sultan Mahmud Begarha, to leave Gujarat. He died in Herat about half a century before the accession of Akbar but his followers—Mahdawis—were very much around and active in Akbar's reign.

Mustafa Gujarati: He was a prominent Mahdawi of Akbar's time who fell afoul of the Islamic clergy for his views. He was brought in chains to debate with the orthodox clergy in Fatehpur Sikri in the presence of Akbar. The Mahdawis believed that a person from the Prophet's family would come to show the path to humanity. Around the millennium of the Islamic calendar (1590–91 CE), there was considerable interest in the possibility of the appearance of a Mahdi, a guide. But the followers of Sayyid Muhammad believed that the Mahdi—Sayyid Muhammad—had come and gone.

Sheikh Alai: A Mahdawi saint who took on the ulema. He was given lashes on the orders of Islam Shah and died.

Sheikh Salim Chishti: Belonging to the Chishti order of Sufism, he had his hospice in Sikri where Emperor Akbar came seeking his blessings for an heir to the throne. When the heir was born, he was named Salim after the saint. Such was Akbar's regard for him that an elaborate capital city was built in Sikri.

Vallabhacharya: The founder of Pushtimarg—the way of fulfilment through divine grace.

Shri Gosainji: Vallabhacharya's second son and successor, Vitthalnath is called Shri Gosainji in devotional *varta* literature. He organized and expanded the Pushtimarg.

Swami Haridas: Vaishnav saint-musician of the Braj region. Tansen is believed to have been his disciple.

Surdas: Saint-poet of Vaishnavite tradition who lived in the Braj region. According to Vaishnavite tradition, Akbar and Surdas did meet but the latter refused to sing the Emperor's praise.

Govindswami: A Vaishnavite poet of the Braj region. According to the Vaishnavite tradition, Akbar came to listen to him in disguise and Govindswami was angry when he recognized the Emperor.

Kumbhandas: A saint-poet of the Braj region who, according to the Vaishnavite tradition, was summoned to Sikri by Akbar. Kumbhandas then expressed his irritation in a piece of poetry.

Dastur Mehrji Rana: The Parsi priest from Surat who came to the Mughal court and is believed to have influenced Emperor Akbar's interest in fire worship.

Rudolf Acquaviva: Was the youngest of the three Jesuit priests and yet named leader of the first Jesuit mission which came to the Mughal court to convert Akbar without success. He belonged to a notable family of Naples. His desire for martyrdom was achieved in Salsette when he was killed while breaking idols.

Antonio Monserrate: Born in Spain, he was part of the first Jesuit mission to Akbar's court. On the orders of Emperor Akbar, he taught Portuguese to Prince Murad.

Francis Henriques: The Jesuit priest who was born in Persia and converted to Christianity from Islam. He came to Akbar's court as a member of the first Jesuit mission with an intention to convert him but failed.

Benoist de Gois: Member of the third Jesuit mission to Akbar's court; stayed at Lahore for eight years.

Jerome Xavier: Member of the third Jesuit mission; related to Father Francis Xavier. He wrote a book in Persian on the life of Jesus for the benefit of Emperor Akbar and others in the Mughal empire.

Emmanuel Pinheiro: Also a member of the third Jesuit mission to the Mughal court. He was the pastor of Lahore.

Hiravijaya Suri: Jain saint who was invited to the court by Emperor Akbar to gain an understanding of his faith. Subsequent to the visit, the Jain community gained major concessions from Akbar.

Vijayasena Suri: He was Hiravijaya Suri's successor in Akbar's court and became a target of the Brahmins.

Bhanuchandra: The Jain saint who had considerable influence over Akbar and taught him the significance of one thousand names of the sun. For this reason, he was bestowed the title 'Patshah Akbar Jalaluddin Surya Sahasranamadhyapak'.

Bhattacharya: A Brahmin who engaged in a theological debate with the Jain saint Vijayasena Suri at the insistence of Emperor Akbar.

Devi: The Brahmin who was pulled up to the balcony of Emperor Akbar's sleeping apartment at night to explain matters of the Hindu faith.

The 'Unknown Brahmin of Mathura': He created a storm by making a temple from the construction material kept for a mosque and using intemperate language against the Prophet. The Sadr-us-Sudur—chief of all clerics—Sheikh Abd-un-Nabi sentenced him to death, creating a crisis for Emperor Akbar.

Chroniclers

Abul Fazl: An intimate courtier who was the official spokesman of the Emperor. He wrote *Akbarnama,* which is a history of Akbar and his ancestors. It was a huge image-making exercise in which Abul Fazl elevated Akbar to the level of a leader with spiritual and divine attributes. However, Abul Fazl could not complete it as he was killed by Bir Singh Bundela because Prince Salim saw him as an obstacle in the path to kingship. Abul Fazl was a very vocal instrument in Emperor Akbar's battle against the clergy.

Mullah Abdul Qadir Badayuni: A bitter but silent critic of Emperor Akbar. Entered the court at the same time as Abul Fazl but did not rise as high as him. Unsettled by Akbar's liberal attitude, he wrote *Muntakhab-ut-Tawarikh,* a highly critical account of his reign from an orthodox perspective. This book was discovered after his death.

Gulbadan Begum: Daughter of Emperor Babur and Dildar Begum, stepsister to Humayun. She was adopted by her stepmother Maham Begum. She wrote an account of Humayun's reign called *Humayunnama.* She was very dear to Emperor Humayun. Gulbadan Begum lived through the reign of three emperors—Babur, Humayun, and Akbar.

Bayazid Bayat: Had joined the service of Humayun in Persia and thereafter served Munim Khan. In this capacity, he had the opportunity to closely observe events associated with Emperor Humayun and Emperor Akbar. He recorded this history to aid Abul Fazl in writing *Akbarnama.*

Jauhar Aftabchi: Emperor Humayun's ewer-bearer, a very close attendant, and a chronicler of the early years of the Mughal dynasty as he saw it.

Abbas Sarwani: On the orders of Emperor Akbar, he wrote *Tarikh-i-Shershahi,* a history of Sher Shah.

Arif Qandhari: An employee of Bairam Khan, he wrote the first history of Akbar's reign called *Tarikh-i-Akbari.*

Banarsidas: He was a trader from Jaunpur who did not personally know Emperor Akbar but lived during his reign and beyond. He documented in his work *Ardhkathanak* the situation around him and the state of his own mind when Akbar died.

Narottam: He wrote *Mancharitra Raso* in praise of Raja Man Singh.

Amrit Rai: He wrote *Mancharit* in praise of Raja Man Singh.

Author of *Dalpat Vilas*: His name is not known to us but it is clear that he was writing for a Rajput prince and was most likely present when Akbar had a fit—*'baalat-i-ajeeb'*—on the full moon night of May 1578 CE. He offers a crucial clue into the troubled mind of Jalaluddin Muhammad Akbar.

Artists

Tansen: Akbar's favourite musician and a prominent Dhrupad composer and performer. He came to the Mughal court from the Rewa court. He was born in Behat near Gwalior.

Keshavdas: Eminent poet who enjoyed a high station at the Orchha court.

Mir Sayyid Ali: Persian artist hired by Humayun. Given the title 'Nadir-ul-Mulk'—rarity of the age.

Khwaja Abd-us-Samad: Persian artist hired by Humayun. Given the title 'Shirin Qalam'—one with sweetness in his pen. He and Mir Sayyid Ali laid the foundation of the Mughal atelier.

Other Poets: Gang, Jadda, Qasim-i-Kahi, Sheikh Rahai, Mullah Sheri, Naziri Nishapuri, Sant, Holrai.

Other Artists: Mansur, Govardhan, Hiranand, Madhu, Basawan, Manohar, Daulat.

Author's Note

None in my time has seen Akbar; had we lived in his era, we might well have. For, throughout his reign of fifty years, Akbar spent about half his time travelling across Hindustan. Barring a few days of this half-a-century of rule, he gave *jharokha darshan* to his subjects every morning, and met—and even spoke in person—with a wide variety of people in his darbar, his *Ibadat Khana* (place of worship) and at gatherings.

This novel begins at a critical juncture in Akbar's life. An 'intense feeling' gripped him, a feeling that was described by a historian of his time as a strange state, a *haalat-i-ajeeb*. Akbar's disciple, the articulator of his inner voice, as also his chronicler, Sheikh Abul Fazl in *Akbarnama*, Nizamuddin Ahmed in *Tabqat-i-Akbari*, and Mullah Abdul Qadir Badayuni in *Muntakhab-ut-Tawarikh* have all described this state but none could claim to fully understand it. In recent times, historians Athar Ali and Iqtidar Alam Khan have tried to explain it. In course of my own investigations, I came across a text called *Dalpat Vilas* which indicates that this 'strange' behaviour was at its most acute at night.

It is evident from this Rajasthani text that its author—whose identity is not known to us—was watching from very close quarters when the state overcame Akbar. The Emperor's 'incoherent' utterances at that moment, as recorded in *Dalpat Vilas*, offer crucial insights into his mind. The symptoms mentioned by the chroniclers of the time could even be diagnosed as bipolar disorder. Alternatively, Jalaluddin Muhammad Akbar's state could now also be diagnosed as temporal lobe epilepsy. It is possible that, after a phase of temporal lobe epilepsy, a person's mind acquires fresh insights and finds solutions to issues it had been grappling with. Akbar's haalat-i-ajeeb could be reflective of a reasoning that is beyond the comprehension of most ordinary human beings. It also seems that Akbar was dyslexic. Obviously, it is not possible to definitively understand Akbar's state because he is not personally available for examination, though it is also true that we aren't always in a position to fully understand personalities physically present around us either. However, if we do analyse Akbar's psyche on the basis of modern scientific knowledge, he could be regarded as a remarkably intelligent person in deep turmoil over the complexities of life and extremely desirous of changing the status quo. The author of *Dalpat Vilas* deserves our gratitude. His account enabled me to partially decode some parts of Jalaluddin Muhammad Akbar's sensitive personality and throw some light on his obvious unease over religious and worldly issues.

Subject to what is briefly explained in the note towards the end of this book, this novel is a work of historical fiction, a period piece. Such a work demands that the author lay down his idea of what part is history and what is fiction in his work; what is the fidelity he observes towards the period and what are the pieces he creates on his own. I believe that an author has a sovereign right to create his characters and his period, but if he is talking of people who once walked in flesh and blood in a period that did exist, he has to observe fidelity towards facts to make the period and the person believable. This, however, does not make the author a helpless chronicler. An author of historical fiction has huge room to manoeuvre. In this space lay the opportunity for me to understand Akbar.

History records facts but seldom surmises as to the state of mind, and definitely not the mental journey which brings people to the point where we see them make momentous decisions. In case of Emperor Akbar, this is all the more true. He did not record his state of mind, but very clearly, he did have a mind of his own. As an author of fiction, I have tried putting myself in his shoes—and mind—to understand why he arrived where he did. In a way, I have tried to enter the backstage to the happenings in the Akbarian arena. This task needs imagination but the story is not imaginary. It is drawn from reality.

Writing a novel devoted to an exploration into the state of mind of Akbar as he took on matters of faith, I had to build a picture in my mind and then reproduce it for my readers. This picture comprises the people and circumstances around Akbar, the memories he inherited, the influence he was open to and how these moulded his thoughts and how these thoughts in turn shaped his actions. For this, I had to draw upon accounts, monuments, inscriptions, and pictures to bring my context to life. So as to not compromise the fidelity of contemporary sources, I have chosen to liberally use excerpts (from the works I consulted) as they help in creating the period piece I intend my novel to be. Where sources fall short or silent, I have exercised the inalienable right of a novelist—that of imagination.

As I went through the texts, pictures, and material remains of those times to piece together Akbar's life and thoughts, very often the historical trail went cold. When facts did not support my quest for details of specific episodes from the life of Akbar and his contemporaries, I tried to reach as close to the 'truth' as was humanly possible. For example, history records Akbar's victories in religious and temporal spheres, but my surmise is that he must also have recollected these on his deathbed. Where I fell short of facts in creating the 'right' ambience, I tried to complete the picture in alternative ways. For example, on the night of the 'strange sensation', *Dalpat Vilas* records that Akbar drew out his dagger in agitation but it gives no description of the dagger. Here I assumed that the dagger was as shown in the miniature purporting to relate to the day immediately following: especially as an eyewitness to the next day's events records that the Emperor was seen in the previous night's clothes. Where sources failed to offer even this bit of detail, I had to fall back on my imagination. There is no record available of the carpet of the room where the Emperor lay dying, but we do have many samples of the carpets of the period. I used one such design to complete a picture of Akbar's last illness. Thus in the setting the novel creates, it strives to be closest to 'truth', if not the absolute truth. However, I would like to emphasize that despite being historical, the novel is entirely mine in the manner it is woven. Only writers of fiction have the liberty to create a work of this nature, not historians!

History has recorded in substantial measure what Akbar and his associates did. For this I am grateful to Sheikh Abul Fazl who wrote *Akbarnama,* which is a detailed account of the Emperor's life and beliefs, and to Mullah Abdul Qadir Badayuni who wrote *Muntakhab-ut-Tawarikh* in secret to spite the Emperor. I am grateful to Rahim, Tansen, Banarsidas, and the Vaishnav poets, whose writings indicate what they and Akbar thought of each other. The accounts of Jesuits, 'Mahdawi' Mustafa Gujarati, and

Jain saints helped me understand the Emperor's mind and faith. I am grateful to these saints and godly persons. I am also grateful to Akbar's grandfather Zahiruddin Muhammad Babur for *Tuzuk-i-Baburi* (*Baburnama* in Persian), to Akbar's aunt Gulbadan Begum for *Humayunnama,* to Humayun's employees Jauhar Aftabchi for *Tazkirat-ul-Waqiat* and Bayazid Bayat for *Tarikh-i-Humayun,* to Arif Qandhari for writing the first history of Akbar's period *Tarikh-i-Akbari,* to Akbar's son Jahangir for *Tuzuk-i-Jahangiri,* to Abbas Sarwani for *Tarikh-i-Shershahi,* to Amrit Rai for *Mancharit* and Narottam for *Mancharitra Raso,* and to Mughal emperors and their nobles for their buildings and paintings, which even now offer an insight into how they lived.

Akbar was not merely a historical figure; he was also acutely conscious that he was making history. And he tried to ensure that future generations see him as he wished to be seen. Every Mughal miniature of his atelier and royal buildings of his time were commissioned by him and made as he wished them made, and each and every word of *Akbarnama* was written by his permission and vetted by him. We may not see these relics the way Akbar wanted them to be seen, but they do tell us how Akbar wanted himself to be seen by people then and thereafter. That is why they valuable clues into his mind.

In a work of fiction—even though historical—I deem it needless to cite references at every step. However, some references and detailed acknowledgments would definitely be in order to unburden myself of the thought that I might be robbing Abul Fazl or Mullah Abdul Qadir Badayuni, their translators, and many others (which includes recent historians) of credit. This is not a work of History but there is substantial history in it within a creative framework. The quotes and details in the novel are drawn from various sources: published English and Hindi translations of Persian or Sanskrit texts or inscriptions and those in other languages; published and unpublished Persian, Sanskrit, and Braj sources; published and unpublished Mughal miniatures (many studied directly in museums); secondary sources, i.e. works of academic historians. Instead of attribution at every quote, I have included a bibliography towards the end along with an author's note. Of course, I have updated, abridged, or simplified the quotes where necessary.

Since the events and characters in the novel are real, I have given a genealogy—including all relevant characters from Zahiruddin Muhammad Babur down to his fifth generation—and a table of significant events to make sense of the complexities of Mughal life and politics.

I originally wrote this novel in a language that Akbar would have spoken if he were alive now. His language lives in today's Hindustani, in which I wrote. At one place, an obscene and colloquial word has been used. Since an original text mentions this word as spoken by Akbar, I have made no effort to camouflage it. This indicates that, in a moment of stress and tension, the Emperor spoke in a language he was comfortable with. Obviously, the particular word was in common usage then, as it is now. I have used many words that were in common usage then but are not understood now or have since changed meaning. I have, therefore, added a glossary. While a word may have multiple meanings, only the meaning relevant to this novel has been included in the glossary. In some places, the articulation of some characters can seem long-winded. I appeal to the readers to be patient as it is important to understand the manner of articulation of those times to get an idea of the age. It must also be noted that in some conversations recorded in medieval times the sentences seem to imply something that is not very obvious from the text but the two persons involved seem to understand. It shouldn't be an obstacle, however, in this book for the reader to comprehend the general drift of such dialogue.

I have chosen to refer to the central character of this work as Akbar Badshah, Badshah Salamat, Abul Muzaffar Jalaluddin Muhammad Akbar, or Arsh Ashiyani (as he was posthumously known). Where a character has referred to 'Badshah Salamat', 'Hazrat Badshah', or 'My King', it means the emperor who is a contemporary of that specific character. Likewise, I have called Humayun as Nasiruddin Muhammad Humayun, Humayun Badshah, or Jannat Ashiyani Humayun Badshah (as he was referred to posthumously) and Babur as Zahiruddin Muhammad Babur, Babur Badshah, or Firdaus Makani Babur Badshah (as he was called posthumously).

In Akbar's time, prominent courtiers, *mansabdars*, and officials had titles attached to their names, which could be taken away, changed, or transferred from one person to another. For example, Abdur Rahim was first awarded the title of Mirza Khan and thereafter Khan-i-Khanan. His father Bairam Khan also had this title of Khan-i-Khanan and after him Munim Khan as well. For this reason, a mere Khan-i-Khanan is not sufficient to identify a person. Likewise, Man Singh was a 'Kunwar' in the lifetime of his father Raja Bhagwant Das. He became Raja Man Singh after his father's death. I have tried to associate each character with the title he had at a particular moment.

The pronunciation of a name, and the way you write it, changes with time and place. This novel has Hindu, Jain, Muslim, Parsi, and Christian characters. There could be a difference of opinion on how to pronounce and write some of these. Some names are not pronounced today as they were in Akbar's time. Some names were even then pronounced differently in different areas, or among different classes or communities in a particular part of the world. For example, the Christian priests would not have pronounced their name the way Sheikh Abul Fazl did. To resolve such issues, I have tried to articulate names as they are understood today. If Birbal is referred to as Birbar in an original text I have quoted, I have not changed it. Everywhere else in the novel, I have referred to him as Birbal or Raja Birbal.

Most places mentioned in this novel exist even today. With the passage of time, some names have changed to a small or large extent. I have mentioned these names as they are written and understood now. If a particular place has disappeared from the map, obviously I have used the name as it was taken when it existed.

I have enclosed a map of the land that Akbar ruled, as also the lands that were relevant to the rule. In addition to all important places within the Mughal empire, the map especially shows those places which are linked to the story in this novel. I am grateful to Faiz Habib who completed the map of Akbar's empire and the world around it in a very short time.

Jalaluddin Muhammad Akbar began a new calendar—Ilahi, also called Jalali or Julusi—which was deemed to have begun from his accession. Although the accession took place on 14 February 1556 CE, which was the second of Rabi us-Sani 963 of the Hijri era, and fourth of Phalgun 1612 of the Vikram era, the Ilahi calendar was deemed to have begun twenty-five days after 'Navroz', which was the first day of the first month Farwardin of this calendar. This was the twenty-eighth day of Rabi us-Sani of the Hijri calendar, the thirtieth day of Chaitra of the Vikram era 1612, and the eleventh day of March 1556 of the Christian calendar. Taking the Ilahi calendar as the base, I have included a table at the end that shows the beginning of each year of the Ilahi calendar along with the corresponding dates in the Hijri, Vikram, and Christian calendars because all four find mention in the novel. For the period preceding Akbar's, I have used Hijri, and for Akbar's period mostly the Ilahi calendar. I have done so because Zahiruddin Muhammad Babur and Nasiruddin Muhammad Humayun measured time by the Hijri calendar and Akbar himself measured it in the Ilahi calendar. Abul Fazl himself in his account preceding Akbar's accession has used the Hijri and in the account after accession the Hijri along with the Ilahi calendar. For the sake of convenience and comprehension, I have given Christian dates along with Hijri and Ilahi dates in this novel. Vikram, Hijri, Ilahi, and Christian calendar dates quoted in original documents, statements, or buildings have been reproduced verbatim.

There is a complexity involved in the conversion of Hijri, Ilahi, or Vikram calendar dates into Christian calendar dates. Just about midway into the reign of Jalaluddin Muhammad Akbar, in 1582, the Christian calendar was changed from Julian to Gregorian, though despite this, until 1752, the English-speaking nations continued to use the Julian calendar. Converting a date of the Hijri, Ilahi, or Vikram calendar into the Christian calendar would yield a difference of ten days between Julian and Gregorian dates. In addition, the day starts with sunset in the Hijri calendar and with midnight according to the Christian calendar. It is generally recommended that the dates before 1582 should be measured in accordance with Julian and the dates after that in accordance with the Gregorian calendar. Given the complexity, however, if the date mentioned varies by a few days, I would seek your indulgence.

In those days, as also now, the idea of good and bad omens held great significance in the life of the commoners as also the elite. A course of action would depend upon astrology or reading of omens in the actions of an animal, bird, or human being. The time of taking action was also decided in a similar fashion. Through similar means, people tried foretelling the future. Such instances occurring in the novel should not be assumed to be unreal. In that age, this was not something people would be ashamed of admitting. It finds a place in the novel as a regular part of people's life in those times.

I have also tried to correct some of the errors that had crept into the original Hindi edition.

Work on this novel began in my childhood. I must have been four or five. While playing with children in my neighbourhood, a boy my age said, 'Muslims are bad people.' Even at that age, this was not a surprise to me. Whatever be the strata or place, a child soon enough gets to hear and speak things of this nature. Obviously, it is a result of the influence of elders. Another child of my age said, 'No. Their Akbar was God.' Even at the age of four or five, I felt as if somebody had saved my honour. When formal education began, I got to learn closely about Akbar. In my school days, a team of the Education Department made a surprise visit to our classroom. When a member of that team linked Akbar's thoughts with the secular stream in India, I began reading about Akbar. I do not know the name of the member of the team but I wish to thank her for the inspiration. After that, I had the privilege of learning at the feet of my teacher Muhammad Amin (Amin Saheb) and understood the real meaning of Akbar's *sulh-i-kul*. I was his lifelong student and he spoke to me about Akbar till his last days. This novel is the result of his teaching and blessings. He is no more but he lives on in the hearts of his students.

Radhika Bordia, Madhuker Upadhyay, Dr Amit Gupta, Sajid Shapoo, and Anand Bordia have been associated with this work since the time it was just in my mind. Their indulgence made the task of understanding and explaining *Akbar* easier.

My heartfelt gratitude to Naved Masood, who patiently guided me through difficult linguistic and historical issues in the course of the writing of *Akbar*, and thereafter in its translation into English. It takes extraordinary dedication to go through a bulky translation twice.

Life would be incomplete without my wife Rumana, our children Tara, Arzoo, and Kabeer, and my siblings Shahida Perveen, Afroz Zaman, and Sheeba Nudrat.

From my first novel till the time I wrote *Akbar*, I had been blessed by Namwar Singh. He was my father's contemporary and belonged to an era that is very dear to me. His loss has robbed me of a guide. If Rajendra Yadav were alive, I could have answered the query he posed every time he met me: 'What have you written? Get it for *Hans*.' I still remember a small note from my childhood which he had sent to Papa with a book—'Khwaja Saheb, do read this book. If you can't, ask Shazi Saheb to read it.' As a result of his encouragement, whatever I wrote in his lifetime was published in *Hans* magazine. Krishna Sobti, a titan of Indian literature, will be deeply missed. Her encouraging words when she released my first novel in the year 2002 gave me strength to keep writing.

How can I *remember* my father Syed Muhammad Khwaja Badiuzzaman? One needs to remember those who may have been forgotten. I can only speak to the one who resides in me and say, 'I have carried your work forward.'

The loss of my mother Sayeeda Khatoon is so fresh in my memory that one is unable to fully express it in words. It seems that life has reached its loneliest point.

I am grateful to Ashok Maheshwari and Satyanand Nirupam of Rajkamal for publishing my works in Hindi, to Ravi Singh for introducing *Akbar* to the English-speaking world, and to Nazeef Mollah for his diligence.

I begin this tale with the words of Sheikh Abul Fazl—who was the articulator of Jalaluddin Muhammad Akbar's thoughts and ideas—from the initial pages of *Akbarnama*.

'Alas, I am no seller of words to seek approval from people. What more blessing can there be than this, that my loyal heart be the receptacle of lordly tales, that my mind be the resting place of these divine subtleties. I frame these night-illuminating jewels as ornaments for the ears of the minds of lovers of wisdom.'

SHAZI ZAMAN

The twenty-second of October 2020 CE

Part One

1

'Gai hai su Hindu khavo! Aur Musalman suar khavo. Naje hudiyar naanje ain khavo to hudiyar karahi vichi vaho ar randho, je hudiyar hunta suar hoi to Hindu Musalman rali khavo. Je gai hoi to Hindu Musalman ral khavo. Je suar hoi to Musalman khavo je gai hoi to Hindu khavo. Kyun oon devimishra hoiga.'

That full moon night, Abul Muzaffar Jalaluddin Muhammad Akbar was in a trance-like state, shouting incoherently, sacrilegiously, asking Hindus to eat beef, Muslims to eat pork. And if that didn't work, to fry lamb in a pan, and if it turned into pork, Hindus and Muslims should partake of it together, and if it turned into beef Hindus and Muslims should have it together; if it became pork, Muslims should have it and if it was beef Hindus should have it, and thus a divine miracle would happen.

Terrified nobles could hear Badshah Salamat's words but not make sense of them.

It was the third of May of 1578 CE, the twenty-third regnal year of the Ilahi calendar. Jalaluddin Muhammad Akbar had crossed the Jhelum barely ten days ago and pitched his camp at Bhera. By royal orders, one of the biggest qamargah—great hunt—of Timuri history had been set rolling. With the river marking a fixed line, beaters and soldiers of the Mughal nobles drew an arc across eighty kos from Khushab to the hills near the border fortress of Rohtas. About fifty thousand soldiers participated in the great game on the frontier of the Mughal empire. With the beaters and soldiers moving in steadily, the terrified animals had now been hemmed in and trapped in Nandana. The final hunt was just a day away.

At sunset, twelve camphor flames were lit in the presence of Badshah Salamat and prayers sung for his long life—

Emperor Akbar who shall live till eternity,
Sits on his throne, royal sceptre above.
O charming Lord of Delhi, you are lieutenant to the Prophet.
You have taken all four directions under your charge,
All kings, nobles obey your command.
Says Miyan Tansen, there is none like you in honouring the talented.

Badshah Salamat drew his lineage from Amir Timur and Changez Khan. Amir Timur was a Turk of the Barlas tribe but married Tukul Khanam whose father was a direct descendant of Chaghatai Khan, the second son of the Mongol king Changez Khan. The Barlas tribe had aligned with Chaghatai Khan during the reign of Changez Khan. Though Amir Timur claimed that he and Changez Khan had a common ancestor, this relationship was in fact only forged by marriage. Besides himself, Amir Timur had also married three of his sons into Changez Khan's family.

A man of wheatish complexion and of medium height, Badshah Salamat Jalaluddin Muhammad Akbar had lustrous dark eyes, black eyebrows, broad shoulders, a straight but small nose, a mole on the left nostril, a slim waist, a broad chest and a well-built body. He was neither fat nor slim. He had long arms and long legs that were peared and suited to horse riding. He did not have a beard but wore a moustache. He had a booming voice.

In accordance with the practice introduced by Badshah Salamat, all Muslims wore their jama—gown-like upper garment—tied under their arm on the right side and all Hindus on their left. With his jama tied on the right side, Badshah Salamat wore on his waist a long, golden-coloured sash and a smaller light pink one tied at the front.

That evening, Jalaluddin Muhammad Akbar sat with his legs folded under him, with one end of the pink sash touching the left leg. Both the long ends of the golden sash hung below his knees. The sash—which he called katizeb—held a dagger in a gold and red scabbard. His long sleeves gathered in ripples near his wrists. The Emperor wore a dark-coloured jama and green yar-i-pairhan. The pyjama had been given the name yar-i-pairhan—friend of the attire—by Badshah Salamat. Ever since Jannat Ashiyani—heaven residing—Humayun Badshah had got his foot entangled in his own dress and tumbled to his death, Badshah Salamat had shortened the length of the jama to the knees. As a child, he had worn a headdress with multiple folds especially designed by Humayun Badshah. After ascending the throne, he gave up the tall headgear of his forefathers and in keeping with the simplicity of his temperament devised a simpler turban. Badshah Salamat called this simple headgear sheesh shobha—that which befits the head. The red sheesh shobha had white embroidery on it. Other than two necklaces—one of pearls—Badshah Salamat wore no other ornaments. A feathered sarpech of gold on the turban stood out as the symbol of sovereignty.

The first chronicler of Badshah Salamat's life and reign Arif Qandhari wrote, 'When powerful Turkish and Indian youth wound their turban, its each twist is so beautiful and luminous that it was like a chain that bound them to His Majesty.'

It had been ten days since Badshah Salamat had been surveying the qamargah from Bhera. It was his habit to listen to books read out to him every night. The chronicle of Babur Badshah's life was a favourite. And at this moment, he was encamped in a place where Babur Badshah had set his foot.

Every night, around this time, Badshah Salamat remembered Darbar Khan, the storyteller. Darbar Khan had inherited the powerful voice and the storytelling ability of his father Taklu Khan, who had been a favourite storyteller of Shah Tahmasp of Persia. Darbar Khan's name was Inayat. He earned the title Darbar Khan after he entered Badshah Salamat's service and was granted a mansab of seven hundred men. In the fourteenth regnal year, when Badshah Salamat embarked on a pilgrimage to the shrine of Muinuddin Chishti at Ajmer, Darbar Khan took leave and came back to Agra on account of ill health. In keeping with his will, he was laid to rest at the feet of Badshah Salamat's loyal dog, whose mausoleum he had built. After his death, Badshah Salamat never found a storyteller like him. But stories don't die with storytellers.

Torches illuminated Badshah Salamat's do-ashiyana manzil—the two-storeyed camp—and the area outside it. In accordance with Timuri tradition, the royal encampment was laid from north to south. At this moment, Badshah Salamat sat facing south and his right hand was towards the west. His camp, the harem, the naqqar khana—which housed the royal ensemble—was contained in an area of 1,530 square yards. In the centre of this area was an open space called a mahtabi, where an awning was placed over a raised platform. In the evening, Badshah Salamat spent his time here. To the left, right, and at the back of this encampment was a three-hundred-yard area earmarked for the royal guards. At the back, at some distance, were the karkhanas—royal workshops—and thirty yards behind that were the bazaars. The walls inside the do-ashiyana manzil were lustrous with brocade and velvet. The outer walls had deep red silk. By convention, no one but the royal camp could wear the deep red colour. Being a full moon night, torches of just a single wicker were sufficient to light up the place. A flame atop a forty-yard pole—akashdiya—supported by sixteen ropes was visible from far and wide, a symbol of the presence of Jalaluddin Muhammad Akbar Badshah Ghazi.

When Badshah Salamat travelled, his cavalcade was no less than a moving city. A hundred elephants, five hundred camels, four hundred bullock-carts, and hundreds of people on foot. As the entourage rested here, another party had already moved ahead to prepare for the next halt.

Badshah Salamat was listening to *Tuzuk-i-Baburi* in his do-ashiyana manzil at Bhera—

'We had turned off from Bajaur with Bhera in our thoughts. Ever since we came into Kabul, it had been in my mind to move on Hindustan, but this had not been done for a variety of reasons. Nothing to count had fallen into the soldiers' hands during the three or four months we had been leading this army. Now that Bhera, the borderland of Hindustan, was so near, I thought something might fall into our men's hands if, riding light, we suddenly went into it. To this thought I clung, but some of my well-wishers, after we had raided the Afghans and dismounted at Maqam, set the matter in this way before me—"If we go into Hindustan, it should be on a proper basis; one part of the army stayed behind in Kabul; a body of effective braves was left behind in Bajaur; a good part of this army had gone into Lamghan because its horses were worn out; and the horses of those who have come this far are so poor that they have not a hard riding in them." Reasonable as these considerations were, yet, having made the start, we paid no attention to them but set off early next day for the ford through the water of Indus. Mir Muhammad the raftsman and his elder and younger brethren were sent with a few braves to examine the river and the ford...'

Firdaus Makani Zahiruddin Muhammad Babur became the king of Transoxiana's Ferghana kingdom at the age of twelve. He sat on the throne of Samarqand at the age of twelve, nineteen, and twenty-two. Firdaus Makani's ancestor Amir Timur had ruled a vast empire from Samarqand. Occupying the throne of Samarqand was a matter of great prestige. In the course of a long period of struggle and after losing his kingdom, Babur Badshah had been driven out of his ancestral Transoxiana and reached Afghanistan and then Hindustan. Before embarking on the Hindustan campaign, he addressed his nobles:

'Strangers and ancient foes, such as Shaibaq (Shaibani) Khan and the Uzbeks, are in possession of all the countries once held by Timur Beg's descendants; even where Turks and Chaghatais survive in corners and borderlands, they have all joined the Uzbeg, willingly or with aversion; one remains, I myself, in Kabul, the foe mightily strong, and I very weak, with no means of making terms, no strength to oppose... In the presence of such power and potency, we had to think of some place for ourselves and, at this crisis and in the crack of time there was, to put a wider space between us and the strong foeman; that choice lay between Badakhshan and Hindustan and that decision must now be made.'

Badshah Salamat was listening to the tale which was at a point where Firdaus Makani Babur Badshah had knocked at the doors of Hindustan and reached the place where the royal entourage was encamped—

'As it was always in my heart to possess Hindustan, and as these several countries, Bhera, Khushab, Chenab, and Chiniot, had once been held by the Turk, I pictured them as my own and was resolved to get them into my hands, whether peacefully or by force. For these reasons, it being imperative to treat these hillmen well, this following order was given—"Do no hurt or harm to the flocks and herds of these people, nor even to their cotton-ends and broken needles."'

Akbar Badshah was listening with eyes closed. As the music of the naubat—the imperial ensemble—began, he looked up. With his own hand, he marked the point to which the book had been narrated and gave the storyteller a reward commensurate with the pages he had read out.

The naubat—of eighteen damamas, twenty naqqaras, four duhuls, three sanjs, nine surnas, and a variety of horn instruments that included four karnas, two seengs, and many nafirs—sounding from the naqqar khana, the room atop the tall gate of the royal encampment at Bhera rang out the message far and wide that

Jalaluddin Muhammad Akbar Badshah Ghazi and his Timuri dynasty were here to stay. It was meant to give comfort to friends and peace-loving subjects and a warning to rebels and foes.

The Rohtas Fort in the vicinity peeped across the border into the fiefdom of Mirza Hakim—Badshah Salamat's stepbrother who ruled from Kabul.

2

The Timuri dynasty had a strong and old association with the place where Badshah Salamat was encamped that night. It was not so long ago that Humayun Badshah had been forced by Sher Shah to flee Hindustan.

People remembered the banquet where Babur Badshah had observed that, when a tough piece of meat was placed in Sher Khan's dish, he had skilfully used his dagger to cut it into small pieces before eating it. Sher Khan was just emerging as a power in Bihar and had joined hands with Babur Badshah. Sher Khan was an Afghan; his grandfather had come to India in the days of Sultan Bahlul Lodhi. Babur Badshah had said about him, 'Keep an eye on Sher Khan. He is a clever man and the marks of royalty are visible on his forehead. I have seen many Afghan nobles, greater men than he, but they have never made such an impression on me. As soon as I saw this man, it occurred to me that he ought to be arrested, for I find in him the qualities of greatness and the marks of mightiness.'

When Sher Khan returned to his quarters, he said to his men, 'The Emperor today looked much at me and said something to the minister, and cast evil glances towards me. This is not a fit place for me. I shall go away.'

And the day did come in the reign of Babur Badshah's son, on the eve of the Battle of Chausa—which was fought on the ninth of Safar 946 Hijri corresponding to 26 June 1539 CE on the banks of the Ganges—when in spite of the heat, Humayun Badshah's envoy found Sher Khan with his sleeves rolled up, preparing the entrenchment with a spade in hand. After ordering a shamiana—an awning—to be pitched for the envoy, Sher Khan sat on the ground informally and after hearing the message of Humayun Badshah said,

'Take this message to your King: "You yourself desire war but your army does not. I, on the other hand, do not desire war, but my army does. For the rest, the decision is the King's."'

Abbas Sarwani's account of Sher Shah's life, which he wrote on the orders of Jalaluddin Muhammad Akbar, tells us that a stream barely a breadth of twenty-five yards separated the two sides, though both were on the same side of the Ganges. Humayun Badshah agreed to give Bengal to Sher Khan on one condition. Since Sher Khan had transgressed his boundaries by encamping opposite the Emperor on the other side of the stream, he demanded that he show his respect by retreating and leaving the passage of the river free to the Emperor, and that when the Emperor crosses, he would advance two or three marches in the track of Sher Khan and then turn back. As soon as the agreement was reached, Sher Khan turned back. Humayun Badshah crossed the stream with his entire army and family and pitched his camp on the other side.

Soon after, Humayun Badshah sent Sheikh Khalil, a descendent of a Sufi saint of the Chishti order, Sheikh Fariduddin Shakarganj, along with many of his men, to Sher Khan. When Sheikh Khalil repeated the terms of agreement in the gathering, Sher Khan consented, but in a private meeting with Sheikh Khalil he went back on this word.

Sher Khan said, 'Afghans hold Sheikh Fariduddin Shakarganj in high esteem. We come from the same fatherland. Can you give me frank advice concerning my well-being? Is peace with the Emperor advantageous, or war?'

After much hesitation, Sheikh Khalil said, 'By asking my advice, you have in two ways placed me in great difficulty. First, since I have come to you as an envoy from the Emperor, it is not right that I should say anything except to his advantage; and second, you have asked me for advice, and those of old have said, "Even if your enemy asks your advice, speak the truth." If I give advice contrary to my own opinion, I shall act dishonestly. For generations past, the Afghans have held my ancestors in reverence; it appears from the miraculous precepts of the Holy Prophet Muhammad, peace be upon him, that it behoves him who gives advice to do so in good faith. I am compelled, therefore, to speak the truth. War with Emperor Humayun is more to your advantage than peace, because his army is in complete disorder; he has no horses or cattle, and his own brothers are in rebellion against him. He only makes peace with you now out of necessity and will not eventually abide by the treaty. Look on this opportunity as so much gained and do not let it out of your grasp, for you will never again have such another.'

Hearing this, Sher Khan strengthened his resolve. Calling his nobles at midnight the next day, he said:

'I have promised peace to the Emperor but I have considered that all the good service I have rendered has bore no good fruit. He makes peace and manifests a friendly disposition towards me because his army is in want of horses and cattle and of every equipment, and because his brothers have rebelled against him. He is but playing with me and eventually will not abide with this peace, but having appeased the rebellion of his brothers on his arrival at Agra and refurnished his army, he will not fail to uproot and destroy me. I have often experienced that the Afghan are braver in battle than the Mughals who only got the country because of the dissension of the Afghans. If my brothers advise so, I will break off the peace and try my fortune.'

The nobles replied, 'By your blessing, dissension has been banished from among the Afghan nation, and we all have been cherished by you. We will not fail in devotion and gallantry to our utmost capability. Your purpose of breaking off the treaty is most wise.'

After taking his army back in accordance with the treaty, Sher Khan said, 'For two days, I have drawn out my army and have returned to my encampment, that I might put the Emperor off his guard, and that he might not suspect that my army was coming towards him. Now, turn. Set your faces towards the army of the Emperor, and let not the honour of the Afghans out of your grasp nor fail to display your utmost devotion, for now is the time to regain the Empire of Hindustan.'

There was such a fierce attack on the right flank of Humayun Badshah that his army fell into complete disarray. Battle drums were immediately sounded and the demoralized troops were mustered with great difficulty. So much so that none came forward to defend Humayun Badshah when an elephant charged at him. The Emperor grabbed a lance and plunged it into the elephant's forehead. An archer seated on the elephant shot an arrow at the Emperor and injured him.

Humayun Badshah shouted, 'Come on! Let's attack!' But nobody came forward. Just then, someone grabbed the Emperor's reins and said, 'This is not the time to make a stand.'

Humayun Badshah was forced to flee Chausa in such a rush that his family was left behind and he almost lost his life himself when his horse was swept away from under him as he tried to cross the river. A water-carrier by the name of Nizam saved him from drowning. In return, Humayun Badshah favoured him by making him the emperor of Delhi for a day and ordered that all nobles perform kornish—a manner of salutation that was only offered to the king—to him. The water-carrier even had the right to grant office to people. Jannat Ashiyani Humayun Badshah's younger brother Mirza Kamran did not attend the darbar as he was ill but he sent a message—'He could have been given some other rewards. Why was it necessary to put him on the throne? At such a time, with Sher Khan so near, what is the Emperor doing?'

On the other side, an Afghan noble Isa Khan told Sher Khan, 'You should write letters describing your victory in the style of firmans—royal proclamations.'

Sher Khan replied, 'You, who formerly were nobles of Sultan Bahlul and Sikandar, have, for the cause of the Afghans, done me the honour of joining yourselves to me. It does not become me to send firmans to you and to seat myself on the throne while you stand around me. The King of Hindustan has escaped alive and still holds much of the country in his possession.'

Isa Khan said, 'It behoves him whom God Almighty brings to empire, and elevates and exalts above the rest of mankind, to observe the rules and etiquette of earlier kings.'

When more Afghan nobles spoke in favour of his becoming king, Sher Khan said, 'The kingly name is a very exalted thing, and is not devoid of trouble. But since the noble minds of my friends have decided to make me king, I agree.'

The astrologers advised: 'An auspicious moment, by the good fortune of your birth hour, has now come. If you, at this moment, seat yourself upon the throne, your army will never face defeat.'

Sher Khan then ascended the throne and assumed the name

of Sher Shah. He struck a coin and had the khutba—the Friday sermon in the mosque that mentions the emperor of the realm—read in his name.

Soon after losing the Battle of Chausa, Humayun Badshah prepared for a battle with Sher Shah once again. This time, the two sides faced each other at Kannauj.

After gathering his forces, Sher Shah sent a message: 'I have for some time entrenched myself here. The Emperor has the power to choose. If he will cross the river, he may fight with me on this side, or if he prefers it, I will cross the river and fight with the Emperor on that side.'

Humayun Badshah replied, 'Tell Sher Khan that if he will retreat some kos away from the water, I will cross the river Ganga and give him battle.'

The battle took place on tenth of Muharram 947 Hijri, corresponding to 17 May 1540 CE, after Humayun Badshah's army crossed the river.

Sher Shah told the Afghans, 'I have used my best exertions to gather you here, I have done my best to train you, and have kept you in anticipation of such a day as this. This is the day of trial.'

The Afghans replied, 'The mighty king has much protected and favoured us. This is the time for us to serve him and show our devotion.'

By afternoon, Humayun Badshah had seventeen thousand troops under him. By the time he fled and crossed the river, he was barefoot, bareheaded, and alone. Such was the rout that he could never take on Sher Shah again.

The akashdiya of the royal encampment at Bhera was casting its light far and wide. Badshah Salamat was thinking of the time he was born to a king who had lost his empire.

Just about thirty-eight years ago, Humayun Badshah had been forced by Sher Shah to flee as far as Lahore.

He had sent a message to Sher Shah from Lahore: 'What kind of justice is this? We have left all of Hindustan for you. Leave Lahore for us and take Sirhind, where you are, as the boundary between us.'

'We have left Kabul for you. You should go there,' Sher Shah had replied.

Humayun Badshah had just left Lahore and crossed Ravi when his stepbrother Kamran Mirza said, 'Can I sit on a corner of Badshah Salamat's carpet in the presence of Sher Khan's envoy so that there may be some distinction between me and my brothers?'

Four days before he passed away, Firdaus Makani Babur Badshah had said in his last darbar:

'For years, it has been in my heart to hand over the throne to Humayun Mirza and retire to a corner of Bagh-i-Zar Afshan. By God's grace, I have obtained all things but could not lead a healthy life as I wished. Now, when illness has laid me low, I charge all nobles and viziers to acknowledge Humayun in my stead. Fail not in loyalty to him. Be of one heart and one mind with him. I hope to God that Humayun also will bear himself well towards nobles and people. Humayun, I commit to God's keeping you and your brothers and all my relatives and people.'

Firdaus Makani Babur Badshah looked towards his nobles, who were his comrades in the conquest of Hindustan, and then spoke to Humayun, 'And I entrust them to you.'

Jannat Ashiyani Humayun Badshah was born of Babur Badshah's wife Maham Begum and Kamran Mirza of Gulrukh Begum. Jannat Ashiyani had always shown special favour to his stepbrother Kamran Mirza but it was not possible to give him space on the royal carpet. Firdaus Makani Babur Badshah had quoted Sheikh Sadi in his *Tuzuk-i-Baburi*—

Ten dervishes can sleep under one blanket,
But two kings cannot find room in one clime.
If a man of God eats half a loaf of bread,
He gives the other half to a dervish.
Let a king grip the rule of a clime,
He dreams of another to grip.

Humayun Badshah wrote back to Mirza Kamran—

Although one's image be shown in the mirror,
It remains always apart from one's self.
It is wonderful to see one's self in another form.
This marvel will be the work of God.

Fleeing from Sher Shah, Humayun Badshah crossed Chenab and then Jhelum, and reached the place where Jalaluddin Muhammad Akbar was camping.

Humayun Badshah had then said, 'With my brothers' concurrence, I shall go to Badakhshan. Let Kabul remain the fief of Mirza Kamran.'

In fact, Mirza Kamran did not wish Humayun Badshah to go to Badakhshan. Kabul lay en route to Badakhshan and perhaps he feared that he would seize Kabul from him if he went that way.

'In his lifetime, Badshah Salamat Firdaus Makani gave Kabul to my mother Gulrukh Begum. It is not right for you to go to Kabul.'

Humayun Badshah replied, 'Badshah Firdaus Makani often used to say, "My Kabul I will give to no one. Let none of my sons covet it. There God gave me all my children, and many victories followed its capture." Indeed in his memoirs, Firdaus Makani often mentions this. What was the good of my showing kindness and brotherliness to the Mirza, if he now keeps on talking this way?'

A short distance away from His Majesty's do-ashiyana manzil in Bhera lay Khushab. A little further away was a valley beyond which the road bifurcated—one going to Kabul, the other to Sind. Kamran Mirza wanted to go first so that Humayun Badshah could be prevented from going to Kabul, whereas Humayun Badshah said that it was his right to go first. Mirza Kamran remained adamant. He had a bigger army than Jannat Ashiyani. Finally, Humayun Badshah went first but did not take the road to Kabul. He turned towards Sind.

It was here that Abul Muzaffar Jalaluddin Muhammad Akbar Badshah—son of Humayun Badshah, son of Zahiruddin Muhammad Babur Badshah, son of Umar Sheikh Mirza, son of Sultan Abu Sayeed Mirza, son of Sultan Muhammad Mirza, son of Jalaluddin Miran Shah, son of Sahib-i-Qiran Qutbuddin Amir Taimur Gurkan, son of Amir Taraghai, son of Amir Barkal, son of Elangar Bahadur, son of Ejil Noyan, son of Qarachar Noyan, son of Sughuchijin, son of Erdamchi Barlas, son of Qachulai Bahadur, son of Tumina Khan, son of Bai Singhor Khan, son of Qaidu Khan, son of Duttumannan Khan, son of Buqa Khan, son of Bodhonchar Khan, son of Alanqoa—was born.

Badshah Salamat's spokesman, his confidant, and the chronicler of his and his family's life, Sheikh Abul Fazl had said: 'If you listen to tales of Mary, believe the same of Alanqoa.'

Sheikh Abul Fazl says in the *Akbarnama* that Badshah Salamat's ancestor, ruler of her age, Alanqoa, was resting one night when suddenly a glorious light cast its rays into her tent and entered into her through her mouth and she became pregnant. Since she was a widow, she sought to clear doubts in people's minds and said, 'If any simpleton unaware of the wondrous power of God falls into the misfortune of evil thoughts and sullies his mind's mirror with the rust of wicked imagination, he will for ever and ever abide in distress and loss. It is better then that I clear the courts of their intellect of such confusion. For this purpose, it is necessary that awakened-hearted truth-knowers and trustworthy persons of sincerity watch by night around the tent, so that the darkness of suspicion and doubt caused by the blackness of their hearts may by the light of divine events and the beholding of hidden radiances be changed into illumination and that evil thoughts may pass from their turbid minds.'

Sheikh Abul Fazl wrote, 'Accordingly, several wakeful and prudent, keen-sighted watchers were placed around the tent, and like night-burning stars, they closed not their eyes. Suddenly in the middle of the night, which is the time for the descent of divine mercies, a shining light, like bright moonlight, just as the lady, the curtain of chastity, had said, came down and entered the tent. A cry was raised by the watchers. For a little while, people were stunned and then their vain thoughts and imaginations were exorcised. Alanqoa bore three sons; the third was Bodhonchar Khan. The sons of these exalted ones are called Niru'un, which means born of light, and they are considered to be the noblest class among the Mughals. Bodhonchar Khan was the ninth ancestor of Changez Khan, the fourteenth ancestor of Sahib-i-Qiran Amir Timur, and the twenty-second ancestor of Badshah Salamat.'

For Abul Fazl, the glorious light entering the womb of Alanqoa was an event of great significance. Linking it to Badshah Salamat's birth, he wrote, 'That day was the beginning of the manifestation of His Majesty, who after passing through diverse stages was revealed to the world from the holy womb of Her Majesty Maryam Makani.'

Whilst Humayun Badshah was on the run, with Sher Shah in pursuit, on the fourth day of Rabi ul-Awwal, 947 Hijri corresponding to 9 July 1540, he saw an elderly person in his dream who was draped in green from head to toe. Giving his staff to Humayun Badshah, he said, 'Don't be disheartened! God will bless you with a child who shall be called Jalaluddin Muhammad Akbar.'

Jannat Ashiyani Humayun Badshah asked, 'Who are you?'

The man replied, 'Ahmed of Jam, The Terrible Elephant. Your son will be of my lineage.'

Humayun Badshah had first laid his eyes on Akbar's mother, Maryam Makani—one who has the stature of Mary—Hamida Banu Begum, a sayyid's daughter, at his stepbrother Hindal's home.

Humayun Badshah's mother Maham Begum said, 'Her father Mir Baba Dost is related to us.'

Ahmed of Jam was both Hamida Banu Begum's and Maham Begum's ancestor. He was a notable saint of Khurasan of the eleventh and twelfth century. When Humayun Badshah reached Persia after fleeing Hindustan, he paid respects at the grave of Ahmed of Jam between Mashhad and Herat.

Humayun Badshah asked his mother about Hamida Banu, 'Is she engaged?'

Maham Begum replied, 'No. She is not married.'

Humayun Badshah said, 'Mir Baba Dost is a relative of ours. It is fitting that his daughter be given to us in marriage.'

About this proposal, his stepbrother Mirza Hindal said, 'I look upon this girl as a sister and child of my own. He is *padshah*. God forbid this becomes the cause of quarrel. He did not come to show his support of us. He came only to get married. If he does this, I will leave him.'

Mirza Hindal's mother Dildar Begum scolded him, 'You are crossing your limits with Hazrat Badshah. *He* has brought you up, because you have not even seen your father.'

When Mirza Hindal refused to take back his words, Humayun Badshah left in anger. His stepmother Dildar Begum wrote to him: 'The girl's mother is acting even more coquettish than she is. It is surprising that you left, insulted by only a few words.'

Humayun Badshah wrote in response: 'What you said has pleased us much. Whatever persuasion you may use, we agree to it.

As for emoluments, whatever you have written shall be done. We shall wait.'

Then one day, Humayun Badshah came to his stepmother Dildar Begum and called for Hamida Banu.

Hamida Banu Begum sent the reply, 'To see a king once is permissible. It is not permissible to see a na-mahram twice.'

Humayun Badshah said, 'If she is na-mahram, we will make her mahram.'

For forty days Hamida Banu refused to agree. Humayun Badshah's stepmother Dildar Begum advised her, 'After all, you have to marry someone. Who better than the Emperor?'

Hamida Banu said, 'Oh yes, I shall marry someone, but he shall be a man whose collar my hand can touch, and not one the hem of whose skirt I cannot reach.'

Finally, Hamida Banu agreed to the marriage. Jannat Ashiyani Humayun Badshah took an astrolabe in his own hands and chose an auspicious hour. After forty days, in the month of Jamadi ul-Awwal, 948 Hijri corresponding to 15 September 1540 CE, which was Monday, the nikah ceremony was performed in the afternoon in Pat city, and Hamida Banu Begum became Humayun Badshah's wife.

After his defeat at the hands of Sher Shah, as they waited for help from the Arghun king of Sind Mirza Shah Hussain, Humayun Badshah's army remained camped outside Bhakkar Fort for months. He had crossed Indus to meet Mirza Hindal at Pat and gone back to Bhakkar three days after the nikah. When Mirza Shah Hussian killed ten thousand of his soldiers by drowning them, the only ray of hope seemed Raja Maldeo of Marwar. In deep distress, he entered Phalodi in Raja Maldeo's kingdom and was relieved when he was welcomed by him. The Raja also sent a coat of armour and a camel loaded with ashrafis—gold coins.

Humayun Badshah dispatched Shamsuddin Muhammad to Raja Maldeo. Shamsuddin Muhammad had saved Humayun Badshah from drowning in Kannauj when he was trying to flee Sher Shah. Humayun Badshah had managed with great difficulty to get hold of an elephant to cross the river but had found it impossible to get out of the river. A soldier had then thrown a rope for him and pulled him up. On being asked, the soldier said that he was Mirza

Kamran's soldier and was born in Ghazni. Humayun Badshah was in dire straits at that time but promised him rich rewards. Later, when the soldier came to see him in Lahore, he was taken in employment. Thereafter, he got attached to Jannat Ashiyani for life.

Sheikh Abul Fazl said about the Battle of Kannauj, 'Now that the period of the showing forth of the final destination of the holy light—which had been carried by Alanqoa—in the holy incarnation of Badshah Salamat was at hand, an untoward event was to happen to ward off the evil eye from this great blessing.'

Humayun Badshah needed and hoped for refuge in Raja Maldeo's territory. His wife Hamida Banu Begum was expecting. His entourage was in distress. Shamsuddin Muhammad's wife was also expecting. Hamida Banu Begum had told her, 'After you deliver your child, you feed my son.'

Akbar Badshah used to call Shamsuddin Muhammad's wife 'jiji'. She was the one at whose breast he had nursed the most. Because of this relationship, Shamsuddin earned the title 'atka'.

Before Shamsuddin returned, Humanyun Badshah received a secret message. After he lost Hindustan, his old librarian Mullah Surkh had joined the employment of Raja Maldeo, who now sent word, 'Beware, a thousand times beware of advancing. March at once from wherever you are, for Maldeo intends to make you prisoner. Put no trust in his words. There came here an envoy from Sher Khan who brought a letter to say, "By whatever means you know and can use, capture that king. If you will do this, I will give you Nagaur and Alwar and whatever place you ask for."'

When Shamsuddin Muhammad returned after meeting Maldeo, he too said, 'This is not the time to stay here.'

The entourage had to leave in such a hurry that there weren't any horses left for Hamida Banu Begum. Humayun Badshah was about to give his own horse to her and mount a camel when a trusted server asked his mother to mount a camel and gave her horse to the Emperor.

Now they marched towards Umarkot in Sind because they were hopeful of its ruler Rana Prasad's help. After leaving Phalodi in Raja Maldeo's kingdom, the entourage thirsted for water. Those were days of summer, and that too in the desert. At one place, there was such a stampede for water that many fell into the well. At the next stop, thirsty horses and camels drank so much water that they died.

When Humayun Badshah reached the fort of Umarkot, he had just seven horsemen with him. All three brothers of Rana Prasad kissed his stirrups and said, 'Time is not auspicious today. The Rana will present himself before the throne tomorrow morning.'

The next day, Rana Prasad offered him seven thousand horsemen and said, 'May Your Majesty's arrival be auspicious. I have two thousand horsemen from the Soda tribe and five thousand from Samicha tribe, who are related to us. They are loyal and ready to sacrifice themselves for the Emperor in the conquest of Thatta and Bhakkar.'

Humayun Badshah then thought of a trick to raise money for the horsemen. After calling for all his nobles, he sent two men back to surreptitiously search their belongings. Of the gold and precious clothes recovered from them, half were returned and half given to the soldiers.

By the time Hamida Banu Begum reached Umarkot, she was seven months pregnant. Reaching Umarkot was a huge relief. There was no scarcity of water and Rana Prasad was a generous host. He made excellent arrangements inside the fortress.

After resting for seven weeks, Humayun Badshah left for Bhakkar but left Hamida Banu Begum at Umarkot. Astrologer Maulana Chand was ordered to remain with her so that he could cast the horoscope after ascertaining the exact time of birth.

It is believed that some wise men were already getting portents of an event that comes once in a thousand years. Shamsuddin Muhammad Atka Khan told his father Mir Yar Muhammad Ghaznavi of a dream where he saw a moon come into his arms. His father interpreted the dream and said that God Almighty would grant a great privilege to Shamsuddin that would exalt their family.

Shamsuddin Muhammad's wife Jiji Anga said, 'One morning, before the birth of Hazrat, a great light approached me and entered my bosom. I felt as if the world-warming sun had fallen into my breast. A strange condition supervened and a great astonishment laid hold of me so that all the parts and particles of my body were moved and shaken, as if by an excess of joy and ecstasy. And the exquisiteness of that delight still suffuses me. And from the time of that white dawn of the morning of majesty and beauty and rose-blooming of fortune and glory, I was on the watch thinking, "Oh God! What will be the result of this sublime feeling!"'

A short while before the birth of Jalaluddin Muhammad Akbar, Hamida Banu Begum was travelling on a camel when her gaze fell upon a mango grove. In that state, she felt like having something bittersweet and asked her stepbrother Khwaja Muazzam to get her some mangoes. While handing her the mangoes, Khwaja Muazzam is said to have noticed a dazzle as if she had mirrors on her forehead.

People say that one day Humayun Badshah was trying to figure out the date of his son's birth through astrological calculations when a divine light became visible from the lattice. Humayun Badshah told those present, 'A rose of the garden of the caliphate will just now come into bloom, and a child of light will emerge from the hidden chamber of magnificence and glory... His greatness will melt the hearts of the enemies of the state in the crucible of destruction, and confer new splendour and glory on our race and family.'

It is said that on the fifth of Rajab 949 Hijri corresponding to October 1542, Humayun Badshah was deep in thought when he suddenly raised his head and said, 'Praise be to God the Gracious, the lamp of our royal family has been relit... I saw a brilliant star—light incarnate of my successor—rise higher and higher, and its size and brilliance increase and embrace the greater portion of the world... Whatever portion of the earth has been shone upon by this world-illuminating ray will come under his light of justice.'

Two days later, when a loyal courtier Tardi Beg came with the news of the birth of a son, it became clear that the birth had happened when Jannat Ashiyani had seen the star in his vision.

3

Sitting in his camp, Jalaluddin Muhammad Akbar remembered that he had reached Hansi after hunting at Hissar on his way to Bhera when Mir Ali Akbar Mashhadi showed him the horoscope that had been cast at the time of birth. It was clearly written there that Humayun Badshah had seen, many days before his birth, that the Almighty was blessing him with a son of lofty fortune. Jalaluddin

Muhammad Akbar bestowed the pargana of Nagina on Mir Ali Akbar Mashhadi.

On the fifth of Rajab 949 Hijri corresponding to 15 October 1542 CE, Rana Prasad's palace was bustling with activity.

Hamida Begum had gone into labour. Servant girls of the palace, with uncovered heads and bangles on their wrists, as well as her personal lady attendants were astir around her. Medicines were being prepared. A makeshift screen covered her bed. Auspicious peepul leaves were strung in a line at the doorway of Rana Prasad. It seemed that the hour of Badshah Salamat's arrival had come. But, standing at the door, the astrologer Maulana Chand looked at his astrolabe and was disturbed. He said, 'In just a short time, a glorious moment will arrive, one that does not occur once in a thousand years. What an advantage if the birth could be delayed!'

Those present snubbed him and said, 'What is the good of your agitation? Such things are not under our control.'

Just then, Hamida Banu Begum was repulsed by the appearance of the local midwife. Her mind was diverted and the moments of ill-omen passed.

When the auspicious hour arrived, Maulana Chand became restless once again, fearing it might pass. Hamida Banu Begum had gone to sleep. Plucking up courage, Maulana Chand sent word that she be woken. He was told, 'It would not be right to waken her. Whatever God Almighty in His good pleasure has determined must happen.'

No sooner was this told to Maulana Chand than Hamida Banu Begum woke up and Abul Muzaffar Jalaluddin Muhammad Akbar came into the world. It was around six minutes past one at night.

When Badshah Salamat was born, his father Jannat Ashiyani Nasiruddin Muhammad Humayun was about thirty miles from Umarkot. He raised his hands in thanksgiving and distributed musk to his nobles who congratulated the King and prayed. Humayun Badshah prayed that the son's name spread as far and wide as the scent of the musk. Jannat Ashiyani was reminded of the dream he had had two years and four months ago in which his mother's and wife's ancestor Ahmed-i-Jam had instructed that his son be named Jalaluddin Muhammad Akbar.

Badshah Salamat's horoscope had been cast by many astrologers. Maulana Chand was the first to cast it in accordance with Greek principles. Then, India's best astrologer at the time, Jotik Rai, prepared it on the basis of Indian principles. Maulana Chand ascertained Badshah Salamat's lucky ascendant as Virgo. According to the horoscope cast by Jotik Rai, Badshah Salamat's lucky ascendant was Leo. Since the two royal horoscopes seemed to be in disagreement, Mir Fathullah Shirazi studied the matter in accordance with Persian and Greek principles and came to the conclusion that the birth was in Leo.

Sheikh Abul Fazl wrote that, according to Indian astrologers, 'Badshah Salamat's auspicious horoscope falls under Leo which is a fixed sign and is significant of perfect supremacy, victory, energy, and superiority. The Sun, which takes more note of kings than of all the other objects in the universe, is the dominant, and this is a clear indication that the Native will be victorious and paramount among famous sovereigns and mighty rulers.'

Jotik Rai said of the horoscope that, 'Notwithstanding the perfect simplicity and unceremoniousness of Hazrat Badshah, such rays of glory and power stream from the forehead of his might as to indicate that the Indian astrologers are not far from the truth when they assert that his noble horoscope belongs to Leo. In their books of stellar influences, it is laid down that the Native of this ascendant is wealthy, victorious over enemies, forgiving towards offenders, ruling according to just and equal laws, and accomplishing his purposes by force of his own reason and by firmness in his own opinions. He will be fond of travel and will reap benefit from it.

'The meeting of Jupiter and Venus in the second house makes the Native a guide in various arts and sciences. As Jupiter is in the house of Mercury, the Native will be endowed with beauty of form, proportional admixture of the elements, gravity of speech, social graces, lofty understanding, and sublime apprehension in theology and divine worship, and will have the ability to accomplish everything in accordance with propriety. Venus in Virgo takes charge of the adornment of virtuous veiled ones and provides for the increase of beauty and elegance.

'As the Sun is in the third house, the Native will accomplish whatever great undertaking he desires to compass, without reference to any other person. He will be powerful and his brethren will not attain his level. Indeed, the star of the brothers' horoscope is occulted. Men will be united and agreed in love of him.

'As Mercury is in the third house, the Native will be talented, versed in business, and disliking idleness, a subduer of difficulties, and a slayer of enemies. His acute thoughts will revel in theology and other philosophies and will attain the rank of ecstasy. And as Mercury is in Libra, he will be famed throughout the world, and his good deeds will be widely known. He will be world-conquering and world-ruling for long periods of time, and excellent contrivances and ingenious plans are indicated.

'As Saturn is in the third house, the Native will enjoy repose and much tranquillity, and will have innumerable servants, but he will act according to his own personal courage and his own ripe reason. As Saturn is in Libra, and in exaltation, the Native will be the master of the treasures of the world, and as Saturn is under the shade of the venerable world-illuminating Sun, his boundless treasures will last for a long time and will remain unaffected by prolonged usage of them. He will make delightful journeys with success and accomplishment of his objects. And there will not be one greater than he upon earth. Elephants will wait at his gate. As he grows in years, his power will increase, and he will, without trouble or pains, acquire great armies and perfect dominion and glory. His power and felicity will be lasting, for there is no slower planet than Saturn, and among its gifts are extension of happiness and permanence of sovereignty.

'The Sun, Saturn, and Mercury are in one sign. He will therefore be friend-cherishing, foe-subduing, knowing well how to maintain amity and enmity.

'Mars being in Sagittarius, mankind will glorify him for Mars is in the triplicity with the ascendant and in the house of its friend. This friendship of Jupiter puts away the sorrows and apprehensions of the people. And he will be happy and joyful. And he will be greatest of the greats and king of kings. The glory of his renown will embrace the world and the fame of his majesty will extend from shore to shore. Many princes and rulers will be subject to him, and being afraid of him, will be obedient and submissive. And as Mars is in the house of Jupiter and the Sun is in sextile to him, the princes throughout the world will place their heads on the line of his command and make the dust of his threshold the adoration-spot of their obedience.

'The Moon is in the sixth house; he may have powerful enemies but they will not reach him, nor be able to withstand the scorching lightning of his wrath and might, and they will always endeavour to gain his friendship so that by borrowing the lights of his alliance, they may be safe from calamity. As the Moon's detriment is in the Capricorn, the weakness of his enemies is signified. And there comes a sweet reasonableness to the Native which enables him to decide disputes according to equity and the real merits of the cases. And having examined various faiths and sects, he will guide every group in the way of good works. His desire is that men should leave the slippery path of imitative routine, and emerge into the straight highway of inquiry. And as Jupiter is in aspect towards him, the royal power and might will be beyond calculation. He will become possessed of worthy children and, as Venus is in aspect, high-minded chaste ladies will have a long life in his service and he will have obedient and amiable children.

'There are certain principles, too, to be found in the books of Indian philosophers which prove the grandeur of this holy nativity. If a planet occupies the dodecatemory of the Moon, the Native will have a long life, and the dust of sickness will hardly touch the garment-hem of his health. If that planet is in the fullness of its powers, he will obtain a great kingdom, and will have long life, abundant blessings, sublime stations and lofty places. Now, as in this horoscope Mars occupies the dodecatemory of the Moon, all these things would be attained to perfection. He will be lord of victorious armies, and be foe-scattering on the battlefields, and everyone on whom the glance of his wrath shall fall, will be melted by his terrible majesty. Since an auspicious planet occurs as the dodecatemory of the Sun, the honoured Native will be eloquent and wise, firm and fortunate. And in emergencies when the brave in battle and men of men may hesitate, the owner of these happy omens will never swerve, but will keep a steady foot on the skirt of fortitude and courage, and the trace of doubt and the smallest vestige of change will not reach the court of his circumspection. Now in this royal horoscope, the meeting of the two stars in a dodecatemory shows abundant auspiciousness. If the Sun be the lord of the ascendant and be in the third house, the noble Native will be advanced to lofty sovereignty. If Jupiter, Mercury, and Venus be in aspect to the Moon, the Native will open up countries and will rule over them. Now in this embellished horoscope, the three planets are kindling the lamp of the dominion. If the cusp of the ascendant or the Moon be in nuhbahr of a sign and four planets or more are in aspect to the Moon, the Native will have twenty-two kingdoms and many countries will be permanently in his possession. Now, in this horoscope, not only are the cusp of the ascendant and the Moon in the nuhbahr, but five planets are in aspect, viz. the Sun, Jupiter, Venus, Saturn, and Mercury. And in this horoscope, the lord of the ascendant—the Sun—is in the third house. If the Native have a brother, the latter will not be long-lived, but many devoted friends will gather around the Native and he will be beneficent, bounteous, and powerful and will enjoy sovereignty free from calamity and prosperity without end.

'The lord of the second house, Mercury, is in the third house and so the Native will do great things and will bring wondrous works to pass. He will devise laws of dominion and wisdom and be a terror to the evil-minded, and no alarm on this account will touch the hem of his lofty spirit.

'The lord of the third house, Venus, is in the second. The Native will assist the helpless and downcast, and deal benignly with well-disposed kindred. And all those who walk rightly will experience his bounty and benevolence and will gather fruits from the gardens of his bounties and liberalities. It is certain that if the lord of the third house be auspicious, the Native will attain great sovereignty. Now in this horoscope, the regent of the third house is the greater lucky star. This signifies a majestic government.

'The lord of the fourth house is Mars and he is posited in the fifth. His venerable father will help him from his place in heaven. His noble children will live long and will be great and famous for their dominion and fortune.

'The lord of the fifth house is Jupiter and is in the second. The Native will have ample treasures and great countries will come under his sway. And as Venus is also in the second house, he will be acute and discerning in musical notes, in subtle harmonies, and in the secrets of melody.

'Saturn, the lord of the sixth house is in the third; so some of the Native's servants will have evil thoughts and be trodden under his foot by his wrath.

'Saturn, also the lord of the seventh, is in the third house; the Native will perform works of majesty and splendour by his well-directed exertions. And there rises the longing in his heart, "Oh! I wish I had a brother who would rise high in my service!"

'Jupiter, the lord of the eighth is in the second house. The Native will gather abundance of goods and incalculable treasures by his own exertions. It may also happen that an inheritance will be enured to him.

'Mars, the lord of the ninth house is in the fifth, that is, the house of Jupiter. This signifies strength of retention. He will have a powerful memory and whatever he transacts with mortals, will be done in a becoming manner. Fitting worship of the Creator is also indicated. And he will excel in good regulations for the prosperity of his subjects and the administration of justice. He will have fortunate and dutiful children and they will be respectful and obedient.

'Venus, the regent of the tenth house is in the second. The Native will be respectful and submissive to his parents and elders of his family.

'Mercury, the regent of the eleventh house is in the third. He will love the attendants and servants of the court and will protect mankind. His enemies will be turned into nothingness without any trouble or exertion on his part.

'The Moon, the lord of the twelfth house is in the sixth. The Native will have many opponents but they will be dispersed and scattered by the reverberating sound of the war-drums of his fortune, and will descend with loss and frustration into the abode of annihilation.

'And if Jupiter or Saturn be in the second house, the fortunate Native will be a great monarch and will prevail over his enemies. And whenever the Moon is in Capricorn, which is the house of Saturn, and is in nuhbahr with Saturn, this is a proof that much of the world will be submissive to the illustrious Native. His territories will be bounded by the ocean and his auspicious reign be long. It is also certain that, if in the horoscope, Saturn be in exaltation, the Native will attain great empire and have a long life. All these indications are there in this auspicious horoscope.'

Those in the know of things say that often when Jannat Ashiyani Humayun Badshah studied the horoscope, he closed his room and danced with joy. He used to say, 'In many ways, this horoscope is better than that of Sahib-i-Qiran Amir Timur.'

Humayun Badshah had promised that Shamsuddin Muhammad's wife Jiji would feed Badshah Salamat. But when Badshah Salamat was born, Jiji had not yet become a mother. Despite this, Badshah Salamat was placed in the lap of Jiji Anga after being bathed and wrapped in a piece of cloth. People say Badshah Salamat wanted to have his mother's milk first. After his mother, he was breastfed by Fakhrunnisa Anga and Jannat Ashiyani Humayun Badshah's private servant Bhawal Anga. After this, he was breastfed by Khwaja Ghazi's wife and then by Hakima. By then, Jiji Anga had delivered her own child and could nurse Badshah Salamat. After her, Koki Anga, Bibi Rupa, Khaldar Anga, and finally Picha Jan Anga breastfed Badshah Salamat.

Sheikh Abul Fazl says, 'It was as if there were divine wisdom, thus implanting varied temperaments into the baby so that the pure entity, advancing by gradations, might become familiar with diverse methods of divine manifestation.'

Jiji Anga would relate an incident that would amaze people. She claimed that Badshah Salamat gave up milk when he turned seven months old. Jiji was in a troubled state when Badshah Salamat spoke from her lap, 'Jiji, do not be distressed. I will only have your milk. Do not reveal this secret of ours to anybody.'

People said Jiji had committed sorcery on the prince, but Jiji Anga said, 'I was thrown into rapture by this intimation. With each passing day, the doors of joy and gladness opened wider and wider before me. I addressed myself to my duties, heart and soul. I kept this a secret until this nursling of dominion occupied the throne.'

Jiji's son told her, 'One day, His Majesty had left Delhi to hunt in Palam, and an enormous and terrifying serpent, such as might move the heart of the daring, appeared on the road. On this occasion, His Majesty performed the miracle of Moses and without any hesitation seized its tail and flung it away.'

That's when Jiji Anga revealed to her son the closely guarded secret of what she had seen and heard. She said, 'His Majesty performed this miracle in his tender years. It is not strange that he has in his maturity performed another, for every act has its time and every speech its season. I did not mention it until now because nobody would have believed it. Instead, people would have attributed it to the fancifulness of my intellect.'

4

A full moon beamed over the royal enclosure at Bhera.

Near the border that lay between Jalaluddin Muhammad Akbar and his stepbrother Mirza Muhammad Hakim, the great game was reaching its final stage. Both were sons of Humayun Badshah, but Mirza Hakim was born of Mah Chuchak Begum and Badshah Salamat of Hamida Banu Begum. Jalaluddin Muhammad Akbar ruled Hindustan while Kabul was with his stepbrother Mirza Muhammad Hakim. Twelve years younger than Badshah Salamat, Mirza Muhammad Hakim was born on the fifteenth of Jamadi ul-Awwal of the year 961 of the Hijri era, corresponding to 18 April 1554 CE.

Sheikh Abul Fazl had rightly said, 'Learned people of earlier times believed that Kabul and Qandhar were two gates of Hindustan. Qandhar from Iran and Kabul from Transoxiana. By protecting these two gates, Hindustan would remain safe from invaders and trade would prosper the world over.'

Near Bhera and Khushab, where Badshah Jalaluddin Muhammad Akbar was at present, Humayun Badshah's stepbrother Mirza Kamran had been captured and produced before him.

Mirza Kamran had once gone to the court of the Afghan ruler Islam Shah to seek help but had failed. Instead, he had faced humiliation. When Mirza Kamran performed kornish at the bidding of the barbak—chief attendant of the court—people grabbed him by his neck and repeatedly shouted, 'Your Majesty! Be pleased to cast a glance hither, for Kamran the son of Kabul's chief seeks blessings.'

After ignoring him for some time, Islam Shah cast an arrogant glance in his direction and said, 'Welcome!'

Mirza Kamran was mocked by all in Islam Shah's court. According to the practice of his time, he wrapped a turban around his cap and wore a sash around his jama. When he entered, the Afghans would say in Hindi, 'Here comes the mor—the peacock.'

When Mirza Kamran asked the meaning of 'mor', he was told, 'It is a name given to a person of great dignity.'

At this, Mirza Kamran had replied, 'In that case, Salim Shah is a first-rate mor and Sher Shah a still finer one.'

This was when Islam Shah put a stop to this joke.

Mirza Kamran had stood like a prisoner in the presence of his brother Humayun Badshah, who was in a dilemma. On one hand was the fatherly advice of Babur Badshah, and on the other, the pleading of the commoners and the nobles.

He remembered the letter sent by his father—

'To Humayun, whom I am longing to see. State of affairs on both sides of the Hindukush have been made known to me on Monday the tenth of Rabi ul-Awwal.

'Thank God a son is born to you. He is a son to you and a beloved to me. May God ever grant you and me tidings as joyful! You have named him "al-Aman"—peace—but have overlooked that common people mostly say "Alaman" or "Ilaman". Besides that, this "al" is rare in names. May God bless and prosper him in name and person. May He grant us al-Aman—peace—for many years and decades to come. May He now order our affairs by His own mercy and favour; not in many decades comes such an occasion as this.

'Kamran and commanders of Kabul have orders to join you. Once this is done, move on Hissar, Samarqand, or whatever direction is in our best interest. May you, by God's grace crush foes, take lands, and make friends happy. God willing, this is the time for you to risk life and wield the sword. Slothful life in retirement does not befit the sovereign.

'He grips the world who hastens,
The world is his who delays not,
A king can take rest from everything,
Except kingship.

'If by God's grace, Balkh and Hissar are won and held, put your men in Hissar and Kamran's men in Balkh. If Samarqand is also won, make it your seat. God willing, I shall make Hissar a crown-domain.

Should Kamran regard Balkh as small, represent the matter to me. I will compensate him from other territories.

'As you know, the rule has always been that when you get six parts, Kamran gets five. Make no change in this rule.

'Treat your younger brother well. Elders must bear the burden. I hope that you will keep on good terms with him. He has grown up as a fine young man. He should not fail in his loyal duty towards you...'

Jannat Ashiyani Humayun Badshah remembered the winter night when Babur Badshah called for him after having a few drinks. By the time he reached, his father had dozed off. When Babur woke up at midnight, he saw his son in front of him. He asked, 'When did you come?'

'When you had called for me,' the son replied dutifully.

A delighted Firdaus Makani Babur Badshah said, 'If God gives you the crown, do not kill your brothers. Pardon them.'

At that time, Humayun Badshah had prostrated and agreed to abide by that.

Now his nobles were clamouring in his presence: 'Mirza Kamran was responsible for the injury to your blessed head at Qibchaq!'

In Qibchaq, Mirza Kamran's soldier had hit Jannat Ashiyani Humayun Badshah on the head. He would have raised his sword again, but an angry Humayun Badshah looked at him and said, 'You stupid little fellow!'

Hearing this, the man had lost his nerve.

A scrap of Humanyun's vest had been carried in triumph to Mirza Kamran. Humayun Badshah learnt later that Mirza Kamran had been overjoyed as he thought his brother was no more. He even displayed the vest as proof of Jannat Ashiyani's death.

Jannat Ashiyani's attention was again drawn to the nobles and commoners facing him.

'His conspiring with the Afghans cost Mirza Hindal his life.'

Babur Badshah had learnt of Mirza Hindal's birth when he had set out to conquer Hindustan. Considering this a good omen, he had named the son Hindal—one who conquers Hind.

Mirza Hindal was stepbrother to Jannat Ashiyani Humayun

Badshah. He was the son of Firdaus Makani Babur Badshah by his wife Dildar Begum. He was adopted by Humayun Badshah's mother Maham Begum. Jannat Ashiyani Humayun Badshah loved Mirza Hindal like his own brother. It is another matter that when Jannat Ashiyani Humayun Badshah was campaigning against Sher Shah, Mirza Hindal had got the khutba read in his name in Delhi and proclaimed himself king. At that time, he had forgiven Mirza Hindal on Mirza Kamran's request.

When Humayun Badshah reached Agra after his rout at Chausa, Mirza Kamran was at Bagh-i-Zar Afshan. Hearing of the Emperor's arrival, he hastened across and paid homage. Humayun Badshah embraced Mirza Kamran. Then both rested in a tent. Mirza Kamran said, 'The Emperor must be tired. Why not rest on the throne and pardon Hindal's sins for my sake?'

Jannat Ashiyani Humayun Badshah said, 'We pardon him for your sake. Write to him to come.'

Alas, Mirza Hindal lost his life because of the person who had asked the Emperor to pardon him.

When Mirza Kamran assembled his troops at Nangarhar near Kabul, Humayun reached there with Mirza Hindal. After taking stock of the situation, Mirza Hindal said, 'Let Your Majesty stay on the hill with Jalaluddin Muhammad Akbar so that a careful watch may be kept from there.'

Mirza Hindal had then tried to boost the morale of his troops, 'Put earlier services in one scale and the service of this night in the other. God willing, whatever claim you can make, you shall have it.'

When Mirza Hindal's toshakchi delayed bringing his bundle, he was asked for an explanation. The toshakchi told him, 'I had just lifted the bundle when somebody sneezed, and therefore put it down. So there was a delay.'

Mirza Hindal said, 'You were wrong. You should have just said "Insha'Allah! May there be blessed martyrdom."'

Then Mirza Hindal said, 'May all my companions bear witness that I abjure all forbidden things and improper actions.'

Those present recited the Fatiha and said, 'May it be blessed.'

When Mirza Hindal approached the trench to raise his troops' morale, he heard the voice of his tabaqchi—the officer in charge of utensils—who was under attack. Dismounting from his horse, he said, 'It is far from brave to offer no help when my tabaqchi is held at a sword's point.'

He himself got down into the trenches and was killed.

Jauhar Aftabchi was in Humayun Badshah's service at the time and used to be in his attendance. He wrote, 'Two days before his death, he had shot a deer with an arrow. The deer turned his head towards heaven three times and passed away. People wondered whether the deer had pleaded to God.'

During the battle, Jannat Ashiyani kept asking but none among the nobles had the heart to tell him about Mirza Hindal's death. A man specially sent by Humayun Badshah returned and recited:

O King, many a Navroz has gone with the wind.
May the hundred-petalled red rose remain.

Jannat Ashiyani understood and was plunged into grief. The nobles came to offer condolences and said, 'It was his good luck to attain martyrdom in your service. Long live His Majesty.'

Jannat Ashiyani was reminded of the day he had attacked Badakhshan and Mirza Kamran had been produced as a criminal with a whip around his neck. In accordance with his orders, the nobles had welcomed Mirza Kamran. Drums were beaten. Mirza Kamran had alighted at Mirza Hindal's tent and was about to sit down, but just before his knees could touch the carpet, he was told that Humayun Badshah has summoned him. Jannat Ashiyani saw the whip around Mirza Kamran's neck and said, 'Alas! This is not needed! Remove it!'

Mirza Kamran did taslim thrice and Humayun Badshah asked him to take a seat on his right. According to protocol, only the favoured were given a place on the right. Mirza Kamran once again did taslim and sat down and once again began to apologize. At this, Humayun Badshah said, 'So far we have met according to the rules of the Tora. Now we shall meet as brothers.'

Both the brothers stood up, embraced, and wept profusely. It seemed as if all was forgotten.

When sherbet was served, Jannat Ashiyani drank half a glass and gave the rest to Mirza Kamran.

After Humayun Badshah and Mirza Kamran washed hands, the other brothers Mirza Askari and Mirza Hindal passed the ewer and basin to their cousin Mirza Sulaiman since he was older than them. When Mirza Sulaiman cleared his nose after washing his hands, Mirza Askari and Mirza Hindal said harshly, 'What kind of boorishness is this? To begin with what business do we have to wash our hands in the presence of the Emperor? However, since he commanded us to do it, we couldn't change his order. But what does all this snorting mean?'

Mirza Sulaiman was embarrassed and Mirza Askari and Mirza Hindal went out to wash their hands.

That day, they all ate together. Jannat Ashiyani Humayun Badshah fondly remembered his sister Gulbadan.

Gulbadan had played in the lap of her father Babur Badshah. She was born of Dildar Begum and was Humayun Badshah's stepsister. She was two years old when Babur Badshah's elder wife, Humayun Badshah's own mother, adopted her. Gulbadan was eight when her father Babur Badshah passed away. She had seen the reigns of Babur Badshah, Humayun Badshah, and then of Abul Muzaffar Jalaluddin Muhammad Akbar. On Badshah Salamat's order, she wrote the *Humayunnama* to help Sheikh Abul Fazl write *Akbarnama*.

As they sat down for the meal, Humayun Badshah said, 'In Lahore, Gulbadan Begum said she wished to see all her brothers together. I have been remembering her words since we sat down this morning. Insha'Allah, our unity be preserved. God knows I harbour no thought of harming anyone, much less my brothers. May God keep you all loyal and cooperative.'

Now Jannat Ashiyani again came out of his reverie. The nobles were all saying in one voice, 'One who breaks the kingdom must be punished.'

Humayun Badshah said, 'My mind is in agreement but not my heart. If this is your wish, put it in writing.'

All the nobles wrote: 'One who breaks the kingdom must be punished.'

Humayun Badshah was reminded of the day he had besieged Kabul which was under the control of Mirza Kamran. Jalaluddin Muhammad Akbar, who was about five then, was in Kabul, in Mirza

Kamran's custody. There were countless among the royal army who were attacking the city whose families were inside. Mirza Kamran had looted their homes, their children were beaten and thrown down from the parapet, and their women hung by their breasts.

One day, when Kabul was under attack by Humayun Badshah's army, the chief of artillery Sumbul Khan spied a child sitting at a place that was under maximum shelling. Humayun Badshah was dumbstruck when he learnt that Mirza Kamran had placed the young Jalaluddin Muhammad Akbar at the parapet to face the shelling.

Now that Mirza Kamran was in custody, Jannat Ashiyani told his special servant Jauhar Aftabchi to keep a watch over him. Mirza Kamran asked Jauhar Aftabchi, 'I have missed six days of fasting during the month of Ramzan. Can you keep them for me?'

'Yes, I can. But Your Highness will be able to do it for himself. Have courage, and don't let yourself dwell on such things.'

Mirza Kamran asked, 'Will they kill me?'

'Only a king knows a king's mind. But nobody breaks his own hand. Moreover, His Majesty Emperor Muhammad Humayun is kind.'

By the time the royal entourage reached Rohtas, Humayun Badshah had taken a decision. He said, 'Blind Mirza Kamran in both eyes.'

On the orders of Humayun Badshah, the overseer of the Farrash Khana Ghulam Ali told Mirza Kamran, 'O Mirza, if these words were ours, would that our tongues had been cut out, but how can one oppose the command of the Emperor! It has been ordered that a needle be drawn across your eyes.'

'Kill me!' Mirza Kamran said.

'Who would dare to kill you?' Ghulam Ali said.

When Ghulam Ali stretched his hand to catch hold of the prince, Mirza Kamran flung money at his face.

Mirza Kamran was dragged out of his tent and pinned down. A needle was drawn across his eyes fifty times. Mirza Kamran did not utter a sound but he cried out when salt was poured in his eyes.

After that he said, 'Oh Lord, I have paid for my deeds in this world, but I am hopeful of the afterlife.'

Humayun wanted to send him to Kabul but Mirza Kamran said, 'I have ruled over Kabul. How can I go there in this condition? I should have been killed. Since the Emperor has spared my life, he can at least allow me to go to Mecca. If I am not allowed, I will kill myself on the way. He will be responsible for my death.'

Humayun Badshah said, 'How can we let him go in this condition?'

Humayun Badshah was persuaded to let him go with great difficulty and when the royal entourage reached Nilab near the river Indus, he permitted Mirza Kamran to go to Mecca.

Jannat Ashiyani went to Mirza Kamran's tent with his close associates but on the condition that Mirza Kamran would not weep. It was midnight when he reached. Mirza Kamran was led by the hand to the rope of the tent. Seeing his brother's blindfolded eyes, Humayun Badshah broke into tears. Mirza Kamran kept quiet because he had already promised not to weep. Taking his shoes off, Humayun Badshah sat down inside the tent. He indicated that Mirza Kamran be seated opposite him on the other side of the tent so that the two brothers could face each other.

Mirza Kamran recited—

The dervish's cap touched the skies,
When the shadow of a monarch like you fell upon his head.

After which he recited—

Whatever comes from you is cause for thanks,
Be it an arrow of cruelty or a dagger of tyranny.

Mirza Kamran asked the names of the people present and then said, 'You all bear witness that if I knew myself innocent, I would have definitely said so at this time when His Majesty visits me. I am certain I am worthy of death. His Majesty has spared my life and allowed me to go to Hejaz. I offer a thousand thanks because he has not taken revenge.'

When Mirza Kamran gave his children in Humayun's safekeeping, Humayun Badshah said, 'I will look after them as my own children.'

5

Seated in the royal enclosure of Bhera, Jalaluddin Muhammad Akbar remembered the time when he had been in the custody of his uncle Mirza Kamran. It was a tradition since Changez Khan's time that the father threw his turban at his son when he walked for the first time. Since Humayun Badshah was on the run at the time, this duty was performed by Mirza Kamran. He threw his turban at Mirza Akbar so that he would fall now but never again in life.

Mirza Kamran performed Haj three times, and in the second year of the Ilahi calendar corresponding to the fifth of October of 1557 CE, he passed away. His real brother Mirza Askari had already been given permission to go to Mecca but he passed away in the second Ilahi year corresponding to 1558 CE between Badakhshan and Damascus.

Humayun Badshah had defeated and sent both the brothers to Mecca. But he did not live long to enjoy his victory. He passed away before the two vanquished brothers.

The special servant of Jannat Ashiyani Humayun Badshah, Jauhar Aftabchi wrote:

'After defeating Iskandar Sur, Hazrat Padshah ascended the throne in Delhi. He had appointed me, Jauhar, treasurer of the province of Punjab and Multan in Lahore, and I prayed for his well-being day and night. Suddenly, I had a vision from the other world and it seemed as if Hazrat Padshah was telling me, "Prepare a place." I went to the top of a high mountain where a carpet of green had been spread. On that carpet stood the Emperor's court tent, and its robe extended beyond the ocean.

'After setting it up, I told Hazrat Padshah, "The place is ready."

'He said, "Take Jalaluddin Muhammad Akbar Padshah there."

'When I heard the word "padshah" from his blessed tongue, I thought to myself, "Hazrat Padshah would always call him Mirza. Has he now appointed him the king?" Anyhow, I took the prince there. The prince had a white shawl in his hand that he was rolling and unrolling.

'I said, "Your Majesty, you haven't been brought here to play."

'As soon as I said this the prince stood up. Giving me a kettle, he said, "What is it to you whether I play or not?" With this. I woke up.

'Seven days after this the crown of world rule was placed on the regal head of Jalaluddin Muhammad Akbar Padshah Ghazi.'

It was a Friday of the Rabi ul-Awwal month of 963 Hijri, which was the twenty-fourth of January 1556 CE. Jannat Ashiyani Humayun Badshah was in the fort that he had abandoned in an unfinished state when he fled from Hindustan. In the Muharram month of Hijri 940 corresponding to around July 1533 CE, in an auspicious hour, he had begun construction of this city called Din Panah near the shrine of Nizamuddin Awliya by the banks of the river Yamuna. Humayun Badshah had placed the first stone with his own hands. When Hindustan slipped from his hands, this city too had come under the control of Sher Shah. By the time Humayun Badshah won back the city, Sher Shah had made many changes in it.

That evening, Jannat Ashiyani was on the first floor of the octagonal structure called Sher Mandal. He had made his library in this elegant red stone building with a cupola. Since Jannat Ashiyani wore a different colour each day, in keeping with the stars, that day he was in the green that he wore on Fridays. He had met his old friends returning from Mecca and had learnt of the welfare of his brothers. After giving a jharokha darshan from the Sher Mandal, he called in his advisers who were experts in calculation. Because it was the night Venus was to rise, he decided he would hold a grand darbar when the star rose.

Descending from the Sher Mandal, he was on the second step when he heard the azan from the nearby mosque that had been built by Sher Shah.

Allahu Akbar Allahu Akbar
Allahu Akbar Allahu Akbar
Ashhadu an la ilaha illallah
Ashhadu an la ilaha illallah
Ashhadu anna Muhammadur rasul Allah
Ashhadu anna Muhammadur rasul Allah
Haiya alal salah
Haiya alal salah
Haiya alal falah
Haiya alal falah

Allahu Akbar Allahu Akbar
La ilaha illallah.

It was Jannat Ashiyani's habit to sit down as soon as he heard the azan. As he stood up and descended after the azan, his foot got entangled in his robe. The staircase was steep and slippery. He tumbled down and suffered a deep gash on the right side of the head. He departed from this world three days later in an unconscious state. His death was kept a secret for seventeen days. A body double gave jharokha darshan during this period. Celebrations were held for his recovery. Even a firman was sent to his son—

'My dearest son, dearest of the empire, may God give him long life. May it be known that on Friday the eleventh of this month after the asr prayers I went up to my library, which is under renovation and stayed there till the maghrib. When it was time for the maghrib prayer, I was in a hurry to descend. I had just descended a few steps from the eleven-step staircase that the azan was heard. I wanted to sit but in the process my foot got entangled in the fur cloth and I tumbled down the staircase. God saved us and save for a minor injury on head and shoulder there was no pain. By God's grace all is well and no harm happened. Our beloved son need not worry. If he hears any false news, he should not believe it because by grace of God there is no reason to worry. Whatever happens will be conveyed daily.'

Sheikh Abul Fazl wrote that some time before the death of Emperor Humayun, Jalaluddin Muhammad Akbar had dreamt that somebody was pulling at his locks. Maham Anga, who had nursed Mirza Akbar in his childhood, asked many people to interpret this dream. Humayun Badshah had said, 'Evil will be far from his head.'

It is said that later Humayun Badshah told Mirza Akbar quietly that this was a dream about his own impending death.

It is believed that the day Humayun Badshah fell from the staircase, Jalaluddin Muhammad Akbar said, 'A great misfortune will befall an eminent person and he will probably die.'

6

When Jannat Ashiyani Humayun Badshah died, Mirza Akbar was on an expedition to Punjab. As his teacher and a warrior, Bairam Khan was accompanying him. On Friday of Rabi us-Sani 962 Hijri corresponding to the fourteenth of February 1556 CE, Mirza Akbar was crowned at Kalanaur. Bairam Khan's employee Arif Qandhari drew a picture of the occasion:

'I can't say whether people saw the fourteenth moon or they saw a fourteen-year-old emperor ascend the throne. The seekers of truth and intelligent ones know that the age of fourteen is equal to forty, just as the moon of the fourteenth is complete.'

The khutba was read in the mosques and new coins were minted in the name of Jalaluddin Muhammad Akbar. Bairam Khan became the Vakil of the empire. Jalaluddin Muhammad Akbar Badshah Ghazi's reign had begun but all powers were with the Vakil, Bairam Khan.

Although Bairam Khan Khan-i-Khanan saved the Timuri empire at a critical juncture, a flashpoint was inevitable on the issue of who would wield power—the Emperor or the Vakil.

Sheikh Abul Fazl writes:

'One of the paramount conditions of authority is that special servants and those in near attendance should abide by fixed rules. In every section of them, there should be prudent persons to oversee their activities, and take precaution against evil companionship, which is the father and mother of wrong ideas, especially when the lord of the age is too occupied with important matters to tend to details. Otherwise, many of the narrow-minded will cease to respect imperial majesty because of their length of service. The wine of familiarity carries them out of their senses. Great seditions emerge from this intoxication.'

In the fifth Ilahi year, corresponding to the summer of 1560 CE, Badshah Salamat wrote a letter to Bairam Khan Khan-i-Khanan—

'My dear Khan Baba, with affectionate salutation and a message of love, we have to state that on account of certain important matter, we have come to the capital of Delhi. We have also come to know that you intend to continue in the service of the court. So we are dispatching Tarsum Beg to intimate to you that we have certain complaints against you. We feel that the heart of good persons will not reconcile to your continuance in service. We write to assure you that certain unpleasant incidents might have occurred between father and son, but there can be no misunderstandings. You are our Khan Baba and we have respect and regard for this relationship. In spite of the recent painful events and of your improper deeds, we still hold you in our affection and treat you with kindness. We still follow the old custom of calling you "Khan Baba". It is better for you to proceed to holy Mecca for which you have sought our permission. You should send someone to receive presents and cash left behind at Sirhind and Lahore so that it can be sent to you.'

Bairam Khan was of Persian descent and was an old loyalist of the Timuri dynasty. Humayun was still a prince when Bairam Khan had joined his service. Soon after, Babur Badshah noticed him and Bairam Khan joined his service. When Jannat Ashiyani became the emperor, Bairam rejoined his service. From Zahiruddin Muhammad Babur to Jalaluddin Muhammad Akbar, he had served three generations of the Timuri dynasty. He was with Jannat Ashiyani Humayun Badshah in the Battle of Chausa and Kannauj.

When Humayun Badshah had fallen on bad days, he ordered Bairam Khan to go to Qandhar and himself took towards Kabul. It was Bayazid Bayat who took his master's letter to Bairam Khan.

Bayazid Bayat had joined Humayun Badshah in Persia. He was from Tabriz and worked in the kitchens of Jannat Ashiyani. Later he joined Munim Khan Khan-i-Khanan, the powerful noble of Humayun Badshah and Jalaluddin Muhammad Akbar's time. Bayazid Bayat had a powerful memory for old events. When Badshah Salamat directed Sheikh Abul Fazl to write a history of him and his family, he also directed those who had witnessed this history to record it. What Bayazid Bayat related from memory was recorded in the *Tarikh-i-Humayun*.

When Bayazid Bayat dismounted from the horse and stood at his place, Bairam Khan said, 'Why don't you come forward?'

Bayazid Bayat said, 'I have a letter from Hazrat Badshah.'

Bairam Khan immediately dismounted from the horse and said, 'Why didn't you tell me earlier?'

Taking the letter, Bairam Khan performed taslim in the direction of Humayun Badshah and then mounted his horse again.

After defeat at Kannauj, Bairam Khan had once run into Sher Shah. To bring him to his side, Sher Shah said, 'A loyal person will not make a mistake.'

Bairam Khan had replied, 'Absolutely. How will a loyal person make a mistake!'

One night, Humayun Badshah was talking to Bairam Khan, who became inattentive. Jannat Ashiyani said, 'We are addressing you.'

Bairam Khan had immediately become attentive and said, 'My king, I was attending but I have heard that in waiting upon princes one should have heed to his eyes, and when serving dervishes one should have heed to his heart, and in presence of the erudite should guard his tongue, and so I was thinking that as all three personalities were collected in Your Majesty, which of them I should observe.'

In Hijri year 952, corresponding to 1545 CE, Sher Shah was shelling the fort of Kalinjar. What happened here gave a fresh chance to Humayun Badshah. Sher Shah gave orders to fire grenades filled with gunpowder into the fort. One grenade struck the wall of the fort and exploded with great force. Its fragments fell among the other grenades, which exploded, burning Sher Shah severely from head to foot. Sher Shah ran using his hands to cover his body and fell unconscious in his tent. Sandal and rose water was sprinkled on his body but his condition deteriorated. Whenever he regained consciousness, he asked about the state of the siege. He gave up his life when he heard of victory over the fort.

Sher Shah had often looked at his white beard in the mirror and said, 'Alas! That I obtained my kingdom at the time of dusk.'

Before departing from the world, Sher Shah had expressed four unfulfilled desires—

'One is, I wish to have depopulated the country of Roh, and to have transferred its inhabitants to the tract between the Nilab and Lahore, including the hills below Nandana as far as the Shivalik; that they might have been constantly on the alert for the arrival of the Mughals, and not allow anyone to pass from Kabul to Hind, and that they might also keep the zamindars of the hills under control and subjection.

'Another is to have entirely destroyed Lahore, that so large a city might not exist on the very road of an invader, where, immediately after capturing it on his arrival, he could collect his supplies and organize his resources.

'Another is, to have built two fleets of fifty large vessels each, as commodious as sarais for the use of pilgrims from India to Mecca; and to have made them so strong, that wind and storm should have not been able to disperse them; and that all people might go to and from that holy place in ease and comfort.

'The last is, to have raised a tomb to Ibrahim Lodhi in Panipat, but on the understanding that opposite to it there should be another tomb of the Chaghatai sultans, whom I may have dispatched to martyrdom; and to have constructed both with such architectural embellishments, that friend and foe might render their tribute of applause, and that my name might remain honoured upon earth until the day of resurrection. None of these aspirations has God allowed me to carry into effect, and I shall carry my regrets with me to my grave.'

After the deaths of Sher Shah and his son Islam Shah, Afghan power weakened. Islam Shah's minor son Firoz Khan was killed by his maternal uncle Mubariz Khan, who sat on the throne of Delhi as Muhammad Shah Adil, alias Adali. It is said that Islam Shah tried to kill his brother-in-law Mubariz Khan many times. He would tell his wife, 'If you want your son to live, beware of your brother. If you wish to save one, don't hope to save the other.'

Islam Shah's wife Bibi Bai would reply, 'My brother spends all his time in amusing himself and he has no desire to be the king; give up the idea of killing him.'

Despite this Islam Shah would say, 'In the end you will regret this at a time when regret will avail nothing.'

When Mubariz Khan decided to kill the twelve-year-old king Firoz Khan, Bibi Bai fell at his feet, 'Ah, my brother, spare the life of this poor harmless boy, and let me take my own way and bear him away to some place where no one will have a trace of him, and where he will have nothing to do with sovereignty, nay, will not even mention the name of kingship.'

Without heeding her, Mubariz Khan cut off the twelve-year-old's head under the very eyes of his mother.

Within a year Ibrahim Khan of Sher Shah's family forced Adali to leave Delhi. Muhammad Shah Adil set up his base at Chunar.

This was the time when Hemu, a person of the merchant class of Rewari, won twenty-two battles and became Muhammad Shah Adil's most trusted aide. Ibrahim Shah who forced Muhammad Shah Adil to flee Delhi was ousted from Delhi by a nephew of Sher Shah. This nephew sat on the throne of Delhi and took the name Sikandar Shah Sur but lost to Timuri forces in 962 Hijri, corresponding to February of 1555 CE, at Machhiwara and then at Sirhind. Delhi once again came under Humayun Badshah. No Afghan sat on the throne of Delhi ever again. The last Afghan emperor of Hindustan was ousted from Delhi but he was not yet finished. He was challenging Mirza Akbar and Bairam Khan in the Shivalik Hills. Hemu was silently observing the situation. The opportunity he was looking for came with news of Humayun Badshah's death.

Hemu mustered fifty thousand infantry, one thousand elephants, fifty-one heavy and five hundred light cannons and marched towards Delhi. On the first of the Zil Hijj month of the Hijri year 963, corresponding to sixth of October 1556 CE, he pitched his tent at Tughlaqabad near Delhi. Tardi Beg was the governor of the Delhi and Agra region, who was very close to Humayun Badshah and had been with him in bad times. Tardi Beg put up a defensive position against Hemu. The next day, when the fighting began, it seemed that Hemu would lose. The royal army chased Hemu's left flank up to Hodal and Palwal and seized a lot of goods. But the tables turned at Tughlaqabad. Standing at a short distance from his main army, Hemu was taking stock of the situation with three hundred elephants and a group of warriors. He saw that Tardi Beg was also observing the battlefield along with a small group of warriors. Seizing the opportunity, Hemu launched a direct attack at Tardi Beg. This assault changed the royal army's victory into defeat. Tardi Beg fled the battlefield. When the victorious royal army returned from Palwal and Hodal around maghrib, Delhi and Agra had slipped out of the grip of Jalaluddin Muhammad Akbar.

Jalaluddin Muhammad Akbar was in Jalandhar when he received this news. The morale of the court was low. Badshah Salamat had been crowned just a few months back. The fear of losing the throne of Hindustan loomed large once again. It was estimated that Hemu had an army of one hundred thousand as against about twenty thousand of the royal forces.

'This is not the right time to take to the battlefield. We should go to Kabul. We can come back with an army and give a fitting reply to the Afghans next year.' One courtier spoke what most had in mind.

Bairam Khan said, 'To lose a country we have won twice after sacrificing hundreds of thousands of lives without fighting is a matter of shame.'

Badshah Salamat said, 'Khan Baba is right. How can we leave this land? We will not leave Hindustan without a fight.'

Orders were given to march towards Delhi. By the time the royal entourage arrived at Sirhind, Tardi Beg had reached there too. Bairam Khan and Tardi Beg both had been loyal to Humayun Badshah. Tardi Beg had been with Humayun Badshah since the early days. But he had also given him trouble. In Umarkot, Tardi Beg had refused to give his wealth for the army. Humayun Badshah had ordered his wealth to be seized. But Tardi Beg was the person who had brought the news of Jalaluddin Muhammad Akbar's birth from Umarkot and Jannat Ashiyani Humayun Badshah forgave all his mistakes on this happy occasion. Even after this, however, he continued to give him trouble. First the Rana of Umarkot and then another close ally, Munim Khan, had deserted Humayun Badshah because of the quarrelsome nature of Tardi Beg. Thereafter, when Humayun Badshah left for Persia, Tardi Beg joined his stepbrother Mirza Askari. When Jannat Ashiyani returned from Persia, Tardi Beg repented and joined him once again. He was granted the jagir of Mewat. When Jannat Ashiyani Humayun Badshah died, Tardi Beg had the khutba read in the name of Jalaluddin Muhammad Akbar in Delhi and sent the insignia of royalty to Punjab. He had also sent Mirza Kamran's son, Mirza Abul Qasim, as homage to the royal court.

One day when Badshah Salamat returned from a hunt in Sirhind, he heard a disturbing piece of news.

In the afternoon, Bairam Khan Khan-i-Khanan had taken Tardi Beg to his tent. At the time of the maghrib prayer, when Bairam Khan stood up to go for ablutions, his men, on a signal from him, had murdered Tardi Beg.

With this news, Badshah Salamat also got a submission from Bairam Khan Khan-i-Khanan—

'I did this out of loyalty. Tardi Beg is a traitor and deliberately fled the battlefield. His insincerity is known to all because his behaviour has been bad from early days till the end. If such follies are forgiven, Badshah Salamat's plans will not be fulfilled. I am repentant at not taking your permission. I had the courage to do this because His Majesty is very forgiving and would never have agreed to a death sentence. If His Majesty had given orders forbidding the death sentence, it would have been unthinkable for me to go against it. Obeying the order would have meant chaos in the kingdom and rebellion in the army. I hope His Majesty will forgive so that others take a lesson.'

Sentencing a mansabdar of a rank of five thousand without permission was an open challenge to royal authority. But Jalaluddin Muhammad Akbar accepted Bairam Khan's decision. At that vulnerable moment, this is all he could do. Hemu had declared himself the 'Vikramaditya' from the throne of Delhi and the Timuri throne was tottering.

Badshah Salamat's army now marched towards Delhi from Sirhind; 'Vikramaditya' Hemu and the Pathans marched towards the royal force. Both sides finally clashed at the same battlefield of Panipat where about thirty years ago Firdaus Makani Babur Badshah had won the throne of Delhi by defeating the Afghans and had laid the foundation of the Timuri empire in India.

7

It had become very hot in that month of Rajab of Hijri year 932, corresponding to April of 1526 CE, when Firdaus Makani Babur Badshah chose Panipat as the place to take on Sultan Ibrahim Lodhi.

While marching towards Panipat, Sultan Ibrahim Lodhi had asked his astrologers, 'Study our horoscope and tell us who will win.'

The astrologers said, 'It seems from the study of the stars that all our horses and elephants will become part of the Mughal forces.'

Sultan Ibrahim Lodhi asked, 'This means we will attain victory over the Mughals?'

The astrologers said, 'This is what will happen.'

Babur Badshah had begun to plan the layout of his troops keeping the city of Panipat to his right. On the left he had ditches dug and placed a line of carts in the front, which were joined by ropes. Between every two carts were six to seven big shields so that musketeers could fire from behind them. During the six days spent in preparation, there was no attack from the side of Sultan Ibrahim Lodhi. The battle took place on the seventh day, when the advance party returned to inform him that Ibrahim Lodhi's army was advancing rapidly. Babur Badshah planned his defence in such a manner that he held charge in the centre. The left, right and the vanguard were in readiness, the right flank being commanded by Mirza Humayun himself. The cavalry was stationed on the left and right for the tulghama technique of warfare, such that when signalled it would gallop in a semi-circular arc from both sides, surround the army of Sultan Ibrahim Lodhi and launch an attack. Firdaus Makani Babur Badshah estimated that his twelve thousand soldiers were facing at least one lakh of Ibrahim Lodhi's troops.

Ibrahim Lodhi's army was marching fast but faltered when it came near and saw the orderly plan of the opposing force. Now it could neither fully halt nor charge forward. Sultan Ibrahim Lodhi found the vanguard of Firdaus Makani Babur Badshah's army too narrow. By the time he could align his army to match the front of the enemy, Babur Badshah sent his two groups from left and right and attacked Sultan Ibrahim Lodhi's army from behind with arrows. He launched an attack with bows and arrows and cannons from the front as well. Ibrahim Lodhi's army too attacked from the left and right flank but the retaliatory assault was so heavy that his army was sandwiched and could not move ahead nor move back.

Seeing the situation, a loyalist had told Sultan Ibrahim Lodhi, 'It would be better for you to leave the battlefield. If you are safe a big army can be raised again and we can take on the Mughals.'

It is said that Sultan Ibrahim Lodhi replied, 'It is a matter of shame for emperors to flee the battlefield. Look around. There are so many nobles, friends and loyal ones who lie martyred around us. How can we run away? My horse's hooves are sunk in blood up to its neck. I ruled as long as I was fated to rule and fulfilled my desires. Now unpredictable fate is on the side of the Mughals, so why should I live? Better that I and my close ones together become one in dust and blood. Don't you see that emperors have camps of the red colour that stands for honour and success? We have now become red with our own blood. How can we don any other colour after donning red?'

Then Sultan Ibrahim Lodhi recited a couplet—

It does not befit manhood to go any other way,
Those in red cannot turn yellow.

The fighting that began in the morning ended by midday, but Sultan Ibrahim Lodhi was missing. Since some thought that he had fled, Babur Badshah ordered that he be chased till Agra. But in a short while, Sultan Ibrahim Lodhi's head was brought to Emperor Babur. His body was in fact found lying in the dirt. His headgear and royal umbrella—the insignia of royalty—lay at a distance.

It is said that Babur Badshah then reached the spot where Sultan Ibrahim Lodhi's body was found and, raising his body from the dust, he said, 'I salute your bravery!'

On the orders of Babur Badshah, Ibrahim Lodhi's body was given a bath and buried at the very spot he died.

Five to six thousand soldiers were found dead by the side of Ibrahim Lodhi alone. In all, fifteen to sixteen thousand were killed. Some of Sultan Ibrahim Lodhi's astrologers fled the battlefield. The rest died or were imprisoned. A person present in the battlefield wrote of the battle in this manner:

It was thirty-two years beyond nine centuries,
In Panipat in India,
On the Seventh of Rajab crisis befell,
Babur won, Ibrahim lost.

After winning the Battle of Panipat, Babur Badshah wrote:

'Hindustan, from Bhera to Bihar, was under the Afghans, whose padshah was Sultan Ibrahim. In proportion to his territory, his army should have been five hundred thousand. But the eastern amirs were in rebellion. His army was estimated at one hundred thousand and his and his commanders' elephants were estimated to be one thousand. Under such conditions, in this strength, we put trust in God and faced the ruler of such a huge army and of domains so wide. As our trust was in Him, the most high God did not make our labour and hardships in vain, but defeated that powerful foe and conquered that vast kingdom of Hindustan.'

Now in the Second Battle of Panipat, Badshah Jalaluddin Muhammad Akbar and Bairam Khan Khan-i-Khanan were three kos from the battlefield. The advance guard of the royal army was stationed very near Panipat. Its commander Ali Quli Khan was such a brave man that he advanced and snatched Hemu's artillery. In retaliation, Hemu launched his attack with full force.

In the battlefield Hemu—or Basant Rai, his real name—was on his elephant named Hawai. His army had fifteen hundred battleworthy elephants. They included elephants who could run faster than Arabian horses, could create chaos among the horsemen, could move tall buildings and easily uproot strong trees. These elephants could pick up and fling men and horses in the battlefield. Musketeers and bowmen rode these elephants. Hemu had thirty thousand able Afghan and Rajput soldiers. In comparison, the advance guard of the royal force was small. It had about ten thousand people, of which five thousand were warriors. They would have faced defeat on account of the elephants but their bowmen launched such a severe attack on the elephants that Hemu's army fell into chaos. An arrow hit Hemu's eye. Seeing this, his army's morale fell. Hemu was trying to flee the battlefield on his elephant Hawai when he was overpowered. Ali Quli Khan did not know Hemu by his face. So to capture the elephant he kept hitting the mahout. At this the mahout said, 'Why kill me? *This* is Basant Rai.'

Before the army with Badshah Jalaluddin Muhammad Akbar and Bairam Khan could commence their march, news reached them that the advance guard had carried the day. Ali Quli Khan presented Hemu in chains to Badshah Salamat.

Bairam Khan Khan-i-Khanan said, 'His Majesty may please kill him by his own hands and become a ghazi.'

Injured and bareheaded, Hemu stood quietly in front of Badshah Salamat.

Badshah Salamat said, 'We will not be able to kill him. We don't think that killing a prisoner would please God.'

Some of the nobles insisted, but Badshah Salamat refused and said, 'I have already cut this arrogant man in many pieces. This happened after Jannat Ashiyani defeated Sikandar Shah Sur. I was drawing pictures in the library of Jannat Ashiyani. A picture got drawn of a man whose hands and feet were cut from his body. When a noble of the court of Jannat Ashiyani asked, I said, "This is Hemu." Until then Hemu was an unknown name for us. That is why none understood and none asked about it.'

People were amazed at this incident. Sheikh Abul Fazl said, 'Certainly, today, tomorrow, yesterday, the present and the absent may be revealed to ordinary compounds of human nature...but in those whose pure essences are manifestations of the divine radiance, the future and the past attend upon the present and the absent is like the present fully visible... One day when I asked His Majesty the circumstances of this miracle, he replied, "An invisible Inspirer had placed an intimation of it on our tongue; he best knows the secret thereof."'

Bairam Khan Khan-i-Khanan understood that Badshah Salamat would not agree. He immediately killed Hemu with his own sword.

So that all—big and small—learnt a lesson, Hemu's body was publicly hung in Delhi. His head was sent to Kabul so that people there saw it too. Bayazid Bayat was present in Kabul at the time. He is known to have said, 'Munim Khan wrote to me: "As soon as Hemu's head arrives, hang it from the Iron Gate, and have the naqqara beaten for celebration." Three or four hours would have passed when the head reached me. I carried out Munim Khan's order and...delivered the good news of the victory over Hemu to the ladies...the ladies were asking whether it was really Hemu's head and whether the news of victory was correct. I sent Munim Khan's letter to them since most of the ladies knew his handwriting. Once they were convinced they promised me a horse and saropa.'

The day after the victory, Badshah Salamat entered Panipat and had a kalla minar—a tower of skulls—made. Thereafter he immediately reached Delhi and had the khutba read in his name.

Hemu was finished. The last Afghan king to sit on the throne of Delhi, Sikandar Shah Sur, became a noble of the Timuri empire. Afghan power was not entirely wiped out but Timuri power was gaining strength.

This power, however, did not reside in Badshah Salamat.

It was with Vakil-i-saltanat Bairam Khan Khan-i-Khanan.

8

By the fifth regnal year, Emperor Akbar had decided that he would take the reins of power in his own hands. It is said his nurse Maham Anga played a crucial role in this decision. On the twentieth of the Jamadi us-Sani month of Hijri 967, corresponding to 19 March 1560 CE, he left Agra for hunting and immediately went to Delhi on the pretext of his mother Hamida Banu Begum's illness. Before Khan-i-Khanan could see through the design, Badshah Salamat reached Delhi and announced among his close ones that Bairam Khan was on the wrong path and that that was the reason he had come to Delhi without informing him.

A crafty Maham Anga told Badshah Salamat, 'When Khan-i-Khanan gets to know that the royal entourage came to Delhi on my advice, he will wreak revenge. I don't have the power to face him. So it is better that I be allowed to go to Mecca.'

To allay her fears, Badshah Salamat sent a message to Bairam Khan, 'Since we have come here without your advice, my companions are very scared. It is best that your conduct be good, so that they can serve with me without fear.'

In that moment of crisis, Bairam Khan Khan-i-Khanan thought of Mirza Kamran's son, Mirza Abul Qasim. Since Badshah Salamat had been worried that Bairam Khan might place someone else on the throne, he had taken Mirza Abul Qasim along when he left Agra on the pretext of hunting.

Badshah Salamat had childhood memories of Mirza Abul Qasim. Three-year-old Mirza Akbar was not with his parents. He was in the custody of his uncle Mirza Kamran in Kabul. On the occasion of Shab-i-Barat Mirza Kamran organized a feast and presented a kettledrum to his son Mirza Abul Qasim. Babur Badshah's sister Khanzada Begum was present when Mirza Akbar began insisting for the kettledrum. Mirza Kamran told them whoever wins in wrestling would get the kettledrum. In Bagh-i-Shahr Ara outside Kabul, Mirza Kamran seated under a canopy on his cushioned seat and nobles in attandance standing with hands folded at the front were awestruck when Mirza Akbar placed his hand behind the waist of his older brother, raised him in the air and brought him down. It is said that Mirza Akbar's well-wishers took this as a good omen and Mirza Kamran as a bad omen. When Mirza Akbar played the kettledrum he had won, his people saw it as the drum of victory.

Now Bairam Khan Khan-i-Khanan was alone. Badshah Salamat had rejected his message of loyalty and detained his messenger. Bairam Khan tried coming to Delhi to prove his loyalty but Badshah Salamat refused him permission and asked him to go on Haj.

When this happened, one after another, the nobles of the empire began to desert Bairam Khan and present themselves in the court of Badshah Salamat. Mullah Abdul Qadir Badayuni, who wrote a secret history of Badshah Salamat's reign, was reminded of this couplet:

When fate smiles on a slave,
Even strangers become relatives
But as soon as good times pass
One's own doors and walls begin to bite.

Bairam Khan reached Bayana and Nagaur from Agra with the intention of going on Haj. From Nagaur he sent back all his insignia of office and authority, naqqara and alam to the royal court. Despite this, Badshah Salamat's well-wishers did not trust him. They did not let Bairam Khan go for Haj, nor did they allow him to come to Badshah Salamat.

Pir Muhammad Khan was Bairam Khan's vakil—representative. Bairam Khan raised an ordinary cleric to such a high station that even the highest nobility were turned back from his doors. He became so powerful that he began to believe that he was the vakil of the sultanate and not merely the vakil of Bairam Khan. It is said that once Bairam Khan felt hungry on the way from Agra to Delhi. Pir Muhammad Khan laid out a spread that comprised three hundred goblets of sherbet and seven hundred dishes. Bairam Khan had been taken aback by the flamboyance of his vakil. He kept quiet but could not forget it. One day in Delhi, Bairam Khan came to see an ailing Pir Muhammad Khan. Since there were orders to not allow nobles in, one slave stopped Bairam Khan at the door. When Pir Muhammad realized what had happened, he came rushing and said, 'The doorman did not recognize you.'

'Nor did you,' Bairam Khan Khan-i-Khanan said.

Two or three days after this, Bairam Khan sent a letter to Pir Muhammad—

'Have you forgotten those days when you had reached Qandhar in dire straits? Keeping in mind your talent, affection and some instances of commendable service, we had then raised you from dust to a high station... It seems that you are not worthy of this wealth and office and there is an apprehension of rebellion. To bring you to your senses we are taking away the insignia of power that have made you so arrogant. It is best for you to hand over the kettledrums, alam and other goods to officers of state.'

Now the noble Pir Muhammad Khan again became Mullah Pir Muhammad. He was imprisoned in the Bayana Fort and then dispatched towards Mecca. He was on his way when he received a letter from Maham Anga's son Adham Khan—'Please stop wherever you are and wait for the good news.'

After getting the message of Adham Khan Koka, when Pir Muhammad Khan stopped at Ranthambhor, Bairam sent his men to capture him. Leaving all his belongings behind Pir Muhammad Khan fled. He had just reached Gujarat when he heard that Badshah Salamat had taken power away from Bairam Khan. When he came back and reached the court, Badshah Salamat gave him a kettledrum, alam and the title of 'Khan' and sent him in pursuit of Bairam Khan to ensure that he left Hindustan as quickly as possible. Chasing Bairam Khan, Pir Muhammad Khan reached Nagaur and sent him this couplet:

In my heart the foundations of love were firm when I came,
My sorrow-laden soul is full of sorrow for you, my companion.

To this Bairam Khan replied:

It was manly of you to have come,
But your delay, after having come near, is cowardly.

Khan-i-Khanan felt hurt that his former employee had been sent on his trail. He now decided to turn towards Punjab instead of Gujarat.

He wrote to the nobles stationed at the border of the empire, 'I was going to Hejaz but got to know that some people had poisoned Badshah Salamat's ears, especially Maham Anga who claims that she has got Bairam Khan sacked. Now I shall teach such people a lesson and then go for Haj.'

In response to this open declaration of rebellion, Badshah Salamat sent a stern firman to Bairam Khan—

'Be it known to the Khan-i-Khanan that whereas he has been nourished and cherished by this sublime family and his duties of good service to this court have been ascertained, and as Jannat Ashiyani Humayun Badshah—may God be bountiful to him on account of the good qualities and sincerity which appeared in him—bestowed favours on him, and confided to him the great office of being our guardian, and whereas, after that king had departed from the defiles of this world to the wide spaces of the eternal world, he with loyalty and sincerity bound upon his waist the girdle of devotion and discharged the office of Vakil, we, observing his alacrity in that service, and his seemingly good disposition, left to him the bridle of loosening and knotting to the utmost extent conceivable. Accordingly, whatever he wished, good or bad, was carried out, and thus in these five years some improper acts of his came to light which disgusted everyone, such as his patronage of Sheikh Gadai so that he made him sadr, and in spite of the offices requiring consummate ability and knowledge, he, on account of his own private companionship and intimacy, chose him from among all the men who were fit for it by capacity and lineage. And in addition to making him sadr and allowing him to endorse decrees with his seal, he exempted him from the ceremony of homage and in spite of his utter ignorance and want of capacity, he gave him precedence in the paradisiacal assemblies over all the sayyids of noble rank and all the distinguished ulema to whom we paid reverence on account of their rank and qualities. He thus showed in the clearest manner his contempt for the purest and holiest family, in spite of his boasting of his love and affection for that lineage. He gave his protégé, who was rejected and despised by everyone, precedence over those who were divinely nurtured. Feeling no shame or reverence before the holy spirits of all our ancestors, he advanced Sheikh Gadai to such a rank that he appeared before us on horseback. To his own menial servants, whose conditions and qualities were well known, he gave the title of "Sultan" and "Khan", and presented them with flags, kettledrums, rich fief and productive territories, whilst he with total want of consideration made the khans, the princes, the officers, and the trusted servants of Jannat Ashiyani, whose rank, claims and qualifications are known to everyone, to be in want of even dry bread. Nay, he aimed at the life and honour of all of them, and he took no thought for old servants and domestics, who had served for years in hopes of reward and had become entitled to kindness and favour, and did not provide them with even the smallest offices which might have been a means of livelihood to them. As for those who in hunts and expeditions had done service and undergone thousands of labours and troubles, he every now and then fabricated lies against them and thirsted for their blood. He committed various immoderate and disproportionate acts. If his own servants committed a hundred faults such as murder, theft, highway robbery, plundering, and these were brought to his notice, he from partiality and hypocrisy took no notice of them; whereas if a small thing were done by the court servants or were slanderously alleged against them, he had no hesitation of imprisoning them or in putting them to death, or in plundering them.'

Badshah Salamat recalled many decisions made by Bairam Khan.

Once Badshah Salamat's mast elephant went out of the control of its mahout. This elephant caused such grievous injury to Bairam Khan's elephant that its intestines spilled out. For this Bairam Khan had the royal mahout done to death.

Once Bairam Khan was enjoying the breeze on the Yamuna river. Just then, a mast elephant of Badshah Salamat's entered the river and began advancing towards his boat. With great difficulty the mahout controlled the elephant and Bairam Khan was saved. When Badshah Salamat got to know of this, he had the mahout bound and sent to Bairam Khan for his satisfaction. Badshah Salamat had not anticipated that Bairam Khan would sentence the innocent mahout to death.

Bairam Khan Khan-i-Khanan had told Shamsuddin Muhammad Atka Khan, 'We do not have any improper thoughts about the esteemed family of Badshah Salamat. We know that Badshah Salamat undoubtedly has noble thoughts about us. That is why we are not apprehensive of a conflict. Still, if Badshah Salamat's behaviour sometimes turns against us, it must be because of your conspiracies. What have we done that you are thirsting for our blood and have turned Badshah Salamat's noble heart against us?'

Shamsuddin Muhammad Atka Khan was so disturbed to hear this that he appeared before Khan-i-Khanan with his entire family. He swore and tried to convince Bairam Khan that he had not spoken against him, nor would he speak against him.

Badshah Salamat listed many instances of insubordination in his firman that had displeased him though he had kept quiet.

'Some in their utter baseness had engaged themselves in his service, and uttered flatteries to him... He in his simplicity believed them to be truth-speakers and patronized them, and supported them. For instance, Shah Quli behaved in an offensive manner and did not pay heed to orders, and Muhammad Tahir gave such a rude answer that he deserved to have his tongue cut out or rather to be put to death. He heard of this and did nothing. Lang Sarban uttered before a number of people and in his presence such rude expressions that he too was deserving of punishment...in many assemblages such deeds were performed by him as to distress and trouble our capacious soul. As we wished to please him, and regarded him as a sincere well-wisher of our family, and fully relied upon his words and actions, we considered all these unseemly actions of his as his extreme loyalty and goodwill, and knowingly and intentionally passed them over with consummate benevolence... But as we were ourselves giving our attention to affairs of government, it was considered that he should take his own position and submit what he judged proper, and that then we should according to our judgment pass orders thereon. As we had on various occasions represented that the time had come when we should address ourselves to the duties of sovereignty, it was thought that on hearing of this good news he would be pleased, and that he would be firm and constant in obedience. But it came to our knowledge that he had utterly forgotten the favour which had been shown to him while holding his office, and the claims of our glorious family from their favour and patronage of him during forty years, and from their support of him from his cradle and had hearkened to the words of the rebellious. They for their own selfish objects wished to enlist him among the rebels, and in this last stage of his life to exclude him from other-world joys and to involve him in eternal disgrace. Accordingly, from perfect devilry, baseness and arrogance, they won him over and have carried him off the road. Into the imperial dominions he has introduced dissensions and has endeavoured to extinguish by a cold breath the lamp of the dominion of this family which has been kindled by the eternal radiance, and kept alight by the hand of the divine power. Seemingly the veil of pride and arrogance has blinded the eyes of his understanding, and that he does not know that—

> *'Who blows out a God-lighted lamp,*
> *Sets fire to his own beard.*

'Since from considering all that sincerity and reliability which were clearly manifested in all his behaviour, it appeared and still appears that these actions originated in wicked men and were in reality far from himself; nor can it be believed that they are his own, for he has been nourished and cherished by this great family, and obedience to our orders is for him right and proper. We directed for the sake of demonstration that he should withdraw himself from these abominable proceedings, and that he should arrest and send to court this lost and abandoned crew who have been the cause of the destruction of his fortune and honour, and who for their own objects support his rebellion and enmity. As we, during these five years, have respected his wishes and have not shown any recusancy, and have not gone beyond his good pleasure in anything that he proposed, whether it was acceptable to us, or inacceptable, he likewise should at once submit to our order, and not be vexed therewith. Whenever he acts according to this order, we shall clear our heart with regard to him and entirely forgive his crimes and offences. And whenever he is inclined to serve, and there is occasion for it, we shall summon him to our service, so that the veil over him may be removed. And as his services are still appreciated and approved by us, though he has received a thousand favours equal to them, we desire that his name, which has for years been celebrated in all countries and cities for sincerity, devotion, obedience, and reliability, may not become notorious for rebellion, contumacy and sedition. Accordingly, we make known to him the duties of obedience. Let him beware of cherishing other thoughts, and let him be assured that if out of ignorance and short-sightedness he leaves the path, and if pride and arrogance ruin his brain and place him among the seceders, we shall proceed against him with our victorious troops, and attended by dominion and prestige, with the determination to put him down, and by the divine favour, we shall abolish him from the earth. There is hope that under these circumstances, when the fortune of our caliphate is preluding, and his is beginning to retrograde, there will be a great victory, and that he shall be overcome by the army of fortune and put to shame and made a prisoner. Let him not show his folly by thinking that he has bestowed so many favours on his own men during these five years in order that they might be of use in time of need. In his shortness of thoughts and ignorance he does not know that fortune is linked to divine favour. Whenever that favour does not exist, an unfaithful servant does not succeed. Accordingly, it is transparent that most of those who called themselves sons and brothers, and who, he thought, never would separate from him, have under the guidance of auspiciousness separated from him. Those who have remained, are separating, one by one, and coming to court. Gradually they will leave him all alone. Under these circumstances, nothing but submission and surrender will avail.

'The head must bend and the neck obey,
For whatever the just prince does is right.'

When the news came that Bairam Khan had left Bikaner for Punjab, Shamsuddin Muhammad Atka Khan put up a barrier at Gunachaur. At first Khan-i-Khanan's army launched such a fierce attack that most of the royal force ran away, but when Bairam Khan's elephants got stuck in a quagmire, the royal archers got the opportunity to attack them. Bairam Khan had to retreat. Many of his men were injured and many captured.

Bairam Khan took refuge in Talwara by the banks of Beas river. With the help of Raja Ganesh of the region he kept up attacks on the royal forces. Alongside these skirmishes, peace talks began as well. Messages went back and forth but a stalemate prevailed.

Now appeared on the scene a person who had been watching Bairam Khan's activities from the safe distance of Kabul for years. This was Munim Khan Chaghatai, who was Humayun Badshah's associate since the days the Emperor was roaming Sind in dire straits. At that time, his loyalty was suspect but when Humayun Badshah returned from Persia, Munim Khan sided with him. He rose to high office and became the governor of Kabul.

When Akbar was young, one day he told Adham Khan Koka, 'Tell Munim to let us go free today.'

Since Munim Khan enjoyed a high status, Mirza Akbar was granted leave. When Humayun Badshah got to know of this, he told Mirza Akbar, 'Yesterday you had asked Haji Muhammad Sultan for leave. Don't do it again.'

When Mirza Akbar left, Humayun Badshah told Munim Khan, 'Munim, I have heard that it was you who let him go. I told the prince it was Haji Muhammad because he is still young. Let us hope he doesn't remember that it was Munim Beg who let him go and then came and told the Emperor lest, sometime when I am not around, he harms you. Haji Muhammad deserves any harm that comes to him because he is rude.'

Even after the death of Humayun Badshah, Munim Khan remained in Kabul. His status was no less than that of Bairam Khan. He had thus given up the idea of coming to Hindustan after the killing of Tardi Beg because he feared that Bairam Khan might mete out a similar fate to him. Munim Khan came to Hindustan only when he was convinced that Bairam Khan had lost favour. After Bairam Khan's defeat at the hands of Shamsuddin Muhammad Atka Khan, Munim Khan appeared before Badshah Salamat at Sirhind. That very day he was given the office and title that Bairam Khan had enjoyed. Now he became Vakil of the sultanate and became Munim Khan Khan-i-Khanan.

One day Bairam Khan sent Munim Khan a message from inside the fort, 'I am forced to seek refuge with the kafirs. If you could come, take me by my hand and take me down the hill... If Badshah Salamat and his ministers need even a drop of my blood, I am willing.'

When Badshah Salamat got the message, he replied, 'Tell Munim Khan that he is like a father to us. He may do whatever he can think of to placate Bairam Khan and bring him here.'

Gathering courage, Munim Khan went straight inside the fort. He and Bairam Khan were meeting for the first time since the death of Jannat Ashiyani Humayun Badshah. Both had been loyalists of Jannat Ashiyani. Remembering him they wept profusely. It was decided that Bairam Khan would appear before Badshah Salamat.

Munim Khan's employee Bayazid Bayat went ahead to inform Badshah Jalaluddin Muhammad Akbar, who was in Maham Anga's tent at that time. Badshah Salamat recognized Bayazid from afar. The servants present cried, 'Is all well?'

Bayazid Bayat said, 'All is well. The Emperor has a lofty fortune. Bairam Khan is coming.'

It was between the evening and the nighttime prayers when it was learnt that Bairam Khan was about to arrive.

In accordance with Badshah Salamat's orders, the nobles welcomed Bairam Khan like earlier times. When the top of Badshah Salamat's camp became visible, Bairam Khan dismounted and hung his sword around his neck like a wrongdoer. He took his turban off and put it around his neck and tied his hands with his own sash.

As soon as he appeared before Badshah Salamat, he placed his head at his feet. When Bairam Khan kissed his feet, Badshah Salamat took him by his shoulders and raised him. Then Jalaluddin Muhammad Akbar hugged his Khan Baba and made him sit at his old place on the right side. His hands were untied and the turban was placed on his head.

Bairam Khan said, 'I would have liked to give up my life for Badshah Salamat. Alas, a lifetime of loyal service has been laid waste. God knows what all is in store for me. I am grateful that in my last days I am privileged to be at Badshah Salamat's feet.'

Munim Khan said, 'I have assured the Khan that he would be given leave to go to Mecca and Medina.'

Badshah Salamat said, 'We would have liked to keep him in our service but since Bairam Khan has made a request, we grant it.'

Badshah Salamat took off his own saropa and gave it to Bairam Khan. The nobles and commoners pooled in to arrange money and articles of necessity for Bairam Khan.

What Sheikh Abul Fazl spoke of Bairam Khan was in fact Badshah Salamat's innermost assessment—

'In truth, Bairam Khan was a good man, and of excellent qualities. On account of bad company, which is the worst evil for mortals, his excellencies were first perceived by him, and his infatuation was increased by excessive flattery...but the house of flatterers did not do him so much harm as did his honest but inexperienced and short-sighted friends. At length, as he in reality belonged to the band of the auspicious of mind and awakened of fortune, he by good guidance did not end in rebellion and contumacy, and lived to repent. By the blessing of service and grace of pardon he attained to happiness, and the king of the world became pleased with him and was gracious. He set off on a pilgrimage to the glorious places, with honour, accompanied by his family, and provided with goods.'

Badshah Salamat's regard for Bairam Khan was evident in Govardhan's painting. Govardhan had begun work in Badshah Salamat's atelier and then worked for Prince Salim and thereafter came back to Badshah Salamat's atelier before the end of the reign. His pictures seem real, as if he knew the characters closely. On Badshah Salamat's orders, Govardhan painted a scene wherein a young Mirza Akbar was learning to shoot under the guidance of Bairam Khan.

On the way to Haj, Bairam Khan stopped in Gujarat. In the Jamadi ul-Awwal month of 968 Hijri, corresponding to January 1561 CE, he was returning for his evening prayers after an excursion to a pavilion located in midst of the Sahastraling Lake in Patan when about thirty to forty Pathans attacked him. The leader of the gang was a person called Mubarak Khan, whose father had died in the Battle of Machhiwara. One Pathan drew his dagger and struck Bairam Khan in his back with such force that the point came out at his breast. Another struck him on his head and finished him. His daily early morning prayer for martyrdom was finally answered. The attack was so fierce that Bairam Khan's close ones could not even take his dead body. Some poor men and faqirs buried him in the precincts of the nearby shrine of Sheikh Hisam, a disciple of Hazrat Nizamuddin Awliya. Later, his body was taken to Mashhad and buried there in accordance with his wishes.

His wife Salima Sultan Begum, his four-year-old son Abdur Rahim, and others who were with him were pursued by the attackers and they reached Ahmedabad with great difficulty. When Rahim was brought to the court on royal orders, Badshah Salamat took the child on his lap and wept. He said, 'Remember, this is my son. Always keep him in front of my eyes.'

Badshah Salamat took upon himself the responsibility of raising Mirza Abdur Rahim. He entrusted Hakim Abul Fath and Kunwar Man Singh with the task of educating Mirza Abdur Rahim.

When Mirza Abdur Rahim would wake up at night and ask for Bairam Khan, on the orders of Badshah Salamat he was told, 'He has gone on Haj. He has gone to the house of God.'

An important individual of the Timuri dynasty lost his life in the battle that was fought with Bairam Khan. While dispatching his stepbrother Mirza Kamran to Mecca, Jannat Ashiyani Humayun Badshah had promised that his children would be protected. Among these children was Mirza Abul Qasim, whom Bairam Khan had probably thought of raising to the throne. Now Mirza Qasim was imprisoned in the Gwalior Fort and then killed on the orders of Jalaluddin Muhammad Akbar.

9

The cries and shrieks of animals caught in the qamargah could be heard at night in Bhera. The hunt had not yet started but the noose was tightening. In the do-ashiyana manzil, Badshah Salamat was reminded of a very crucial incident from his seventh regnal year. The Vakil of the sultanate, Shamsuddin Muhammad Atka Khan and Munim Khan Khan-i-Khanan were working in the Diwan Khana of Agra Fort. A few months earlier, Badshah Salamat had taken the office of Vakil from Munim Khan and given him the responsibility of assisting the new Vakil, Shamsuddin Muhammad Atka Khan.

While Munim Khan had convinced Bairam Khan to appear before Badshah Salamat, the actual feat of defeating Bairam Khan was performed by Shamsuddin Muhammad Atka Khan. That is why when Bairam Khan's office and title were bestowed upon Munim Khan, Shamsuddin Muhammad Atka Khan wrote a petition to Badshah Salamat—

'After prayers and expressions of devotion, it is represented that when this well-wisher arrived at Delhi, and when His Majesty bestowed royal favours on him and gave him the flag, the kettledrum, tumantogh of Bairam Khan and made him governor of the Punjab, it appeared right that this well-wisher should perform service corresponding to such favours and preferment, so that none of the loyal might say anything against his promotion. When the news came that the disloyal and the seditious had by letters and messages brought Bairam Khan into the neighbourhood of Firozpur, an order was issued that the pillars of the empire should assemble and should represent what should be done for the welfare of the state. In that meeting the letter of Bairam Khan to Darvesh Muhammad Khan was produced. It was there written, "I am the slave and bondsman of His Majesty, but I wish to take vengeance on His Majesty's vakils." Each well-wisher stated at that meeting what he thought should be done to baffle Bairam Khan. As two days ago the paraphernalia of the said Khan's dignity has been bestowed on this well-wisher, he decided that the occasion of doing good service has arrived. There was much talk and discussion among the pillars of the empire, and both small and great were gathered there and this faqir claimed the right of move and proposed that the affair of Bairam Khan should by God's favour and unending auspices of the King come to him, and added, that wherever he met him, or came in sight of him, should he slacken in his advance, he would be worse than slave girls and bad women. The pillars of empire said, "The putting down of Bairam Khan is a great undertaking. So long as His Majesty does not go in person it will not be possible to capture him." When the pillars of the empire were of this opinion, your servant did not say much, but represented to his Lord that Muhammad Qasim Khan and Mahdi Qasim Khan had got leave and gone towards Multan and Lahore. It might be that this servant could also go in employment of a scout of his Lord and report day to day everything that occurred. This well-wishing servant's application was favourably received, and an order was given that he should go, accompanied by the great officers, and suppress Bairam Khan. An order was also given that a thousand men should be enrolled as auxiliaries. He took leave and halted four or five days in the neighbourhood of Rohtak and in pargana Meham, but there was no sign of the auxiliaries. On a representation being made to his Lord, fifteen men, out of all the thousand were sent. As there were many veterans present, the anxieties which are part of warfare came home to them. As also it was the rainy season, and there was mud and water, there was some delay in marching. Men made use of Maham—Maham Anga—as a go-between, and told a hundred thousand tales, such as that the Atka marched every day two kos and did not advance because he was afraid, and that matters would not progress in his hands. He should be deprived of his fief and allowances. Maham acted upon what men said and without giving weight to twenty years' service and affection, represented whatever they said to the Emperor. Your Majesty knows that this was so. My son Aziz Muhammad could not stand men's words and allusions, and wrote, "Father, men's words have killed us. Whatever is your fate will happen. By all means act quickly and dispose of the affairs of Bairam Khan." This well-wisher knew what was designed. In reliance upon the divine favour and the King's fortune he advanced to suppress Bairam Khan. Now the fear of Bairam Khan has been disposed of by Your Majesty's fortune; a number of his attendants and leaders have been killed, and all his relations have been arrested and brought to court. God deliver us! If things had turned out otherwise, one knows what would have happened. Probably the truth of the case has been represented to you by Bairam Khan. After the victory, all the well-wishers who were not present at the battle and whose services are known to Your Majesty, received tenfold presents and favours. As yet no one had asked after the well-wishers who were in the engagement when Jan Muhammad Sultan Behsudi, who was two days in Jalandhar Fort, was recommended and received the title of Khan. Besides him, everyone has received presents and pensions tenfold more than their services. When after all these, this well-wisher and his son Yusuf Muhammad, who wielded his sword in that great battle, had their turn, the favour shown to them was the order of the first day that the name "atka" should appear on the firman. Aalam panah!—protector of the world—this well-wisher regards Maham Anga as a mother, and says no evil of her. May God make lawful what I am about to say! This well-wisher took his life in his hands for the behoof of Your Majesty and taking with him his twelve-year-old son encountered Bairam Khan and his ten to twenty relatives and servants. None of the great officers came from their pargana to help me. And the men who were with me acted in a way which Bairam Khan has probably represented. In such a manner did they behave to this old servant. All the bodyguards of Bairam Khan, who were in Your Majesty's service as spies have by Your Majesty's favour received titles and grants of two or three crores. Yusuf Muhammad Khan encountered with the sword Bairam Khan and his khans, and Your Majesty gave him the title of Khan. The authorities gave him an order for one crore, but it has no assignment. They gave one crore as reward to this servant who has been exalted by the title of "Khan-i-Azam". Out of the whole of it, the authorities assigned only forty lakhs on Firozpur. Protector of the World! All the retainers of this well-wisher have for a lifetime been serving with their brothers and sons in expectation. And now by Your Majesty's good fortune each has been exalted by the title of Khan and Sultan. As the flag, kettledrum and tumantogh of Bairam Khan have been presented to this humble one, and as after the victory over Bairam Khan, jama-i-daqu [fur garment given as an honour] and robe of victory and the insignia of his dignity have been granted, and his rank bestowed upon him, he is hopeful that his office also will be assigned to this humble one.'

When within a year, Badshah Salamat took away the powers of the Vakil from Munim Khan and granted them to Shamsuddin Muhammad Atka Khan, it dealt a blow to two people. Munim Khan Khan-i-Khanan and Maham Anga did not take Atka Khan's promotion too well. Munim Khan quietly began to instigate Maham Anga's son Adham Khan, a young man intoxicated by youth and prosperity.

In the do-ashiyana manzil of Bhera, Jalaluddin Muhammad Akbar was reminded of the day when two persons close to the Timuri dynasty had lost their lives. It was the seventh regnal year of Badshah Salamat, corresponding to the summer of 1562 CE. Adham Khan Koka and his men entered the Diwan Khana of Agra Fort, where the Vakil of the sultanate, Shamsuddin Muhammad Atka Khan was busy working. Munim Khan Khan-i-Khanan was by his side. Seeing Adham Khan, the people in the Diwan Khana stood up. Shamsuddin Muhammad half rose. Putting his hands on his dagger, Adham Khan swaggered towards him and told one of his men, 'Why do you stand still?'

The man dealt a grievous blow on the breast of Shamsuddin Muhammad Atka Khan, who was caught completely unawares. When he tried to run towards the door of the Diwan Khana, another of Adham Khan's men struck him with his sword and killed him.

Chaos reigned in the Diwan Khana. Munim Khan feared he would be accused of being a co-conspirator. So he not only fled Agra but also destroyed the bridge of boats over the Yamuna river so that no one could easily give him chase. On the other hand, Adham Khan, far from fleeing, ascended the staircase and tried to enter the harem but the khwaja sara—the eunuch guardian of the harem—Niyamat closed the door from inside.

Hearing the commotion, Badshah Salamat woke up. Quickly wearing his loincloth, he came out bare-bodied, with a scimitar in his hand. Even in that state, he had on his headgear with a sarpech and a red sash around his waist. Badshah Salamat did not come out the door at which Adham Khan stood. As soon as he came out the other door, he met Rafiq Charmansab, who had been a family retainer of Babur Badshah's sister Khanzada Begum. Badshah Salamat asked, 'Whose body is this?'

Rafiq Charmansab replied, 'My Emperor, it is your Atka.'

'Who killed him?' Badshah Salamat asked.

'Adham Khan,' Rafiq Charmansab said.

Just then Badshah Salamat saw Adham Khan Koka, who was coming towards him. A furious Emperor asked in Hindustani, '*Gandu*, why did you kill our Atka?'

'He was disloyal,' Adham Khan replied.

Badshah Salamat's hand was on his scimitar but Adham Khan ran and caught his hand and said, 'Majesty, just think! Just a small dispute!'

Badshah Salamat looked at Adham Khan's face. He was a koka to Badshah Salamat. Adham Khan's mother Maham Anga had been a nurse to him. Jalaluddin Muhammad Akbar could never forget the day when as a child Humayun Badshah's brother Mirza Kamran had placed him in the line of cannon fire. Maham Anga had sat as a human shield between cannon fire and Mirza Akbar.

In front of Badshah Salamat lay the dead body of his wet nurse Jiji Anga's husband Shamsuddin Muhammad Atka Khan. The murderer of Shamsuddin Muhammad Atka Khan, Adham Khan, whose mother Maham Anga had brought up Badshah Salamat, stood in front of him.

Badshah Salamat was reminded of Adham Khan's misdeeds. When Adham Khan had sent the details of victory over Baz Bahadur of Malwa, he had kept the war booty for himself, just sending some elephants to the court. A displeased Jalaluddin Muhammad Akbar immediately left for Malwa. Travelling day and night he reached Sarangpur in sixteen days, taking Adham Khan by surprise. Kissing his stirrups, Adham Khan had presented new clothes to the Emperor. At first Badshah Salamat refused to accept them but upon seeing Adham Khan Koka's agitation he had finally agreed. Close on the heels of Badshah Salamat, when his mother Maham Anga reached Malwa, Adham Khan gave an account of the spoils of war and presented women from Baz Bahadur's harem, and his courtesans and goods. When the royal cavalcade was returning to Agra from Sarangpur, Badshah Salamat learnt of another trick Adham Khan had played. Two dancing girls of Baz Bahadur's harem, who were meant for Badshah Salamat's harem, were surreptitiously taken into custody by Adham Khan. When this became known, the royal cavalcade was stopped and men were sent for the girls. But Maham Anga had the girls put to death so that Adham Khan's complicity was not revealed.

Badshah Salamat could not forget the night he had spent on Adham Khan's terrace in Malwa. It is said that Adham Khan had resolved that he would get Badshah Salamat killed if he as much as peeped down the terrace into his harem.

Badshah Salamat released his hold on his scimitar and freed his hand from Adham Khan's. His hands reached out to take Adham Khan's sword.

Seeing this, Adham Khan placed his hand on his sword which Badshah Salamat immediately removed from there. After this Emperor Jalaluddin Muhammad Akbar dealt him such a powerful blow that his koka fell off. He then told people standing nearby, 'What are you doing standing idle! Tie this madman's hands and feet!'

On the orders of Badshah Salamat, Adham Khan Koka was flung from the terrace. He did not die the first time. So he was thrown head first a second time. This time his neck snapped and he died.

Badshah Salamat then went to Maham Anga and said, 'Mama! Adham Khan killed our Atka. We have inflicted retaliation upon him.'

'You did well,' Maham Anga replied.

Maham Anga was under the impression that Adham Khan Koka had been imprisoned. Later, when she learnt the truth, she decided to go to her son's house. Badshah Salamat felt Maham Anga would not be able to bear the sight of Adham Khan. So he consoled and stopped her from going there.

Neither could Shamsuddin Muhammad Atka Khan's family believe that Adham Khan had died. They too wanted to wreak revenge upon Adham Khan. Finally, when Badshah Salamat allowed their representative to see the dead body of Adham Khan, the Atka family was pacified.

The bodies of Shamsuddin Muhammad Atka Khan and Adham Khan were sent to Delhi and Badshah Salamat himself walked some distance with the funeral procession. Although Adham Khan Koka died a short while after Shamsuddin Muhammad Atka Khan, he was buried a day before him. Adham Khan's death was such a blow to Maham Anga that she too passed away after the fortieth-day ceremony of Adham Khan. By Badshah Salamat's orders, a magnificent octagonal mausoleum with arched verandahs on all sides was built for Maham Anga and Adham Khan Koka near the shrine of Qutbuddin Bakhtiyar Kaki.

Shamsuddin Muhammad Atka Khan's mausoleum was built by his son Mirza Aziz Koka near the shrine of Hazrat Nizamuddin Awliya. This square mausoleum was built of red stone. It was inlaid with stones of many colours with Quranic verses carved on marble.

Munim Khan Khan-i-Khanan, who had fled Agra, was persuaded to return.

A few days after this incident, Badshah Salamat asked Munim Khan, 'What do people say of our sultanate?'

Munim Khan said, 'May His Majesty live a hundred and twenty years! Ever since you ordered Adham Khan's killing for the death of your Atka, and of Muazzam for the killing of Bibi Fatima's daughter, people praise you a lot. Your justice was perfect.'

Khawaja Muazzam was the stepbrother of Badshah Salamat's mother Hamida Banu Begum and had been pardoned many times for his follies. But Badshah Salamat finally ran out of patience when Khwaja Muazzam's mother-in-law Bibi Fatima came with a petition.

'Now he is taking my daughter to his pargana. He could not take my daughter's life here because of the fear of Badshah Salamat but what will happen there?'

Bibi Fatima had been in the service of Humayun Badshah and now occupied a high position in the harem of Badshah Salamat. Her daughter Bibi Zehra was married to Khwaja Muazzam.

Hearing Bibi Fatima's petition, Badshah Salamat immediately

crossed the Yamuna on a boat and disembarked at Khwaja Muazzam's house to counsel and chastise him.

When he heard of the arrival of Jalaluddin Muhammad Akbar, Khwaja Muazzam said, 'I will not meet His Majesty.'

Just then Bibi Zehra came out of the bath and Khwaja Muazzam plunged his dagger into her. Then, throwing away the weapon, he put his head out of the window and said, 'Go and tell everyone. I have killed her.'

When the dagger was shown to Badshah Salamat, he lost his cool. When he entered the house, he found Khwaja Muazzam's hand on his sword. Badshah Salamat said, 'What is this? If you try drawing your sword, you will get such a blow on your head that you will not survive.'

Khwaja Muazzam lost his strength and sank to the floor upon hearing this.

Badshah Salamat asked, 'Why did you spill the blood of an innocent woman?'

When Khwaja Muazzam began babbling nonsense in reply, he was dealt blows with hands and feet and silenced. He was dragged by his hair to the river and an attempt was made to kill him by drowning. Even in this state he insolently criticized the saints just so that Badshah Salamat should hear it. When attempts to drown him failed, he was imprisoned in the Gwalior Fort where he eventually lost his mind and died.

Hearing Munim Khan speak of the death of Adham Khan and Khwaja Muazzam, Badshah Salamat said, 'We have done far bigger things. I wonder why people do not mention them. You know of it but do not speak for it might hurt some people.'

Munim Khan said, 'How can it be that I keep silent before Hazrat about something I know?'

Badshah Salamat said, 'I called Atka's clan from Lahore and scattered them like stars and gave them fiefs in various parts of Hindustan. This is far more significant than what you mentioned.'

The Atka clan had been scattered. With the death of Adham Khan and Maham Anga, their family too began to lose its clout. Munim Khan got back the office of Vakil after some time but this office lost the prominence it had earlier enjoyed. Munim Khan's prestige at court diminished but now a crucial phase of his life began—that of commanding the army in the battlefield.

10

At this moment, Badshah Salamat was not too far from his stepbrother Mirza Hakim's territory. He had let Kabul stay with Mirza Hakim. Badshah Salamat was reminded of the winter of his eleventh regnal year, corresponding to 1566 CE, when Mirza Hakim had entered Punjab. When the ruler of Badakhshan Mirza Sulaiman drove Mirza Hakim out of Kabul, he had tried to capture Lahore. It was a delicate situation for Badshah Salamat. The Uzbek nobles had rebelled in the east. Badshah Salamat had just left for Lahore when the Mirza clan of Sambhal too rebelled. Very quickly, he foiled Mirza Hakim's attempts by capturing Lahore. Now that the Uzbek nobles knew that Badshah Salamat would turn upon them, they took a step that closed forever the possibility of peace between them.

The Uzbek nobles' rebellious nature was evident within a short time after Badshah Salamat's accession. Powerful Uzbek nobles like Ali Quli Khan-i-Zaman, Bahadur Khan, Sikandar Khan, Ibrahim Khan and Abdullah Khan had fiefs in Awadh, Jaunpur, Banaras, and Malwa. Together they were so powerful they were defying the state. Of these the most powerful was Ali Quli Khan-i-Zaman. His father Haidar Sultan Uzbek Shaibani had fought for Shah Tahmasp of Persia in the famous Battle of Jam in 935 Hijri, corresponding to the September month of 1528 CE. He came to Hindustan with Humayun Badshah. He had fought valiantly in the Battle of Qandhar that Jannat Ashiyani won. After him, Ali Quli displayed bravery in Humayun Badshah's campaign to recapture Hindustan and rose to a high rank. He was granted the title of Khan-i-Zaman for defeating Hemu in the Second Battle of Panipat and was thenceforth known as Ali Quli Khan-i-Zaman.

He fell in love with the son of a camel-driver, Shaham Beg. He would prostrate himself before him and call him 'My King!' This brought him a lot of disrepute. He was called to the court and asked to desist from such activities. When this did not have any effect, Badshah Salamat became angry. When the Afghan power reared its head in the post-Bairam Khan era, Ali Quli Khan-i-Zaman defeated them but did not send the booty to the Emperor. In the seventh regnal year, corresponding to the July month of 1562 CE, when Jalaluddin Muhammad Akbar launched an expedition to the east, Ali Quli Khan-i-Zaman and his brother Bahadur Khan arrived at the royal court, which was then assembled at Kara by the banks of the Ganga, with elephants and precious goods.

Uzbek nobles were sometimes defiant, sometimes compliant. Badshah Salamat too would at times use power against them and at times forgive them. This continued for a while. Once Munim Khan Khan-i-Khanan was stationed at Buxar to crush their rebellion. Ali Quli Khan-i-Zaman sent Agha Sarv-qad who had been in service in the harem of Babur Badshah and had once been a confidant of Munim Khan. Ali Quli had thought that Agha Sarv-qad would gather intelligence about the royal forces but on the contrary Munim Khan gathered from her information about the circumstances of Ali Quli Khan-i-Zaman. Munim Khan sent a message to Ali Quli Khan-i-Zaman through Agha Sarv-qad—

'What has entered your mind? Give up your deplorable activities and take refuge at the Emperor's court. Tell me if you have any requests. I will communicate them to His Majesty and settle your issues. Else I will write to the Afghans, who you deem to be your supporters, and tell them to arrest you and bring you here.'

Finally, it was decided that both would meet midstream in the Ganga near Buxar. Both the armies kept watch on the banks. Ali Quli Khan-i-Zaman and Munim Khan Khan-i-Khanan reached the middle of the river in their separate boats. When just a short distance away, Ali Quli Khan-i-Zaman jumped into Munim Khan's boat. Meeting for the first time after the death of Humayun Badshah, they embraced and wept profusely. Both then placed their hands on the Quran and took an oath of loyalty to Badshah Salamat.

Such oaths did not stop the Uzbek nobles from rebelling. Now that Badshah Salamat had driven Mirza Hakim out of Lahore, both sides resolved to fight to the finish. The Uzbek nobles declared Mirza Hakim their emperor. A khutba was read in Mirza Hakim's name from Jaunpur. Coins were minted in his name. No compromise was now possible.

Sheikh Abul Fazl says, 'Only the acute and the truth-discerning know the difference between the good and the evil in the world. Just as poison and medicine both are used in cure, in spiritual remedies as well both kinds of people are needed. Evil ones are encouraged so that they meet their end. What happens if he falls from the wall? What happens if he falls from a hill? If he falls from the highest heaven, he would be reduced to dust. That is, what would happen if he falls from the sky of fidelity to the dusty abode of disloyalty?'

Badshah Salamat took the road from Lahore to Agra and from there marched eastwards. Chasing Ali Quli Khan-i-Zaman, he reached Rae Bareli. It was the monsoon season and the Ganga was in spate. Despite this, he crossed the river from Manikpur and reached within half a kos of the enemy camp. Oblivious of the danger, Ali Quli Khan-i-Zaman and his brother Bahadur Khan drank and watched dance that night. Reports of the royal army's arrival kept coming in all night but they paid no heed. The next day, which was the ninth of June 1567 CE, in the twelfth regnal year, when Jalaluddin Muhammad Akbar's kettledrums sounded, his royal standard became visible, and then Badshah Salamat appeared himself, Ali Quli Khan-i-Zaman was taken completely by surprise. In a hurry he took to the battlefield.

That very day a few of Badshah Salamat's loyalists were pondering rumours that were causing gloom. One of them said, 'Why don't we in one voice spread the news that the heads of Ali Quli Khan-i-Zaman and Bahadur Khan are being brought?'

This rumour spread like wildfire and became known all across Agra.

Badshah Salamat had entrusted Munim Khan Khan-i-Khanan with the responsibility of Agra in his absence. Munim Khan spoke to Badshah Salamat's loyalist Sheikh Mubarak Nagauri about the low morale of the people in the city.

Sheikh Mubarak's ancestors belonged to Prophet Muhammad's Quraysh tribe. In the fifteenth century, Sheikh Mubarak's great-great grandfather Sheikh Musa came to Sind from Yemen. From there the clan came to Nagaur, where Sheikh Mubarak was born. He was educated at Nagaur and then at Ahmedabad. Ahmedabad was then a major centre of Islamic learning. Here Sheikh Mubarak read the Maliki, Shafi'i, Hanafi and Hanbali schools of Islamic jurisprudence of Sunnis and also the jurisprudence of the Shiites. It is said that when Sheikh Mubarak reached Agra from Gujarat, he met Sheikh Alaul Balaul, to whom the people of the city would come with their problems. Sheikh Alaul Balaul told Sheikh Mubarak, 'Settle down in this auspicious city. You will have capable children. You will attain great wisdom and great happiness. But sorrow, conspiracies and disrepute that will tear your heart also await you. Don't be disheartened. Finally, all will be well.'

In Agra, Sheikh Mubarak settled down at the place where Firdaus Makani Babur Badshah had built the Chahar Bagh. He began to spend his time in imparting religious instruction. Sher Shah and Islam Shah tried to grant fiefs to him but the Sheikh refused. In time, two of his sons attained high stations in Badshah Salamat's court. They were Sheikh Abul Fazl and Sheikh Faizi.

While Badshah Salamat was on the expedition to the east, Munim Khan requested Sheikh Mubarak to arrange a Sufi service and to find out what is to happen. Sheikh Mubarak's face wore a happy look the next day. He told Munim Khan, 'Last night it was intimated to me that the heads of Ali Quli and Bahadur will soon be brought.'

The forces of Badshah Salamat and those of Ali Quli Khan-i-Zaman came face to face near Allahabad. At first Badshah Salamat remained on his elephant Bal Sundar but took the seat of the mahout. Thereafter he mounted a horse and rushed into battle. Ali Quli Khan-i-Zaman's brother Bahadur Khan was captured by the royal forces and his soldiers ran away. Ali Quli was asking about his brother when an arrow struck him. The next arrow struck his horse and he was thrown off. He was trying to extricate the arrow from his body when mahout Somnath reached the spot with the royal elephant Narsingh.

Ali Quli Khan-i-Zaman said, 'I am the commander of the army. Take me alive to the Emperor. You will be honoured.'

'Thousands like you are dying unknown. Those wishing ill of the Emperor are better off dead.' With these words the mahout Somnath crushed Ali Quli Khan-i-Zaman under his elephant.

The writer of the secret history of Badshah Salamat's reign Mullah Abdul Qadir Badayuni said, 'With its feet and trunk the elephant ground his bones to powder and made his body like a sack full of chess pieces.'

When a man arrived with the head of Ali Quli Khan-i-Zaman, his vakil recognized him. In sorrow he banged his head on that of Ali Quli Khan-i-Zaman's and said, 'Alas! This is the head of Ali Quli.'

Then somebody said, 'He always chewed betel leaf on the right side of his mouth. His teeth on the right side would be black.'

As soon as the head was identified Badshah Salamat got off his horse and thanked God.

When Ali Quli Khan-i-Zaman's brother Bahadur Khan was brought in, Badshah Salamat asked, 'How are you, Bahadur?'

Like Ali Quli Khan-i-Zaman, his brother Bahadur Khan too had once been close to Jannat Ashiyani Humayun Badshah. During a campaign a weary Emperor Humayun had placed his head in the lap of Bahadur Khan, who had sung him to sleep. Today he stood as a wrongdoer before the son of Jannat Ashiyani.

'Grace of God in all circumstances,' Bahadur Khan replied to Badshah Salamat.

Badshah Salamat wanted to spare his life but he was beheaded on the advice of the nobles.

A proclamation of victory was issued on the occasion—

'Grace and help of God, which is always with Badshah Salamat's sultanate! The rebels ran away after our frontal attack and our brave warriors who broke the defence of the enemy killed a large number of them and packed Ali Quli off to his final destination and brought Bahadur to Badshah Salamat. The rest of the rebels were scattered and in a sorry state ran barefoot to the jungles and hid there. About one hundred elephants were captured in the war and this army, which has become a symbol of victory, got much war booty. Praise be to God for His numerous and unending bounties and gifts. That is why when the news of this victory is heard, people should get busy praying to God and also surely note that wishes are granted as a result of Badshah Salamat's favour.

'Written on the order of Badshah Salamat. To remain in force and obeyed till eternity.'

The heads of the two brothers were sent to Agra, Delhi, Lahore and beyond that to Kabul as well so that doubts of all classes of people be put to rest and they see the fate meted out to those issuing coins in the name of Mirza Hakim.

11

The tall akashdiya lit up the wilderness of Bhera far and wide and could be seen from a long way off. The royal encampment was not too far from the sultanate of Badshah Salamat's stepbrother Mirza Hakim.

Badshah Salamat was being read his favourite book, *Akhlaq-i-Nasiri*—

'The king should keep his secrets concealed, so that he can change his mind without sounding contradictory. This is also necessary for the reason that the enemy would become vigilant if he gets to know the plans. The need to keep secrets has to be combined with the need to consult intelligent people. This is possible by only consulting men who are intelligent and have administrative abilities and who would not publicize their opinion. Such matters should definitely not be shared with persons of weak intelligence, like women and children. When a matter has been decided, one should mix the first steps in the desired direction with steps opposite to it. One should not go to extremes in either direction because it might evoke suspicion or give away the actual plan.'

Badshah Salamat's close courtier Abul Fazl wrote, 'Badshah Salamat believed that travel and hunting provided occasion to provide justice to the subjects. During the hunt he acquires a knowledge of the events of the world and puts down oppressors. He thinks that perhaps he may fall in with some good man and thereby get wisdom. Someone may quietly communicate religious knowledge to him, and his heart may be at rest from the questions of why and wherefore. Badshah Salamat was travelling and enjoying the hunt but in reality he was making an effort to win people's hearts with all his might.'

While on his way to Bhera, Badshah Salamat had stopped at Ajmer.

Those days he would go to the urs of Sheikh Muinuddin Chishti every year in the month of Rajab. He had an old association with the shrine. After Bairam Khan's removal, one night he had left Agra on a hunt. Passing through Mandhakar on his way to Fatehpur, he found minstrels singing of the miracles of Khwaja Muinuddin Chishti. He immediately made up his mind to visit Ajmer.

Khwaja Muinuddin Chishti belonged to Seistan but had become associated with the Sufi tradition that began a hundred miles east of Herat in the town of Chisht. He was fifteen when he lost his father. One day when Sheikh Ibrahim Majzub—the ecstatic—of Qunduz passed by his garden, Khwaja Muinuddin Chishti offered him a seat under a tree and offered him grapes. Sheikh Ibrahim Majzub chewed some sesame seeds and then put them into the mouth of Khwaja Muinuddin Chishti. It is said that this aroused spiritual illumination in him and he became free of worldly bonds. He sold all his possessions and distributed the proceeds among the dervishes. After that, he studied in Samarqand and Bukhara. Then in Harwan, he learnt to control his desire by the most difficult means under the notable Sufi of the Chishti order, Sheikh Usman Harwani, who made Khwaja Muinuddin Chishti his khalifa—spiritual representative. After that Khwaja Muinuddin Chishti travelled far and wide. Travelling to Baghdad, Hamadan, Tabriz, Kharqan, Astarabad, Herat, Hissar Shadman, Balkh and Ghazni, he finally reached Hindustan before Muizuddin Muhammad seized Delhi. After spending some time in Lahore and Delhi, he came to Ajmer and settled there.

Khwaja Muinuddin Chishti's piety and simplicity won people over. He believed that helping the helpless and feeding the hungry was the highest form of worship. When he was asked what was expected of a true ascetic, he said that according to the sharia, one who fully obeyed the commandments of God and abstained from what God had forbidden has truly renounced the world. But on the Sufi path, one had to fulfil nine conditions to be called a real dervish. On Khwaja Muinuddin Chishti's bidding, his disciple wrote down the nine conditions for all to know—

'Do not earn money. Second, do not borrow money from anyone. Third, do not reveal to anyone nor seek help from anyone if one has eaten nothing, even for seven days. Fourth, if one gains plenty of food, money, grain or clothing, do not keep anything for the following day. Fifth, one should not curse anyone, and one should pray to God to show the right path to one's enemy. Sixth, one should consider one's virtuous deed to be due either to the kindness of one's pir, to the intercession of Prophet Muhammad or to divine mercy. Seventh, hold the evil inside you responsible in case you do something wrong. Desist from wrongdoing. Be afraid of God and beware of deeds that will take you towards evil. Eighth, observe fast during the day and pray at night. Ninth, be quiet and speak only when necessary. According to the sharia, it is wrong to speak continuously as also to remain absolutely silent. Bring only those words on your lips which would please God.'

Khwaja Muinuddin Chishti believed that the haji circumambulated the Ka'ba and the arif—one who knows God—circumambulates the heart. He believed in ecstatic love for God. There was no difference between the lover, the beloved and love itself.

About three hundred years before Badshah Salamat came into this world, Khwaja Muinuddin Chishti left this world on the sixth of Rajab of 663 Hijri, corresponding to 16 March 1236 CE at the age of ninety-seven. He was buried in Ajmer right at the spot where he had spent much of his time. He brought the Chishti order of Sufism to Hindustan in the twelfth century. After him Hazrat Khwaja Qutbuddin Bakhtiyar Kaki of Delhi, Baba Farid Shakarganj of Pakpattan, Hazrat Nizamuddin Awliya of Delhi and Sheikh Salim Chishti of Sikri took the Chishti tradition forward.

After hearing of the miracles of Sheikh Muinuddin Chishti from the minstrels, Badshah Salamat dispatched the royal harem with Maham Anga and himself left with his hunting party by another route on the fourteenth of January 1562 CE in the sixth regnal year. This was Badshah Salamat's first pilgrimage. After this he was often in Ajmer. Badshah Salamat developed a spiritual link with the shrine and a temporal one with Ajmer. He could keep an eye on the affairs of Gujarat from here.

The royal entourage was camped by the river. Badshah Salamat recalled that his son Sheikhu ji was hesitant to enter the water that day. Badshah Salamat had taken hold of him and given him a few dips. Sheikh Salim Chishti had given his own name to Badshah Salamat's heir. That is why Badshah Salamat never called his son by his name. He always called him Sheikhu ji. Sheikhu ji was nine now. When Badshah Salamat had been that age, he had already developed an inclination to meet holy persons. In Hijri 959, corresponding to 1551 CE, Jannat Ashiyani Humayun Badshah had sent him to

Ghazni. There Mirza Akbar had met Baba Bilas, who lived in a cave. He wore a short loincloth and a thin shawl, and had white hair and a white beard. Baba Bilas had seen signs of spiritual and temporal success on the forehead of the prince and congratulated him for the simultaneous possession of supremacy within with worldly glory. When the nine-year-old prince seated on a flower-patterned carpet and the elderly Baba Bilas seated on a tiger skin had discussed religious issues, the rest of the people had stood in respect.

Badshah Salamat had lost many children after their birth when he knocked at the doors of Sheikh Salim Chishti. Sheikh Salim Chishti had built his hospice on a hillock in Sikri near Agra. His fame had spread far and wide. Even in the bitter cold he wore a thin cloth and bathed twice a day. He had travelled for Haj once through the sea and once overland. In all, he had performed Haj twenty-two times. Fourteen times during the first visit and eight in the next.

In the hospice on the Sikri hillock, Jalaluddin Muhammad Akbar asked Sheikh Salim Chishti, 'How many sons will I have?'

Sheikh Salim Chishti said, 'God will give you three sons.'

Badshah Salamat said, 'I will give the first son to your guardianship.'

Sheikh Salim Chishti then said, 'I also accept him as my son.'

Badshah Salamat's favourite court musician Miyan Tansen had sung:

The soft-hearted, son-bestowing Sheikh Salim Chishti has illuminated the realm of faith,
His name drives away worries and kufr,
Gharib Nawaz—patron of the poor—have mercy on your slave Tansen and give him faith!

The moment Badshah Salamat realized that his wife Maryam Zamani—Mary of the age—daughter of Raja Bharmal of Amber, was expecting, she was sent to Sikri along with many functionaries of the harem, so that the heir to the Timuri dynasty was born near Sheikh Salim Chishti. Badshah Salamat also came there for some time.

From the hillock in Sikri, Badshah Salamat could clearly see the battlefield of Khanwa. Had Firdaus Makani Babur Badshah lost the battle that took place sixteen kilometres from Sikri, on the thirteenth day of the Jamadi us-Sani month of 933 Hijri, which was sixteenth of March 1527 CE, Timurids would have lost power. Emperor Babur took the field against Rana Sanga, who had acceded to the throne of Mewar after a long struggle with his brothers. He had fought many battles with Ibrahim Lodhi and had lost one leg.

After defeating Ibrahim Lodhi, people close to Babur Badshah had been getting weary of Hindustan. Babur Badshah called them and said:

'There can be no supremacy and grip on the world without means and resources. Without land and retainers, sovereignty and command are impossible. By toil of several years, by encountering hardships, by long travel, by flinging myself and the army into battle, and by deadly slaughter, we through God's grace, beat these masses of enemies to take their land. And now what necessity has arisen that we should without cause, abandon countries taken at such risk of life? Was it for us to remain in the harsh poverty of Kabul? Henceforth, let no well-wisher of mine speak of such things! But let not those turn back from going who have decided to depart.'

This put to rest the concerns of people but Khwaja Kalan, who was Babur Badshah's close friend—and they had fought many battles together—was so weary of Delhi that he got a couplet written in marble on the wall of his house in Hauz-i-Khas.

If safe and sound I cross Sind,
Blacken my face if ever I wish for Hind.

Babur Badshah took it as an affront and wrote in reply:

Give a hundred thanks, Babur, that the generous Pardoner has given you Sind and Hind and a vast kingdom,
If you cannot endure the heat, and say, 'I would see the face of cold,' there is Ghazni for you.

Now the fear of Rana Sanga of Mewar gripped the army of Babur Badshah. Its morale was low. Emperor Babur wrote:

'Our people of higher and lower ranks were anxious and timid. No manly word or brave counsel was heard from any anyone. There was no bold speech from the viziers who were meant to speak out or from the amirs who were to seize lands.'

The gold and silver implements used in Emperor Babur's assembly were broken and distributed among the poor. All the wine was thrown away. Salt was put into the best wine brought from Ghazni to turn it into vinegar. A firman was issued banning consumption, manufacture, sale or transport of intoxicants throughout the kingdom. He then called the nobles to remind them—

Who comes into the world will die,
What lasts and lives will be God.

Firdaus Makani Babur Badshah said:

'God has allotted to us such happiness and good fortune that you die as a martyr and kill for His cause. Therefore must each of you take oath upon His Holy Word that he will not turn away from battle so long as there is life in the body.'

Emperor Babur wrote:

'All those present, great and small, took the Quran joyfully into their hands and made a vow. The plan worked admirably and had a favourable effect on all who saw or heard, near or far, friend or foe.'

After reading the Fatiha, all said, 'Our Emperor! God willing, we shall not shy from war while there is life in us.'

Firdaus Makani Babur Badshah's army was arrayed in the field of Khanwa near a hill. Troops attached directly to the Emperor were in the centre. There were troops to the left and right of the centre as well. The right flank of the army was led by Mirza Humayun, the son of Firdaus Makani Babur Badshah. The left flank was also in readiness. Ahead of the army was a line of carts joined together by chains and wheeled tripods. Taking shield behind them were men with artillery and matchlock. There was enough space between the carts for cavalry to pass through and charge. Matchlock men could advance and fire from behind the wheeled tripods. Firdaus Makani also stationed men to be in readiness for a fierce tulghama attack when the need arose. With the battle lines drawn, royal orders were given that the men remain stationed in their place and not enter the battlefield without instructions.

Firdaus Makani Babur Badshah has written:

'According to Indian calculation a territory yielding one lakh of revenue furnishes hundred horsemen, and a territory of one crore revenue will support ten thousand. The dominions of Rana Sanga yielding ten crores furnished a lakh horsemen. Many chiefs who had never served under him before pledged their allegiance and increased his army.'

Firdaus Makani was faced with the combined might of Rana Sanga and Harauti, Nagaur, Jalor, Sirohi, Dungarpur, Dhoondhar, Amber, Marwar, Merta, Chanderi, Meerut, Raisen, Sarangpur, and Jarhal. Hasan Khan Mewati with his twelve thousand soldiers and Sikandar Lodhi's younger son Mahmud Lodhi with ten thousand men were with Rana Sanga. The Rajputs and Afghans had joined hands against Emperor Babur, who assessed that these chiefs had a combined strength of two hundred thousand, much higher than his own army.

One watch of the day had elapsed when a fierce fight broke out on the right and left flanks. Rana Sanga's left flank launched a strong attack on the right flank of Firdaus Makani's army. But for the reinforcements that were rushed, the defence could have been breached. Now from this flank led by Mirza Humayun, the matchlock men and artillerymen launched an attack from behind the carts. There were repeated onslaughts on the left flank of the royal forces by Rana Sanga's right flank, which were repelled by Firdaus Makani's army. When the soldiers earmarked for the tulghama attack were ordered they surrounded the army of Rana Sanga and attacked it. With the battle showing no sign of abating, royal orders were given for the elite imperial soldiers to come out from behind the carts. With arrows and swords, these soldiers charged at the army of Rana Sanga from both sides. Firdaus Makani ordered the carts in front of the centre to move forward and himself launched an attack on the army of Rana Sanga. Seeing Emperor Babur advance, his men charged ahead with greater enthusiasm. By the time the day ended, the left and the right flank of the royal army had broken the left and the right flank of Rana Sanga. But before they were completely vanquished, there was a powerful offensive from Rana Sanga's side. His soldiers penetrated deep into the left and right flank of the centre. This attack was repelled, and Rana Sanga lost the battle.

Hasan Khan Mewati, Raja Rawal Udai Singh of Dungarpur, Rai Chandrabhan Chauhan, the son of Chanderi's ruler Nripat Rao,

Manikchand Chauhan, Dilip Rai, Gangu, Karam Singh, and Rao Bikrasi lost their lives. Thousands more were killed. A kalla minar was built of enemies' heads. Rana Sanga fled to Chittor. Men sent to capture him were unsuccessful. Babur Badshah said, 'It was a delicate moment. I should not have relied on anyone. I should have gone myself.'

After the victory at Khanwa, Babur Badshah thanked God. He added 'ghazi' to his name after this victory.

The battle was fought at Khanwa but Firdaus Makani had set up his camp by the lake at Sikri. Thanking God for the victory at Sikri—expressing shukr—he changed the name of the village to Shukri. He laid out a garden there called Bagh-i-Fatah—the garden of victory. It was decided after the death of Babur Badshah that the expenses incurred on those reciting the Quran and reading the Fatiha at his mausoleum would be borne out of the revenue from Sikri.

Jalaluddin Muhammad Akbar had never met his grandfather. He was born twelve years after the death of Babur Badshah. He would hear about Emperor Babur from members of the family and would have the *Tuzuk-i-Baburi* read out to him.

Looking at the ablution tank of the Bagh-i-Zar Afshan at Agra, Firdaus Makani Babur Badshah had once said, 'I am tired of kingship. Tahir the ewer-bearer is more than enough for me. I will hand over the rule to Humayun.'

Hearing him speak thus, Emperor Babur's sister Khanzada Begum and the children began to weep—'May God keep you safe on the throne for long years and numerous generations and may your children live long at your feet.'

Shortly after this, Firdaus Makani Babur Badshah's son Mirza Humayun fell ill. He was at his fief in Sambhal then. On the orders of Emperor Babur, he was brought to Delhi and from there by river to Agra. At Agra the royal physicians tried their best to heal him but failed.

One day, when Babur Badshah came to see his son, his wife, Humayun's mother, Maham Begum said, 'You have no concern for my child. You are an Emperor. Why would you grieve? You have other sons. My grief is that I have only this one.'

Emperor Babur replied, 'Maham, I have many children but none is as dear as your Humayun! I have built this empire for him because he has not his equal in distinction.'

Babur Badshah was discussing, one day during this period of his son's illness, the treatment with wise men of his age by the Yamuna river in Agra. Mir Baqa, a close courtier, who was an expert in the field of religion and philosophy, said, 'It has come down to us from learned men of earlier times that the only recourse left after physicians fail is to give away in charity one's most precious thing.'

Babur Badshah said, 'The most precious thing that Humayun has is me. I sacrifice myself for him. May the Creator accept me.'

The courtiers said, 'God willing, he will soon be fine and live his full lifetime in the shadow of Your Majesty's favour. Why say such things? The learned men of earlier times meant that the most precious of worldly possessions should be given away. The precious diamond that had been miraculously found in the battle with Ibrahim Lodhi should be given away.'

Soon after winning the Battle of Panipat, Babur Badshah had dispatched his son Mirza Humayun to Agra with instructions to take the treasury under control, especially the famed diamond which was believed to weigh eight mithqal. Mirza Humayun looted the treasury but could not find that diamond. In course of interrogation, one servant pointed towards the zenankhana—the female quarters. Mirza Humayun entered the zenankhana and assured the wailing ladies that they would be treated honourably. Then with trembling hands, Ibrahim Lodhi's mother handed over a gold box. When Mirza Humayun opened the box, he found the diamond that Emperor Babur had spoken of. Mirza Humayun presented the precious diamond to Babur Badshah, who accepted it and gave it back to Mirza Humayun. Gem appraisers believed that this diamond cost as much as half a day's combined expenditure of all the populated regions of the world.

Having heard the advice of his courtiers, Babur Badshah said, 'What is the value of worldly possessions? Is this worth giving in return for Humayun's life? I will sacrifice myself. He is in pain and I cannot bear to see his pain any more.'

Babur Badshah kept the fast of Hazrat Ali every Wednesday. This time around he was so distressed that he kept it on Tuesday itself. It was extremely hot. It is said that Babur Badshah prayed during the fast, 'O God! If a life may be exchanged for life, I, Babur, give my life and my being for Humayun.'

After saying this, Babur Badshah circumambulated three times Mirza Humayun.

People say that Firdaus Makani immediately felt a heaviness and he said, 'I have taken it upon myself! I have taken it upon myself!'

It is said that Mirza Humayun got up immediately and was cured. Firdaus Makani Babur Badshah developed fever and his condition began to worsen. He took to bed. A pain in his stomach kept growing. The physicians told Mirza Humayun, 'Our misfortune that no medicine is proving effective. Now we can only hope that God will treat him.'

The physicians felt his pulse and said, 'This is the effect of the poison given by Sultan Ibrahim's mother.'

They were referring to an incident that took place after the Battle of Panipat. Babur Badshah had written a letter to his wife Maham Begum, who was then in Kabul, and related the whole episode—

'The wretched old woman, Ibrahim's mother heard that I ate food made by Hindustani cooks. Three or four months earlier, as I had not had Hindustani food, I ordered Ibrahim's cooks to be brought and out of fifty or sixty had kept four. So she sent a man to Itawa and got a tola of poison wrapped in paper and gave it to Ahmed Chashni Geer through an old woman servant. In Hindustan, the person responsible for tasting food is called "chashni geer". That poison Ahmed gave to the Hindustani cooks in our kitchen, promising them four parganas if they would somehow get it into our food. Following the first woman servant, the wretched woman sent a second one to see whether the food had been poisoned. Well was it that Ahmed put the poison not into the cooking pot but on a dish. He did not put it into the pot because I had strictly ordered the tasters to supervise the Hindustanis and make them taste from the pot while the food was cooking. Our graceless tasters were neglectful when the food was being dished up. Thin slices of bread were put on a porcelain dish; on these less than half the poison was sprinkled, and over this buttered fritters were laid. It would have been terrible if the poison had been strewn on the fritters or thrown into the pot. In his confusion, the man threw the larger half of the poison into the fire.

'Late Friday evening when the cooked meats were laid out, I ate a good deal of a dish of hare and also much fried carrot, took a few mouthfuls of the poisoned Hindustani food without noticing any unpleasant flavour, took also a mouthful or two of dried meat. Then I felt sick. As some dried meat eaten the previous day had an unpleasant taste, I thought my nausea due to the dried meat. After retching two or three times I was near vomiting on the tablecloth. At last I saw it would not do, I got up, went retching to the toilet and on reaching it vomited much. Never had I vomited after food, not even after drinking. I became suspicious. I had the cooks arrested while the vomit was given to a dog that was to be watched. Until the first watch of the next day it was listless; its belly was swollen and however much people threw stones at it, it did not get up. It remained in that state till midday. It then got up and did not die. One or two pages who had also eaten of that dish vomited a good deal the next day. One was in a bad state. In the end all recovered.'

Emperor Babur wrote to Maham Begum:

'Calamity struck, but all's well that ends well.

'The cook was taken away for torture. He revealed all the details. On Monday I ordered the grandees, amirs and viziers to be present. Two men and two women were brought for interrogation. They confessed details of the matter. The taster I had cut in pieces and cook skinned alive. One of those women I had thrown under an elephant, the other blown to pieces.

'On Saturday I drank a bowl of milk. On Sunday I drank some earth of Lemnos dissolved in spirits. On Monday, I mixed some earth of Lemnos and opiate in milk and drank it. The milk really shook up my insides. On Saturday, the first day of this medication I excreted some pitch-black things like burnt bile.

'Thank God, no harm has been done. I had not known how precious life is. As is said, "He who has been near to death knows the worth of life." God has given me a new life. With what words can I thank him!

'All has passed off well and for good. Have no fear or anxiety in your minds. Written on Tuesday the twentieth of Rabi ul-Awwal in the Chahar Bagh.'

The attempt to poison Firdaus Makani Babur Badshah had been made a long time ago but the physicians attending upon him told

Mirza Humayun that he was still under the effect of that poison. Finally, all treatment failed and Babur Badshah grew weak. Four days before his death, he held his last court and told his nobles, 'For years, I had wished to hand over the reins of the sultanate to Humayun Mirza and go and sit in one corner of Bagh-i-Zar Afshan. By the grace of God, all wishes were fulfilled but for this one...'

People began to weep and Babur Badshah too became tearful.

On the fifth of Jamadi ul-Awwal of the Hijri year 937, corresponding to Tuesday, 25 December 1530 CE, Babur Badshah left his sultanate and this world at the age of forty-eight. The family went into mourning. But the death was kept a secret from the outside world. A Hindustani noble Araish Khan advised, 'It is not proper to keep such matters a secret because it is common in Hindustan for looting to begin when kings die.' So a man clad in red mounted an elephant and declared that Firdaus Makani Babur Badshah had become a dervish and had handed power to Emperor Humayun. On Friday, a khutba was read in the name of Emperor Humayun in the Jama Masjid of Agra.

Sheikh Abul Fazl says of Firdaus Makani Babur Badshah:

'... His personality had all eight principles necessary to rule the world. First, lofty fortune. Second, a high degree of courage. Third, power to conquer. Fourth, administrative capacity. Fifth, desire to improve the cities. Sixth, devotion to welfare of the subjects. Seventh, ability to keep the soldiers happy. Eighth, power to restrain the army from evil.'

In his will Firdaus Makani Babur Badshah had instructed his son Mirza Humayun—

'My son! The territory of Hindustan is inhabited by people professing different faiths. Praise be to God who bestowed the kingship of this land to you. You should cleanse your heart of all religious prejudices and dispense justice according to the practice of that religion. You should particularly abstain from sacrificing cows. This would capture the hearts of the people of Hindustan and people would get attached to the kingly office. You should not destroy temples or houses of worship of any community living in your kingdom. You should dispense such even-handed justice that people should feel satisfied with their ruler and the ruler with his people. Islam can flourish better with the sword of kindness than the sword of oppression. Close your eyes to sectarian dispute between Shiites and Sunnis, otherwise it would weaken Islam. Consider the different communities in your territory as the four humours in the human body; in their balance depends the health of the state. The achievements of Hazrat Amir Timur Sahib-i-Qiran should always be before you for these can consolidate your power.'

Emperor Babur had stayed in Agra for four years. During this time, he would go to meet the elderly ladies of his family every Friday. One day his wife Maham Begum complained, 'It is so hot. What will happen if you don't go this one Friday? Would the ladies feel insulted?'

Referring to his grandfather, Emperor Babur replied, 'Maham, I am amazed that you say such a thing! His Majesty Abusaid Sultan Mirza's daughters are deprived of father and brothers. If I don't take care of them, how will it be done?'

After Babur Badshah passed away, Jannat Ashiyani Humayun Badshah too did his best to look after his relatives. Maham Begum, the wife of Emperor Babur, had become worried about the future of her daughters after his death. She had told her daughter Gulbadan, 'It is hard for me to imagine that after my death the Emperor's daughters should see their brother in Gulbarg Bibi's house.'

Somehow Emperor Humayun got to know this. As long as he lived in Hindustan, he would come to Gulbadan Begum's house to meet his stepsisters. Gulbadan Begum used to say, 'After my father, the Padshah, and my mother passed away, His Majesty was so compassionate towards me that I never realized I was an orphan.'

Once when Humayun Badshah had gone and met his stepsisters and stepmothers, his wife Bega Begum taunted him, 'How many days have you been visiting this garden? Not one day have you come to our place. The path to our tent hasn't been spiked with thorns. We hope you will deign to visit our quarters too and make merry. How long will you remain inattentive to us? We too have a heart. You have honoured other places thrice by your visit and spent a whole day and night in amusement.'

Emperor Humayun replied, 'Why such a complaint first thing in the morning? You know that I have been to our elders' tent. It is my duty to see to them. Indeed I am ashamed before them because I see them so rarely.'

12

Emperor Jalaluddin Muhammad Akbar was facing the elegant pleasure pavilion that Emperor Babur had built in midst of the lake in such a manner that water would pass from underneath it. It had two lower platforms and a higher one, upon which an awning would be spread for Firdaus Makani Babur Badshah to relax. Like Agra, Sikri was also a waterfront city, the difference being that Sikri faced a lake, not a river.

Badshah Salamat noticed a small mosque near the hospice of Sheikh Salim Chishti on the hills of Sikri that was not built by an emperor, nor by any noble. When Badshah Salamat had begun construction of the Agra Fort five years ago, a thousand cartloads of red sandstone were sent daily from Sikri. This first building in Sikri of Badshah Salamat's reign was built by quarrymen of that time.

Sikri's skyline was now rapidly changing. Once Maryam Zamani shifted there, Badshah Salamat ordered construction of a beautiful palace to house the royal harem near the hospice of Sheikh Salim Chishti. This palace was called 'Rang Mahal'. Orders were also given for the construction of a new hospice and mosque.

On the seventeenth of Rabi ul-Awwal of 977 of the Hijri era, corresponding to the thirtieth of August 1569 CE, there was a flurry of activity in the newly built Rang Mahal.

This red sandstone palace, comprising two courtyards, was the first structure in Sikri to be built on the orders of Badshah Salamat. The parapet of the Rang Mahal gate and that of the inside of the courtyards had ornate work. The slender columns had a decorated base and capital.

That day Raja Bharmal's daughter Maryam Zamani gave birth to Prince Salim in this building. Sheikh Salim Chishti's daughter breastfed the newborn child.

The painting that Badshah Salamat had commissioned of the significant occasion shows a gaggle of Timuri and Indian women and girls gathered around the mother and the newborn. A lady in Turkish headgear is giving the mother something to drink, while an Indian girl sits with the newborn Salim on her lap on a carpet with a flowery pattern. Another Indian girl stands nearby with a vessel, a second holds a smoking olibanum and at a slight distance a third is pounding something in a pestle. The other girls are busy cooking. A naubat is sounding outside the zenankhana, within the palace compound. The naqqara, karna and jhanjh echo through the palace. Two Indian women dance, while two sing, one clapping her hands and the other playing on a dholak. Below the palace, food is being distributed and money showered on alm-seekers and performers.

A lady in Turkish headgear emerged from the gathering and gave the time of birth to seven astrologers who were assembled across the curtain. They cast the prince's horoscope according to Greek and Indian principles.

Badshah Salamat was not present to take part in these celebrations. He was twelve kos away in Agra. It was a Hindustani tradition that the father was not meant to immediately see the face of the child he had sought as a boon.

There was rejoicing at the royal court at Agra when Sheikh Salim Chishti's son-in-law Sheikh Ibrahim came with the good news. An order was given to release prisoners. Badshah Salamat sat cross-legged in a light-coloured jama and green yar-i-pairhan. The dagger in the right side of the golden sash had a green scabbard with golden work on it. As always Badshah Salamat wore a turban with multiple folds.

Sheikh Abul Fazl wrote:

Time arranged an assembly of enjoyments
The cup-bearers sat and the glass rose up
There was a banquet more joyous than life's foundation
A cup-bearer unequalled as a drawer of cups
They made an illumination for the world
There was a vernal assemblage...
The King came and the desire of friends was fulfilled
He sat at the feast by the cup and the relish
His diadem he raised to the sky
His forehead he fastened to the ground
He issued a proclamation for enjoyment
He invited the world as his guest
The cup-bearer opened the lid of the goblet
The treasurer opened the door of the treasury
The skirt and the wallet of the sky were filled
In order that it might shower pearls on the earth.

Two women in Turkish headgear danced very near Badshah Salamat's throne. Two other women in Turkish headgear were playing the daira, while another played the nai. Next to them a man played a ghichak. A short distance away from this group and right in front of Badshah Salamat's throne, a man juggled swords. Nearby there was another threesome—all males—with two of them playing the naqqara and the third the surna. Further away from Badshah Salamat, almost on the corner of the court near the wall was a Hindustani man playing a huruk that was strung around his left arm. He was accompanied by a woman with cymbals in a short choli with long braided hair and an uncovered head. They sang the glories of valorous men.

Tansen asked people to celebrate—

Sing songs of happiness on this auspicious day,
Play the mridang, been and rabab,
String bandanwar [auspicious peepul leaves] on the door beams.

With the birth of an heir, Jalaluddin Muhammad Akbar decided to set up a new city to establish Timuri power near the abode of Sheikh Salim Chishti. In a matter of a few years, Sikri was transformed to such an extent that a chronicler of Badshah Salamat's age, Arif Qandhari, wrote:

'Land that was barren like the dry hearts of lovers began to glow like the rosy cheeks of the beloved. The wild land which had been home to foxes now had trees, mosques, bazaars, baths, sarais and other fine buildings.'

Badshah Salamat had already taken a vow that if his wish was realized, he would travel from Agra to Ajmer on foot. Because Sheikh Muinuddin Chishti's urs fell in the Hijri month of Rajab, he made the resolve in that month to fulfil his vow. On Friday, the twentieth of January 1570 CE of the fourteenth regnal year, Badshah Salamat set out, travelling ten to twelve kos every day through Mandhakar, Fatehpur, Khanwa, Juna, Karoha, Basawar, Toda, Kalawali, Kharandi, Disa, Hansmahal, Phoolmahal, Sanganer, and then near Neota, and thereafter Jhak near Muizzabad, Sakhun and Kajbil, finally reaching the shrine of Khwaja Muinuddin Chishti in Ajmer.

At Ajmer, Badshah Salamat spent time in prayer and distributed gifts. While there, Badshah Salamat learnt of a dispute between those claiming to be descendants of Khwaja Muinuddin Chishti and the attendants of the shrine over the division of gifts. It was alleged that the claim regarding lineage was false and that the putative descendants had kept all the gifts for themselves. Badshah Salamat had the matter investigated and found that their claim of being the descendants of Khwaja Muinuddin Chishti was indeed not true. Badshah Salamat handed over the charge of the shrine to Sheikh Muhammad Bukhari, who was a notable sayyid of Hindustan and was known for his learning and trustworthiness.

Abul Fazl writes that when Badshah Salamat set out on foot to Ajmer after the victory of Chittor to fulfil a vow and Shaguna the scout had gone ahead in advance and conveyed the news of Badshah Salamat's arrival, the dervishes of the shrine said, 'His Holiness the Khwaja had appeared in a vision and had announced that the spiritual and temporal king be restrained from coming on foot.'

Sheikh Abul Fazl went to the extent of conveying through the dervishes what Khwaja Muinuddin Chishti thought of Badshah Salamat. According to Sheikh Abul Fazl, Khwaja Muinuddin Chishti said, 'If he knew the amount of his own spirituality he would not bestow a glance on me.'

Hearing this message, Badshah Salamat agreed to ride thereon but did travel the last leg of the journey on foot.

A few years before the Chittor victory, Badshah Salamat was hunting cheetahs in Gwalior. He got to know that the Sufi saint Sheikh Muhammad Ghaus and his relatives had a good stock of oxen which could be useful for royal hunts. Sheikh Ghaus gifted him all the bulls he had when Badshah Salamat came to meet him. After presenting sweets and perfume, he asked Badshah Salamat, 'Are you a spiritual disciple to any saint?'

Badshah Salamat said, 'No.'

The Sheikh took Jalaluddin Muhammad Akbar's hand and said, 'We have taken your hand.'

Badshah Salamat smiled and kept quiet at the time but later said, 'That night we returned to our camp and had a drinking party. There was a lot of merriment about how we got hold of the bulls and despite him holding our hands, we did not fall into his trap.'

In the royal camp at Bhera, Badshah Salamat was being read the *Tuzuk-i-Baburi*—

'The year I took Kabul and Ghazni, overran Kohat, the plains of Bannu and lands of the Afghans, and went on to Ghazni by way of Duki and the Ab-i-Istada, people told me there is a tomb in the village which moved when durood was recited. I discovered that it was a trick, presumably of the servants at the tomb, who had put a screen above it which moved when pushed, so that it seemed as though the tomb was moving, just as the shore does to those passing in a boat. I ordered the attendants to stay away from the screen. Then no matter how many times they recited the durood, no movement happened. I ordered the screen demolished and a dome built over the tomb. I forbade the attendants to ever play the trick again.'

While moving towards Bhera, Badshah Salamat had gone for a hunt on his way to Merta. He then travelled through Marot, Amber, Kotputli and reached Narnaul, where he met Sheikh Nizamuddin Narnauli of the Chishti order. It is heard from Mullah Abdul Qadir Badayuni that the dervishes of the hospice would partake of the oil of mal kangni on his orders and would get to know the secrets of the other world. From his youth till his old age, he would walk down to Mehrauli to pray at the shrine of Khwaja Qutbuddin Bakhtiyar Kaki. When he became very old, he started celebrating the urs of Qutbuddin Bakhtiyar Kaki in Narnaul itself.

Sheikh Abul Fazl says, 'Badshah Salamat's far-seeing glance did not fall upon his own treasure, and as he did not find in the wearers of rags, or in the learned of the age, any notes of the spiritual and celestial mysteries which are attached to the table of the bounty of God, his thirst for truth increased. Hence it is that the intimates of the majestic council of God have described as eternal that pain of seeking after God which is the zenith of truth. The incomparable Deity does not come into the heart of the mortals, nor does the foot of the search become worn out.'

From Narnaul, Badshah Salamat reached Delhi and stopped by to pray at the tomb of Jannat Ashiyani Humayun Badshah, near the shrine of Hazrat Nizamuddin Awliya.

He was reminded of Sura al-Nisa of the Quran as soon as he entered the char bagh of the tomb—

But those who believe
And do deeds of righteousness—
We shall soon admit them
To Gardens, with rivers
Flowing beneath, to dwell
Therein for ever.

Jannat Ashiyani Humayun Badshah's tomb was patterned on this description of paradise. The water canal of its char bagh went underneath the tomb and emerged on the other side. Orange and lemon trees, that Jannat Ashiyani Humayun Badshah liked, were planted in the garden. In accordance with the hasht bihisht—eight heavens—plan of architecture, there were eight rooms around the central domed chamber, which was octagonal. The first floor of the tomb had a similar plan. There was a cenotaph below the central dome but the real grave of Jannat Ashiyani Humayun Badshah was in the basement under it. The building of red sandstone was highlighted with white marble and the exterior of the dome was entirely faced with white marble. Jannat Ashiyani used to join boats to make a structure which looked somewhat like this. An octagonal pool would form with the boats joined. Jannat Ashiyani Humayun Badshah's mausoleum had an octagonal central chamber in place of this pool.

Jannat Ashiyani did not get this paradisiacal resting place easily. As in life, so in death, he had remained unsettled. At first he had been buried in the fort of Sher Shah where he had stumbled on the staircase and died. Thereafter, when Hemu took Delhi, he was shifted and buried at Sirhind. When Jalaluddin Muhammad Akbar's army defeated Hemu, Jannat Ashiyani once again got a place in Sher Shah's fort. When the tomb was ready he found his final resting place.

Badshah Salamat recited the Fatiha at the grave of his father Jannat Ashiyani Humayun Badshah. After praying at the tomb, he stopped at Hauz-i-Khas and Sarai Bawali, hunted at Palam and thereafter proceeded on his journey. As per the tradition, a naqqar khana—an ensemble—travelled on elephants and camels with Badshah Salamat's entourage. The damama, naqqara, seeng and sanj made such thunderous music that people far and wide knew that the Emperor was on his way. Crossing Meham and Brahma, he reached Hissar. Cheetahs were found here in large numbers. Badshah Salamat hunted here as well.

After this, Badshah Salamat reached Hansi. Sheikh Jamal of Hansi was one of the successors of Sheikh Fariduddin Shakarganj. Sheikh Farid trusted Sheikh Jamal so much that whenever he appointed somebody to a particular area he would ask the person to get the appointment letter countersigned by Sheikh Jamal. It is said that Sheikh Farid wanted to appoint his nephew to the vilayat of Delhi. When he sent the letter a second time, Sheikh Jamal tore it apart. Later, he countersigned the appointment of Sheikh Nizamuddin Awliya for Delhi.

After praying at the shrine of Sheikh Jamal Hansvi at Hansi, Badshah Salamat crossed Gohana and Sunam and reached Shadiwal when his lips expressed a heartfelt wish: 'If the scarf of social life were not on my shoulder, I would restrain myself from eating flesh.'

Badshah Salamat used to say, 'Men are so accustomed to eating meat that were it not for the pain, they would undoubtedly fall to on themselves. Would that my body were so vigorous to be of service to eaters of meat who would thus forgo other animal life, or that as I cut off a piece for their nourishment, it might be replaced by another.'

When the royal entourage reached the town of Tihara, which means 'yours', Badshah Salamat thought, 'All belongs to God, what is mine!'

Crossing Mamdot, Ispani, Kotri, and Bhati Ibrahim Ki Talwandi, Badshah Salamat reached Lakhi Qiyampur. After this he crossed the Sutlej. He completely bypassed Lahore. In case somebody in the royal entourage wondered why Badshah Salamat took a longer route instead of the straight one Sheikh Abul Fazl had a reply. He said, 'Sovereignty and saintship go shoulder to shoulder in the personality of Badshah Salamat.'

The large royal entourage reached Pakpattan after crossing Sutlej. Badshah Salamat prayed at the shrine of Sheikh Farid Shakarganj. Flowers lay strewn across the grave. The arched gateway of the tomb had floral patterns. The saiban—royal parasol—that always remained over the head of the Emperor as a symbol of power, lay outside the door of the shrine. A close vizier Raja Todar Mal respectfully stood behind with folded hands as Badshah Salamat prayed barefoot on his knees.

After camping here for fifteen to sixteen days, Badshah Salamat crossed the Ravi river. Thereafter Chenab was crossed from near Chiniot. Badshah Salamat had then crossed Jhelum and reached Bhera, where his entourage was camped at the moment, and a huge qamargah was underway. If the wild animals of Bhera felt the tremor caused by the royal entourage, Badshah Salamat's stepbrother Mirza Hakim too would have heard it. Mirza Hakim would have surely been taken by surprise because the royal entourage bypassed the main route, zigzagged its way praying at various shrines, and appeared suddenly near the border.

Badshah Salamat was being read the *Akhlaq-i-Nasiri* in his do-ashiyana manzil—

'...when a matter has been decided, one should mix the first steps in the desired direction with steps opposite to it. One should not go to extremes in either direction because it might evoke suspicion or give away the actual plan.'

13

There was a matter beyond the spiritual and temporal that was deeply worrying Badshah Salamat. For this he prayed at the dargahs, spent time in the company of Sufis and prayed to the Almighty.

Jalaluddin Muhammad Akbar looked out of the window of his do-ashiyana manzil to look at the sky. He could see a bright moon. He felt relieved that the inauspicious comet was not visible any more.

About six months ago he had reached Manohar Nagar from Ajmer, with a stopover in Amber, when a bright comet appeared in the west. People would look at it from their terrace and wonder what evil could befall. Badshah Salamat gave Raja Todar Mal the responsibility of talking to astrologers to find out the effect of the sighting of this comet.

Raja Todar Mal enjoyed such prestige that the poet Gang said:

As Tansen to music, Birbal to intelligence,
Akbar amongst Emperors, is Todar Mal amongst ministers.

Raja Todar Mal was from Lahore and came from the Khatri caste. He was a very important minister of the empire. He had just left Ajmer for Punjab when the idols he used to worship were misplaced in the confusion of moving camp. Since he used to attend to work and eat and drink only after worshipping his idols, he gave up food and sleep when the idols couldn't be found. Only after Badshah Salamat counselled him did he recover to some extent and attend to his duties.

After analysing the stars, the most competent astrologer of the age, Jotik Rai said, 'The King of the dominion from whose direction the comet rises will die. The prince towards whose dominion its angle is inclined will lose his possessions. The dominion towards which it is in a falling angle will suffer from sickness, pestilence and destruction. It is because of Badshah Salamat's good fortune that it has risen in the west and is inclined towards the north. Because of the holy personality of the Emperor, Hindustan is safe from the malefic influence of this inauspicious star.'

However, despite the assurance of Jotik Rai, Badshah Salamat did not take chances and gave a large amount of money in charity in accordance with the practice of Hindus and Muslims. People said that Hindustan escaped the evil influence of the comet, but Persia did not. The comet had just been sighted when a caravan from Persia arrived with the news that Shah Tahmasp had passed away shortly before the sighting of this comet. It was learnt that Shah Tahmasp's third son Sultan Haidar had been killed by his own sister Pari Khanum. Thereafter, Shah Tahmasp's second son Shah Ismail killed many of his brothers as soon as he acceded to the throne. After the sighting of the inauspicious comet, Pari Khanum got her brother Shah Ismail poisoned.

People said that the practice of maligning the first three caliphs of Islam and the Umayyad caliphs under emperors of Persia had now ended. Badshah Salamat said, 'This country is bearing the consequences of its ingratitude.'

This happened when Badshah Salamat was about a year old and Jannat Ashiyani Humayun Badshah's entourage was fleeing from Mirza Kamran and Mirza Askari. They were camped at the border of Qandhar when they had to leave suddenly. Mirza Akbar was left behind and fell into the hands of his uncle Mirza Askari. It is said that Mirza Askari took the young child from Maham Anga's lap and tried to humour him but Badshah Salamat did not even smile. People remember that the one-year-old child reached out for a ring hanging from Mirza Askari's neck by a red thread. When Mirza Askari placed the ring around Mirza Akbar's neck, well-wishers took it as an auspicious sign.

Jannat Ashiyani Humayun Badshah's entourage passed through difficult routes. Once they were stranded in snow all night. There was such scarcity of food that they had to kill a horse and eat it. They hoped for help from the Baluch people but their chief told Emperor Humayun, 'Mirza Kamran and Mirza Askari have sent a firman which says, "Badshah Salamat might come your side. If he does, beware a thousand times! Capture him and hand him over to us." But I will not do this. I will put at stake my family's life. Please go where you please. May God protect you.'

Now Humayun Badshah was perplexed and could not decide where to go. He said, 'Let us go back to the land of our ancestors.'

Bairam Khan, who was with him, replied, 'What will Badshah Salamat gain from a land where his father gained nothing? Let's go to Iran. People there are hospitable. The Shah there has helped Firdaus Makani Babur Badshah twice. And then it is the land of my ancestors. This humble servant is aware of the situation there.'

There was strong logic in what Bairam Khan said. Since there was nowhere to go but Iran, they moved towards it.

When Shah Tahmasp got the letter of Seistan's governor Ahmed Sultan Shamlu and Herat's governor Muhammad Khan Sharfuddin Oghli Takalu, he ordered that Jannat Ashiyani Humayun Badshah be given a grand welcome—

'The untroubled progress and approach of the King, the angel of honour, are a great boon. Follow the instructions given in this order. Appoint five hundred prudent and experienced men, each of whom should have a spare horse and necessary accoutrements, that may go forth to meet the King, the lord of fortune, with one hundred swift horses which have been sent from the sublime court for the use of the Emperor, together with golden saddles; and let the governor select from his own stable six swift horses, quiet, of good colour and strong, and such as may be fit for the rising of that royal cavalier of the field of glory and success; and let him place on them azure and embroidered saddles, with housings of gold brocade and gold thread, such as may befit the riding-horse of that majestic King; and let him make over each horse to two of his own servants. A splendid, special side-dagger ornamented with exquisite jewels which came to us from His Majesty, our father the King, together with a golden scimitar and a jewelled girdle, has been sent for the Alexander-like king for victory and conquest and good augury. Four hundred pieces of velvet and satin from Europe and Yezd have been sent, so that one hundred and twenty coats may be made for the King's special use, and that the remainder may be for the servants attached to the victorious stirrup of that fortunate prince; also two-pile gold-brocaded velvet carpets and coverlets of goat's hair and satin lining, and nine pairs of large carpet of twelve cubits, twelve tents, crimson, green and white have been sent.

'Let arrangements be made day by day for sweet and pleasant drinks, with white loaves kneaded with milk and butter and seasoned with fennel seeds and poppy seeds. Let them be well made and be sent to His Majesty. Let them also be sent for each member of the staff and for his other servants. At the places where the Emperor will halt, let there be arranged and pitched on the previous day, cleansed, pleasant, white, embroidered tents and the awnings of silk and velvet, and also pantries and kitchens and all other outhouses, so that every requisite apparatus be in readiness. When he, in his glory and fortune, shall direct a halt, let rose water sherbet and wholesome lemon juice be prepared and poured out, after having been cooled with snow and ice. After the sherbet, let conserves of apples of Mashhad, watermelons, grapes, with white loaves made as already directed be tendered; and let care be taken that all the beverages be examined by the Emperor, and that rose water and grey ambergris be added to them. Each day let five hundred dishes of varied food be presented together with the beverages.

'Three days after five hundred people set out, let your relatives and clansmen Qara Sultan, Tatar Sultan and Jafar Sultan go forth to offer welcome. And during those three days let the officers and troops be inspected. Be careful to give your servants Turkoman and Arab horses, for there is no finer decoration for a soldier than a good horse. And be it arranged that when the officers come to wait upon the Emperor, they kiss the ground one by one. Be it seen that on the occasion of riding there be no altercation between the officers' servants and the Emperor's, and that no annoyance of any kind happen to the Emperor's servants. During the time of riding and of marching, let the officers remain with their own troops and serve the Emperor from a distance, but at the same time of being on guard, let each officer display his alacrity in the vicinity of the quarters which shall have been fixed for the Emperor, and let them, having taken in their hands the staffs of service, serve in the manner that one would serve one's own king, and let them adopt and bring into practice the utmost attentiveness. Let this mandate be shown to the governor of every territory to which the Emperor may come, and care be taken that the officer render his service, and let entertainments be so conducted that the total of the food, sweetmeats and liquids be not less than fifteen hundred dishes, until the Emperor reaches Mashhad. And let each of the aforesaid officers, on the day when he is host, tender a present of nine horses, of which three will be for the Emperor's personal use, one for the chief Amir Bairam Khan Bahadur, and the five others for such of the select officers as may be fitting. Let all nine horses be produced for auspicious inspection, and mention which of them are for His Majesty. By every possible means keep the servants in attendance of the Emperor pleased, and show utmost sympathy. Soothe the hearts of this body of men, which have been clouded somewhat by the revolutions of unequal fate, with affection and sympathy, as is proper and pleasing at such seasons. Continue this practice throughout till they come to our presence. Thereafter, what is proper will be executed by us. After food has been partaken of, let sweetmeats and various conserves, which shall have been perfumed by rose water, musk and grey ambergris, be brought in.

'The governor of the province, after performing the duties of service and hospitality, shall put his mind at ease about his province, and escort the Emperor up to Herat, the capital, not omitting the most minute points of service and attendance. When he shall arrive at twelve farsakh from the said province, the governor will leave experienced officers in charge of our dear son, that they may take care of the city and wait on the son. The remainder of the army from the city and provinces and its boundaries, consisting of the Hazaras,

Nikodari and others, to the number of thirty thousand, which number must be exact, shall go forth with the governor to offer welcome. Tents, awnings and necessary furniture will be conveyed by strings of camels and mules, so that a well-ordered camp may come under the Emperor's auspicious glance. When the governor is honoured by attendance on the Emperor he will, before making any other remarks, convey to him many prayers for his welfare on our behalf. The governor, when he has come on duty, will request leave, in order that he may entertain the Emperor, and will station himself for three days there. On the first day he will invest the Emperor's troops with handsome khilats of satin and brocade from Yezd, and of silk of Mashhad and Khaf, and let them all have velvet cloaks, provide various foods in accordance with the rules already prescribed, so that tongues may speak in praise of it. Let there be made a list of his troops, and let it be sent to the sublime court. Let the utmost zeal be displayed in service, and let the march from the said quarters to the city occupy four days, and let the entertainment of each day be the same as on the first. And it is appropriate that at every entertainment the honoured sons of the governor bind, like servants and waiters, girdles of service on their loins and perform worshipful ministration, and that, in thanksgiving that such a king, who is a gift of God, has become our guest, they display their utmost alacrity in service; and let there not be any failure, for the more zeal and devotion are displayed in respect of the Emperor, the more will be approved by us.

'On the day before he reaches the city, let there be erected at the head of the avenue of the Bagh-i-Eidgah tents, with crimson satin on the inside and Isfahani carpets on the top. And let care be taken that at every place where the Emperor's gracious heart may take pleasure, he be approached by you in an agreeable way, with the hand of respect placed on bosom, and that it be represented to him that camp and army and all its paraphernalia are a present to him. Also, while on the march, continually keep him pleased by conversation of a reassuring nature. And you yourself on the day before he will arrive at the city, leave that station after obtaining your dismissal, and proceed to our son. Next morning, bring out our dear son from his residence for the purpose of giving a welcome. Put on him the suit which we sent him last year on Navroz. Let tents and camels and horses be presented to the Emperor, so that he may mount the next day. The camp may also march, and let the governor be the guide. When the son shall come out of the city, strive that all the troops mount in a prescribed order, and that they proceed to welcome the Emperor. When an arrow's flight from the Emperor, let the governor advance and beg him not to dismount. If he agrees, let him return immediately and dismount the son; and let the son go quickly and kiss the thigh and stirrup of the Emperor and show all the points of service and respect and honour which are possible. Should the Emperor not agree, and should he dismount, let our son dismount before him. Let him kiss the Emperor's hands and do homage and then mount after the Emperor mounts. And let the governor be in attendance on the Emperor, and close to the son, so that if the Emperor should put any questions to the son, and the son, out of bashfulness, be unable to reply, the governor may give a proper reply.

'In the quarters aforesaid let that son show hospitality to the Emperor. Let three hundred dishes of varied foods be at once presented. At midday let twelve hundred courses of varied foods be presented on dishes known as "Muhammad Khani", and also on other plates of porcelain, gold and silver, placing covers of gold and silver over them. After that, let sweet conserves, such as may be available, and sweetmeats and comfits, be presented. After that let twenty-seven handsome and good horses be taken from the son's stables, and velvet and brocade cloths with straps of fine linen woven with silk be placed on them, and let white straps be put on multi-coloured velvet, black straps on red velvet and yellow straps on green velvet. Let these be presented to the Emperor. It is proper that Hafiz Sabir Qaq, Maulana Qasim Qanooni, the harpist, Ustad Shah Muhammad, Hafiz Dost Muhammad Khafi, Ustad Yusuf Maudud and other famous singers and musicians who may be in the city, be always present, and whenever the Emperor desires, please him by singing and playing. And let everyone from far and near who may be worthy of that assemblage be in attendance so that he may be present when called upon, and that they may by every possible means make his hours pleasant to him. And on arrival at the quarters, let his servants be brought before our son, who shall, with the munificent ways which are hereditary with him from his ancestors, entertain them, giving each a suit of clothes and a horse befitting his condition, and let not the largesse to each be less than three tumans. Also let twelve times nine pieces of silk, including velvet, satin, European and Yezdi kamkhab and Syrian silk and other choice materials, and three hundred gold tumans in thirty purses be given, and let there be given to every soldier and servant three tumans.

'Musicians and singers should always be present for entertainment in the assemblies of the Emperor. People should always be present to attend to his needs. He should always be kept happy. Let him spend three days touring the avenue, the gardens and the Gazargah. When he travels from the Chahar Bagh to Bagh-i-Eidgah at the end of the avenue, the professional and trade guilds should display their ware, with one amir being with each guild to guide the display of art and craft. It is excellent that the Emperor should first come to the city, which is the light of the eyes of mankind.

'On the third day, let it be proclaimed that all the men and women of the city shall assemble on the morning of the fourth day in the avenue, and that in every shop and market, where carpet and cloths shall be spread in order, the women and maidens will be seated, and, as is the rule in that city, the women will engage in pleasant sayings and doings with the comers and goers. And from every ward and lane let the singing ladies come forth so that the like of it will not be seen in any other city of the world. And bid all people come forth to offer welcome. After all this has been arranged, let the King be respectfully asked to mount the horseback. Our son will proceed alongside the Emperor, in such a manner that the head and neck of the latter's horse be in front. The governor will follow close behind, so that, if he should put any questions about the buildings, the palaces and gardens, you may make suitable reply. When he enters the city, he will visit Chahar Bagh. And let him alight in the small garden which was made at the time of our residence in that city for our living and reading and writing, and which is at present known as the Royal Garden. Make the baths in the Chahar Bagh white and clean, and also other baths, and make them fragrant with rose water and musk, so that whenever he is inclined, he may have a place for bodily repose.

'On the first day our son will show hospitality with abundance of provisions, and when the Emperor shall have gone to his repose, the governor will order each of his amirs to host a banquet in the gardens. Then let the governor display hospitality in the manner that will be described below. When the Emperor enters the city, you will make a report on the same day and dispatch it to the court. Let a good writer be appointed to write a full diary from the day of the reception to the day the Emperor comes to the city, and let it be sealed and dispatched by the governor, and let all the stories and remarks, good or bad, which pass in the assemblage, be reduced to writing and be sent by the hands of trusty persons, so that we be fully informed of all that occurs.

'The entertaining by the governor will be as follows—three thousand dishes of food, sweetmeats, syrups and fruits will be prepared. Necessary furniture will be arranged as follows—first, fifty tents and twenty awnings, and the large store tent which was reported to have been prepared for the Emperor's personal use, with twelve pairs of carpets of twelve cubits, ten cubits and seven cubits, and seven pairs of carpets of five cubits, nine mares, ninety camels of angelic temperament, two hundred and fifty porcelain plates, large and small, twenty-one of the platters mentioned above, a clean and well-tinned vessel with cover, and two sets of nine camels shall be presented by the governor on the occasion of the entertainment.

'Let the amirs conduct their entertainments as follows—let them present food, sweetmeats and comfits to the extent of fifteen hundred plates, and also three horses, a string of camels and a string of mules, which shall have first been seen and approved by the governor. The governors of Ghorian, Pushanj, and Kusu will show hospitality in their own country. The governors of Khwaf, Turshiz, Zava, and Muhavvalat will entertain at Sarai Jam al-Jam, which is five farsakhs from Mashhad.'

Shah Tahmasp wrote instructions to the governors of his provinces on ways to look after Jannat Ashiyani Humayun Badshah but what he really had in his mind he wrote to the Turkish Sultan Sulaiman:

'One of the most powerful emperors of the world, Emperor Humayun had an army of five hundred thousand and twelve thousand elephants. Then he became so arrogant that he began to claim divinity. When he would appear before the people once in a while, it was deemed a divine spectacle. Shariat disappeared from his sultanate and his army, and evil prevailed all over. One day he called his close people, fortune tellers and astrologers and told them of a dream in which he saw that the moon, the sun and the stars have come down to the foot of his throne. These people said that dream means that the Sultan of Turkey, Shah of Iran, the Shah of Turan and other kings would soon present themselves at the court of Humayun and be under him, and these emperors' sovereignty would depend upon his pleasure. From Hind came Humayun to be my slave!'

Before meeting Humayun Badshah, Shah Tahmasp called his vakil Bairam Khan and said, 'Cut off your hair and wear a taj.'

This was no royal taj. It was a Safavid headgear called 'Taj-i-Haidari'. According to the Safavid tradition, Hazrat Ali had appeared in a dream to Shah Tahmasp's grandfather Sheikh Haidar and asked him to create a special headgear—a taj. A turban wound twelve times around a cap, this was a symbol of allegiance and discipleship to the Safavid emperor. It was wound twelve times in memory of the twelve Shiite Imams. Shah Tahmasp's father Shah Ismail had declared the Shiite Islam to be the state religion of Iran. The Safavid emperors drew their lineage from the seventh Imam Musa al-Kazim, who is believed to draw lineage from Hazrat Ali. The Safavid emperor, in whose court Bairam Khan now presented himself, believed that they were descendants of the son-in-law of Prophet Muhammad and the fourth Caliph of Islam, Hazrat Ali. The Safavid emperors believed that they were meant to guide their subjects in matters religious as also temporal.

Bairam Khan replied, 'We are the subject of another monarch. We shall follow his commands.'

An irritated Shah Tahmasp said, 'He is a subject only to himself.'

Bairam Khan observed that Shah Tahmasp immediately ordered the execution of some people on the charge of their being Sunnis. This was a clear signal for the Hindustani guests.

Shah Tahmasp had sent a saropa—a robe—for Humayun Badshah. And also an unbroken colt. Jannat Ashiyani donned the saropa. His personal servant Jauhar Aftabchi was present there. He says, 'When the Emperor easily mounted the wild horse, Shah Tahmasp's people took it as an auspicious sign and understood that the Emperor would bring good fortune.'

What happened after cannot be easily forgotten.

When Jannat Ashiyani entered the court, Shah Tahmasp came

to the edge of the carpet to receive him. He gestured to Emperor Humayun to take a seat by the bolster on the right and seated himself beside him. Shah Tahmasp had arranged for a musical performance for Jannat Ashiyani at this first meeting. Sitting by the side of an impressive Shah Tahmasp, who had a jet-black moustache and beard, Emperor Humayun wore the robe presented by the Shah over a red-coloured jama and wore a Hindustani headgear. To the right of Emperor Humayun were those who had come with him from Hindustan, who were also in jama, pyjama and Hindustani headgear. They wore sashes in the Hindustani style. There was a sword tied to the waist of Shah Tahmasp but Jannat Ashiyani Humayun Badshah carried no arms. His men from Hindustan, standing to his right, did have swords on their shoulders. The painting in Iran that depicts this meeting shows that even in a seated position Shah Tahmasp was slightly taller than Emperor Humayun.

When this meeting happened in the Jamadi ul-Awwal month of 951 Hijri, corresponding to about July–August 1544 CE, Shah Tahmasp had already been ruling for two decades. His views were becoming rigid. The phase where he took Persian art to new heights was now ending. It is said that he learnt painting at the hands of the legendary artist Bihzad. But now with changing views he was drifting away from the art of painting.

From among the many artists he removed from his employment, Emperor Humayun took two master painters, Mir Sayyid Ali and Khwaja Abd-us-Samad, under him. Mir Sayyid Ali was given the title of 'Nadir-ul-Mulk'—a rarity of his age, and Khwaja Abd-us-Samad the title of 'Shirin Qalam'—one with sweetness in his pen. Thus the foundation of a tasvir khana—an atelier—was laid, where Jalaluddin Muhammad Akbar's history was captured in pictures.

Jannat Ashiyani Humayun Badshah was extremely fond of paintings. Once in Umarkot, during his difficult days, he had just taken his clothes off and given them for washing when a bird entered his tent. Immediately closing the tent, he plucked some of its feathers. He called an artist to paint the bird and then freed it.

Once Nadir-ul-Mulk Mir Sayyid Ali painted a polo field with players on a grain of rice with this couplet written on each corner of the grain:

There is a burden of a thousand asses on each grain,
A whole world can be filled easily into a single heart.

Shirin Qalam Abd-us-Samad enjoyed a very high status. Once, at a gathering in his own house, a high-ranking amir of the empire Mirza Aziz Koka complained to the son of Khwaja Abd-us-Samad, 'You are not kind to me. What love your late father Abd-us-Samad, the artist, showed me! Why, all the pictures and paintings that you see in this private chamber were made by his august hand.'

In the tasvir khana he inherited, Jalaluddin Muhammad Akbar made innovations that changed the method of painting as also the number of paintings produced. Line drawing, being the most crucial part of the work, was done by the most consummate masters. Filling the colour was the job of another artist, and sometimes making the face was entrusted to a third artist. Artists were allocated functions according to their abilities. This system ensured a fast production of paintings. The deficiency Badshah Salamat experienced in reading and writing was made up by paintings. He would say, 'There are many who hate paintings but such men I dislike. It appears to me as if a painter has a quite peculiar means of recognizing God; for a painter in sketching anything that has life, and in devising its limbs, one after another, must come to feel that he cannot bestow individuality upon his work, and is thus forced to think of God, the giver of life, and will thus increase in knowledge.'

When Badshah Salamat got his nobles' portraits painted, Sheikh Abul Fazl said, 'Those who have passed away have received a new lease of life, and those who are still alive have immortality promised them.'

After offering Emperor Humayun a seat in the court, Shah Tahmasp asked him about the journey. After that he came straight to the point and asked, 'Will you wear the taj?'

'The taj is a symbol of honour. I will wear it,' Jannat Ashiyani Humayun Badshah replied.

The moment Shah Tahmasp placed the new taj on the head of Humayun Badshah, the courtiers fell in prostration before Shah Tahmasp saying 'Allah, Allah'.

An important king had become a disciple of Shah Tahmasp of Persia.

Jannat Ashiyani Humayun Badshah, referring to the people who had come with him, said, 'Let the mirzas be seated.'

Refusing point blank, Shah Tahmasp replied, 'Our regulations do not permit this.'

14

After ascending the throne, Jalaluddin Muhammad Akbar did not wear the taj that Jannat Ashiyani Humayun Badshah had taken off in the presence of Shah Tahmasp, nor did he ever wear the Taj-i-Haidari which the Shah had placed on the head of Emperor Humayun, making him a disciple.

It is heard from Bayazid Bayat, the servant of Humayun Badshah, that a qamargah was arranged for the two emperors in Sulluq—

'At a spring called Savuq Bulaq countless wild animals had been herded for the hunt. The Emperors remained there for one week. Once the fodder and the meat from this hunt had been consumed, the soldiers drove prey from a distance of ten days and another qamargah was arranged at Takht-i-Sulaiman. A large number of birds and animals were hunted. In an attempt to escape the qamargah, several deer threw themselves in the river but were killed with arrows and swords by soldiers and servants. Soldiers stationed at points from where the animals escaped were punished, and several were given the death penalty.'

Jannat Ashiyani himself got caught in a trap in Persia.

Arrangements were made for a bonfire for the comfort of Humayun Badshah. A pile of firewood had been gathered when Shah Tahmasp's message arrived. The Shah said, 'We will support you, only if you adopt our religion. Otherwise, all people of your religion will be put into this fire.'

Jannat Ashiyani replied, 'We have firm faith in our religion. We have no great desire for sovereignty. Whatever happens is God's will. Allow us to proceed to Mecca. This territory lies on the route to Mecca.'

Shah Tahmasp said, 'I want to declare a war against the Sunnis. Good that a Sunni emperor himself came under our control. We will not let you to remain in your religion.'

Shah Tahmasp's Vakil Qazi Jahan told Jannat Ashiyani, 'You are not alone. Because of you nearly seven hundred people will lose their lives. God forbid, your circumstances will force you to deny God and Prophet if they tell you to, and you will have no option.'

Emperor Humayun said, 'What does this mean? Let them give in writing.'

On behalf of Shah Tahmasp three papers were given to Humayun Badshah. Two he read and returned. After reading the third, he said, 'Doesn't the Shah think that there should be no compulsion in religion?'

Those in the know of things are aware that Jannat Ashiyani was a Sunni at heart like other emperors of the Timuri family. But he had no option at a time when seven hundred people stood the risk of being burnt to death. Hindustan was under Sher Shah, Kabul and Qandhar with his brothers. There was nowhere to go.

On the first day of the month of Shawwal of the Hijri year 950, corresponding to the twenty-ninth of December 1543 CE, shortly before crossing into the kingdom of Shah Tahmasp, Emperor Humayun had written a letter to him from Garmsir—

'After the performance of the duty of expressing good wishes and sincere friendship, which is the distinguishing pleasure trait of intimate friends, be it known that, notwithstanding the want of service and abundance of remorse, I beg to present myself like an atom in the presence of the sun of the firmament of splendour and magnificence, His Majesty, Zill-i-Ilahi—the shadow of God—who is the receptacle of wisdom, the manifestation of the perfect attributes of God, and beg to state that, although I had not outwardly placed myself among his exalted servants, but my heart was always attracted towards His Majesty's court of ample joy and abundant light. On account of vicissitudes of time, I have reached the airless and dark defile of Sind from the plains of the spacious kingdom of Hindustan.'

Because of the fear of Mirza Kamran, Emperor Humayun had to enter Persia without waiting for Shah Tahmasp's reply. He got the reply to his letter while on his way to Herat—

'The gracious letter which His Majesty of royal dignity, of exalted rank, repository of justice and equity, king of great power had sent, in the contents of which the incidents that had occurred in every direction to his dynasty, were made known, has been received. As out of firmness of friendship and confidence, he has turned his face to this direction, and as, following the tradition of the king of exalted sovereignty, whose abode is in paradise...'

Shah Tahmasp remembered Babur Badshah, who too had taken help of a Persian emperor—Shah Ismail—captured Samarqand and wore the taj of discipleship which was later worn by Humayun Badshah as well. Emperor Babur had the khutba read in Shah Ismail's name and inscribed the name of Shah Ismail along with those of the twelve Imams on the coins. In doing so, he alienated the Sunnis. Yet the Persian kings continued to believe that Babur betrayed them in the battle against the Uzbeks.

Shah Tahmasp further wrote—

'... He has considered the acquisition of security and hopes in dependence on this great dynasty, undoubtedly amends for the rectification of wrongs will be made with the invisible help of the Lord Imams, the Innocent Ones, and the favour of my successful and auspicious person, and all his objects and desires will be attended with success and triumph. Now I am waiting for his respectful arrival and our meeting.'

Humayun Badshah then sought permission to go to Mashhad. It was clear from his letter that he had knowingly entered a Shiite kingdom—

'Every desire which may be depicted in the power of imagination and conception of a man was fulfilled by the grace of God without obligation to any created being except that he had not had the honour of the great bliss and high position of going round the abodes of the innocent Imams round which the angels walk, and especially the holy sepulchre, the mausoleum of al-Riza.

'It is he whose foot-dust is the collyrium of our eyes,
It is he who is our guide and Imam in the world and hereafter.

'That is, the Imam, nourisher of the poor, the holy king, Abul Hasan Ali bin Musa al-Riza.'

When Jannat Ashiyani reached the mausoleum of Imam Riza in Mashhad, the doorkeeper could not open the chain of the gate. Jannat Ashiyani took two steps back. Then facing the shrine, he said, 'O Imam, everyone who comes to your blessed threshold with wishes gets them fulfilled. This slave has taken refuge at the gate of the blessed shrine and is hopeful that his wishes would be fulfilled.'

People say that after this the chain fell open when he placed his hand on the gate. He then circumambulated the shrine and recited the Fatiha.

What was the content of the third letter read by Jannat Ashiyani Humayun Badshah? Jalaluddin Muhammad Akbar tried to drive the thought away but did not succeed.

Jannat Ashiyani read out the basic tenets of Shiism in the presence of Shah Tahmasp and accepted the Shiite ideology. He also agreed to have the name of the twelve Imams read in the khutba.

After Jannat Ashiyani Humayun Badshah returned from Persia and captured Hindustan again, a close one said in anger, 'My King, I can see that your entire army is comprised of Shiites.'

Jannat Ashiyani said, 'Why do you say this?'

The man replied, 'All around such is the name of your soldiers. Yar Ali, Kashf Ali, Haidar Ali. One does not find anybody with a name of any other companion of the Prophet.'

Jannat Ashiyani threw down his pen in anger and said, 'My grandfather himself was called Umar Sheikh and there is nothing more I can say.'

Then he got up and went into the harem. When he returned he said that his faith is strong.

Though he became a Shiite in Persia to save his skin, the threat persisted even after that.

Word had reached Shah Tahmasp that Humayun Badshah had amused himself with divining arrows in Hindustan, writing his own name on twelve good quality arrows and the Shah's name on eleven poor quality ones, to decide who was more powerful. When the two met in Persia, Shah Tahmasp asked him the reason. Humayun Badshah replied, 'One third of the world is Khurasan, which is yours, and two-thirds of the world is Hindustan, which is ours.'

Shah Tahmasp replied, 'This is the result of your arrogance. You were so hard on the country that your subjects turned against you.'

Jannat Ashiyani replied, 'You are right. However, this world is a divine workshop. We seek refuge in God. What choice do we have?'

It is said that, one day, Shah Tahmasp asked him the reason for his defeat in Hindustan.

'The hostility of my brothers,' Humayun Badshah replied.

'Your treatment of your brothers was not right,' the Shah said.

It was time for lunch and the Shah's brother Bahram Mirza was in attendance to help them wash hands.

Shah Tahmasp told Humayun Badshah, 'This is how brothers should be treated.'

An angry Bahram Mirza poisoned the ears of Shah Tahmasp that Emperor Humayun would deceive them the way his father Babur Badshah had.

If the brother poisoned the Shah's ears, the sister saved him. Shah Tahmasp's sister Sultanam Begum said, 'We are always praying for the Shah but you are surrounded by enemies—Ottomans, Uzbeks, Circassians and Franks. If you kill Humayun Badshah, you will create more enemies, for his sons and brothers will one day take revenge. If you cannot help him, it is advisable to let him go.'

While Humayun Badshah and his wife Hamida Banu Begum were living there as guests, the Shah's sister Sultanam Begum hosted a banquet. Tents were pitched outside the city. Pavilions, tents, parasols and arches were set up in an enclosed area. Sultanam Begum asked Hamida Banu Begum, 'Are such parasols and arches found in Hindustan?'

Despite being a guest, Hamida Banu Begum replied, 'Khurasan is two-sixths of the world and Hindustan is four-sixths. It is clear that what is found in the two-sixths will certainly be found better in the four-sixths.'

Because of Sultanam Begum, Shah Tahmasp decided to help Humayun Badshah. He ordered a big feast. On the first day various kinds of food were laid out. On the second day, Shah Tahmasp sat him by his side, and horses, camels, and necessary provisions for the royal household were presented for inspection. The Shah assigned him his son along with twelve thousand cavalry and told Humayun Badshah that a troop count would be held in Seistan.

Shah Tahmasp then stood up and said, 'Muhammad Humayun Badshah, the little we have is yours.'

Now Humayun Badshah threw a party. When Shah Tahmasp entered Humayun Badshah's tent, there was an impressive gathering of singers and instrumentalists. Hindustani food had been cooked at the Shah's request, of which he particularly enjoyed the khushka pulao.

One day Shah Tahmasp asked Humayun Badshah, 'You have so many capable and loyal nobles, despite that you lost your kingdom? Who are these people?'

Humayun Badshah replied, 'Some are Afghans and some Rajputs.'

'How are the relations between these two?' Shah Tahmasp asked.

'Not good,' Humayun Badshah replied.

Shah Tahmasp then advised, 'Encourage Afghans to get into trade. Build relationships with Rajputs, marry them because it is not possible to rule Hindustan without winning the hearts of the landlords.'

15

Ruminating in the royal enclosure of Bhera, Jalaluddin Muhammad Akbar was reminded of another tragic incident fourteen years ago.

In the eighth regnal year, corresponding to the winter of 1564 CE, Badshah Salamat had hunted around Delhi and then offered prayers at the dargah of Hazrat Nizamuddin Awliya. He had just reached the crowded intersection at Maham Anga's madrasa. A cloth merchant was measuring his fabric. People were peering from the terrace to catch a glimpse of Badshah Salamat. An Indian girl pepped out of her window. The saiban above Badshah Salamat's head symbolizing the security his subjects enjoyed under his shadow, the jhanjh, nai, seeng and naqqara were heralding the presence of Emperor Jalaluddin Muhammad Akbar, when an arrow shot from the first floor of the madrasa struck his right shoulder. All hell broke loose. The archer had shot the arrow with the intention to kill but the Emperor escaped with light injuries. The arrow was taken out and while still on horseback the Emperor showed it to all. The assailant was immediately captured. He was Faulad Habshi, a slave of Mirza Sharfuddin Hussain.

Mirza Sharfuddin Hussain had been sent by the ruler of Kashghar, Sultan Abdul Rahim, to condole the death of Humayun Badshah and offer compliments to Badshah Salamat on his accession. Having joined Badshah Salamat's court in the first regnal year, Mirza Sharfuddin Hussain soon gained a mansab of five thousand with the help of Maham Anga and her son Adham Khan. He received the fief of Ajmer and Nagaur. Since he was a high-born from his mother's side, Badshah Salamat married his stepsister Bakhshi Banu Begum to him. In the eighth regnal year, for unknown reasons he rebelled and became a renegade.

Sheikh Abul Fazl said, 'Let no one think that to show this man favour above his rank was to transgress the laws of justice. The place of Justice is one thing, and the station of benevolence is another. Though in matters of this kind an increase of trust on part of the Emperor is a means of applying a test, and of ascertaining character, by administration of the world's wine.'

When people wanted to interrogate Mirza Sharfuddin Hussain's slave to ascertain the cause of the attack, Badshah Salamat said, 'Don't ask! God knows what all this slave would say and which loyalists would fall under suspicion. Don't let him speak. Finish him off.'

None understood why Badshah Salamat took this step. However, there definitely was disquiet in Delhi at that time about Badshah Salamat's wedding plans.

By now Badshah Salamat had married many times. He had married Ruqayya Begum, who was the daughter of Humayun Badshah's brother Hindal. He had married Salima Sultan Begum, who was the daughter of Humayun Badshah's sister. She had been wedded to Bairam Khan earlier. Although Bairam Khan had extracted a promise out of Emperor Humayun that Salima Sultan Begum would be married to him after Hindustan is won, the wedding was solemnized in the beginning of Badshah Salamat's reign. In addition, Jalaluddin Muhammad Akbar had married the daughter of Raja Bharmal of Amber. But none of these marriages caused an unease such as that prevailed in Delhi then.

What happened was that Fatima, the widowed daughter-in-law of Sheikh Buddh, a notable person of Agra, entered into a relationship with Baqi Khan, who was the elder brother of Adham Khan and the son of Maham Anga. This relationship turned into a matrimonial alliance. The lady began taking another daughter-in-law of Sheikh Buddh to marriage ceremonies and other gatherings. This lady was very beautiful and was wedded to a man called Abdul Wasi. When Badshah Salamat chanced upon her on some occasion, he sent a marriage proposal for her. Mongol law dictated that it was obligatory upon the man to divorce his wife if the emperor took fancy to her. So Abdul Wasi pronounced talaq thrice and departed to the Deccan with this comment: 'God's earth is wide.'

Now Fatima began to instigate Badshah Salamat at the behest of Sheikh Buddh. She said that Badshah Salamat should marry into other prominent families of Delhi and Agra so that all feel equal in the eyes of the Emperor. When Badshah Salamat reached Delhi, he expressed his desire to forge matrimonial relations with prominent families of the city. Middlemen and eunuchs were sent to prominent families to look for maidens for Badshah Salamat. While this search was on, an attempt was made on Badshah Salamat's life near the madrasa of Maham Anga. The assailant's motive was not known, nor did Badshah Salamat let it be known. The attack happened from inside the madrasa of Maham Anga and the attacker was the slave of a person married to Badshah Salamat's stepsister. With the death of Faulad Habshi, the mystery of whether it was Badshah Salamat's relatives who were behind the attack or those Delhiites who were not yet ready to give their daughters in marriage to the Timuri emperor, was closed forever. Those who tried to get to the bottom of the conspiracy noticed that Badshah Salamat gave up the idea of marrying into the families of Delhi after this attack. Mullah Abdul Qadir Badayuni—the writer of the secret history of Badshah Salamat's reign—said, 'God gave him sense. By the miracle of the saints he was saved.'

16

The *Akhlaq-i-Nasiri* was being read out to Badshah Salamat in the royal enclosure at Bhera—

'If a man's wife has poise and nobility of mind, he should not prefer another wife to her, even if the other woman be superior in beauty, property, lineage and family. This causes disruption in the household, because women are jealous by nature and deficient in intelligence. Only kings are allowed to have more than one wife because their aim is to have a large number of descendants and their wives are like slaves to them. Even kings must be careful because a man is to the household what a heart is to the body. One man cannot run two households just as one heart cannot sustain two bodies.'

In the first regnal year of Badshah Salamat, Majnun Khan Qaqshal was sent to Narnaul as the administrator. When Sher Shah's slave Haji Khan besieged him, Raja Bharmal of Amber came to his rescue and sent him safely towards the royal court. When Badshah Salamat got to know of this, he asked for Raja Bharmal to be called to the court with full honours. A major mishap was averted as Raja Bharmal was about to depart after getting the robe and reward. The elephant on which Badshah Salamat was mounted went out of control. This caused chaos all around. People ran for their lives. But when the elephant ran towards the Rajputs, they bravely stood fast. Badshah Salamat did not forget this. A few years later when he was on his way to Ajmer to seek blessings, a courtier told him that Raja Bharmal had fled to the hills because of Mirza Sharfuddin's harassment. When Jalaluddin Muhammad Akbar's entourage reached Dausa on the way to Ajmer, most inhabitants had fled the place. Badshah Salamat said, 'We wish to serve humanity. Why are these people fleeing? It seems they have been oppressed by Mirza Sharfuddin Hussain. That is why they are also scared of us.'

By the time Badshah Salamat reached Sanganer, Raja Bharmal presented himself and was honoured at the court. Raja Bharmal gave proof of loyalty and offered his eldest daughter in marriage to Badshah Salamat. The offer was accepted and Raja Bharmal was sent off to make preparations for the wedding that was to happen once Badshah Salamat returned from Ajmer. On the way back, the royal party camped at Sambhar and Raja Bharmal's daughter was wedded to Jalaluddin Muhammad Akbar. When Raja Bharmal bade farewell to his daughter, he also sent his son Bhagwant Das and grandson Man Singh to Agra with Badshah Salamat. Within two years of this wedding Badshah Salamat abolished jizya—the tax on non-Muslims—throughout his empire.

'Rana ji cannot have food with those who have married their sisters and daughters to the Turks.'

They say it was the eighteenth regnal year, corresponding to the summer of 1573 CE, when Man Singh came to Udaipur and had to hear this. Despite Man Singh's best efforts at cajoling, Maharana Pratap Singh did not agree to offer his services to Badshah Salamat.

Maharana Pratap Singh had acceded to the throne of Mewar in highly unusual circumstances just about a year ago. By tradition, the throne of Mewar was never vacant. That is the reason all grieving happened at the residence of the royal priest. And while this happened, the palace was decked up. The eldest son did not participate in the last rites of the king. He was enthroned the moment the funeral procession left. Maharana Pratap Singh's father Udai Singh had married eighteen times and had twenty-four sons and twenty daughters. When his son Jagmal was not seen at the funeral it became clear that the King had decided to give the throne to the son who was ninth in the list of heirs, instead of the eldest son Pratap.

Those supporting Maharana Pratap Singh said, 'On what ground is the eldest, the most eligible and the bravest Pratap ineligible? An enemy like Emperor Akbar is hounding us, Chittor is crumbling, Mewar is getting ruined. Would there be any doubt about disaster if a problem arises from within the family?'

When those supporting Pratap Singh reached the Maharana's palace after the last rites, they found Jagmal seated on the throne. Taking hold of Jagmal by his hand, they forced him off the throne and seated him in the place reserved for the king's brother. With the throne vacated, Pratap Singh was seated on it.

They say that the charan—the bard—named Jadda had sent four dohas in the praise of Abdur Rahim Khan-i-Khanan—

O Khan-i-Khanan! I am amazed,
How a heart like the Meru Mountain is created in a soft body.
Khan-i-Khanan says, fire is blazing in the oven,
Strange that man whose heart is soft as water is afire, one as dry as reed is alive.
Khan-i-Khanan says, praise be to His ways of making humans,
He needs not a heart like Meru Mountain or mani, He needs complete submission.
Khan-i-Khanan says, He burns the entire world in the fire of love.

Khan-i-Khanan tried rewarding him with a hundred thousand rupees for each doha but Jadda requested instead that the pargana of Jahazpur be granted to Jagmal. It is said that Khan-i-Khanan used his clout to grant Jadda's wish and sent him this doha:

The Jadda on the earth is like amber in the sky,
Jadda is a class apart, there being none like him.

Jagmal might have received the pargana of Jahazpur but the age of Maharana Pratap Singh had dawned on Mewar.

17

About four years ago, at the end of the twelfth regnal year, corresponding to Tuesday, the twenty-third of February 1568 CE, the strong fortress of Chittor fell to the army of Badshah Salamat. The previous night, the walls of the fort had been breached from a number of places but the forces of Chittor were able to hold back the royal army. At a point where the wall had been breached, Jalaluddin Muhammad Akbar saw in the flash of cannon fire a man in an armour with a thousand nails. Badshah Salamat picked up his favourite gun Sangram.

Badshah Salamat was fond of guns. He was a good marksman. His innovations led to the manufacture of such powerful guns of which, even when filled to the top, there was no fear of bursting. Now guns could be fired off without a match. A slight movement of the cock was sufficient. Out of the thousands Badshah Salamat chose one thousand and five guns as khasa—special ones—for his personal use. Of all the khasa guns Sangram was dearest to him. It was his first khasa gun. He would take it for hunts as also into the battlefield. By Badshah Salamat's order, a record was kept of the game killed by each gun and it was found that one thousand and nineteen animals had been killed by Sangram.

Now he fired his Sangram, and told Raja Bhagwant Das, 'A good hunter knows when he has hit the mark.'

An hour had not passed when Chittor's forces disappeared and flames were reported from a number of places. Courtiers were speculating about it when Raja Bhagwant Das said, 'This is jauhar. When defeat is imminent and men have been killed, women enter the pyre made of sandalwood, dry wood and oil.'

By the morning it became clear that Badshah Salamat's Sangram had claimed the life of Jaimal, the governor of the fort. The Chittor

Fort was finally at Badshah Salamat's feet after a siege of four months. He entered the fort on an elephant. Three hundred royal elephants also entered the fort. An elephant crushed Patta, the brave warrior of Chittor, to death in front of Badshah Salamat's eyes. Even in this situation a Rajput attacked the tusk of the royal elephant Madhukar and said, 'Give my regards to the Emperor.'

There was massacre from dawn till the afternoon. Almost thirty thousand died. Badshah Salamat knew very well what had been said in the *Akhlaq-i-Nasiri* about conduct in such times—

'Once victory is gained, as far as possible, whoever can be captured should not be killed. There are many advantages in taking prisoners, such as holding them hostage or to ransom, or placing them under an obligation. There is no benefit in killing people. There should be absolutely no killing or enmity because after victory the enemy becomes a subject or slave. It is said that when Alexander continued killing people even after conquering a town, Aristotle reproached him: "You had an excuse to kill your enemies before victory. After victory, what is your excuse for killing your subjects?" It is more creditable for a king to be pardoning because he has the power to do the opposite.'

The chronicler of Badshah Salamat's history Sheikh Abul Fazl says, 'On the former occasion on third of Muharram of 703 Hijri, when Sultan Alauddin took the fort after six months and seven days, the peasantry were not put to death as they had not engaged in fighting. But on this occasion there was a general massacre because the peasantry had shown great zeal and activity.'

The Battle of Chittor was personally fought by Badshah Salamat. He suffered huge losses in this tiring campaign. In the twelfth regnal year, corresponding to the twentieth of October 1567 CE, the royal tent had been pitched near Chittor Fort. The very next day Jalaluddin Muhammad Akbar circled the two-kos-long circumference of the hill on which the Chittor Fort was situated. Within a month the siege was completely laid. When royal warriors began to get killed while frontally attacking the fort, Badshah Salamat forbade them and said, 'This should not be called courageous. This is rashness.'

Thereafter, orders were given to find ways for mines to be laid at three places and fill them with gunpowder so that the walls of the fort be breached, and at two places a pathway be made on the hills which reached right up to the fort. Five thousand artisans got down to the work of making a sabat—covered pathway—which would enable the army to approach the fort and breach its walls. This came under attack from inside the fort and about two hundred people died every day in their effort to make the sabat. The workers were liberally paid in gold and silver and the construction of the sabat was speedily pushed forward. The mines were also advancing by Badshah Salamat's orders.

This caused consternation among the Rajputs inside the fort. The Maharana was not present inside the fort at this time. After hearing reports of the arrival of Badshah Salamat, he gave the reins of the fort to Jaimal and hid in the hills along with his family and five thousand Rajputs. During the entire period of battle, he came nowhere near.

Now two Rajput chiefs were sent from inside the fort to Badshah Salamat to seek peace.

People far and wide in Chittor could feel the royal presence through the forty-yard-tall akashdiya. They looked at it and said, '*Akbar cha diva*'—Akbar's lamp.

Rawat Sahib Khan Chauhan and Dodiya Thakur Sanda, who had come from inside the Chittor Fort told Badshah Salamat, 'Maharana has gone into the hills. Those inside the fort are innocent. Please lift the siege of the fort because it is a tradition from the times of earlier emperors that they oblige after receiving tribute.'

After hearing the Rajput sardars, Jalaluddin Muhammad Akbar said, 'Until the Rana comes, the fight will not stop. Ask for whatever else you wish.'

Dodiya Thakur Sanda said, 'Now what else can we ask for? Since you command, I just ask this much that in case I die fighting, my body be cremated according to Hindu rites.'

Badshah Salamat granted this wish and then got ready for a major offensive. But this assault became a major cause of regret.

By now the mines had been driven up to the foot of the fort. Gunpowder was placed on both sides of the Lakhauta Gate. One hundred and twenty maunds on one side and eighty maunds on the other. The plan was to trigger a simultaneous blast at the two places to breach the wall of the fort so that the army could enter it.

But an unforeseen accident happened when one mine exploded first. It breached the wall of the fort. The royal soldiers rushed swiftly towards the breach and so did the soldiers of Chittor to save the fort. Just then the second mine exploded with such ferocity that it could be heard fifty miles away. Two hundred of the royal force and forty of the forces of Chittor were killed instantly. Their limbs were blown away and scattered all over.

This was a big setback to Badshah Salamat. Twenty of those who died were personally known to him. Badshah Salamat had already said before this accident that for the two mines to ignite simultaneously, they should be fired from two different places. He had cautioned that the second mine might ignite later in case both were fired from one place. And this is what happened.

After this calamity, Badshah Salamat decided to pay full attention to the completion of the sabat. Putting his life in danger, he would inspect the site and fire shots. Once a person standing two removes from Badshah Salamat was shot at from inside the fort but he did not suffer much injury. In response, Badshah Salamat picked up his gun but he could not see the gunman. He could just see the barrel of the gun projected from the firing hole. When Badshah Salamat took aim at the gun, it struck the gunman as well. It was later found that Badshah Salamat had hit Ismael, who was the chief of the musketeers.

Once a cannonball burst very close to him. It killed twenty people of the royal army but Badshah Salamat was himself unhurt.

Finally, the sabat was completed. A path that was covered on the top and also on the two sides was ready for use. It was so high that an elephant rider with a spear in his hand could pass under it and so wide that ten horsemen could ride abreast. Once this path took the forces up to the fort, it did not take long for it to be breached. From here Badshah Salamat fired at Jaimal with his Sangram and won this difficult battle.

To mark this, it is said that Maharana Pratap Singh ordered the naqqara to always follow in the rear and not be in the front either in a procession or in battle. Badshah Salamat commemorated the battle in many ways. On his way back to Agra from Chittor, he issued the 'Fatehnama-i-Chittor'—Chronicle of the Chittor Victory—

'Praise be to Allah who made good His promise, helped His

servant, honoured His soldiers, defeated the enemies. After Allah there is none. All Praise and thanksgiving to He who opened the doors of forts and kingdoms. In whose grasp are the keys to the conquests of the just and religious sultans...the Merciful one whose omnipotence has ensured the victory of the believers. The Omnipotent one enjoined the task of destroying the wicked infidels on the dutiful warriors. "Fight them! Allah will chastise them at your hands and He will lay them low and give you victory over them." Glorified is He. His sovereignty is not dependent on any friend or helper. Allah has assigned to us government of Hindustan which is one of the biggest countries of the world. The Supreme Sovereign's office has sent the message for our sultanate. People kept secure from the hardships and misfortunes of the age are God's trust. Under our benevolent protection, people are discharging the obligations of worship of the Almighty. We are thankful for this great favour. Proceed whither we wish, we shall be victorious. In whatever direction we proceed fortune will come forward to greet us... We spend our precious time to the best of our ability in war and jihad, with the help of God, who gives strength to our ever increasing empire. We are busy in subjugating the places which are under the possession of the infidels, may God forsake and annihilate all of them, and thus raising the standard of Islam everywhere and removing the darkness of polytheism and violent sins by the use of the sword. We destroy the places of worship of idols in those places and other parts of Hindustan.

'Praise be to Allah, who guided us to this, and we would not have found the way had it not been that Allah had guided us. This is to say that during these victorious times, after the elimination of Ali Quli and his ungrateful faction, we arrived at the capital Agra. Then for recreation of hunting we stopped near Chittor. There it was brought to our notice that Rana Udai Singh, may God annihilate him, from whom it was expected that he would come forward to welcome, pay respects and kiss the royal threshold or would send his son with tribute, is collecting provisions in the fort of Chittor, which is his hereditary place of residence and is distinguished in the forts of India in strength and grandeur, with the intention of entrenching himself there. Since the thoughts of war and jihad dominated the enlightened mind, the Emperor was displeased. Despite the fact that most of the royal troops had returned to their fiefs after the last victory and only a few, who happened to be present at the capital, accompanied the royal cavalcade on this hunting expedition, we decided to pay attention to defeating the infidel.

'The people of Islam were busy praying. O Allah! Bestow on us endurance, make our foothold sure, and give us help against unbelievers...good tidings were coming from heaven. There was attack in groups against the wicked unbelievers and the opening of the fort was seized. They stood without flinching and got an upper hand. They felled them one upon the other with the stroke of their bloodthirsty sword, leaving around heaps of the slain. The remnant were fleeing in different directions as frightened asses fleeing from the lions. May they go to the lowest part of hell. The star of success and good fortune rose with the sublime message that victory comes only by the help of Allah, the Mighty, the Wise. The victorious troop entered the fort. In accordance with the divine command to kill the idolaters, those defiant ones who were still offering resistance having formed themselves into groups of two to three hundred persons, were put to death and their women and children taken prisoner.

'According to Allah's promise, immense booty and spoils in cash and kind were acquired. The roots of the people who were unjust were cut off. All praise is due to Allah.

'The pillar of the mighty state, the confidant of the resplendent khilafat, the foremost among the great khans of the age, the climber of the ladder of authority and dignity, the devoted and sincere, the intrepid horseman, having high rank in bravery, Mubarizuddin Mir Muhammad Khan Bahadur, and the pillar of the mighty state, the best among the loyal ones of the age, the rider of the field of battle and valour, Qutbuddin Muhammad Khan Bahadur and the rest of the khans, nobles along with the sayyids, ulema, sheikhs, the qazis of shariat and other dignitaries, residents, chaudharis, qanoongos, the subjects and peasants of Punjab, being jubilant at the glad tidings carried by this auspicious "Fatehnama", which is a foretaste of the victories to follow, should offer infinite thanksgivings. They should also pray in the auspicious moments, when the prayers are more likely to be granted, for the long life of our noble self, the perpetuity of the empire and for the grant of greater ability to us for fulfilling the obligation of jihad, divine worship and acts of piety. They should pray that day by day doors of fresh victories and success be opened before us.

'After the management of the affairs of Chittor we have with determination turned the reins towards the capital Agra.

'The horse beneath the thigh and the canopy of victory above us.
Victory keeping company and divine help guiding the way.'

Badshah Salamat fought many battles after Chittor and won each one of them but he did not commit a massacre ever after, nor did he issue a proclamation of victory of this nature.

On his return, Jalaluddin Muhammad Akbar honoured Jaimal and Patta in a grand manner. The statues of the two brave warriors were installed at the Delhi Gate of the royal fort at Agra. The statues of Jaimal and Patta were made in red sandstone and the elephants they were seated on of black marble.

After the Chittor victory, but before the victory at Haldighati, when Kunwar Man Singh reached Mewar, a feast was laid out for him at the banks of Udai Sagar Lake. It is said that when Man Singh sat down to have his meal, he found Maharana Pratap Singh missing. When he asked, he was told, 'Maharana has an upset stomach.'

'I very well know how to treat an upset stomach. I have been your well-wisher until now but be careful now onwards.'

When Kunwar Man Singh's reply reached Maharana Pratap Singh, he sent his reply through Thakur Bheem Singh. Referring to a town of Amber, he said, 'If you come on your own strength we shall receive you right up to Malpura. If you come on the strength of your phoopha, you shall be dealt with wherever opportunity arises.'

Maharana Pratap Singh made a pointed mention of Man Singh's 'phoopha' Jalaluddin Muhammad Akbar. Man Singh left the feast and stood up. To not show disrespect for food he picked up a few grains and put them in his turban and said, 'To protect your honour we gave up ours and gave our women to the Turks. But if such is your wish, you will live in crisis because this land will not be able to keep you.'

Thakur Bheem Singh said, 'I will attack the elephant on which you come with a spear, for my name is Bheem Singh.'

As an angry Kunwar Man Singh was leaving, Thakur Bheem Singh said, 'Come back soon with your phoopha.'

It is said that the Maharana got all the food and silver and gold utensils thrown into the lake as soon as Kunwar Man Singh left. The place where the feast was laid was dug up two feet and was purified with the water of the Ganga. All the Rajputs too bathed and changed.

Within three years the moment came when Bheem Singh and Man Singh came face to face.

When Badshah Salamat sent Kunwar Man Singh against Rana Pratap, Mullah Abdul Qadir Badayuni too expressed a desire to go to the front. Badshah Salamat had given Mullah Abdul Qadir Badayuni the responsibility of leading the namaz congregation on Wednesday because he had a good voice. When he expressed his wish to the highest officer in matters of religion, Sadr-us-Sudur Sheikh Abd-un-Nabi, the latter accepted it but gave his vakil the responsibility of taking it to Badshah Salamat. When the matter did not progress for some time, Mullah Badayuni expressed his desire to Naqeeb Khan, a person close to him. Naqeeb Khan said, 'If a Hindu were not leading the army, I would have myself sought permission to fight.'

Mullah Abdul Qadir Badayuni said, 'I am willing to fight under any genuine underling of Badshah Salamat. What difference does it make whether it is Man Singh or someone else. Our intentions should be genuine.'

When Naqeeb Khan presented the petition Badshah Salamat said, 'He has just been made imam of the royal court. How can he go?'

Naqeeb Khan said, 'He is very keen on taking part in the jihad.'

Then Badshah Salamat asked Mullah Badayuni, 'Are you very keen?'

Mullah Abdul Qadir Badayuni replied, 'Yes.'

'Why?'

Mullah Badayuni replied, 'I want to colour my black beard with blood to show my loyalty to Badshah Salamat.'

Hearing this Badshah Salamat said, 'Insha'Allah you will return with the news of victory.'

At this Mullah Badayuni stepped forward to kiss Badshah Salamat's feet. Since only a chosen few were granted this privilege, Badshah Salamat withdrew his feet.

Mullah Abdul Qadir Badayuni was leaving the darbar when Badshah Salamat called him back and himself picked fifty-six ashrafis and gave them to him.

Mullah Badayuni then took leave of Sheikh Abd-un-Nabi, who said, 'It is a hadith that when two armies meet in the battlefield, it is the best time and place for a wish to be fulfilled. Remember me in prayers at that time. Don't forget.'

It is said that Maharana Pratap entered the battlefield of Haldighati with twenty thousand and Kunwar Man Singh with eighty thousand soldiers. Maharana Pratap Singh divided his army into two. Hakim Sur Afghan began by launching such an attack on the advance and vanguard of Kunwar Man Singh's army that it faced serious reverses. The Sayyids of Barha gave a tough fight from the right flank and there was heavy loss of life and equipment on both sides. In the meanwhile, Maharana Pratap Singh himself led the second part of his army and launched an attack on the left flank, causing disarray. Seeing this situation, war drums were sounded and it was declared that Badshah Salamat was coming himself. Out of enthusiasm, the rear flank of the royal army took charge and the tides of the battle began to turn. Luna, the elephant from Maharana's side, inflicted injury upon the royal elephant, Gajmukt. But when the mahout was hit with a bullet, Luna turned back. Maharana's elephant Ramprasad was fighting Panju Ranmadar of the royal forces when an arrow hit the mahout and Ramprasad was captured by the royal forces.

Launching a direct attack on Kunwar Man Singh, Thakur Bheem Singh said, 'Here comes Bheem Singh. Beware!'

Thakur Bheem Singh's spear could just hit the howda of Kunwar Man Singh. Thakur Bheem Singh was killed in the battle.

Now Maharana Pratap Singh and Kunwar Man Singh came face to face. The Maharana said, 'Show whatever valour you can, here comes Pratap Singh!'

Maharana Pratap Singh's spear could also just hit the howda of Kunwar Man Singh, who was unhurt, but two legs of Maharana Pratap Singh's horse were struck by the dagger that was affixed to the elephant's forehead. The horse was injured. Maharana Pratap escaped on his injured horse and was never ever captured by the royal forces.

The poet Narottam wrote in his *Mancharitra Raso*—

Battle was so fierce that none knew the name of the countless who perished,
Angry warriors from the two sides fought.
King, nobles and flagbearers fought,
Even the unknown warrior protecting the flag fought.
All fought for the honour of their master,
Undoubtedly, Raja Man was the winner, and Pratap fled the battlefield.

People speculated why Kunwar Man Singh did not pursue Maharana Pratap Singh. One said that Kunwar Man Singh's forefathers had been loyal to Mewar and that is why he allowed Maharana Pratap Singh to flee. Some said that the royal forces did not have the strength for pursuit due to extreme heat. Whatever be the reason, Badshah Salamat showed his displeasure by not allowing Kunwar Man Singh to appear in the court for some time.

After the battle, Mullah Abdul Qadir Badayuni remembered a line of Mullah Sheri on the valour of Kunwar Man Singh—'A Hindu wields the sword of Islam.'

When Mullah Badayuni appeared in the court with Maharana Pratap Singh's elephant Ramprasad, Badshah Salamat asked, 'They have written ever so many praises of you. Tell me truly, in what army have you served, and what exploits have you performed?'

The Mullah replied, 'In the presence of Badshah Salamat, this humble servant speaks even the truth with a hundred fears and tremblings, how can he speak that which is not the truth?'

After hearing the full account of the battle, Badshah Salamat gave ninety-six ashrafis to Mullah Badayuni and asked, 'Have you met Sheikh Abd-un-Nabi?'

Mullah Badayuni replied, 'From the dust of the road I came to the court. How could I have seen him?'

Badshah Salamat gave him a shawl for Sheikh Abd-un-Nabi and said, 'Tell him that it is from us. We have made this on purpose for him. He may please wear it.'

Sheikh Abd-un-Nabi was very pleased with the shawl. He asked Mullah Badayuni about the prayer in the battlefield. Mullah Badayuni replied, 'I recited the prayer, "O God! Pardon believers male and female, and keep those who keep the religion of Muhammad, and abandon those who abandon the religion of Muhammad."'

The Sadr-us-Sudur of the empire Sheikh Abd-un-Nabi said, 'That was sufficient, praise be to Allah.'

18

During the Battle of Chittor, a person appeared in Badshah Salamat's court who became a lifelong confidant.

In accordance with protocol, Badshah Salamat's throne was placed at a slight elevation and was cordoned off with gold railings. In an enclosure cordoned off with silver and wooden railings stood the nobles. In keeping with court etiquette their feet were bare and heads covered.

The eldest son of Sheikh Mubarak Nagauri, twenty-year-old Sheikh Abul Faiz, who wrote poetry under the name of Faizi, stood far behind in the court, hoping to catch the Emperor's eye. He was worried.

Sheikh Mubarak had no dearth of enemies at the court. When Badshah Salamat heard of Faizi's poetry he summoned him. Rivals at the court sent soldiers to cordon his house as if he was being forcibly brought. When Faizi left for Chittor, his entire family was apprehensive about the intentions of the enemies.

Faizi was looking at the Emperor from beyond the railings of gold and silver. This was an opportunity that could change the family's fortunes. Once he had gone along with his father Sheikh Mubarak to meet Sadr-us-Sudur Sheikh Abd-un-Nabi to seek a land grant of a hundred bigha. Sheikh Abd-un-Nabi had refused to grant the land on the ground that father and son were of Shiite faith. They had been unceremoniously sent away. Since then Faizi had been trying to meet the Emperor. Finally, at the court assembled some distance away from the Chittor Fort, the moment arrived when Faizi won Badshah Salamat's heart.

Following royal protocol, Faizi placed his right palm on the forehead and bowed his head thrice in taslim. None but the Emperor could be greeted in this manner. This convention began in Badshah Salamat's childhood when his father Humayun Badshah gave him a turban. Since the turban was too big for the head of young Mirza Akbar, he held the turban in his palm to prevent it from falling off as he bowed to offer salam. Humayun Badshah loved this so much that he made it a rule.

From outside the railings of gold and silver, Faizi recited to the Emperor:

O Emperor! I am outside the cage,
Allow this sweet-tongued parrot to enter the cage.

Badshah Salamat looked at the young man standing beyond the railings. Faizi's poetry had won his heart.

In matters of faith, Faizi was a troubled soul. He would say,

Sometimes Faizi is like a pious man in the mosque,
At times he is the idol-worshipper sitting in Somnath.

At the battlefront of Chittor, Badshah Salamat found a courtier who would become an associate in the biggest battle of his life. Faizi said of Jalaluddin Muhammad Akbar:

This king, whose wisdom shows the path to God,
He is an ocean, inseparable even for a moment from God,
People call him shadow of God,
I say, not shadow, he is the divine light.

Some years later, when Badshah Salamat was leaving on the eastern campaign, Sheikh Abul Fazl, the younger brother of Faizi, came to the court. He presented a commentary of the Ayat al-Kursi and won praise for it.

Sheikh Abul Fazl was born on the sixth of Muharram of the Hijri era, corresponding to the fourteenth of January of 1551 CE. By the age of fifteen he had completed his education. He loved being alone. Therefore, he did not take a liking to any occupation. Sheikh Abul Fazl described his state in these words:

'I had grown weary of the learned men of my land. My brother, relatives and friends were unanimous in asking me to obtain the boon of serving Badshah Salamat. I was not inclined to do so, for I had not opened a far-seeing eye. My father impressed upon me that the Emperor is the leader of the caravans both of society and seclusion. The multiplicity of external associations does not withhold him from essential unity. From him comes the resolution of spiritual and temporal matters.'

This was a crucial moment in Badshah Salamat's life. He had won Gujarat and was now looking east to completely overcome the Afghan power. When Sheikh Abul Fazl wrote Badshah Salamat's history and praise in *Akbarnama,* he mentioned that it was necessary to win new territories to establish peace and justice and free these regions of tyrants.

19

It was the fourth of August of 1574 CE, corresponding to the nineteenth regnal year, when the people of Patna heard a noise that shook the earth under them. Despite heavy rains, Badshah Salamat reached Patna from Jaunpur by the river route. Munim Khan Khan-i-Khanan had gone two kos ahead on the river to receive him. Artist Govardhan of Badshah Salamat's atelier painted a picture of the reception in neem-qalam. Munim Khan was paying obeisance at the court held on the banks of the Ganga. Seated on an engraved throne, one foot on the footrest that was laid on a carpet of flowery pattern, with a canopy above, Badshah Salamat was addressing Munim Khan.

Cannons, guns and fireworks fired from the boats raised so much smoke that it was dark all around. The cannons had been fired for Badshah Salamat but were heard loud and clear by the self-styled Afghan king Daud Khan Karrani, who had been entrenched at Patna for many months. He had not allowed Munim Khan's siege of Patna to succeed. Munim Khan tried to instil fear in Daud Khan Karrani. He invited him to become a mansabdar to avert Badshah Salamat's march on Patna. The news of Badshah Salamat's arrival at Jaunpur had reached Daud Khan Karrani. Yet he was not expecting Jalaluddin Muhammad Akbar to reach Patna during the monsoon. In anxiety he sent a message—

'I do not approve for myself the title of sovereign...now obedience to the Emperor has taken possession of this heart. Whatever fief is given, I would consider it a piece of good fortune. Owing to youth and lack of wisdom, I have committed faults. So I would not kiss the threshold until I make amends by my service.'

Rejecting Daud Khan Karrani's plea, Badshah Salamat said:

'We, by virtue of our being the Zill-i-Ilahi, receive little and give much. Our forgiveness has no relish for vengeance, provided that Daud has light from the torch of truth, and will rub his forehead on the threshold of fortune, so that the hand of our grace may disperse the dust of destruction from the crown of his fortune. Otherwise let him do one of the three things so that the lives and goods of so many thousands may not be an offering to ruin. First, let someone from his party come to our camp and be a spectator, and someone from our side go to his army and be a sentinel, so that no one on either side engage in war, and let us two come into the field of battle and fight with one another with all the arms that he knows, so that whoever by divine decree, and the help of heaven, shall be the conqueror shall have the kingdom. If his courage be not equal to this, let him choose someone of his soldiers who is distinguished for valour and strength of arm, and skill in combat. We shall also send one of our strong-armed ones, whose countenance shall be decked with might, against him. These two combatants will contend in the arena. The army of whichever of them conquers shall be victorious. If in his army there be no such lion-heart, then let him choose one of his host of elephants, and we too shall produce an elephant as majestic as heaven. Victory shall be on the side of whichever of them prevails.'

Daud Khan Karrani was unnerved by Badshah Salamat's offer. After surveying the situation for two days, Jalaluddin Muhammad Akbar ordered attack on Hajipur from where supplies were reaching Patna. Six thousand men and a strong fleet of war-boats launched an attack at night. This onslaught lasted till the next evening. Hajipur was captured and the heads of Afghan warriors arranged in a boat and sent to Daud Khan Karrani. The very next day Daud Khan Karrani fled Patna in a drunken state. Thousands of Afghan warriors lost their lives in the stampede. Badshah Salamat entered Patna with his army through the Delhi Gate of the city.

Badshah Salamat then gave Munim Khan Khan-i-Khanan the responsibility of completely uprooting Afghan power from Bengal and then proceeded to Delhi to pray at the grave of Humayun Badshah and the shrine of Khwaja Muinuddin Chishti at Ajmer. Fulfilling his vow at Ajmer, he placed the kettledrums of Daud Khan Karrani at the shrine and returned to Fatehpur Sikri.

Afghan power had been uprooted from Bihar, Bengal and Orissa when, fourteen months later, an epidemic broke out in the army and Munim Khan Khan-i-Khanan breathed his last.Munim Khan's last words were:

'Take care of the organization of the treasury, elephant stable and articles of buyutat. Let Majnun Qaqshal, Muhammad Murad Khan and other khans strengthen the administration of their parganas and vilayats and remain there. Send information to the court and act according to imperial instructions.'

Soon afterwards Daud Khan Karrani's head was presented to Badshah Salamat. Sheikh Abul Fazl writes that the same day Badshah Salamat had told his close ones, 'Last night, in a dreamlike state, a window opened from the spiritual world, and we got to know that in a short time news would arrive of victory over the eastern region and the people there would find daily-increasing justice.'

Actually, Daud Khan Karrani was captured when his horse got stuck in a morass. When he asked for water, it was given to him in a shoe. When Daud Khan Karrani refused, he was given water in a vessel. Fair complexioned with a moustache and a short beard, Daud Khan Karrani could only be finally beheaded in the third attempt. His head was filled with hay and sprinkled with perfume and dispatched to Badshah Salamat.

Once when Daud Khan Karrani had appeared to hold talks for peace, Munim Khan Khan-i-Khanan stepped forward and received him at the edge of the carpet. Daud Khan Karrani unloosened his sword and took it off. Munim Khan gave him the robe sent by Badshah Salamat. A sword and a sash were also tied to his waist. In the painting made by Hiranand, the artist of Badshah Salamat's atelier, Daud is shown trying to put his second arm into the robe, with the first already in. It seems as if he is finding it difficult to wear the robe sent by the Emperor. Obviously the picture was painted after Daud Khan Karrani had once again rebelled and thereafter dispatched to the other world.

Later Badshah Salamat told Raja Todar Mal, 'It has come to our notice that many Afghans have settled in the towns and villages of Punjab. Although some claim to be traders and some farmers, it seems they are wicked. It seems they exploit the poor from time to time and these matters were not promptly inquired into. Also, the weak were unable to produce evidence. We feel this body of men should be scattered so that people obtain relief from the burden of oppression, and also that the Afghans might not become vagabonds.'

When Badshah Salamat returned from the east after defeating the Afghan power, Sheikh Abul Fazl came to Fatehpur Sikri's Jama Masjid with the intent to see the Emperor. Seeing Badshah Salamat from afar, he thought, 'Whether the Emperor sees you or not, yet you are seeing that holy light. Though I may not be favoured by a glance from the Emperor, I have attained vision and understanding by beholding that holy one.'

Sheikh Abul Fazl was not expecting it but Badshah Salamat recognized him from a distance and sent for him.

This was the time His Majesty's views were undergoing a critical transformation and the two brothers—Sheikh Abul Fazl and Sheikh Faizi—were to find a crucial place in the new scheme of things.

20

The full moon above the Bhera sky and the akashdiya under it lit the royal camp. One of the biggest hunts of Timuri history was to take place the next day. But what transpired during the day had caused tremors from the do-ashiyana manzil of Badshah Salamat down to the camp bazaar.

It was around late afternoon. The Thakurs of the royal entourage had been playing kabaddi for some time when they learnt that Badshah Salamat was coming their side. First they thought that Badshah Salamat would also play kabaddi. So they remained in their underwear. When they learnt that Badshah Salamat would go to Sheikh Jamal's camp, the Thakurs quickly changed and did kornish to the Emperor there itself.

Sheikh Jamal's family had for long lived in Chandwar and Jalesar near the province of Akbarabad. His sister was the 'Sar-Amad'—superintendent—of the palaces of the harem. Because of her influence, Sheikh Jamal was a mansabdar of the rank of one thousand. People say that Badshah Salamat had cured him with an antidote when his enemies had poisoned his water and he had fallen ill.

Before going into the camp of Sheikh Jamal, Badshah Salamat ordered Peshrau Khan to put up the abgah tent.

Peshrau Khan was Badshah Salamat's family retainer. He had studied in Tabriz. Shah Tahmasp of Iran had gifted him to Humayun Badshah. He was in the service of Humayun Badshah and then Badshah Salamat's. His name was Mehtar Saadat and Peshrau Khan his title. It was his responsibility to put the royal camp in place before Badshah Salamat's arrival.

After Peshrau Khan had put up the abgah tent, Badshah Salamat urinated and wore a lungi. Then taking the prince in his arms he took seven to eight dips in the river.

After changing in Sheikh Jamal's camp, Badshah Salamat was about to reach his court when he stopped to inspect the tethered deer. Here occurred the incident that stunned the royal entourage.

Badshah Salamat chanced upon the Thakur who had not appeared for kornish. He asked, 'Where have you been?'

'It took me long to wear clothes to meet the court etiquette. My fault,' the Thakur replied.

Badshah Salamat gave him four or five lashes one after another.

After this, when the Thakur by the name of Prithideep arrived, Jalaluddin Muhammad Akbar asked, 'Where were you?'

Prithideep said, 'My advisors did not allow me to come.'

At this Prithideep too got seven or eight lashes.

When Badshah Salamat asked his advisors, they said, 'We have done nothing, Your Majesty. His uncle did not allow him to come.'

Just as the first lash fell on Prithideep's uncle, he stabbed himself with his dagger. Losing his cool Badshah Salamat said, 'Kill him, kill the bastard!'

Badshah Salamat called for an elephant to kill Prithideep's uncle but when the elephant did not move forward, in anger he went to his do-ashiyana manzil.

Out of fear, the Thakurs retired to their camps, worried about the consequences of Badshah Salamat's anger.

Just then it was learnt that Kunwar Man Singh had arrived. He was the son of Raja Bhagwant Das and grandson of Raja Bharmal of Amber. His aunt—father's sister—was married to Badshah Salamat. By virtue of this marriage Badshah Salamat was Man Singh's phoopha. This was Badshah Salamat's first marriage among the Rajputs. Thereafter he married many other Thakurs' daughters but his bond with Amber was the strongest. Kunwar Man Singh enjoyed a high status at the royal court and Badshah Salamat had bestowed the title of farzand—son—upon him.

Only a few years ago, Badshah Salamat had thrown a drinking party after victory over Surat. It was nighttime and people got talking about the tradition of bravery in Hindustan. It was claimed that some Rajputs would hold a double-headed spear horizontally with two among them running at it from opposite directions, letting the points pierce their chests and come out at their backs.

Jalaluddin Muhammad Akbar stood up when he heard this. Fixing the hilt of his sword to the wall he placed the point at his breast and said, 'If Rajputs can do this, so can we.'

What happened after this is captured in the picture made on the orders of Badshah Salamat by Daulat, the painter of the royal atelier, and by the description given by Abul Fazl. Silence fell upon the drinking party. Anxiety was writ large on faces. None knew what to do. At that moment Kunwar Man Singh showed his presence of mind. Advancing swiftly, he gave such a blow that the sword fell down. It made a cut between Badshah Salamat's thumb and index finger. The nobles present in the assembly immediately removed the sword. Badshah Salamat flung Man Singh on the floor and began to beat him. In his light-coloured jama, red-coloured yar-i-pairhan and a white turban, Kunwar Man Singh was struggling in the grip of Badshah Salamat. There was such commotion that people outside the darbar began to ask the janitor about the activity inside. However, a noble standing nearby managed to break Man Singh free. In doing so, he twisted Badshah Salamat's wounded finger. But very soon it was healed.

As soon as Kunwar Man Singh reached the do-ashiyana manzil

and kissed the feet of Jalaluddin Muhammad Akbar, Badshah Salamat said, 'Just see how that bastard Rajput has stabbed himself in his stomach. If he is alive, bandage his wounds. If he is dead, burn him.'

Outside, the akashdiya was burning bright. River Jhelum was flowing past the royal camp and those of the Thakurs.

By the time Kunwar Man Singh arrived, Prithideep's uncle had succumbed to his injury. When Kunwar Man Singh returned to the royal camp, he found that Badshah Salamat had already got the news and was shouting. Zain Khan Koka, Fatehullah Khwajagi and Sheikh Farid Murtaza Khan Bukhari stood in front of him. They had terror on their faces.

Zain Khan Koka was a prominent mansabdar of the empire. He had a strong built. He did not keep a beard but had a big moustache that turned downwards. His mother Picha Jan Anga had breastfed Badshah Salamat. He was of Persian descent and his father Khwaja Maqsud Ali of Herat had devotedly served Maryam Makani Hamida Banu Begum.

A short distance away from Badshah Salamat stood Shah Fatehullah, who was in the royal service and considered close to the Emperor because of his sagacity.

Next to Shah Fatehullah stood Sheikh Farid Murtaza Khan Bukhari. People say that four generations ago his forefather Sayyid Abdul Ghaffar had ordered his coming generations to give up the madad-i-ma'ash jagir—fiefs granted to religious persons—and become soldiers. Sheikh Farid joined Badshah Salamat's service at a young age and became close to him due to his loyalty and ability.

Kunwar Man Singh saw Badshah Salamat shouting.

'Hindus should eat beef, Muslims should eat pork, and if not this, fry a sheep in the pan. If it turns into pork, Hindus and Muslims should have it together. If it turns into beef, Hindus and Muslims should have it together. If it becomes pork, Muslims should have it. If it becomes beef, Hindus should have it. A divine miracle would thus happen.'

21

Recently Badshah Salamat had suffered a big shock at Fatehpur Sikri.

The qazi of Mathura complained to the Sadr-us-Sudur Sheikh Abd-un-Nabi that a Brahmin had constructed a temple with the material kept to make a mosque. When restrained, the Brahmin spoke ill of the Muslims and also of the Prophet. When the Brahmin did not even respond to the summons of Sheikh Abd-un-Nabi, Badshah Salamat sent Sheikh Abul Fazl and a very close courtier, Raja Birbal. Having brought back the Brahmin, Abul Fazl reported that the allegation of blasphemy was true. Now some of the ulema gave a fatwa to impose a fine, some to impose death penalty. Sheikh Abd-un-Nabi himself repeatedly asked the Emperor's permission to give the death penalty to the Brahmin. Badshah Salamat did not give permission. He was in a dilemma. In a personal gathering he just said, 'It is up to the ulema to decide on matters of sharia. Why ask us?'

Sheikh Abd-un-Nabi enjoyed a very high stature in the eyes of Jalaluddin Muhammad Akbar. Sheikh Abd-un-Nabi, son of Sheikh Ahmed bin Sheikh Abdul Quddus, belonged to Gangoh. He belonged to the family of Imam Abu Hanifa, though he himself was of the Chishtiyya order and it is said that he could hold his breath for one pahar—one watch—while doing zikr, the Sufi practice of taking the name of God. After receiving education in hadith in Mecca and Medina he gave up the practices of the Sufis. He got the office of Sadr-us-Sudur in the reign of Badshah Salamat. This office carried so much weight that his views on matters of faith were believed to be the most significant. He had the power to give land grants to ulema and other religious persons. Badshah Salamat keenly observed the way this power over matters of faith and land grants was exercised but he kept quiet for now. As things stood, he held Sheikh Abd-un-Nabi in such high esteem that he would go to his house to listen to the hadith.

The mosque that Sheikh Abd-un-Nabi got built in Delhi had this inscription in marble above the doorway, which was composed by Faizi:

During the reign of the Emperor Akbar, may God perpetuate his beneficent person,
A holy edifice, like which there is none in all the countries, was built,
By the Sheikh-ul-Islam, the pilgrim of the two sacred cities, and the universally acknowledged chief of the learned in hadith,
Sheikh Abd-un-Nabi Numani, the mine of learning and the spring of beneficence.
The date of the foundation of this building, Faizi asked Wisdom. It said, 'Khair baqa.'

The individual letters in 'khair baqa', literally 'the best place', added up to 983, the Hijri year for the construction of the mosque.

Once the colour saffron was applied to Badshah Salamat's jama on the occasion of his birthday. This angered Sheikh Abd-un-Nabi so much that he threw his staff, which struck Badshah Salamat's jama. Sheikh Abd-un-Nabi had such high standing that Badshah Salamat kept his anger in check and remained quiet. When he complained to his mother Maryam Makani Hamida Banu Begum, she consoled him and said, 'Let it be. Nothing to fret about. It would be written in books that a poor saint threw his staff at a powerful emperor, who controlled himself because of his regard for the sharia.'

Not long after, Sheikh Abd-un-Nabi had a meal with Badshah Salamat that had saffron in it. Sheikh Abul Fazl asked, 'If saffron is sinful, then how can eating it be permissible? And if it is permissible to have saffron, then what was your objection all about?'

People say that Sheikh Abd-un-Nabi had become arrogant because of the high office he held. When he would do wuzu in the Diwan Khana he would be unmindful of the water spilling onto the nobles. Badshah Salamat had once ordered that Sheikh Abd-un-Nabi's signature would be essential to confirm the old land grants held by the imams—men who led the prayers in mosques. Those who had access and recommendations got their work done but those who did not had to bribe the servants of the Sheikh to reach him.

Sheikh Abul Fazl had seen the days when Sheikh Abd-un-Nabi, Makhdum-ul-Mulk Mullah Abdullah Sultanpuri and all other ulema had conspired against his father Sheikh Mubarak and complained to the Emperor, 'Sheikh Mubarak is a "Mahdawi", a "bida'ati" and deeply misguided.'

Badshah Salamat said, 'When your advice is sought in worldly matters, this case is completely that of faith. So the matter is completely in your hands. Call him before the court and take action according to the sharia and the views of the leading men of learning.'

When the soldiers who had been sent to get Sheikh Mubarak found the house empty, they took his ten-year-old son Abul Khair in custody. When the ulema said that the Sheikh's disappearance was proof of his guilt, Badshah Salamat said, 'Why such anger against an aged dervish? What is this hue and cry all about? Sheikh likes to go on short excursions. He must have gone for rest and recreation. Why have you brought this child? Why are there guards at his house?'

In this moment of crisis, Sheikh Mubarak pleaded with Mirza Aziz Koka, who told Badshah Salamat, 'Is the world coming to an end? In this court, madmen with evil intentions live peacefully and good people are being harassed... Sheikh Mubarak does not have any land grants from the state. He has qualities of a dervish. It is not proper to cause harm to such a person.'

Badshah Salamat replied, 'All big people are after his life. They want the death penalty for him. They have prepared fatwas. They don't allow anybody to live in peace. We know where Sheikh is but chose to turn a blind eye. Tomorrow morning let someone get the Sheikh to the darbar and let the ulema be called.'

Such were the times that Sheikh Mubarak and his sons Sheikh Abul Fazl or Faizi could be sentenced to death if it were proved that they were Shiite or Mahdawi. So they thought better of it and did not turn up for a debate with the ulema despite the recommendation of Mirza Aziz Koka. They did appear in the court when the anger of the ulema subsided after some time.

A respected Mahdawi saint Sheikh Alai had criticized the luxurious lifestyle of Makhdum-ul-Mulk Abdullah Sultanpuri at the court of Islam Shah, and took all the clerics of the court to task. Abdullah Sultanpuri was an orthodox Sunni cleric. He had lived through the reigns of many rulers. Jannat Ashiyani Humayun Badshah had given the titles of 'Makhdum-ul-Mulk' and 'Sheikh-ul-Islam' to him. Abdullah Sultanpuri had enjoyed a high position at the court of Islam Shah. Once, Islam Shah saw Makhdum-ul-Mulk Abdullah

Sultanpuri coming towards him. He asked his servants, 'Do you know the person coming this side?'

'Who is he?' the servants asked.

'Babur Badshah had five sons, of them four have left Hindustan. This one is left behind.'

One of the servants asked, 'What is the point of associating with such a bad person?'

Islam Shah replied, 'What can be done? How can I get one better than him?'

Then Islam Shah seated Mullah Abdullah Sultanpuri on his throne and gave him a rosary of pearls that cost twenty thousand rupees.

Sheikh Alai told Mullah Abdullah Sultanpuri, 'You are a learned but a thief of a clergyman. You engage in numerous illegal practices. Even now the sound of musical instruments is coming from your house. In accordance with the true traditions of the Prophet, a fly which settles upon filth is better than learned men who go from door to door and have made kings and emperors the object of their ambition.'

When Sheikh Alai explained the meaning of the ayats of the Quran, of the weaknesses of the world, and described the Day of Judgment, Islam Shah was so impressed that he sent refreshments for him from inside the palace. The Sheikh refused to eat anything and said, 'Your food belongs to the Muslims. Contrary to the principles of Islam you have possessed more than is yours by right.'

In those difficult times Sheikh Mubarak supported Sheikh Alai but this could not save him.

Islam Shah had called Sheikh Alai close to him and said in a low voice, 'Just say in my ear that you repent having made these claims. You shall be then free to go where you wish and do what you please.'

When Sheikh Alai disregarded these words, Islam Shah ordered him to be lashed. The Sheikh was already ill. He died at the third lash. His body was trampled to pieces under a wild elephant. His burial was forbidden.

Sheikh Mubarak would say, 'There is no religion that is free of flaws, nor is there a religion that is completely flawed. So if a man heeds to the voice of his conscience and supports something that is at variance with his religion, his intentions should not be seen as wrong.'

These views of Sheikh Mubarak turned the ulema of the court against him.

Sheikh Alai was the disciple of Sheikh Abdullah Niazi, who had first been the disciple of Sheikh Salim Chishti and then had become a Mahdawi. Sheikh Alai and Sheikh Abdullah Niazi had made Bayana their home and from there had worked to strengthen the Mahdawi sect. Makhdum-ul-Mulk Abdullah Sultanpuri had appealed for action against Sheikh Abdullah Niazi when Islam Shah once passed through Bayana.

Sheikh Abdullah Niazi came to the Emperor Islam Shah and said, 'Assalam Alaikum.'

The governor of Bayana seized him by his neck, bent it forward and said, 'My friend, this is the way to salute the kings.'

The Sheikh replied in anger, 'I only know of the form of salutation that is prescribed by sunnat.'

On the orders of the Emperor the Sheikh was heavily beaten. Then the royal entourage left him for dead and moved on. He recovered somehow and left Bayana. People say he later left the Mahdawi way.

In Fatehpur Sikri, near the hospice of Sheikh Salim Chishti, was an abandoned building which was once the cell of Sheikh Niazi. The place came to life again when Jalaluddin Muhammad Akbar built the Ibadat Khana here.

Those days Badshah Salamat would pray in solitude. In the morning he could be seen sitting on a stone slab of an old cell. This cell was near the royal palace but there was no habitation behind it. Mullah Abdul Qadir Badayuni says that Badshah Salamat won so many victories that he began to sit here to thank God. But this was not the only reason. Badshah Salamat was a free thinker at heart. He would look at each religion and each sect with an open mind. He would say:

'Although I am the master of so vast a kingdom, and all the appliances of government are to my hand, yet since true greatness consists in doing the will of God, my mind is not at ease in this diversity of sects and creeds, and my heart is oppressed by this outward pomp of circumstances. With what satisfaction can I undertake the conquest of empire? How I wish for the coming of some pious man, who will resolve the distractions of my heart.'

A wide variety of ideas would occur to Badshah Salamat and he would express them—

'The faqirs of Hindustan say that keeping death in mind, we should do good work. Not to think of life and one's youth. But we think that good deeds should be done without thought of death. So that we do good just because they are good and not for fear or hope...

'We don't find any reason in the people of Hindustan blowing the conch or ringing the bell in worship. This must be as a warning or a reminder...

'Treading the path of reason and rationality is far above the logic that this humble self can come up with. If past practices were meant to be followed, the prophets would only have walked in the footsteps of the previous prophets.

'Being a pir means having the power to know and cure the suffering of people, and not growing a beard, wearing a long coat and creating a furore over worldly matters.'

Around the twentieth regnal year, corresponding to 1575 CE, in the month of March, Badshah Salamat gave orders to build the Ibadat Khana—the House of Worship—near the Anup Talao. It had four porticos. When completed, a dhrupad was sung to congratulate the Emperor on the construction of this new temple—

Congratulations on the building of a new temple,
Wish you a thousand years of rule, Your Majesty.
Instead of writing in praise of those who can't see the future,
We make effort to learn the mystery of the Emperor who himself knows the mysteries of music;
Live eternally like Lord Indra;
The society would reform through his body,
Which has been made in the fire of the twelve gunas.

Badshah Salamat said, 'We have organized this assembly so that the facts of every religion, whether Hindu or Muslim, be brought out in the open. The closed hearts of our religious leaders and scholars be opened so that Muslims know who they are. They are unaware. They only think of Muslims as those who recite the kalma, consume meat and perform sijda by prostrating themselves on the ground. Muslims in fact are those who wage jihad on their self and control their desires and temper, and surrender to the rule of law.'

Raja Birbal had recited a poem to Badshah Salamat which said:

When we can offer jaggery and sugar made of sugarcane to the gods,
When cotton flowers burst to give us clothes to cover ourselves,
When jute plants rot to give us paper on which the Quran and
Puran is written,
In like manner, poet Brahma says to Emperor Akbar, could the
broken and the rotten be shown the right path.

But this reform was not easy. Once when Badshah Salamat had organized an assembly in the honour of Sheikh Ziaullah, the son of the prominent Sufi Sheikh Muhammad Ghaus, in the Ibadat Khana and called the sayyids, the sheikhs, the ulema and the nobles, a dispute arose over who would sit where. Finally, to end the dispute, Badshah Salamat decided that the nobles would sit towards the east, the sayyids towards the west, ulema towards the south, and the sheikhs towards the north, and he would go to each of them himself to talk.

Now Badshah Salamat had Abul Fazl and Faizi to debate with the ulema. Sheikh Faizi had taunted the ulema in the Ibadat Khana—

You are always busy in heated debate and discussion
It yielded nothing but perspiration.

When Makhdum-ul-Mulk Mullah Abdullah Sultanpuri first saw Sheikh Abul Fazl in the early years of Badshah Salamat's reign, he said, 'How much damage this man would cause to religion!'

One night the ulema created such a ruckus in the Ibadat Khana that Emperor Akbar had to tell Mullah Abdul Qadir Badayuni, 'In future report any of the ulema who talk nonsense and cannot behave themselves, and I shall make them leave the hall.'

Asaf Khan was sitting next to Mullah Abdul Qadir Badayuni. Asaf Khan's father had a special place at the court of Shah Tahmasp of Persia. Two of Asaf Khan's brothers became viziers in Persia. Asaf Khan's name was Ghiyasuddin Ali Qazwini. Badshah Salamat had given him the title of Asaf Khan and the position of 'Bakhshi'—in charge of the mansabs of the province—for displaying valour in the Gujarat campaign.

Commenting on Badshah Salamat's command, Mullah Abdul

Qadir Badayuni told Asaf Khan in a low voice, 'If I carried out this order, most of the ulema would have to leave.'

Badshah Salamat noticed that Mullah Abdul Qadir Badayuni had said something to Asaf Khan. He asked, 'What did you say?'

Badshah Salamat was very pleased with the answer.

Mullah Abdul Qadir Badayuni was born in Toda in the year 947 of the Hijri era, corresponding to 1540 CE on the twelfth of August. At the age of twelve he went to Sambhal for education. Six years after that he came to Agra and became a disciple of Sheikh Mubarak. A few years later when his father died, he went to Badayun. Badshah Salamat immediately made him part of his gatherings when he returned to Agra for a second time. Mullah Badayuni says, 'I was made part of the gathering where the ulema were trumpeting the depth of their knowledge and thought nothing of anybody... By the grace of God, and by virtue of my wisdom and the fervour of my youth, I could speak my mind and often be better than them.'

Although both Sheikh Abul Fazl and Mullah Abdul Qadir Badayuni reached Badshah Salamat at the same time, Sheikh Abul Fazl became Badshah Salamat's voice. Mullah Abdul Qadir could not mount an attack on the ulema in the manner that Abul Fazl did.

Mullah Abdul Qadir Badayuni did not attain any high office and was merely given the responsibility of leading the prayers once a week. He wrote of his plight—

You have made me a courtier and a mansabdar of twenty,
My mother should not know that I am a man of no consequence.

Abul Fazl was also made a mansabdar with a rank of twenty at the time but he progressed swiftly. Mullah Badayuni reached home and quietly wrote down his state of mind one day—

'Mullah Muhammad of Yezd reviled the Companions of the Prophet...and tried hard to make His Majesty a Shia. The bastard Birbar, Sheikh Abul Fazl and Hakim Abul Fath Gilani crossed their limits and turned the Emperor away from religion. The Emperor began to reject prophethood, revelation and miracles, and began to advance a faith of his own.'

Around that time Sheikh Mustafa Gujarati was brought to Fatehpur Sikri as a prisoner.

The Hijri era was reaching its thousand years. There was a belief that the day of reckoning was near and before that would appear a man from the family of the Prophet. He would strengthen the religion and Muslims would follow the path shown by him. He would be the '*Mahdi*'.

Sheikh Mustafa Gujarati himself believed that the Mahdi had come and gone. This Mahdi was Sayyid Muhammad of Jaunpur. People say that Sayyid Muhammad and his fifteen hundred bairagis were with the Sharqi Sultan of Jaunpur when he attacked Dalpat Rai of Gaur. The Sultan and his forces were defeated but Sayyid Muhammad did not give up battle. People say there was such a ferocious attack that Dalpat Rai was cut into two; when his throbbing heart fell on the ground, Sayyid Muhammad saw in it the outline of the idol that Dalpat Rai worshipped.

At that moment, Sayyid Muhammad said, 'When an idol can leave such an impression on the heart, what would happen if the light of the Almighty were manifested?'

People say that Sayyid Muhammad was overwhelmed by this incident and went into a spiritual trance for twelve years. In the Hijri year 901, corresponding to around 1495 CE, after the circumambulation of the Ka'ba, he openly declared himself the Mahdi. He made this declaration again when he reached Ahmedabad. Under the pressure of the ulema, the Sultan of Gujarat, Mahmud Begarha, forced him to leave the place. Then he left for Barli, where again he declared himself the Mahdi. He said, 'I was hesitant but I received repeated injunctions from the Almighty to declare myself the Mahdi. The Almighty asked me if I was afraid of the people and not of Him.'

While leaving Gujarat, Sayyid Muhammad said, 'On the Day of Judgment, the faces of the rulers and the learned men shall be blackened. If I am on the right path, they should have helped me. If I am not on the right path, they should have arrested me, talked to me and shown me the right path. Failing to bring me to the right path, they should have killed me because wherever I go, I would preach my tenets which according to them would misguide the people. They would be held responsible for the consequences.'

Sayyid Muhammad breathed his last about half a century before Badshah Salamat's accession, on the nineteenth of the Ziqad month of 910 Hijri, corresponding to the twenty-third of April 1505 CE, at a place called Farah in Herat.

Sayyid Muhammad claimed that as a Mahdi, God had given him the responsibility of restoring Islam to its pristine purity. He said that he only followed the path shown by God, His Prophet and the Quran. Sayyid Muhammad believed that the recitation of '*la ilaha illallah*'—no god but Allah—purged the hearts of the believers. This zikr—recitation—was so important that even discussion on religion was not justifiable grounds for interruption. He said clearly that he was the Mahdi referred to in the traditions of the Prophet. A Mahdawi was not allowed to offer namaz behind the non-Mahdawis. So much so that jizya could be levied upon the non-Mahdawis. Sayyid Muhammad's message was only for the Muslims. He did not speak against the non-Muslims, nor did he expect them to give up their faith.

Sayyid Muhammad believed that one should keep changing one's place of residence. It was deemed inappropriate to stay at one place for any length of time. Wherever he or his adherents stayed was called a daira. Life was lived according to the sharia in the daira. It was not permitted to save provision even for the next day. Many would turn the vessels upside down at night so that flour, water or even salt was not saved for later.

After Sayyid Muhammad, the Mahdawis believed that the Mahdi has come and gone and would not come any more. Now people just needed to wait for the Day of Judgment. That is why when Mustafa Gujarati was brought in chains before Badshah Salamat and the court, Sadr-us-Sudur Sheikh Abd-un-Nabi said, 'O Emperor, please do justice. The majority of the people say that the Mahdi will come, while these few Mahdawis say that the Mahdi has come and gone. Therefore, O Emperor, please ask what Sheikh Mustafa has to say.'

Sheikh Mustafa Gujarati enjoyed a high stature among the Mahdawis and had a large following in Gujarat. His father had become a Mahdawi at the hands of Sayyid Muhammad.

During the Gujarat campaign, Maulana Muhammad bin Tahir of Patan had taken off his headgear and said, 'I will not wear this until the Mahdawi heresy is eliminated.'

Badshah Salamat had himself placed the headgear on him and

promised to take stern measures. But no such measures were taken.

In Ajmer, during a debate with Mustafa Gujarati, the ulema had said, 'The ulema of Mecca have given a fatwa for the death of Miyan Mustafa.'

Badshah Salamat asked Mustafa Gujarati, 'Have you been to Mecca?'

Mustafa Gujarati said, 'No.'

Badshah Salamat asked, 'Have the ulema of Mecca come to Gujarat?'

Mustafa Gujarati said, 'No.'

Jalaluddin Muhammad Akbar said, 'What kind of people are they! Without coming to Gujarat and without inquiring about the aims of the Mahdawis, they have issued a fatwa for the death of the Mahdawi merely on the basis of what their enemies had to say.'

In the court of Fatehpur Sikri when, after this, the debate took place, Mustafa Gujarati said, 'Has the Emperor heard about Prophet Joseph and his brothers?'

The Sadr-us-Sudur of the empire said, 'I have heard it many times.'

Badshah Salamat told Sheikh Mustafa Gujarati, 'Please tell. We have not heard it from you.'

Sheikh Mustafa Gujarati said, 'O Emperor, ten brothers were the children of one mother. Joseph and Bin Yamin were from the other mother. Joseph's brothers, out of jealousy, said that Joseph should be killed, thrown at a place where there was no human being, or thrown into a dry well. However, they told their father that they would take Joseph out to play with. They took him and threw him into the well of Kin'an. Later they sold him to a trader. Joseph's brothers were many but Joseph was alone. But who was a liar amongst them?'

Badshah Salamat said, 'All brothers of Joseph were sinners and liars.'

Sheikh Mustafa Gujarati replied, 'Joseph's brothers were many. How could they be sinners and liars?'

Badshah Salamat said, 'You are turning it on us.'

Sheikh Mustafa Gujarati said, 'I related the story of Joseph to you because the number of mullahs and sheikhs is great and they say that Imam Mahdi will come. I am alone and my brothers are few and we say that Imam Mahdi has come and gone. Who are the liars? O Emperor, please do justice!'

Badshah Salamat agreed that Joseph was right.

Sheikh Mustafa Gujarati continued, 'If that is so, we Mahdawis, who say that Imam Mahdi has come and gone, are on the right path, because we are few. Allah says, "... Among them are some who have faith, but most of them are perverted transgressors." At every point of time, every prophet has been opposed by a majority and only a few people reposed faith in them. Similarly, at the time of Imam Mahdi also, many people opposed and refused to accept him and only a few accepted him. Hence it is proved by convincing argument that Imam Mahdi had come and gone. Besides, O Emperor, before creating Adam, Allah told all angels, "I will create a viceregent on earth." They said, "Wilt Thou place therein one who will make mischief therein and shed blood?—whilst we do celebrate Thy praises and glorify Thy holy (name)?" He said, "I know what ye know not." And He taught Adam the names of all things; then He placed them before the angels and said, "Tell Me the names of these if ye are right." They said, "Glory to Thee: of knowledge we have none, save what Thou Hast taught us: in truth it is Thou who art perfect in knowledge and wisdom."

'The point to be noted here is that the angels were all in the heavens and had been created out of light. In spite of this, they were jealous of Adam. Then why should not people, who are sinful and madly wedded to worldly desires, not be jealous of Imam Mahdi, his followers and seekers of Allah? When the angels repented and reposed faith in the commandments of Allah in humility, they were accepted by Allah. Similarly, these people, who refute Imam Mahdi, listen to the arguments in proof of Imam Mahdi; those who are blessed with the faith, repent with modesty and humility and accept Imam Mahdi. They thus become the loved of Allah. Satan has sinned. He refused to prostrate before Adam and said, "I am better than Adam." He was arrogant. A few thousand years have passed. He did not repent. Similarly, the person who is not blessed with faith, does not repent. He is very arrogant. He does not accept Imam Mahdi and is therefore a kafir. Allah said, "If they do fail to judge by what Allah hath revealed, they are those who rebel."

'Prophet Muhammad has said, "Whoever disbelieved Mahdi,

verily, he is a kafir." This hadith is reported in *Tabqat al-Fuqaha*. O Emperor, please do justice. Allah says, "O David, We did indeed make thee a viceregent on earth: so judge thou between men in truth (and justice)." And Prophet Muhammad has said, "May Allah bless him who does justice and curse of Allah be on him who does not do justice."'

Hearing this Badshah Salamat said, 'O Sheikh Mustafa, may Allah bless you and may He shower His bounties on you.'

Then turning to the ulema, Badshah Salamat said, 'You too present some arguments in reply to the Sheikh's arguments.'

The ulema asked, 'How many years have passed since Imam Mahdi came and went away?'

Sheikh Mustafa Gujarati replied, 'Imam Mahdi came in 905 Hijri. In the tenth century he claimed to be the Mahdi. He supported the religion of Prophet Muhammad. We followed him. Historians have by consensus quoted the hadith that, according to Abu Huraira, Prophet Muhammad had said that Allah would send at the head of every century a person who will revive the religion for this umma.'

Sheikh Mustafa Gujarati recited a couplet—

The sun has arisen in the sky,
What is the use if a blind eye does not see.

The Sheikh said, 'The sun is overhead and my shield is in my hand. If the ant does not pick up the grains of sugar, tell it not to pick! If the blind man does not see, tell him not to see! Allah says in the Quran, "... And get two witnesses, out of your own men..." In other words, Allah has asked us to call two men from among our men as witnesses. Allah has not asked us to call two witnesses out of impotents. He has not asked for the evidence of eunuchs. Prophet Muhammad has said that the seeker of worldliness is a eunuch, the seeker of life in the hereafter is a woman and the seeker of Allah is a man. Prophet Muhammad has said that fasting is obligatory upon a person who has seen the crescent moon of Ramzan and if others accept his wisdom, fasting is obligatory on them too. Similarly, we have seen the arguments of Quran and hadith and listened to the evidence of Allah and His Prophet, and therefore it is obligatory on us to accept Imam Mahdi. It is for this reason that we have accepted and say that Imam Mahdi has come and gone. And on my saying so, many people have accepted the Imam. And if somebody does not accept, his abode will be in hell. O Emperor, I have presented evidence from the Quran, Prophet Muhammad and the reliable books. Please now ask your ulema also to present evidence from the Quran, hadith and reliable books and give their arguments to show when Imam Mahdi, according to them, has to come.'

In this gathering at Fatehpur Sikri, Badshah Salamat told the ulema, 'Sheikh Mustafa has argued his case and you have listened to him. Now you can present your arguments.'

The ulema kept quiet.

Sheikh Mustafa Gujarati said to the Emperor, 'You may listen to one more argument. In the Quran, Allah says about people who read Quran but do not act according to it, "The similitude of those who were entrusted with the (obligations of) Taurat, but who subsequently failed in those (obligations), is that of a donkey which carries huge tomes (but understands them not)." In other words, people who read the Quran but do not act according to it are like the donkey which is loaded with stones or wood on its back. Prophet Muhammad has said, "The scholar, who does not act according to his knowledge, is like a donkey."'

Then Sheikh Mustafa Gujarati quoted a Hindi doha—

O half-wit, you are loaded with the burden of a donkey,
You are led by your ear and you are asked to walk quietly.

Sheikh Mustafa Gujarati continued to speak, 'Allah says, "They are like cattle—nay more misguided..." So they do what Allah has created them for. They praise Allah. But some people do not remember Allah and do not worship Him. For this reason, they will always burn in hell. Dogs, pigs, donkeys and quadrupeds will not be tormented in hell but people who oppose Allah and His Prophet and die in a state of opposition will always burn in hell. They are worse than animals. Allah says, "Ye People of the Book! Why do ye clothe truth with falsehood, and conceal the Truth, while ye have knowledge?" You have the knowledge of Prophet Muhammad being the true apostle of Allah. Similarly, Imam Mahdi's attributes are obvious. Why do they conceal it? But what can one who is blind see? Prophet Muhammad has said that the fly which sits on filth is better than the ulema who go to the doorsteps of kings. How can such people accept Imam Mahdi? But people who seek the truth and who are just and who have forsaken the profane world, will surely accept Imam Mahdi and have actually accepted him. Allah says, "Those who disbelieve, among the People of the Book and among the Polytheists, were not going to depart (from their ways) until there should come to them Clear Evidence." In other words, they believed that Prophet Muhammad would come but when he actually came with Clear Evidence, they refuted him. Similarly, the ulema and the sheikhs arrived at a consensus that Imam Mahdi will come in 905 Hijri but when he came the imams and the sheikhs made schisms, except for a few who were just and seekers of Allah. They said, "This is not the Mahdi that was promised." This is given in *Tafseer-i-Taveel* by Abdur Razzaq Kashi.'

Sheikh Mustafa Gujarati said, 'O Emperor, I will write a letter to you, and please ask your ulema and sheikhs to write a similar letter that the persons who argue without the support of Quran and hadith should be made to blacken their faces, ride a donkey and go round the bazaars of the town, while people should be allowed to stone them.'

Sheikh Mustafa Gujarati gave a paper to Badshah Salamat but the ulema and the sheikhs did not. An elderly person from among the ulema said, 'We are not as well versed in Quran and hadith as Sheikh Mustafa is. He studies the Quran and hadith day in and day out.'

Badshah Salamat said to the ulema, 'You have studied so much but you cannot argue on the basis of Quran and hadith. Quran and hadith are fundamental. Why did you not become well versed in Quran and hadith?'

Badshah Salamat lost his cool at the Sadr-us-Sudur of the empire, Sheikh Abd-un-Nabi.

'Blacken the faces of these ulema and sheikhs and take them around the town on donkeys.'

No sooner had Badshah Salamat said this than people present in the court began to beg forgiveness and the meeting ended.

Sheikh Mustafa Gujarati was brought to the court for debate once again after a few days. All the ulema offered the zuhr prayers in congregation but Mustafa Gujarati did not join it. He offered the namaz on his own.

Sheikh Abd-un-Nabi told Badshah Salamat, 'Please ask Sheikh Mustafa why he calls Muslims as kafirs?'

Sheikh Mustafa Gujarati replied, 'O Emperor, please ask Abd-un-Nabi whom have I called a kafir, or am calling a kafir. Also please ask Abd-un-Nabi to produce some evidence to prove his allegations.'

The mullah said, 'If you do not call us kafirs why did you not say your prayers under our leadership?'

Sheikh Mustafa Gujarati asked Badshah Salamat, 'O Emperor, which religious order do you belong to and who is your spiritual guide?'

Jalaluddin Muhammad Akbar touched the lobes of his ears and bowed his head in respect and said, 'I am the disciple of Hazrat Khwaja Muinuddin Chishti.'

Sheikh Mustafa Gujarati said, 'Suppose somebody were to say that Hazrat Khwaja Muinuddin Chishti had deviated from the religion or that he had gone astray and had misled other people, what would you say?'

Badshah Salamat said, 'I would call such a person kafir and would kill him with my own hands.'

Sheikh Mustafa Gujarati said, 'My spiritual guide is Imam Sayyid Muhammad Mahdi. If somebody were to say that Imam Mahdi and his followers are apostates and are misleading the people, how can I say my prayers under the leadership of such a person? Besides, I do not call anybody a kafir. But there is a hadith that Prophet Muhammad said, "Whoever refused to accept Imam Mahdi, verily, he is a kafir." This hadith is reported in the book *Tabqat al-Fuqaha*. I am only relating this hadith. I do not call anybody a kafir on my own.'

Then Sheikh Mustafa Gujarati asked Badshah Salamat, 'Please ask the mullahs, what is the punishment under the sharia for falsely slandering somebody?'

The ulema did not reply.

Sheikh Mustafa Gujarati replied, 'Allah says in the Quran that people who falsely slander should be given eighty lashes. The mullahs have become liable to this punishment. Allah says, "And those who launch a charge against chaste women, and produce not four witnesses (to support their allegations),—flog them with eighty stripes; and reject their evidence ever after: for such men are wicked transgressors..."'

Badshah Salamat said, 'O mullahs and sheikhs, you have falsely slandered Sheikh Mustafa and therefore you are liable to the Quranic punishment.'

Sheikh Mustafa Gujarati said, 'O Emperor, Prophet Muhammad has said, "May Allah bless him who has done justice and curse him who does injustice."'

'O Sheikh Mustafa, these mullahs and sheikhs are devout persons and guide the people in religious affairs. Why did you not say your prayers under their leadership?' Badshah Salamat asked.

Sheikh Mustafa Gujarati replied, 'Prophet Muhammad has said that the seeker of the world is impotent, the seeker of the hereafter is a woman and the seeker of Allah alone is a man. O Emperor, please do justice. Ask Abd-un-Nabi and all other ulema to produce one commandment from the books of hadith and fiqh asking a man to say his prayers under the leadership of impotents. Many books have mentioned the prohibition of an impotent person from leading a group of men in prayers. Therefore, I did not say my prayers in the congregation led by an impotent.'

Badshah Salamat laughed and said, 'O Sheikh Mustafa, you have spoken the truth.'

He then told the ulema: 'Sheikh Mustafa did not say his prayers under your leadership because you are impotent and to say one's prayers under the leadership of a eunuch is not allowed. Now answer him. And produce an argument based on the Quran and hadith and reliable books to prove that saying one's prayers under the leadership of eunuchs is permissible.'

When nobody replied, Badshah Salamat said, 'O Mustafa Gujarati, you have given a fitting reply. May Allah bless you!'

Sheikh Mustafa Gujarati stood in chains in the presence of Sadr-us-Sudur Sheikh Abd-un-Nabi and other prominent ulema of the court in Fatehpur Sikri. He said: 'If you wish to listen I want to relate another story. There was a eunuch sitting among a group of God-fearing devout men. These men of God were talking about Allah, Prophet Muhammad and Mecca. One of them said that he had been to Mecca. Great rewards from Allah await those who go to

Mecca. He had seen the wonders of oceans and forests. This created a desire in the mind of the eunuch to go to Mecca. He went to his house, took some food for the journey and set off for Mecca. He had hardly gone a couple of leagues when his legs and loins began to ache. He saw a tree on the way and tried to reach it. He found reaching it very difficult. With great effort, he somehow reached the tree and started lamenting like a woman and fell down. He saw a man approaching from a distance. When he came near, the eunuch asked him how far Mecca was. The man asked how long he had been travelling. The eunuch said that he had started from his house, which was a couple of leagues from the place, the same day and intended to go to Mecca. The traveller said, "O eunuch, return home because when you see the ocean you would die of fear." The traveller went his way. The eunuch felt scared of what the traveller had said. He returned home. His relatives scolded him for undertaking the journey. They said that going to Mecca was a task for men.'

After relating the story, Sheikh Mustafa Gujarati said to Badshah Salamat, 'As Prophet Muhammad has said, the seekers of Allah alone were men and seekers of the world were eunuchs. Hence, they do not follow the Prophet, they do not renounce the world. They go to the kings and nobles and seek pensions and other worldly possessions. For this they indulge in flattery and sycophancy. They cannot repose trust in Allah and they cannot become pious. The seekers of the world were like the eunuch who returned from his intended journey to Mecca.'

Badshah Salamat said, 'May Allah bless you and may He shower His bounties on you.'

Jalaluddin Muhammad Akbar asked the ulema to respond to Sheikh Mustafa Gujarati. The ulema kept quiet.

Badshah Salamat used to say, 'We are so fond of debates on philosophical matters that we are distracted from all other issues. We forcibly restrain ourself from listening to them, lest the necessary duties of the hour be neglected.'

Sheikh Mustafa was released, despite opposition from the ulema. He was permitted to return home but he could not reach Gujarat. He had been ill during debates with the ulema and had been vomiting blood. He died in Bayana.

22

Badshah Salamat remembered that Makhdum-ul-Mulk Abdullah Sultanpuri had asked a person called Mirza Muflis a question. Before Mirza Muflis could reply, Sheikh Abd-un-Nabi asked another question. Mirza Muflis told Sheikh Abd-un-Nabi, 'Little slave, wait until I explain what the big slave has asked.'

This conversation was talked about even up to Mecca.

Sometime after this, he said, 'My name may mean "muflis"—bankrupt—but through the good fortune of petitioning Your Majesty I will be honoured with more cash and goods than are necessary for travel to the holy places.'

Badshah Salamat gave him more gold and gifts than he needed. Mirza Muflis passed away in Mecca and was buried there.

Makhdum-ul-Mulk Abdullah Sultanpuri was soon going to see bad times. At the instigation of Badshah Salamat, he was harassed in many ways. In one gathering, it was said:

'Makhdum-ul-Mulk once gave a fatwa that Haj is no longer binding, and is even hurtful. When asked, he said that both the routes to Mecca were impracticable because people going through Persia were harassed by the Qizilbash and those going by the sea had to suffer indignities at the hands of the Portuguese, whose permits had pictures of Mary and Jesus stamped on them. Taking this route is like following idolatry. Hence both the routes are closed.'

In the same gathering, it was alleged about him:

'Towards the end of each year, he used to make over all his wealth to his wife and escape paying the zakat but before the year ended he took it back.'

There were many occasions when Badshah Salamat felt disappointed with the ulema.

A relative of Sheikh Muhammad Ghaus of Gwalior fell in love with a singing girl of Agra. When Badshah Salamat learnt of this, he gave the girl to a courtier of his. The failed lover broke into the guarded castle one night and eloped with his beloved. On the advice of Badshah Salamat, Sheikh Ghaus's son Sheikh Ziauddin counselled the two. When they appeared, Badshah Salamat said that they be married. When Sheikh Ziauddin did not agree to this, the dejected lover killed himself with a stroke of a dagger. Now the issue arose of the burial of the lover. Sheikh Ziauddin said, 'He is a martyr to love and ought to be buried as a martyr.'

Disagreeing with Sheikh Ziauddin, Sadr-us-Sudur Sheikh Abd-un-Nabi said, 'He had committed adultery and was unclean.'

The singing girl did not survive more than a few days after her lover's death. She spent the last days sweeping her lover's tomb.

Badshah Salamat was fond of *Husn-o-Dil*—'Beauty and the Heart', a love story that had a happy ending. He had got this love story, written by Fattahi Nishapuri, illustrated. The story begins in the city called 'Jism'—Body. The prince of this city was called 'Dil'—Heart. Dil was in search of nectar. He dispatches his representative 'Nazar'—Perception—to get it. After many trials and tribulations, Nazar reaches a kingdom in the East which is called 'Ishq'—Love. The princess of this kingdom 'Husn'—Beauty—resides in the garden where flows the stream of nectar. The princess has the picture of a person whose name, place or identity is unknown.

A picture in this story shows Princess Husn in a pleasant setting in a grand sprawling building. On the wall behind her six-cornered seat of gold are painted the images of fairies, and the stream of nectar flows in front of it. When Nazar meets Husn, he immediately recognizes that the picture the princess has is that of Prince Dil. He tells Princess Husn, 'This is the image of the prince of the West called Dil, whose beauty and exploits are talked about the world over.'

Hearing this, Husn falls in love with Dil and the two are eventually united after many ups and downs.

23

Sheikh Abd-un-Nabi's fortunes finally began to dip when Badshah Salamat asked for the ulemas' opinion on a personal matter.

'How many freeborn women may one legally marry by nikah?' Badshah Salamat asked.

The ulema replied, 'It is forbidden to keep more than four freeborn women as wives at a given point of time.'

By now Jalaluddin Muhammad Akbar was married to his maternal and paternal cousins, and the daughter-in-law of Sheikh Buddh of Agra. He had married into the families of Raja Bharmal of Amber, Rai Kalyanmal of Bikaner, Raja Jaichand of Nagarkot and Rawat Askaran of Dungarpur. He had had two matrimonial alliances with Bikaner.

Badshah Salamat told the ulema, 'In our youth we were not particular about this. We married the number of women we pleased, both freeborn or slaves. What remedy can there be for this?'

After hearing various views, Badshah Salamat said, 'We have heard from Sheikh Abd-un-Nabi that one of the mujtahids had allowed as many as nine wives.'

The ulema said, 'Yes, a mujtahid Ibn-i-Laila was inclined to this. Some had even allowed eighteen from a too literal translation of the verse of the Quran: "Marry whatever women you like, two and two, and three and three, and four and four." But this interpretation is rejected.'

Badshah Salamat was perplexed. He inquired from Sheikh Abd-un-Nabi, who replied, 'I had merely wished to point out that a difference of opinion existed on this. I had not issued a fatwa on this.'

Badshah Salamat lost his cool and said, 'The Sheikh has misled us. He told us at that time a very different thing than what he is telling now.'

To find a way out for Badshah Salamat, the ulema gave a fatwa, 'By mut'a a man may marry as many women as he wishes. Such mut'a is permitted as legal among those who follow Imam Malik. The Shiites loved children born in mut'a wedlock more than other children, contrary to the Sunnis.'

There was so much debate on this point that Badshah Salamat called for Mullah Abdul Qadir Badayuni and asked, 'What do you think about this?'

Mullah Badayuni replied, 'This entire controversy ends at one point. Mut'a is legal in the eyes of Imam Malik and the Shiite ulema, and illegal in the eyes of Imam Shafi'i and Imam Abu Hanifa. Should a qazi of the Maliki sect decide that a mut'a is legal, it becomes legal even for the Shafi'is and Hanafis. This is the crux of the matter. The rest is all idle talk.'

Emperor Jalaluddin Muhammad Akbar immediately appointed a Maliki as qazi who pronounced a fatwa for mut'a.

Sheikh Abd-un-Nabi soon got into more trouble when he was accused of killing innocent individuals.

A Shia was killed in a Shia–Sunni conflict in Kashmir. For this a Sunni mufti was imprisoned and then done to death. When two Shias Mir Muqeem Isfahani and Mir Yaqub Hasan Khan arrived with gifts from the ruler of Kashmir, it began to be said that Mir Muqeem was behind the killing of the Sunni mufti. Sheikh Abd-un-Nabi got both Mir Muqeem Isfahani and Mir Yaqub Hasan Khan killed.

When on top of all of this, Sheikh Abd-un-Nabi began to insist on execution for the Brahmin of Mathura, it caused considerable disquiet in the royal harem. Many of Badshah Salamat's wives began to ask for the Brahmin's release. Wives of the harem had a powerful voice in Timuri families but this time their plea had no effect. Badshah Salamat held Sheikh Abd-un-Nabi in high regard and could not easily refuse his request but it was becoming tough for him to agree as well. When Sheikh Abd-un-Nabi persisted in asking, Badshah Salamat said, 'We have given our reply. You know it.'

With this ruling, the Sheikh pronounced the death sentence upon the Brahmin as soon as he reached home.

The Brahmin's death created a storm. The wives in the harem and the Hindus in the court said, 'You have pampered these mullahs so much that they have ceased to listen even to you and show their strength by awarding the death sentence to people without your approval.'

This affected Badshah Salamat so much that one night he put this issue before the muftis and some other people in the Anup Talao gathering at Fatehpur Sikri.

Towards the west of the Daulat Khana-i-Khas lay the area where Badshah Salamat met important people. This was a space in the middle of the square Anup Talao where people had gathered.

In the gathering, one person said, 'From the witnesses presented, it is proved that what Sheikh Abd-un-Nabi did was wrong.'

Another person present said, 'It is strange that Sheikh Abd-un-

Nabi belongs to the family of Imam Abu Hanifa and the Hanafis believe that in case any kafir blasphemes the Prophet, it does not mean that the Muslims are absolved of the responsibility of protecting the kafirs. A lot has been said about this in the books on Hanafi jurisprudence. It is difficult to understand how the Sheikh went against what his ancestors have said.'

Suddenly Badshah Salamat beckoned Mullah Abdul Qadir Badayuni, who was sitting afar, to come close. Badshah Salamat said, 'Are you too aware of this principle that there could be ninety-nine traditions for a man's death and a single one for his release, but the mufti should prefer that one tradition?'

Mullah Badayuni said, 'Yes, it is as Badshah Salamat says. It is said in Arabic, "Verily, people should be exonerated if there is doubt."'

For the convenience of Badshah Salamat, Mullah Badayuni repeated in Persian what he had said in Arabic.

Hearing this, Badshah Salamat felt sorry and said, 'Maybe Sheikh Abd-un-Nabi was unaware of this. That's why he got the poor Brahmin killed. But how can I believe that he is unaware!'

Mullah Badayuni said, 'There is no doubt that the Sheikh is a great scholar. There must have been a reason why he decided to go against this tradition.'

Badshah Salamat asked, 'What could be the reason?'

Mullah Abdul Qadir replied, 'To remove the thought of rebellion from the hearts and minds of common people.'

When Mullah Badayuni presented a tradition of Qazi Ayaz in support of his argument, some people retorted, 'Qazi Ayaz was a Maliki. His judgments would carry no weight among the Hanafis.'

Badshah Salamat looked at Mullah Badayuni and asked, 'What do you say to this?'

Mullah Badayuni said, 'Qazi Ayaz was a Maliki but if a mufti passes a judgment on the basis of his fatwa, it is in accordance with the sharia.'

For quite some time Mullah Abdul Qadir Badayuni kept debating this. People present at the Anup Talao saw that Badshah Salamat's moustache had begun to bristle like that of a tiger. Many people signalled to Mullah Badayuni from behind the Emperor to stop arguing.

Listening to the arguments of Mullah Abdul Qadir Badayuni, His Majesty finally lost his cool.

'You are talking nonsense!'

The Mullah became quiet, did his taslim and came back to his place.

When Jalaluddin Muhammad Akbar reached Bhera, he had a huge burden of religious disputes on his chest. He was losing patience. Miyan Tansen had told Badshah Salamat:

Slowly, slowly, slowly, all happens at a slow pace.
Slowly rule, slowly meditate, slowly enjoy life.
Slowly to pilgrimage, slowly to fasting, slowly control oneself,
Learn patience in the company of saints.
Says Tansen to Emperor Akbar,
This huge empire has itself been created slowly.

24

Badshah Salamat would often think back to what Sheikh Mubarak had said at the time of the first victory in Gujarat—

'God has bestowed upon the people such a great boon and blessing in the holy personality of Hazrat Badshah. Because of his nobility and his excellent administration, Hazrat Badshah had become the leader of the spiritual world. For this reason, such gracious victories have been unveiled.'

Barely three months had passed after his return after the Gujarat victory when bad tidings reached Fatehpur Sikri. Gujarat was about to slip out of his hands. The governor Mirza Aziz Koka had been confined to Ahmedabad. Ibrahim Hussain Mirza and Muhammad Hussain Mirza of the Mirza clan had rebelled. Their father Muhammad Sultan Mirza was related to the second son of Amir Timur, Umar Sheikh Mirza, and Jalaluddin Muhammad Akbar was related to the third son of Amir Timur. Muhammad Sultan Mirza's son Ibrahim Hussain Mirza was married to Gulrukh Begum, the daughter of Badshah Salamat's uncle Mirza Kamran. Thus they were both Timuri and close relatives. Muhammad

Sultan Mirza was highly respected in the court of Jannat Ashiyani Humayun Badshah and thereafter in Badshah Salamat's. He and his sons were given fiefs by Badshah Salamat in Sambhal. When his stepbrother Mirza Hakim came from Kabul and besieged Lahore in the eleventh regnal year, Badshah Salamat marched to suppress him. In that hour, Muhammad Sultan Mirza's sons Ibrahim Hussain Mirza and Muhammad Hussain Mirza raised the banner of revolt and plundered their way to Delhi. From there they went to Malwa. From Malwa they reached Gujarat, where they captured Champaner, Bharuch, and Surat. The royal forces and the Mirza clan came face to face yet again when Ahmedabad became part of the empire in the seventeenth regnal year. After a tough battle with Badshah Salamat's army at Sarnal, Ibrahim Hussain Mirza had to flee. He later died of injuries in Punjab. His wife Gulrukh Begum had to take refuge in the Deccan with her son Muzaffar Hussain Mirza. Muhammad Hussain Mirza was defeated by Mirza Aziz Koka at Patan. He too fled to the Deccan after defeat. Badshah Salamat had barely entered Fatehpur Sikri after entrusting the province of Gujarat to Mirza Aziz Koka when Muhammad Hussain Mirza came back from Deccan and captured many parts of Gujarat. He besieged Mirza Aziz Koka in Ahmedabad in such a manner that he could neither come out, nor could anyone reach him. Mirza Aziz Koka lost his nerve and began sending pleas to Badshah Salamat and letters to his mother. Mirza Aziz Koka's mother Jiji Anga had breastfed Badshah Salamat. For this reason, Badshah Salamat used to say, 'We and Mirza Aziz Koka are joined by a stream of milk.'

Weeping profusely Jiji Anga told Badshah Salamat, 'Do whatever. I want to see my son's face.'

Badshah Salamat immediately dispatched the royal harem and thousands of soldiers. Bhagwant Das and many other nobles were sent along to protect the harem. Badshah Salamat said, 'They are going ahead of me but will reach after me.'

Raja Bharmal, Raja Todar Mal and many trusted nobles were entrusted with the security of Fatehpur and Kunwar Man Singh was ordered to join Badshah Salamat with Kachhwaha Rajputs.

In the month of Rabi us-Sani of 981 Hijri, corresponding to 1573 CE, on Sunday the twenty-third of August, accompanied by three hundred people, Badshah Salamat mounted a she-camel and began the march. They travelled right up to dinner time, when they stopped at Toda. Early morning on Monday they left Toda for Hansmahal. Then after stopping for a while, they travelled at a fast pace and reached Muizzabad. Despite fatigue, Akbar mounted a chariot at midnight and gave instructions that even if overpowered by sleep he ordered them to slow down, the instruction should be ignored and they should maintain their rapid advance. On Tuesday morning by breakfast time he reached the shrine of Khwaja Muinuddin Chishti and sought blessings. After stopping at Ajmer for the day, he mounted a horse and reached Merta on Wednesday morning. Following a short halt, Badshah Salamat continued the march and reached Jaitaran by the time a watch of the day had passed. The entourage stopped here for a short time. A watch of the day remained when a swift march was resumed. By midnight Badshah Salamat reached Sojat in Jodhpur. After resting just until dawn the entourage was about to leave when it was learnt that the advance army and the harem sent ahead was at Pali. With a chosen few, Badshah Salamat left for Pali but after a short distance he learnt that the report was false. Badshah Salamat decided to return and enter Gujarat through Sirohi. This was a shorter route but Badshah Salamat's well-wishers advised that the route that ran through Jalor should be taken instead because they felt the route running through Sirohi was not safe. When Badshah Salamat did not agree, the scout Shaguna was told to guide the entourage through Jalor but give out that they are going through Sirohi. The royal entourage travelled at night and lost its way. On Friday morning when they reached a village, Badshah Salamat realized that they were on the way to Jalor. He became angry, halted there for a while and resumed the march. By the afternoon they reached Jalor. Here the royal harem and the advance army met them. In Jalor, Badshah Salamat spent some time in the harem. Then at midnight he mounted a swift horse and halted at Pattanwal at midday on Saturday. Leaving after seeing the moon of the first day of the month, they did not halt until the end of Sunday, when they reached Disa, on the Banas river, which was twenty kos from Patan. Resuming the march at midnight, he reached Balisana, which was five kos from Patan, by breakfast time.

Badshah Salamat's entourage travelled at such a rapid pace that on the way they met forces sent in advance and left many behind.

Without waiting for those left behind, the army was ordered to gather in Balisana. Keeping a select band of a hundred soldiers to be with himself, Badshah Salamat divided the forces into left, centre and right flanks. The centre was entrusted to Abdur Rahim, the son of Bairam Khan. This young man, aged sixteen, who had been given the title of Mirza Khan, had childhood memories of this area. His father Bairam Khan had been murdered in Patan and he and his mother had fled the place to save their lives. Some time ago when Badshah Salamat came here to conquer Gujarat, he had brought Abdur Rahim along so that he could see his father's grave. He had then told Abdur Rahim about the martyrdom of Bairam Khan. Badshah Salamat also granted the fief of Patan to Mirza Abdur Rahim.

The leadership of the left flank was entrusted to Mir Muhammad Qilan Khan. The right flank was under the charge of Vazir Khan. Many soldiers were in the vanguard with Muhammad Quli Khan Toqbai and Tarkhan Diwana.

An army of about three thousand began its march from Balisana. Shaguna, the scout, was sent ahead to tell the royal garrison in Ahmedabad to come out to meet Badshah Salamat's forces when it reaches there.

After a full night and a small part of the day, the royal entourage reached Kadi. It would have been easy to capture the fort here. But Badshah Salamat decided against it to avoid letting the enemy get a whiff of their arrival. He thought it best to halt after two kos so that the army could take rest. The royal forces again began their march on Wednesday and reached up to the banks of the Sabarmati. They could see the fort of Ahmedabad beyond the river. A journey that usually took two to three months was completed by Badshah Salamat's army in nine days.

Tansen had written about Badshah Salamat's army—

Here comes the army of the mighty emperor Akbar,
Subjects and kings of the seven islands and eight directions
tremble with fear.
Such is his speed that day and night have turned into moments,
Jalaluddin Muhammad's army moves as if victory is its second
nature.

Shah Humayun's son is like sandalwood and sword,
Tansen submits that valuables be given him to ward off the
evil eye.

When Muhammad Hussain Mirza saw Badshah Salamat's army on the other side of the Sabarmati, he shouted and asked, 'Whose army is this?'

A soldier Subhan Quli Turk of Bairam Khan's time replied, 'This is Badshah Salamat's army that has come to teach a lesson to the disloyal.'

Muhammad Hussain Mirza said, 'My men left Fatehpur fourteen days ago. If this is the royal army, where are the royal elephants who are never separate from the royal army?'

Subhan Quli Turk replied, 'How would elephants mighty as the mountain travel with the army and cover four hundred kos in nine days?'

Now when Badshah Salamat took stock of the armour of the fighting forces, he found that Rupsi's son Jaimal had on a heavy outfit.

Rupsi was a Kachhwaha Rajput and a brother of Raja Bharmal of Amber. He had been in Badshah Salamat's service since the sixth regnal year.

When Badshah Salamat asked Rupsi's son Jaimal, he replied, 'Your Majesty, this is what I have at this moment. My own armour has been left behind.'

Badshah Salamat immediately replaced his armour. Taking off the old one, Jaimal wore the new armour. No sooner had an elated Jaimal done his taslim and left than Badshah Salamat's eyes fell upon Karan, the grandson of Raja Maldeo of Jodhpur, who did not have any armour upon him. Badshah Salamat gave Jaimal's armour to him. It hadn't struck Badshah Salamat that Rupsi would not tolerate his family armour on the body of a Jodhpur man.

When an angry Rupsi asked for his family armour, Badshah Salamat said, 'We have given you a piece of armour from our side. It is an omen for victory. What you are saying is not proper.'

Rupsi could not give a reply to Badshah Salamat. Throwing off his armour, he said, 'I will go just like this.'

Jalaluddin Muhammad Akbar said, 'Our brave men would fight

without armour! So it will not agree with valour that we should go armed into the battlefield. We shall also face the arrows and swords like this.'

Badshah Salamat's armour had inscribed on it Quranic verses and that this was the personal armour of the Emperor of lofty fortune—

'Pairhan-i-khas-i-buland Iqbal Shahanshah Akbar Ghazi.'

His shield had twelve zodiac signs. It was steel with gold patterns with an inscription that again referred to the Emperor with a lofty fortune—

'Buland Iqbal Shahanshah Akbar.'

At this critical moment Bhagwant Das raced his horse and came up to Rupsi. He counselled Rupsi and controlled the situation. Rupsi apologized. Bhagwant Das said, 'Your Majesty, Rupsi had taken bhang. There is nothing more to it. Please forgive him.'

Badshah Salamat forgave Rupsi and the matter was resolved.

Now Badshah Salamat moved towards his white galloper.

Badshah Salamat was as fond of horses as he was of elephants. His six personal stables had forty horses each from Arabia and Persia. There was a steady stream of horses that came in and went out of the stables. Traders brought horses from Persia, Transoxiana, Arabia, Turkey, Turkestan, Badakhshan, Shirwan, Kyrghyz, Tibet and Kashmir. The horses were also sent out of the stables as gifts and also for other purposes. In all, the royal stables had twelve thousand horses. At Badshah Salamat's orders, the horses from the personal stables wore a quilt of chintz, a covering for the mane, a woollen towel, a saddlecloth that was woven in hair, the lining being of felt, and a rope to tightly bind the saddlecloth to the horse's body, bridle and headstall.

Badshah Salamat was about to mount when the horse sat down. When people present saw it as a bad omen, Bhagwant Das said, 'Your Majesty, congratulations for the victory!'

Badshah Salamat replied, 'May you have a long life. But how come?'

Bhagwant Das replied, 'I have observed three good signs all along the way. It is written in our religious texts that when the army is ready for attack and the horse sits down as the general mounts it, it is an omen for victory. Secondly, kindly see how the winds have changed direction. Old men have written that this stands for victory. Thirdly, I have observed that a great number of vultures, kites and crows have been flying overhead. This has also been considered an omen for victory by experienced people.'

In the swift journey between Fatehpur and Ahmedabad, Badshah Salamat had felt the urge to hunt after leaving Jaitaran. Just then a blackbuck was seen. Badshah Salamat said, 'If a swift leopard catches it, this would be a sign that Muhammad Hussain Mirza will be captured.'

With this he let loose his hunting leopard from the cage and the blackbuck was caught.

When a tiger was spotted towards the left side on the way to Jalor, Badshah Salamat's entourage wanted to kill it. Stopping them, Badshah Salamat said, 'Experienced men of India believe that a tiger or tiger-like animal coming on one's left is a good omen. It should not be killed.'

Jannat Ashiyani Humayun Badshah used to feed raisins to a white rooster. It would crow when the night ended so that the attendants wake up. One day it was in front of him when he thought, 'If luck is on our side, this cock would sit on my shoulder and crow.'

Jauhar Aftabchi was in the service of Jannat Ashiyani at the time. He says that the cock immediately sat on Jannat Ashiyani's shoulder and crowed. An elated Jannat Ashiyani immediately had a silver ring put around the cock's neck.

Seeing the royal forces at the door, Muhammad Hussain Mirza left his associate the Abyssinian Ikhtiyar-ul-Mulk Gujarati to guard the city and came out with his army. Badshah Salamat was hopeful that as the royal army launched its attack, Mirza Aziz Koka would pluck up courage and come out from the other side. But when there was no movement from the side of Mirza Aziz Koka, Badshah Salamat himself entered the river on horseback. When the royal army reached the other side of the river, Muhammad Hussain Mirza attacked the vanguard with fifteen hundred Mughals. Muhammad Hussain Mirza's Afghan and Abyssinian soldiers launched an assault on the left flank of the royal army. Seeing the reverses his army was suffering at the hands of about seven thousand soldiers, Badshah Salamat raised a cry, '*Ya Muin!*'

With this cry, Badshah Salamat and his soldiers launched a vigorous attack. It was a tough battle. A moment came when Badshah Salamat found himself surrounded by enemies with just two of his own people with him. Somebody from the enemy's side struck the neck of Badshah Salamat's horse with a sword. Badshah Salamat struck back with a spear which pierced that man's armour and entered his body. When Badshah Salamat tried to extract the spear, its head broke and the injured soldier fled. Another soldier aimed a blow at Badshah Salamat's thigh but could not cause any harm. Now a rumour spread in the army that there was some bad news about Badshah Salamat. The army was about to lose heart when Badshah Salamat cried out, 'Brave men! Come up quickly and dispose of these wretches.'

When more royal forces came in from behind and began a massacre of Muhammad Hussain Mirza's army, Badshah Salamat went to one side of the battlefield to observe.

This battle strategy was described by the Christian priest Monserrate, who came to Badshah Salamat's court sometime after the battle, in this manner:

'The army of horsemen forms a semi-circle on the battlefield. They hold fort on left, right and the central flanks. Behind the cavalry is their infantry and behind them the elephants... The assault happens in such a manner that the enemy is besieged... Mongols never expose their entire army in the battle. If there are six thousand fighting at the front, there would be twenty thousand hiding behind, who would come out to help those fighting at the front in case the situation gets out of hand. These soldiers often turn defeat into victory.'

Badshah Salamat thanked God for the victory and was trying to find out whether Mirza Aziz Koka had come out of Ahmedabad when he learnt of bad news about another 'koka'.

Picha Jan Anga, who was the mother of Zain Khan Koka and his older brother Saif Khan Koka, had also breastfed Badshah Salamat. This bond was deeper than that of milk. People speak of an incident that happened in Badshah Salamat's childhood. Picha Jan Anga was pregnant with Saif Khan Koka. Until now, she had only borne daughters. Her husband told her clearly that if a daughter was born again, he would cease to be a husband to her. In anxiety, Picha Jan Anga sought Maryam Makani Hamida Banu Begum's permission to abort the child. When she came out after meeting Hamida Banu Begum, the young Akbar said, 'Don't ever mention this to anyone. God would bless you with a son.'

Mirza Akbar was very young at the time, but heeding his words, Picha Jan Anga did not abort the child and Saif Khan Koka came into this world. That is the reason Saif Khan Koka believed that he owed his life to Badshah Salamat. When last seen in the battlefield near the Sabarmati river, he was crying 'Ajmeri, Ajmeri' in a wounded state and looking for Badshah Salamat. Badshah Salamat later learnt that Saif Khan Koka fought bravely and was martyred after inflicting heavy losses upon the enemy.

Badshah Salamat was deep in sorrow when two of the royal soldiers brought in Muhammad Hussain Mirza. Badshah Salamat looked at this man who was related to him and now stood before him as a criminal. When both the soldiers claimed to have captured Muhammad Hussain Mirza, Badshah Salamat's close courtier Raja Birbal asked the Mirza himself, 'Who caught you?'

In an injured state, Muhammad Hussain Mirza said, 'Badshah Salamat's salt.'

When Muhammad Hussain Mirza asked for water, Badshah Salamat's attendant gave him a blow on his head and said, 'Water for such a disloyal one!'

Badshah Salamat restrained his attendant and got water for Muhammad Hussain Mirza from his own vessel.

Jalaluddin Muhammad Akbar reproached Muhammad Hussain Mirza but decided to spare his life. His hands that were bound behind him were now bound in the front. He was given into the custody of Rai Singh.

Rai Singh was a fourth-generation descendant of Raja Maldeo and was the son of Rai Kalyanmal of Bikaner. When Ibrahim Hussain Mirza captured Nagaur after the defeat at Sarnal, Rai Singh took him on and defeated him. After this, when Badshah Salamat embarked on his blitzkrieg to Gujarat, Rai Singh was sent in advance. He fought bravely alongside Badshah Salamat against Muhammad Hussain Mirza.

But when Muhammad Hussain Mirza's foster brother Shah Madad was brought in, Badshah Salamat could not control his anger. Shah Madad had killed Bhagwant Das's brother Bhupat in the Battle of Sarnal when Badshah Salamat had won his first victory over Gujarat. Badshah Salamat had felt Bhupat's loss deeply. He had sent Prince Salim's mother, Raja Bhagwant Das's sister, to Amber to be present at the mourning for Bhupat. Badshah Salamat immediately killed Shah Madad with his spear. The soldiers reduced his corpse to pieces.

Barely an hour had passed since Muhammad Hussain Mirza's life was spared when Ikhtiyar-ul-Mulk Gujarati led a charge at the spot where Badshah Salamat was present. At that very moment the Rajputs under Rai Singh pulled Muhammad Hussain Mirza down from the elephant and killed him with a spear.

Ikhtiyar-ul-Mulk Gujarati's soldiers fled in such confusion that the royal forces attacked them with the arrows out of their own quivers. Ikhtiyar-ul-Mulk was himself caught while trying to flee. When a soldier called Sohrab Beg caught him, he said, 'You look like a Turkman. Turkmans are followers of the blessed Ali. I am a Sayyid from Bukhara. Don't kill me.'

Sohrab Beg replied, 'I know you. I have followed you. You are Ikhtiyar-ul-Mulk.'

Saying this, Sohrab Beg beheaded Ikhtiyar-ul-Mulk with one stroke of his sword.

The calm that had now set in was broken when the royal forces became alert to another army marching towards it. But this was Mirza Aziz Koka's army which had come out of the fort of Ahmedabad after Ikhtiyar-ul-Mulk's siege was lifted. Badshah Salamat embraced his foster brother.

Sohrab Beg came and placed the head of Ikhtiyar-ul-Mulk at the feet of Badshah Salamat. By the order of Jalaluddin Muhammad Akbar a tower of two thousand heads was made. The heads of Ikhtiyar-ul-Mulk and Muhammad Hussain Mirza were sent to Agra and Fatehpur where they were hung at the city gates so that people may learn a lesson.

After the victory, Badshah Salamat stayed there for eleven days. At the successful conclusion of the Gujarat campaign, when he set his foot in Fatehpur Sikri after forty-three days, the city celebrated.

Tansen wrote:

Overjoyed men and women in large numbers,
Come out to receive their dear one.
Amidst the sound of the shehnai,
Been, rabab, cymbals and drums.
There is an air of festivity,
The infantry and the cavalry too join in the mirth.
O Tansen! The whole city is euphoric,
With scent and rose sprinkled, the air fragrant.

Badshah Salamat was still on horseback at the big Elephant Gate when the three princes kissed his feet. The nobles and clerics welcomed him. Badshah Salamat was again reminded of Sheikh Mubarak's words.

Sheikh Mubarak had said, 'God has bestowed upon the people such a great boon and blessing in the holy personality of Hazrat Badshah. Because of his nobility and his excellent administration, Hazrat Badshah had become the leader of the spiritual world.'

Badshah Salamat liked this so much that he began to mention it often in the court. Seeing the way the wind was blowing, Sheikh Mubarak's son, Faizi's brother, Sheikh Abul Fazl said, 'Whenever a monarch, well-meaning and with every good intention, leaves the direction of religion, education and justice entirely to a body who are outwardly respectable, and himself assumes in their regard the mantle of indifference, the influence of the truthful and the righteous wanes and the crooked men of learning and the courtiers unite in intrigue. Bigotry has full sway. Families are subverted and reputations ruined.'

In the wilderness of Bhera, Badshah Salamat remembered a question he had posed to the ulema—'Is there any problem in inscribing "Allahu Akbar" on coins and the imperial seals?'

In keeping with his temperament, Haji Ibrahim gave a blunt response, 'This gives a different impression. If you say, "*Wal zikr Allahu Akbar*", the reference is to Allah's greatness, there would be no scope for doubt.'

Haji Ibrahim had agreed to participate in the discussions of the Ibadat Khana but refused to observe the protocol of the court. In matters of faith, he did not mince his words.

Badshah Salamat lost his cool at Haji Ibrahim's reply and said, 'This is not a claim to divinity. We only want to show that the words are similar. What is the logic of taking this matter in that direction?'

Jalaluddin Muhammad Akbar used to say, 'There is no claim to prophethood in Hindustan. The reason is there are claims to divinity here.'

What the ulema did not permit was articulated by Tansen with ease. He said:

The mighty Emperor sits on the throne as incarnation of God,
He serves the land, gifts platefuls of gold.
Whoever comes, gets his wishes fulfilled,
Tansen says of Shah Jalaluddin Akbar,
He has taken birth to do good to virtuous people.

Badshah Salamat was put in mind of the ease with which he had once in the early years of his reign resolved an issue.

In Thanesar, a sect by the name of Puris had the right to sit by the banks of a tank. The pilgrims visiting here would distribute alms that would come to the ascetics of the Puri sect. One day ascetics of the Kur sect forcibly removed the ascetics of the Puri sect. The Puri sect appealed to Badshah Salamat who was then in Ambala: 'Though we do not have the strength to encounter them, yet we would, trusting in God, engage in a fight with them and would either shed our own blood or take the place from them.'

To this the Kurs replied, 'The place belongs to us by inheritance, though the Puris had settled there for some time. Now we would sit there, and the site would remain ours as long as there was life in our bodies.'

Badshah Salamat reached Thanesar and counselled both the sects. Neither agreed and fighting broke out. When Badshah Salamat found that the Puris were losing, he sent his soldiers to assist them. Badshah Salamat saw the battle seated on his brown horse, people holding the symbols of authority—tumantogh, saiban, and alam—behind him. Now the royal forces and the Puri ascetics launched such a fierce attack that the Kurs fled. The head of the sect, Anand Kur, and many other ascetics lost their life. Satisfied, Badshah Salamat marched on.

25

It was a bright full moon on the sky of Bhera. Badshah Salamat was shouting, 'Hindus should eat beef, Muslims should eat pork, and if not this, fry a sheep in the pan. If it turns into pork, Hindus and Muslims should have it together. If its turns into beef, Hindus and Muslims should have it together. If it becomes pork, Muslims should have it. If it becomes beef, Hindus should have it. A divine miracle would thus happen.'

The courtiers could not make sense of this or of what happened next.

Badshah Salamat took off his headgear and said, 'Call the barber and get my head shaved.'

A hush fell on the gathering. In the early years of his reign, Badshah Salamat had given up the ways of his ancestors and begun to keep long hair like the Hindus. Tonight, he suddenly decided to shorten his long and beautiful hair.

When the terrified barbers ran away, Badshah Salamat took off his own dagger from the red and golden scabbard and began cutting his hair. Mustering his courage, Shah Fatehullah caught hold of Badshah Salamat's hands. Zain Khan Koka and Sheikh Farid took away the dagger from his hands.

Shah Fatehullah said, 'If you wish to have a haircut, please do.'

At Shah Fatehullah's bidding, all the nobles present took off their headgear. After Badshah Salamat's haircut, every courtier present got a haircut. But Badshah Salamat's anger did not subside. No one could understand what he was raving about. At midnight, Shah Fatehullah gently took him inside.

A few miles from Badshah Salamat's do-ashiyana manzil, the panting wild animals were trapped in an unyielding noose. With the river on one side, soldiers had laid a semi-circular siege of about sixty miles between Bhera and Girjhak.

Badshah Salamat had inherited this Timuri and Changezi tradition. Seven generations ago, Amir Timur's army had fallen on bad times during a campaign against the powerful Mongol Khan Tokhtamish. The Khan drew his lineage from Jochi, the eldest son of Changez Khan and had the ambition to once again consolidate the disintegrated Mongol power. Amir Timur's army of two hundred thousand had been away from Tashkent for about four months and was falling prey to hunger and fatigue and there was no sign of Tokhtamish yet. At that time Amir Timur ordered the qamargah. The middle flank of the army was ordered to stay where it was. The left and the right flank moved ahead to complete the circle and squeeze it. After various kinds of animals got trapped inside this circle, Amir Timur hunted, followed by his army. Two hundred thousand soldiers played this game which made them ready for the assault against Tokhtamish.

Even before Amir Timur, this was a Mongol way of gathering and storing meat for the winter and to be ready for war. The Mongol soldiers would make a large circle and then begin squeezing it. When the circle became tight enough, the arrow shot by the Khan began the game. If any animal escaped the siege or anyone hunted before his turn, the soldier responsible for this was punished.

In the Timuri and Changezi tradition, this was not a mere hunt. This was a way of keeping an area under control and keeping the army fit. Badshah Salamat himself was so fond of hunting that each kos minar from Agra to Ajmer had horns of deer shot by him.

After becoming free of Bairam Khan, when Badshah Salamat passed through Hissar-i-Firoza, huntsmen told him that cheetahs were found in this region. Pits were dug on the instructions of Badshah Salamat and many cheetahs caught. They were encaged and made part of the royal cheetah khana. This was the first time that Badshah Salamat personally hunted them. And what's more, when a rope was being tied around the neck of one of them, Badshah Salamat was firmly holding the cheetah by its ears.

Shortly after this, Badshah Salamat played the first big hunt of his life. He was hunting and travelling from Malwa to Agra when a tigress launched a ferocious attack to save her five cubs. People in the royal entourage were terrified but Badshah Salamat killed the tigress in one stroke from his horseback. The cubs fell prey to the arrows, swords, and spears of the entourage.

In the twelfth regnal year, corresponding to 1567 CE, on the eleventh of March, Jalaluddin Muhammad Akbar played the biggest qamargah he had played till then. In a ten-mile area near Lahore, beaters and soldiers had begun to squeeze the circle. When the battue was completely formed and about fifteen thousand animals were trapped, Badshah Salamat hunted day and night for five days with bow and arrow, sword, lance and musket. Even Badshah Salamat's cheetah hunted. After this came the turn of the nobles and the attendants of the harem. Then the attendants of the court hunted and in the end the cavalry and infantry.

The current siege in Bhera was the biggest qamargah of Badshah Salamat's entire life. Arif Qandhari wrote of Badshah Salamat's intentions:

'Wherever he would go with his men to hunt, not only were the people accompanying him terrified, even the animals and birds of the area were terrified. If the birds could get news of his arrival, they would have gone under water like a duck, if they could. If the duck could fly and flee, it would have. Out of fear the dog would bark at the deer. The lion would steer clear of the hunters. Badshah Salamat travelled like this for some months. Although his intention was to hunt, his foremost purpose was to know the state of his subjects. Oppressors were punished. Secondly, he wanted to inspect his army. He would have gone to Kabul if he had the time but gave it up for want of it.'

The nobles and the Rajputs spent their night in anxiety about what Badshah Salamat might do in the morning. After worshipping, the Hindu nobles adorned themselves with the sacred signs of shankh and chakra and waited, ready for death, when Badshah Salamat passed by their camps in clothes he had been wearing since night.

Badshah Salamat told the Rajputs, 'Be ready. We shall attack the Firangis.'

Then Badshah Salamat took off his headgear. Cutting it into pieces, he gave a piece of it with Gangajal—the sacred water of the Ganga—to each of them and said, 'When we attack the Firangis, we will ask for this token.'

It was at that time in Bhera, under a tree that was in fruit, all of a sudden, that a strange sensation overpowered Badshah Salamat. He was lost in thought. People around him felt that he was communicating with the other world.

This had happened to Badshah Salamat many times before. It was noticed the first time when Jannat Ashiyani Humayun Badshah had sent someone to Mirza Akbar. The person was surprised by what he saw.

'I found him lying down. His lustrous countenance was serene and looked as if he were asleep. In truth he was communicating with the angels. His blessed hand moved occasionally as if in contemplation. From time to time there fell from his pearl-dropping tongue such expressions as, "Insha'Allah, I will bring the cream of earth's surface under my sway and fulfil the desires of the sorrowful of the seven climes."'

Abul Fazl tried to explain what happened under the tree in Bhera—

'A sublime joy took possession of his bodily frame. The description of it cannot be comprehended by the feeble intellect of the common people. Nor can every enlightened sage attain an understanding of it. A few of the farsighted ones understand a little out of much of it by help of the ecstasy of vision. Until the boon companions of the banquet of Hazrat Badshah have drunk the wine, what do they know of religious experience? And without tasting it, how would you know where it comes from?

'A number of clear-sighted ones of the holy assemblage thought that he had gained his religious destination and has found what he desired. Some thought that he had met one of the holy spirits. Some others thought that the beasts of the forest had with a tongueless tongue imparted divine secrets to him.'

Perhaps in that moment Badshah Salamat had a thought that he often spoke of, 'There are many things in hunting that are similar to the duties a king has. Undoubtedly the foremost of them is to grant a life.'

What happened next was beyond anybody's expectation. Preparations for the qamargah had been on for several days now. The beaters and soldiers had been tightening the siege to make it so compact that it be ready for Badshah Salamat's hunt. Numerous lions, blue sheep, goats, rabbits, foxes, bears, nilgais, jackals and deer had been herded and now trapped in the battue. Badshah Salamat got a picture made of the moment. He sat under a tree in Bhera on a piece of red clothing spread on a rock, wearing a brown jama and green yar-i-pairhan. There was a dagger in the sash. The red headgear had patterns in white and there was a sarpech on it. He wore two strings around his neck. His eyes were locked on to a dead blue sheep. Attendants stood behind him with sword and musket. That was the moment when he suddenly ordered the siege to be lifted and each and every animal to be allowed to leave. Badshah Salamat's state caused consternation all around. A falconer stared at another attendant who was biting his finger in bewilderment.

Fast runners were dispatched so that no animal life was lost. Thousands of animals were suddenly freed. Right under that tree in Bhera, Badshah Salamat distributed alms to the faqirs. He got a pavilion made and an elaborate garden laid out at the spot. He named the spot mini-Mecca.

About fifty thousand soldiers prepared for a qamargah at the border Badshah Salamat shared with his stepbrother Mirza Hakim. Calling off the qamargah, Badshah Salamat also gave up the idea of going to Kabul and decided to turn back after a show of strength to his stepbrother.

Badshah Salamat said, 'My sole wish is that the Mirza may emerge from the defile of savagery and be encompassed with princely favours. Inasmuch as he is young and inexperienced, and is associated with persons of small capacity, perchance he may on our approach turn away from the altar of fortune and go and take refuge with Uzbeks. Though able and farsighted men have regarded a younger brother in the light of a son, yet something tells me that the existence of a dutiful son is doubtful, and the meeting of brothers impossible. It is far better that I hearten him with good counsel from a distance. It may be that his somnolent fortune shall awake and that he shall take the path of obedience, cease to stray, and become a traveller to the abode of bliss. If under the influence of the evil ones he has hurried away from the high road of obedience and the pleasant abode of service, and has fallen into the thornbrake of ingratitude, it becomes a magnanimous nature to act contrary to the nature of the short-sighted.'

The presence of such a huge army at the border was enough to terrify Mirza Hakim. Now Mirza Hakim's sister Sakina Banu Begum was sent to him with the message that if he heeded to Badshah Salamat, Prince Salim could be married to his daughter.

This was not the first time people had seen Badshah Salamat in such a state. But it was definitely the last such occasion. After that day, nobody ever saw him in that state. Having rested for five days in the do-ashiyana manzil, Badshah Salamat left for Fatehpur Sikri by a straight route and with a strong resolve.

Part Two

1

There was tumult in the city, there was chaos all around.
All doors were closed, traders did not sit in the bazaar.
Good clothes and good ornaments, all were hidden under the earth.
Account books buried elsewhere, cash and other material safely hidden.
In every home weapons were gathered, people wore ordinary clothes.
Wrapped in rough blankets, women began to dress plainly.
None could make out the difference between the high and the low, rich and poor seemed the same.
No thieves or robbers were to be seen, people were scared for no reason.
This chaos lasted ten days, then there was peace.
A letter received from Agra said all was well.
It said, Emperor Jalal ruled for fifty-two years,
Now in the month of Kartik, Samvat 1662, he died.

The Jain poet Banarsidas wrote of the chaos around the time when Badshah Salamat passed away. Banarsidas's grandfather Mool Das was the storekeeper of a Mughal noble in Narwar, and his maternal uncle Madan Singh Chinalia was a prominent jeweller of Jaunpur. His father Kharak Singh had undertaken the job of collecting the land revenue of four parganas for Dhanna Rai, the diwan of the Afghan sultan Sulaiman of Bengal. Thereafter he traded in jewellery in Allahabad. Banarsidas himself traded in jewels and many other things but did not achieve much success. When Jalaluddin Muhammad Akbar died in the Kartik month of Vikram Samvat 1662, corresponding to October 1605 CE, Banarsidas was in Jaunpur.

When Badshah Salamat fell ill with a stomach ailment in the Agra Fort, he told Hakim Ali Gilani about it. Hakim Gilani felt his pulse and said, 'Better if Hazrat Badshah abstains from eating, so that the wind in the stomach comes out. Tomorrow when you feel better, treatment will begin to get the strength back into the body.'

That day Badshah Salamat did not eat anything. The next day Hakim Gilani asked him to have broth without any ghee. Not liking this food, Badshah Salamat became perturbed and went into the zenankhana. When the weakness increased the next day all the royal hakims gathered together. Hakim Gilani and Hakim Jamaluddin Muzaffar began to wrangle over the line of treatment. Hearing of this, Badshah Salamat said, 'We are giving ourself to the care of Hakim Ali. He may do as he deems fit.'

Hakim Ali Gilani began the treatment in earnest but high fever and loose motions sapped Badshah Salamat's energy.

Twenty-three years ago, in this very season, Badshah Salamat had suffered a stomach ailment. For a long time, he resisted medication and handed out advice to others instead. Finally, when the loyal ones insisted, the treatment began. Indian physicians did not administer medicine to cure constipation but under the Unani system of medicine this was required. Gathering courage, Sheikh Abul Fazl said, 'I admit that all are true and well-intentioned. What can come of various methods?... If laxatives are not used, an easy matter will become difficult.'

Then some years ago while travelling in Malwa, he suffered so much pain in the stomach that for many days he could not travel on horseback.

Now in the very last phase of his life, Badshah Salamat was bedridden in his sleeping quarters by the river Yamuna.

Badshah Salamat had completely rebuilt the Lodhi fort of Agra even before he built Fatehpur Sikri. A brick fort was converted into a majestic fort of red sandstone. Five hundred buildings that opened towards the Yamuna were constructed in the style of Bengal and Gujarat. On the other side of the fort was the Hathipol—the Elephant Gate—that opened into the city, through which people entered the complex. Here at this gate stood in silence the statues of Jaimal and Patta.

In his history of Badshah Salamat's reign, Arif Qandhari said:

'It will not be hidden from the minds of the skilful engineers and artisans that a good name for kings is achieved by means of lofty buildings. It is said, the name of sultans lasts longer on account of their buildings.

'When the Creator, God, brought into existence the created things of the world, and created the length and breadth of the sky and the earth, He did not order anyone in their creation. When the world became manifest, a voice said, "Have a look My creation." And then He said, "Do they not look at the sky above them, how We have made it?"

'From this preface, it is clear that the advantages of buildings cannot be expressed in words. Great men have said, "The honour of man is his building and the aspiration of man is his house."

'In accordance with these remarks, the King of the world and monarch of the earth, may he rule over the world till eternity, has constructed the fort of the dar-ul-khilafat of Agra.

'The Almighty specially favoured the one who is worthy of kingship, who endowed his kingship with justice and wisdom.

'The Creator of the two worlds gave divine guidance to the sultan of sultans, Zill-i-Ilahi, sultan on the land of Allah, helper of the creatures of Allah, Abul Muzaffar Jalaluddin Muhammad Akbar Badshah to lay the foundation of a fort in the dar-ul-khilafat of Agra, which is among the greatest regions of Hindustan. Skilled architects and masters at an auspicious hour laid its foundation. Nimble-handed masters of art, each one of whom was the foremost of the clime, attended to the subtleties of its fineness. Two thousand master stone masons and two thousand master workers in clay and lime worked for the construction of the fort every day. Eight thousand labourers, who carried stone and lime to the place of work, worked on that fort. A thousand carts of red stone were brought from the village of Fatehpur Sikri and up to one hundred boats brought via the Jumna from the capital Delhi, pellet stones.

'A fort of red sandstone was created on the banks of the Jumna, which like the palaces of sublime heavens, obtained the status of "the Garden beneath which rivers flow".'

The *Hamzanama* was being read out, and shown, to Badshah Salamat, as the Yamuna flowed quietly. The storyteller was at a point where Amir Hamza had dealt a heavy defeat to King Marzuq, the king of the Franks—

'When the ill-starred Marzuq fled the fortress, the princes of the age, the champions, and the Sahib-i-Qiran killed many Firangis that night. The fire of the battle blazed forth. The next day the Sahib-i-Qiran was informed. He entered the fortress and met his sons, warriors, and champions, and showed great kindness.'

With tired eyes, Badshah Salamat looked at the large painting from the *Hamzanama*.

This exciting tale of vanquishing demons, foes and sorcerers is woven around the personality of the uncle of Prophet Muhammad, Amir Hamza. The story begins in Iraq, where a poor but bright boy Buzurjmihr dislodges the evil vizier of King Qubad and takes his place himself. The vizier's widow gives birth to the son who becomes the enemy of Buzurjmihr and Amir Hamza. Amir Hamza is himself born in miraculous circumstances. When the next emperor Anurshivan learns from his vizier Buzurjmihr that a woman in Arabia is pregnant with a child who would be his nemesis, he orders all pregnant women to be killed. Yet Hamza escapes. In time, Anurshivan learns of the exploits of Hamza who is called to the darbar. Now begins a series of exploits that takes Sahib-i-Qiran Amir Hamza to far-flung regions of the world. After eighteen years of separation, Amir Hamza wins his love and marries the daughter of Emperor Anurshivan.

At this moment, Amir Hamza's tale was at a very critical point. The painting being shown to Badshah Salamat displayed the fort of the Firangis being stormed by Amir Hamza's army. Firangi women were peeping from above. There were corpses below. Plunder had begun inside the fort, and the king of the Firangis was about to flee in a boat along with his favourite horse.

The storyteller said, 'Let us return to the story. The Sahib-i-Qiran asked about Marzuq. Prince Alamshah said, "O Lord, we searched far and wide for Marzuq, but no matter where we looked we could not find any trace of him because he got into a ship and set sail."

'The Sahib-i-Qiran said, "I need someone to bring news of Marzuq..."'

Large-sized ferocious characters were peering out of the large canvases of the *Hamzanama*. They had been made by fifty artists under the supervision of Mir Sayyid Ali of Persia. By royal orders, fourteen hundred pictures were made in a span of fifteen years, which Badshah Salamat would look at with a lot of joy. This also happened to be the period when Badshah Salamat won major victories.

On the floor of Badshah Salamat's bedchamber was a deep red carpet which displayed a hunting scene with a floral pattern around it. A strange animal-like bird Simurgh was hunting a lion-elephant hybrid animal, and this animal was hunting seven elephants simultaneously.

Today Jalaluddin Muhammad Akbar was in no state to even rise from his sandalwood bed. The arms that had crafted the empire were now refusing to budge. A flickering life was returning to the times when 'Sultan-ul-Islam', 'Kahaf-ul-Anam', 'Amir-ul-Momineen', 'Zill-i-Ilahi', 'Mahabali', and God-incarnate had fought fierce battles with the forces of this world and of faith, and won many of them.

In these last moments, he was reminded of his own doha—

Gatherings ended with Pithal, raga ended with Tansen,
Joys of meeting and having conversation ended with Birbal.

It seemed as if Tansen's voice from the past sang of a lifetime of struggle. In the light-coloured, long jama that came up to the feet, a dagger on the left side of the waist, a tall and dark Miyan Tansen sang standing in his mellifluous voice in the darbar—

Kashi, Kashmir, Kamru, Karnatak, Bundi, Bundelkhand,
Malwa, Multan, Mewar, Khurasan, Balkh, Bukhara, Gokulmand.
Bijapur, Bang, Badakhshan, Rum, Siam and Bharat,
Says Tansen, the universe fears Humayun's son Jalaluddin Akbar.

In his fifty-year reign, Badshah Salamat won every contest in the battlefield. None from outside dared attack Hindustan. Badshah Salamat believed, 'Emperors should always try to annex new regions, or else neighbours take up arms. The army should always engage in war or else it becomes lazy.'

The grandeur of Badshah Salamat's darbar dazzled the world. Miyan Tansen had said of it:

Emperor Akbar who shall live till eternity,
Sits on his throne, sceptre above.
O charming Lord of Delhi, you are lieutenant to the Prophet.
You have taken all four directions under your charge,
All kings, nobles obey your command.
Says Miyan Tansen, there is none like you in honouring the talented.

When the ruler of Badakhshan came to Fatehpur Sikri to seek help, five thousand elephants, with housings of European velvet and

Turkish cloth of gold, and chains of gold and silver were drawn up in a line on both sides of the road. Between each pair of elephants were placed cheetahs with golden collars and coverings of velvet and fine linen, and oxen-cars with fillets of embroidered gold. Also stationed were Arabian and Persian horses with golden saddles. Despite the simplicity Badshah Salamat displayed in his persona, his clothes were worked in gold thread. The sarpech on the taj had the ruby from Badakhshan, which Maryam Makani Hamida Banu Begum had gifted to him on the occasion of the birth of his first son. Such was his opulence that twenty million tankas filled in a pond measuring twenty feet in length and breadth and three feet in depth was distributed by Badshah Salamat to nobles, learned men, and the poor and the needy.

Filippo Sassetti, the trader from Florence, wrote:

'A prominent ruler of this region, who is a descendant of Timur, who is called the Great Mughal, has a very elaborate court. He is constantly on the move with his nobles. He buys a lot of goods... Whenever any foreigner, whoever and from wherever, alights at Khambhat, he is welcomed by four servants of the court, who also make arrangements for their stay and take care of their needs. Then the trader would unload all his goods without any fear. The goods are valued after adding his profit to the cost.'

In the twenty-fourth regnal year, corresponding to 1579 CE, the royal storehouse caught fire, and the tents and awnings of brocade, Firangi velvet, scarlet, silk, and precious varieties of carpet were reduced to ashes. But it is said that Badshah Salamat was not unduly mindful of the loss.

2

As the memories came flooding back, Badshah Salamat was reminded of an incident that happened a long time ago.

It was some years after returning from Bhera. An old man stood in silence amidst the regal grandeur of the darbar at Fatehpur Sikri. Once upon a time, he had enjoyed such a high stature that Badshah Salamat would pick up his shoes, and high-ranking nobles waited to meet him. Today, he stood as an ordinary criminal and was at the receiving end of Badshah Salamat's harsh words. The earlier days were still fresh in people's minds when Sheikh Abd-un-Nabi had been Sadr-us-Sudur. There was none higher to him in matters of religion. But now after returning from Bhera, Badshah Salamat was not inclined to deem anybody higher than himself in matters of faith.

Tiring of the ulema, Badshah Salamat had complained to Sheikh Mubarak, who replied, 'Your Majesty is the imam and mujtahid of the age. What need have you of these ulema for assistance in issuing your commands, whether religious or secular. They have no lot or part in true knowledge, beyond a groundless reputation!'

Badshah Salamat said, 'Since you are my teacher, why don't you free me from dependence on these mullahs?'

Mullah Abdul Qadir Badayuni was closely watching Badshah Salamat at that time. He wrote:

'That year the Emperor was anxious to unite in his person spiritual as well as secular leadership. He held it to be an insufferable burden to be subordinate to anyone, as he had heard that the Prophet, peace be upon him, and his lawful successors, and some of the most powerful kings, as Amir Timur Sahib-i-Qiran and Mirza Ulugh Beg Gurkan, had themselves read the khutba, he resolved to do the same, apparently in order to imitate their example, but in reality to appear in public as the mujtahid of the age. Accordingly, on the first Friday of Jamadi ul-Awwal of the year 987, in the chief mosque of Fatehpur, which he had built near the palace, His Majesty began to read the khutba.'

This was a very crucial moment in the life of Jalaluddin Muhammad Akbar. He announced from the pulpit of the Jama Masjid that he was subordinate to no one, not just in worldly matters but also in matters of religion.

Built at the highest point of the hillock at Sikri, the Jama Masjid was a very elegant structure and was the biggest mosque of his empire. This red sandstone building reflected Badshah Salamat's aesthetic sense. With a vast open space, it had bays and verandahs on its sides. Arches were built into the entire wall on the western side, that is, towards the Ka'ba. In front of the middle arch at the pulpit stood Badshah Salamat. On three sides of this arch were inscribed Quranic verses from the Sura at-Tauba in golden letters on blue—

The mosques of Allah
Shall be visited and maintained
By such as believe in Allah
And the Last Day, establish
Regular prayers, and
Pay Zakat, and fear
None (at all) except Allah
It is they who are expected
To be on true guidance.

Do ye consider the giving
Of drink to pilgrims,
Or the maintenance of
The Sacred Mosque, equal
To (the pious service of) those
Who believe in Allah
And the Last Day, and strive
With might and main
In the cause of Allah?
They are not equal
In the sight of Allah:
And Allah guides not
Those who do wrong.

Those who believe, and emigrate
And strive with might
And main, in Allah's cause,
With their goods and their persons,
Have the highest rank
In the sight of Allah:
They are the people
Who will achieve (salvation).

There was a big dome almost above the central arch where Badshah Salamat stood, and there was one on the left of it and one on its right. The exterior of the mosque had a huge gateway in the centre, flanked on either side by delicate archways. Above these was a row of chhatris—canopies. On special occasions these chhatris were lit and coloured fabric bound on them, making the mosque absolutely captivating to behold.

Badshah Salamat's khutba echoed in the three domes and could be heard far and wide from the hills of Sikri.

Facing Badshah Salamat, on the far end, was the Badshahi Darwaza, used by the nobles and the Emperor himself to come to the mosque from the palace, darbar and the offices. To the left was the shrine of Badshah Salamat's spiritual guide Sheikh Salim Chishti, which was not just made in the Gujarat style but also by artisans from Gujarat. Sheikh Salim Chishti's dargah was nearing completion now. Its marble was soothing to the eye even in the harsh daylight. The chhajjas were supported by carved serpentine brackets. In a square chamber under the dome was the mazar of Sheikh Salim Chishti, and all around it was an enclosed corridor with a marble screen on the outer walls. A black line in one corner of the veranda denoted the spot where Sheikh Salim Chishti used to pray. To the right of Jalaluddin Muhammad Akbar was the Buland Darwaza, built in memory of the Gujarat victory. This imposing gate of red stone and marble had Quranic verses inscribed on it. This gate at the hills of Sikri was visible from a long way off and stood as a symbol of the strength of Badshah Salamat's empire. This city built according to the liking of Badshah Salamat had drawn influences from the Delhi Sultanate, Khurasan, Transoxiana, Malwa, and Rajasthan but the biggest influence was that of Gujarat, where the buildings showed a synthesis of Hindu and Jain styles.

Abul Fazl, who articulated Badshah Salamat's innermost thoughts, said, 'The spoken word steps forward on man's tongue, and enters, with the assistance of the conveying air, into the windows of the ears of others. It then drops the burden of its concrete component, and returns, as a single ray, to its old place, the realm of thought...'

Badshah Salamat began the khutba but could not complete it. At this crucial juncture he stammered and began to tremble. His close courtier Sheikh Faizi had written a poem for this occasion but Badshah Salamat could barely recite three couplets of it—

In the name of God who gave us sovereignty,
Who gave us a wise heart and a strong arm,

Who guided us in equity and justice,
Who expelled every thought from our heart except justice.
His attributes are beyond our comprehension,
Exalted be His Majesty, Allahu Akbar.

Badshah Salamat could not speak beyond this. The Friday congregation saw that he left his khutba unfinished and handed the responsibility to the khatib of the court Hafiz Muhammad Amin.

Sheikh Abul Fazl wrote, '...but occasionally an idea takes a different turn by means of man's fingers, and having passed along the continent of the pen and crossed the ocean of the ink, alights on the pleasant expanse of the page, and returns through the eye of the reader to its wonted habitation.'

The attempt to read the khutba at the mosque was not successful but within two months there came a declaration that caused considerable disquiet among the laity and the clergy. Sheikh Mubarak wrote the mahzarnama—a memorandum—to which all the prominent ulema put their seal of approval—

'Whereas Hindustan is now the centre of security and peace, and the land of justice and beneficence, a large number of people, especially learned men and lawyers, have immigrated and chosen this country for their home. Now we, the principal ulema, who are not only well versed in the several departments of the Law and in the principle of jurisprudence, and well acquainted with the edicts which rest on reason or testimony, but are also known for our piety and our honest intentions, have duly considered the deep meaning, first, of the verse of Quran: "Obey God, and obey the Prophet, and those who have authority among you", and, secondly, of the genuine Tradition: "Surely the man who is dearest to God on the Day of Judgment is the Imam-i-Adil; whoever obeys the Amir, obeys Thee; and whoever rebels against him, rebels against Thee", and, thirdly, of several other proofs based on reasoning or testimony; and we have agreed that the rank of "Sultan-i-Adil" is higher in the eyes of God than the rank of a "mujtahid". Further, we declare that the King of Islam, Amir of the faithful, shadow of God in the world, Abul Fath Jalaluddin Muhammad Akbar Badshah Ghazi—whose kingdom God perpetuate—is a most just, a most wise, and a most God-fearing king. Should therefore in future a religious question come up, regarding which the opinions of the mujtahids are at variance, and His Majesty in his penetrating understanding and clear wisdom be inclined to adopt, for the benefit of the nation, and as a political expedient, any of the conflicting opinions, which exist on that point, and issue a decree to that effect, we do hereby agree that such a decree shall be binding on us and on the whole nation.

'Further, we declare that should His Majesty think fit to issue a new order, we and the nation shall likewise be bound by it, provided always that such order be not only in accordance with some verse of the Quran, but also of real benefit to the nation. Further, that any opposition on the part of his subjects to such an order passed by His Majesty shall involve damnation in the world to come and loss of property and religious privileges in this.

'This document has been written with honest intentions for the glory of God and the propagation of Islam and is signed by us, the principal ulema and lawyers, in the month of Rajab of the year 987.'

Sheikh Mubarak had written the mahzarnama in his own hand and added below it along with his signature, 'I am most willingly signing it. For years I had been looking forward to it.'

When the Sadr-us-Sudur of the empire, Sheikh Abd-un-Nabi, and Makhdum-ul-Mulk Abdullah Sultanpuri resisted signing it, they were forcibly made to sit at a place where the courtiers took off their shoes. Nobody would greet them. Finally, by force or of their own will, all prominent ulema of the empire, including these two, affixed their seal onto this mahzarnama.

This mahzarnama caused such commotion in Fatehpur Sikri that Mullah Abdul Qadir Badayuni said:

'In this year low and mean people, who pretend to be learned, but were in reality fools, collected evidence, that His Majesty was the sahib-i-zaman, who would remove all differences of opinion among the seventy-two sects of Islam and the Hindus. Sharif Amuli brought proof from the writings of Mahmud of Basakhiwan that he had said that, in the year 990, a certain person would abolish lies... And Khwaja Maulana of Shiraz, the heretic of Jafrdan, came with a pamphlet by some of the Sharifs of Mecca, in which a tradition was quoted to the effect that the earth would exist for seven thousand years, and as that time was now over, the promised appearance of the Mahdi would immediately take place. The Maulana also brought a pamphlet written by himself on the subject. The Shias mentioned similar nonsense connected with Ali, and quoted the following rubai, which is said to have been composed by Nasir-i-Khusrau, or according to some by another poet—

'In 989, according to the decree of fate,
The stars from all sides shall meet together.
In the year of the Leo, the month of Leo, the day of Leo,
The Lion of God will stand forth from behind the veil.

'All this made the Emperor the more inclined to claim the dignity of a prophet...'

When Badshah Salamat learnt of these rumours, he said, 'Good God! How could it enter into the narrow thoughts of the ignorant that recent creatures belonging to a dependent existence and of feeble intellect should ascribe to themselves a share in divinity? And when the leaders of humanity have by thousands of miracles expounded the prophetic office, why should an opinion like this be believed? How could such a notion come into my mind? Why does such an evil thought bewilder the superficial and the worshippers of externals?'

But events one after another gave birth to more and more doubts in people's minds. One night the people of Sikri saw a charpoy being pulled up to the balcony, which was close to Badshah Salamat's sleeping chamber. Badshah Salamat had inscribed on the walls of the bedchamber in gold:

Undoubtedly the building has a high reputation,
May the Emperor enjoy it,
Just casting a glance at this beautiful place gives light,
So the master of this exalted place be forever happy,
The royal building is a source of envy to the sublime paradise,
Undoubtedly it is paradise itself.

From the jharokha—balcony—Badshah Salamat began conversation with the prominent Sufi, Sheikh Tajuddin. These were nightlong interactions. Mullah Badayuni said, 'Sheikh was one of those who weakened His Majesty's belief in our faith. He even said that the kafirs would go to hell but perhaps it is unlikely—nor can it ever be proved—that they would be there for ever.'

Badshah Salamat also got Mullah Muhammad Yezdi up to

the balcony of the palace at night. Mullah Badayuni saw this and quietly recorded, 'Mullah Muhammad Yezdi said inappropriate things about the first three Caliphs. He called the companions of the Prophet, their followers and next followers, and the saints of earlier times, infidels and adulterers, represented the Sunnis as despicable, and pronounced every sect except the Shias as erring and leading into error.'

Some people misled the Sunnis into believing that Badshah Salamat was becoming a Shia. Sheikh Abul Fazl replied to this, 'In His Majesty's sublime gatherings, proof of the Shiite and the Sunni sect was discussed and His Majesty selected what was preferable.'

In this atmosphere, Tansen observed from close quarters and recorded Dastur Mehrji Rana's arrival in Sikri—*'Eeyahu Parsi parhe so qabool'*—

What the Parsi says is true
O Lord, what the Parsi says is true
Like sandalwood on aloe
Like the shrukhar tree
Shah Mehryar with a long beard
There is light on your face
What the Parsi says is true.
So says Tansen,
Listen, O Shah Akbar
This is a flower from paradise
What the Parsi says is true.

Mullah Abdul Qadir Badayuni felt that Dastur Mehrji Rana had changed Badshah Salamat's way of thinking. He wrote in his book, 'Fire-worshippers also came from Navsari in Gujarat, proclaimed the religion of Zartusht as the true one, and declared reverence to fire to be superior to every other kind of worship. They also attracted the Emperor's regard... He ordered that the sacred fire should be made over to the charge of Abul Fazl... From early youth, in compliment to his wives, the daughters of the Rajas of Hind, he had within the female compartment continued to offer hom. On the new year of the twenty-fifth year after his accession he prostrated himself both before the sun, and before the fire in public, and in the evening the whole court had to rise up respectfully when the lamps and candles were lighted.'

Dastur Mehrji Rana's impact on Badshah Salamat is reflected in a khyal—

Mehrji Rana was a good soul,
He was a man of God,
Padshah Akbar wore the sadra,
Such is the spectacle of religion.

It is said that when Dastur Mehrji Rana reached Badshah Salamat's darbar, some Brahmins performed a miracle—

The jagatguru lifts the plate to the skies,
It looked like the sun, and there seemed two suns in the sky,
Seeing two suns, all were amazed.

People say that Dastur Mehrji Rana prayed and brought the plate down.

Badshah Salamat had been very kind to Dastur Mehrji Rana and his sons—

'Allahu Akbar

'Firman Jalaluddin Muhammad Akbar Badshah Ghazi.

'At this time, a royal order, signifying favour, has acquired the honour of publicity, that, whereas, about three hundred bigha of land measured by the Ilahi gaz, together with palm and date trees which are growing on that land, have been assigned in the environs of the town of Navsari, from the Sarkar of Surat, for purpose of livelihood of Parsi Kaikobad, son of Mahyar, from the assignment of the jagirdar, from the season of the kharif, so that from year to year, spending the income thereof, in maintaining his life, he may be engaged in praying for the increase of the wealth and good fortune of His Majesty. It is incumbent upon the present and future governors, tax-collectors, karoris and jagirdars of that district, that, according to what is written, and measuring the above mentioned land, and preparing a chak, they shall transfer it to the above mentioned person. And that trying to bestow care in the settlement and perpetuity of that land, shall make no change or modification. And that on account of land-tax and imposts on manufacturers and capitation taxes and the rest of the taxes, such as imposts and presents and fines and village assessments and marriage fees and darogha's fees and tax gatherer's fees and five per cent tax and two per cent tax and qanoongoi, and burdens for cultivation and gardening and zakat of duties on manufacturers and assessments, no molestations shall be given him every year, after the ascertainment of the grant and all civil taxes and all royal revenue. And excusing and absolving him of all charges, they should not harass him, and should not ask every year for renewed firmans and parvanchas in this matter. And when this firman comes with the royal signet of his Most Exalted Majesty, they should rely upon it.'

Miyan Tansen said:

Emperor Akbar is like a sun to the subjects,
That drives away darkness,
This sun drives away fear,
The source of fire, water, colour, poetry and indulgence,
May there be a sceptre above Shah Akbar as long as this eternal God lives.

Sheikh Abul Fazl said, 'Indeed every man acknowledges that we owe gratitude and reverence to our benefactor; and hence it is incumbent upon us, though our strength may fail, to show gratitude for the blessings we receive from the sun, the light of all lights, and to enumerate the benefits which he bestows. This is essentially the duty of kings, upon whom, according to the opinion of the wise, this sovereign of the heavens sheds an immediate light. And this is the very motive which actuates His Majesty to venerate fire and revere lamps. But why should I speak of the mysterious blessings of the sun, or of the transfer of his greater light to lamps? Should I not rather dwell on the perverseness of those weak-minded zealots, who, with much concern, talk of His Majesty's religion as of deification of the Sun, and the introduction of fire worship? But I shall dismiss them with a smile.'

Sheikh Abul Fazl's brother Sheikh Faizi went to the extent of saying:

In the morning the Emperor with a station as high as the sky
Cast a glance at the sun with a pure heart,
The sun opened the secrets of monotheism onto that blessed face,
So you say, this is my God, this is Akbar.

Words like these would agitate Mullah Abdul Qadir Badayuni—

'Birbar convinced His Majesty that all grows from the sun. The ripening of the grain, the growing of vegetables and fruits, the brightening in the life of the people and of the world is all because of the sun. And that is the reason people pray towards where the sun rises, not where its sets.'

The parapet of Fatehpur Sikri became a focus of attention for people hoping to gauge Badshah Salamat's views and the company he was keeping.

One night, people were surprised to see a Brahmin called Devi being pulled up to Badshah Salamat's bedchamber. Devi told him about Brahma, Mahadev, Vishnu, Krishna, and Ram. After this conversation, the idea of rebirth found a special place in the heart of Badshah Salamat.

The Brahmins even found a past-life connection with Jalaluddin Muhammad Akbar—

'A Brahmin of high calibre called Mukund was doing penance with his twenty disciples in Prayag. Learning that Babur, the mlechchha king, had destroyed the idols of gods, Mukund Brahmin was saddened and gave up his life by entering the fire. His twenty disciples followed him. Once Mukund Brahmin had partaken of a hair of a cow along with its milk. For this reason, he was reborn a mlechchha. A son was born to Humayun when he was in Kashmir, and a voice came from the sky, "Your son would have a lofty fortune. He is born of a boon—a var—obtained all of a sudden—akasmaat. So he would be called Akbar. He will not follow the ways of the mlechchhas. Shridhar, Shripati, Shambhu, Varenya, Madhuvrati, Vimal, Devvan, Som, Vardhan, Vartak, Ruchi, Mandhata, Mankari, Keshav, Madhav, Madhu, Devapi, Sompa, Sur and Madan are the twenty disciples of the Mukund Brahmin of the previous birth, who is born, as luck would have it, in your house in this form."

'A happy Humayun fed the hungry, and lovingly brought up his son. When the son attained the age of ten, Humayun came to Delhi and became the king after defeating Sheshshak—Sher Shah. Humayun ruled for a year and after him his son Akbar became the ruler.

'After the coronation, seven of his disciples from the past birth—

Keshav, Madhav, Madhu, Devapi, Sompa, Sur, and Madan—also took birth again and came to Akbar's court. Keshav, the disciple of Mukund Brahmin, took birth as Gansen—Tansen—in Akbar's time. Madhav of the previous lifetime was born as Vaijvak—Baiju Bawra—and became famous. Madhu of the previous birth was born as the singer Haridas who knew all the ragas. He was a famous Vaishnav, who followed the path of Madhvacharya. Devapi of the earlier lifetime became famous as Birbal in Akbar's time. He was a Brahmin of the western region and was blessed by the presiding deity of the voice, Saraswati. Sompa, born in the house of Gautam in the previous birth became Man Singh and became the general of "arya-bhup shiromani"—the biggest ruler—Akbar. Sur was born a Brahmin in the southern provinces. He was a pandit. His name was Bilvmangal. He became Akbar's friend. The Brahmin Madan of eastern provinces became famous as Chandal in Akbar's time. He was an expert in dance and drama based on the life of Krishna and the gopis.

'These seven became part of Akbar's court, and the thirteen others found their esteemed place elsewhere. Well versed in Puranas, Shridhar became famous as Tulsisharma. Learning from a woman, he became a solitude-loving Vaishnav poet in the tradition of Shri Ramanand, the disciple of Raghavanand. Shripati of the previous lifetime became the famous blind poet Surdas in Akbar's time. He followed the path of Madhvacharya. He wrote of the Krishna-lila. Shambhu of the previous lifetime was born as Haripriya in the family of Chandrabhatt in Akbar's time. He worshipped Vishnu and followed Ramanand. Varenya of the previous life became the famous saint Agradas in Akbar's time. He followed Ramanand. Madhuvrati of the previous birth, who was learned and well versed in religion, language and prosody, became famous as Kilak in Akbar's time and was a follower of the Ramanand sect and wrote Ram-lila. Vimal of the previous birth became famous as Divakar in Akbar's time. He became a follower of Ramanand and wrote of the pious life of bhagwati Sita. In the same manner, Devvan took birth as Keshav in Akbar's time. He became a follower of Vishnuswami. He wrote *Kavipriya* and reached his end. He attained heaven by writing *Ram-Jyotsna*. Som of the previous lifetime took birth as Vyasdas. He became a follower of Nimbaditya. He attained heaven after writing a book on raslila. Vardhan was reborn as Charandas and became famous as such. A follower of Raidas, he wrote a book called *Gyanmala*. Vartak was reborn as Ratnabhanu. He was a creator of the Jaimini language and a follower of the Ropan stream. Ruchi was reborn as Rochan. He followed the sect of Madhvacharya. He attained heaven after many lyrical lilas. Mandhata of the previous lifetime was born a Kayastha called Bhupati. He did an elegant translation of Bhagwat in Hindi, in line with the teachings of Madhvacharya. Mankar of the previous lifetime took a female form and became famous as Meera, the daughter of a king. She was a follower of Madhvacharya. Her writings would be auspicious for Kaliyuga.'

Now people began to hear of Badshah Salamat's close links with the region of Braj. His visit was described in a dhrupad—

Shah Chhatrapati Akbar visits the Braj region,
Kings of the seven islands, nine regions and ten directions tremble.
Cavalry, infantry, elephants, and brave warriors,
With bows, arrows, swords and spears.
Not one blot on the clothes of Humayun's son,
How formidable was the army of Jalaluddin Muhammad.

The region of Braj was not far from Fatehpur Sikri. It is said that Badshah Salamat, having listened to the poetry of Surdas, asked when he met him, 'Surdas ji, God has made me powerful and all the talented people sing my praise. Why don't you sing my praise too?'

Surdas sang the following words in reply: 'No space in my heart.'

Badshah Salamat thought, 'Why would he sing my praise? He would sing if he had the greed to seek something from me. He is a man of God.'

Finally, Surdas sang: 'Seeing God is like nectar for the thirst that the eyes have.'

Badshah Salamat asked him, 'Surdas ji, you can't see. How do you know what this thirst is that the eyes have? How come this metaphor?'

When Surdas kept quiet, Badshah Salamat said, 'His eyes are with God. He sees there and describes what they see.'

Badshah Salamat then thought, 'He should be given something but he has been initiated into Vaishnavism. He has no desire.'

People say that when Badshah Salamat heard that the Vaishnav poet Govindswami sang very well, he went out to listen to him in disguise.

Badshah Salamat was fond of travelling incognito among people. In the sixth regnal year, corresponding to about 1560–61 CE, a large group from Agra had camped outside the city on the way to the shrine of Salar Masud Ghazi in Bahraich. Badshah Salamat went to their gathering incognito but some petty criminal recognized him and the word began to spread. To convince people otherwise, Badshah Salamat rolled his eyes upwards. When people saw this they said, 'Such eyes and expressions can't be that of an emperor.'

As Govindswami sang the Raga Bhairav, Badshah Salamat was sure he would not be recognized. But suddenly, as he sat listening, these words escaped his lips, '*Wah, wah!*'

Recognizing him, Govindswami said, 'This raga has lost its value.'

At this Jalaluddin Muhammad Akbar said, 'I am the Emperor.'

Govindswami replied, 'If you are the Emperor, keep to it. But this raga has lost its value because you listened to it.'

Badshah Salamat then thought, 'I am the ruler of one country. For him, the grandeur of three worlds is meaningless. Why would he obey my command?'

It is said that Badshah Salamat heard an artiste sing the poetry of the Vaishnav poet Kumbhandas and said, 'Would there be anyone like him who sees God in this manner?'

The artiste replied, 'Saheb, he lives even now!'

An excited Badshah Salamat asked for Kumbhandas's whereabouts. The artiste replied, 'There is a village near Shrigovardhan called Jamunawat. He lives there.'

When Badshah Salamat's men reached the residence of Kumbhandas he was in Parasoli. Reaching Parasoli, these men said, 'Badshah Salamat has asked for you.'

Kumbhandas said to them, 'I am no servant to the Emperor. What do I have to do with him?'

Badshah Salamat's men said, 'How do we know what you have been called for? We are under orders from the Emperor to get Kumbhandas ji. Here is a palanquin and a horse. Please mount and come with us. We have to take you.'

Kumbhandas had no option. Wearing his shoes, he said, 'Brother! I have never mounted a conveyance. I will go on my own.'

When Kumbhandas reached Sikri on foot, Badshah Salamat said, 'Kumbhandas ji, come. Please be seated.'

Badshah Salamat's elegant tent had precious stones and frills. Even so Kumbhandas felt his home Braj was far better because Shrigovardhannath ji played there.

Badshah Salamat said, 'Kumbhandas ji, you have written much poetry in praise of Vishnu. That is why we have called you here. Sing for me some poetry in praise of Vishnu.'

Kumbhandas thought, 'The real patron of my voice is Shrigovardhandhar. But now that I cannot avoid it, I better sing something to ensure he does not ever ask for me. Let me say harsh words. If he minds, so be it.'

Kumbhandas remembered, 'One who has been adopted by Lord Krishna is always safe. He would come to no harm even if the whole world turns against him.'

Then he recited—

Devotees have no need of Sikri.
One walks one's shoes threadbare, God's name forgotten,
And salutes those whose face brings no joy.
O Kumbhandas, without Lord Krishna, these are false destinations.

They say Badshah Salamat felt unhappy when he heard this but said to himself, 'If he had any greed he would sing my praise. He is a true devotee of his Lord.'

Irritated with Badshah Salamat, Mullah Abdul Qadir Badayuni said, '... Hindu infidels, who are indispensable, and of whom half the army, and country, will soon consist and as whom there is not among the Mughals or Hindustani Muslims a tribe so powerful, he could not have enough. But to other people, whatever they might ask for, he gives nothing but kicks and blows...'

When it began to be murmured in Fatehpur Sikri that Badshah

Salamat had turned Hindu, Sheikh Abul Fazl was forced to respond, 'This rumour is spread because His Majesty, being of an open mind, would meet Hindu holy men, raise the rank of Hindus and be kind to them in the interests of the welfare of the country... There were three reasons these rumours spread by evil men gained currency. First, people following different religions gathered in the darbar, and because there was something good in every faith, everybody got some bit of praise. Secondly, because of sulh-i-kul, people of various kinds got spiritual and worldy success. Third, the crooked ways of evil people of the age.'

Rumours were still rife when Sheikh Abd-un-Nabi and Makhdum-ul-Mulk Abdullah Sultanpuri made it public that they had been forced to sign the mahzarnama. If this allegation was true, the mahzarnama itself would become invalid, rendering Badshah Salamat's claim to leadership of the world of religion infructuous. Severe punishment was meted out to the two. Badshah Salamat made them Mir-i-Haj—leaders of the Haj delegation. Gifts for the people of Mecca and alms for the poor were sent through them. They were instructed to stay there forever and keep an eye on the proper disbursement of money and keep their own behaviour good. The Sharif of Mecca was advised not to allow these two to return to Hindustan.

Badshah Salamat's ancestors had close ties to Mecca.

After winning Hindustan, Firdaus Makani Babur Badshah wrote:

'On Saturday the twenty-ninth of Rajab examination and distribution of the treasures began. To Humayun were given twenty lakh from the treasury, and, over and above this, a treasure house was bestowed on him just as it was, without ascertaining and writing down its contents. To some begs ten lakh were given, eight, seven or six to others. Suitable money-gifts were bestowed from the treasury on the whole army, to every tribe there was, Afghan, Hazara, Arab, Baluch, etc., to each according to position. Every trader and student, indeed every man who had come with the army, took ample portion and share of bounteous gifts and largesse. To those not with the army went a mass of treasures in gifts and largesse, as for instance, seventeen lakh to Kamran, fifteen lakh to Muhammad Zaman

Mirza, while to Askari, Hindal and indeed to the whole train of relations and young children went masses of gold, silver, textiles, jewels and slaves. Many gifts went to begs and soldiers on that side. Valuable gifts were sent for various relations in Samarqand, Khurasan, Kashghar and Iraq. Offerings were sent to holy men in Samarqand and Khurasan; so too to Mecca and Medina.'

Firdaus Makani Babur Badshah sent to Mecca a copy of the Quran that he had transcribed. He had copied this in a calligraphic style he had invented—khat-i-Baburi.

Jalaluddin Muhammad Akbar suddenly recalled that the guard at the gates of Ka'ba had stopped his mother Maryam Makani Hamida Banu Begum and asked, 'Any mahram with you? Is your husband with you?'

Maryam Makani Hamida Banu Begum pointed towards Mirza Sharfuddin and entered the Ka'ba.

When Badshah Salamat heard of it he was so enraged he wanted to kill Mirza Sharfuddin, who fled to escape the Emperor's wrath.

Maryam Makani Hamida Banu Begum's husband Jannat Ashiyani Humayun Badshah never went for Haj. And when Badshah Salamat expressed a desire, the courtiers said, 'There were other tasks for the great ones of the social order and their worship was of another character.'

It had become easier to perform Haj after the victory over Gujarat. That is why a caravan had begun to go for Haj and a Mir-i-Haj was appointed with the custody of money meant for distribution as alms during Haj. A few years after the victory over Gujarat, six hundred thousand rupees and twelve thousand robes were sent with the caravan. When Badshah Salamat was seeing off the Mir-i-Haj with money and goods, his body was draped in the ahram—the cloth hajis wear—and he was barefoot and bareheaded. Like Haj pilgrims, he had a haircut. He even walked some distance with the caravan. Around that time, he gave an order that anybody who so desires can perform Haj at government expense, but this practice was discontinued not long after.

Makhdum-ul-Mulk Abdullah Sultanpuri and Sadr-us-Sudur Sheikh Abd-un-Nabi never got along well. Both had tried harming each other. Abdullah Sultanpuri had alleged that Sheikh Abd-un-Nabi had sentenced two people to death for heresy on unjust grounds. He had said that namaz should not be performed behind Sheikh Abd-un-Nabi because he was not a dutiful son and had piles. In reply, Sheikh Abd-un-Nabi severely rebuked Abdullah Sultanpuri in full view of others. With such a history of mutual acrimony, the two were together in Mecca now.

Mecca was then passing through a golden period of its history. In 1517 CE, Turkey's Ottoman Sultan Selim had annexed Egypt. Mecca and Medina now came under Turkish supervision because they were under the sultan of Egypt.

While leaving Egypt, Sultan Selim told his governor, 'I hope to serve the Prophet well. I have no desire for anything from Egypt. I have conquered only the title "The Servant of the Holy Cities" and I have left in trust to His Excellency the Prophet all the revenues of Egypt. Bear witness that from now on you are the agent of the waqf of God. So serve it well.'

The Turkish Sultan accepted the Sharif's rule over Mecca and Medina and the Sharif accepted the suzerainty of the Sultan. The name of the Sultan was read in the Friday khutba in Mecca. Beginning from 1524 CE, Sharif Abu Numay II's sixty-year rule saw peace and prosperity in Mecca. The generosity of the Sultan and of the people of Turkey, and Sharif's excellent rule made Mecca a lively place. The Ka'ba was repaired and countless madrasas, and lodges for Haj pilgrims and the poor were built.

It raised alarm when it was learnt at the court of Constantinople that Badshah Salamat had called himself Sultan-ul-Islam and Amir-ul-Momineen because these were titles that the Sultan of Turkey held. On top of it, news spread that Jalaluddin Muhammad Akbar's prophetic prescience and revelation were being talked about in Hindustan. Badshah Salamat was himself aware that his religious views were causing disquiet in Mecca and that Sheikh Abd-un-Nabi had been fanning it.

After sending money to Mecca, Sheikh Abul Fazl prepared the letter that was sent by Badshah Salamat to Sharif Abu Numay II—

'All praise to God who is almighty and salutations to the Prophet—the chosen leader and to the other blessed creatures of God, especially the group of the noble believers.

'We keenly desire welfare and prosperity of our subjects who have been entrusted to us by God. May they be prosperous and happy and fulfil their duties of worship and obedience. We hope that human beings, especially the poor and the helpless among them, remain protected from tyranny. Through divine grace the responsibility of distributing His munificence to people has been entrusted to us. Similarly, those who reside in that auspicious abode, especially the group of people that is associated with that holy place, which is the landing place for the descent of the army of angels, should also be bestowed imperial favours. Therefore, each year an esteemed imperial servant is to be appointed a Mir-i-Haj. He will carry gifts and stipends in cash and kind, which shall be distributed according to the status of various groups. This could not be sent in Hijri 989 due to rebellion of some of the faithless servants. We departed to Punjab and then to Kabul with a large army and elephants to eliminate the rebels and protect the poor from seditious elements. All the wicked rebels were killed. We are grateful to God for our success.

'Being forgiving and generous, we pardoned Mirza Hakim and reinstated him at Kabul provided he revives sharia and seeks to improve the lot of the people of God. The evilness of the rebels had prevented the charities from being sent. We hope that the gifts would henceforth be sent regularly and there would be no occasion of a default.'

Badshah Salamat had been hearing of Mirza Hakim's rebellious activities but he would say, 'He reminds us of Jannat Ashiyani. One can get a son but how would one get a brother?'

However, this time around, Badshah Salamat decided to take direct charge of the campaign. Mirza Hakim had entered Punjab but learning of Badshah Salamat's arrival, he rushed back towards Kabul. He hurriedly crossed the rivers Ravi and Chenab. But while crossing Jhelum from somewhere near Bhera, many of his people drowned. Badshah Salamat ordered that they should not be pursued, lest Mirza Hakim's boat sinks.

Badshah Salamat said, 'If that unfortunate one does not understand matters, and does not acquire enlightenment, why shall we, who have such glory of wisdom, erase his existence. He may, in time, gain sense and the highway of vision may be manifested to him. Moreover, in the balance of application, brother is weightier than a son.'

Badshah Salamat reached the banks of the river Indus with a huge army. The vanguard unit cleared the path. After them came the drum-beaters on elephants, making a sound that shook the earth. Badshah Salamat followed and a short distance after him came his attendants, the cavalry and then the elephants. Some people of the entourage would measure the travel distance so that it could be of use later. When Badshah Salamat alighted, he was received by a row of elephants on one side and horsemen on the other.

From here Badshah Salamat sent a message to Mirza Hakim with the intention of counselling him—

'Whenever a majestic prince who has abundance of power withholds his hand from chastisement and addresses himself to counselling, and the utterance of truth, and has no other design than to show goodwill and graciousness, those who are fortunate and of happy star, but who have made a slip, come to his assembly with ashamed faces and hearts receptive of truth, and amend their conduct by submission and supplication. The wicked and the evil-fated ones remain in their dark and dangerous position, and make use of subterfuges and tricks, and gloss over their evil deeds. Now let that brother, who holds the position of a son, receive knowledge, and gather eternal bliss. Princes of illustrious houses, and the great men of every land receive radiance from our benevolence. Why should he who is so connected to us sit in the defile of unrecognition? How long shall he do so? How long will he, in company with base people, move about in the hollow of loss? It behoves him not to give ear to the buzzings of fly-like men but to come and pay homage at our threshold so that our love for him may be impressed on all, far or near, and that he may spend the few days of life in a proper manner, and that his worldly rank and future position may be exalted, and that he may end his days with a good name. The wretched and tiny ant is not withheld by feebleness from entering on the desert of purpose; perchance it may after the manner of the fortunate arrive at the pinnacle of desire! Why should a son of a man possessed of such enlightenment fall into the fool's sleep of carelessness and not make even half a step in the wide plain of search?

'If you desire to be successful, why test what has already been tested? How long will you keep yourself on the edge of the sword? If from shame and evil behaviour you do not come to court, and out of fear do not apply your heart to service, the tale of our daily increasing graciousness from the beginning of the reign till now—which is the vernal season of fortune—and of our bounty and our forgiveness of great criminals, is patent to all, far and near!'

There was no appropriate response to Badshah Salamat's initiative. Camping by the Indus, he ordered Prince Murad to cross the river with a large army. Badshah Salamat had hoped that Mirza Hakim would see reason when he hears of the movement of this force. But there was also an apprehension that he might get alarmed and seek external help. That is why, having dispatched Prince Murad, Badshah Salamat weighed the situation from this side of the river.

After waiting for some more time for an appropriate response, he crossed the river and advanced. Soon after Badshah Salamat's movement, two messages were received from Mirza Hakim in which he expressed repentance. Badshah Salamat asked Sheikh Abul Fazl to ascertain the opinion of twenty mansabdars and inform him. When Sheikh Abul Fazl saw that all of them were in favour of pardoning Mirza Hakim and returning, he told them, 'It is proper to finish the work which is nearly completed, and then to punish or forgive.'

Sheikh Abul Fazl's statement angered the mansabdars. One of them said, 'Though I know that the degree of your knowledge is being revealed, and that truth-speaking is being displayed, yet in the troubled state of society it is indispensable that one should act along with one's contemporaries and especially with those who are powerful in the state.'

Sheikh Abul Fazl replied, 'It has been reckoned as one of the worst things to conceal what is fitting for the time, in a meeting for uttering confidences, and in the pure place of counsel, and to speak contrary to one's real sentiments. Such a course is destructive of realm and religion. Why should I for the sake of security in an outward world, which is soon to be destroyed, knowingly choose what is deadly injurious spiritually? Seeing I have not spoken foolishly for the sake of applause I am hopeful that no dust will fall upon my skirt.'

Finally, it was decided that every mansabdar would tell his opinion to Badshah Salamat and, unless he asks, Sheikh Abul Fazl's views should not be disclosed. But Badshah Salamat did ask about Abul Fazl's views after hearing the opinion of the mansabdars.

Being unwell Abul Fazl was absent that day. In his absence the mansabdars said, 'He too agrees with this opinion.'

An angry Badshah Salamat said, 'Apparently the officers are afraid of the cold of Afghanistan. I will leave them all behind and go there with my disciples.'

The next day when Abul Fazl appeared in the darbar after his recovery, Badshah Salamat asked, 'Why did you change your opinion?'

An alarmed Abul Fazl asked, 'Was what they allege me to have said spoken to one person's ear, or was it uttered in that meeting?'

When one after another, the mansabdars began telling Badshah Salamat that the matter was uttered in the meeting, Abul Fazl was shaken. It was luck that one mansabdar unexpectedly said, 'In that meeting Sheikh Abul Fazl was speaking against this set of men. Perhaps the conversations they rely upon may have taken place elsewhere.'

After this, Badshah Salamat set aside the views of the mansabdars and moved towards Kabul. But a fierce battle took place near Kabul, before he could reach there, between the forces of Prince Murad and Mirza Hakim, and the latter fled.

Badshah Salamat entered the city of Kabul, where a generation ago he had become a pawn in the battle between two stepbrothers, and Kamran Mirza had placed him at the parapet of the fort to face the cannons of Jannat Ashiyani Humayun Badshah.

Even after winning Kabul, Badshah Salamat refused to take the life of his stepbrother Mirza Hakim. He said, 'Why should the sons of men employ their God-given strength in accomplishing the desires of the juggling sensual soul? And why should I for the sake of my own repose endeavour to take the life of a brother? Or ungratefully allow a follower to be slain? If Mirza is going the wrong road, thinking he is right, he is doing a religious act, otherwise he is suffering from the malady of ignorance. We ought not to trouble those who are suffering pains in the desert of unwisdom.'

Although Mirza Hakim agreed to send his son but not to be present himself, Badshah Salamat pardoned him and returned after restoring the territory to him.

When the rebels of Bengal and Bihar declared Badshah Salamat's stepbrother Mirza Hakim the emperor, the qazi of Jaunpur, Mullah

Muhammad Yezdi declared that it was a religious duty—farz—to rebel against Badshah Salamat. Qazi Yaqub of Bengal said that this rebellion was the scourge of God because Badshah Salamat had taken away the land grants of the ulema.

Mullah Muhammad Yezdi was called to Agra on some pretext. When he was eighteen kos from Agra, Badshah Salamat's orders were received that Mullah Muhammad Yezdi should be separated from his soldiers and sent to Gwalior by the river route. Mullah Muhammad Yezdi and his soldiers were sent off to Gwalior in separate boats. When the boat reached deep waters, Mullah Muhammad Yezdi was killed by drowning.

Sitting in Mecca, Sheikh Abd-un-Nabi and Mullah Abdullah Sultanpuri had learnt of the rebellion of the mansabdars in the east and that of Mirza Hakim in the west but they left for Gujarat before they could know that the rebellion had been crushed. Badshah Salamat was unaware of the designs of these two. From his side he had ordered Sheikh Abd-un-Nabi and Abdullah Sultanpuri to discharge their responsibilities in Mecca and not to return home. He had thus made a special mention of this in the firman he sent to Mecca—

'Sheikh Abd-un-Nabi, Makhdum-ul-Mulk Abdullah Sultanpuri and Hakim-ul-Mulk have been dispatched. Each of them is carrying an amount mentioned in the register for the sharifs and the qazis. Some funds are not to be allocated and are to be kept in secret. For our satisfaction an acknowledgment should be stamped with the seal of the Sayyids and the qazis.

'Nothing against the sharia has been said on our behalf. It is learnt that some elements have out of jealousy and animosity levelled certain allegations against Muinuddin Hashmi Shirazi. We do not know of anything the Sheikh has done that is against the sharia. From the time of his joining the imperial service till now, we have only heard of him being on the right path, following the sharia. The Sheikh should be protected from wicked persons. It is surprising that falsehood spread by mischievous elements is blindly believed by men of inferior judgment and torture is inflicted as a consequence. Such wicked people should be punished and exiled from that holy abode of Mecca and never again be allowed to come back.

'Pray for us in the holy place...'

By the time Sheikh Abd-un-Nabi and Makhdum-ul-Mulk Abdullah Sultanpuri arrived, Badshah Salamat received a troubling piece of news from Mecca.

The twenty-seventh day of the Zil Hijj month of the year 804 of the Hijri calendar, corresponding to the twenty-eighth day of July of 1402 CE, was a very significant day in the history of Badshah Salamat's family. On this day, Amir Timur had taken Sultan Bayazid by surprise by his sudden arrival at Ankara. After a crushing defeat, Sultan Bayazid was put in a cage like an animal and taken to the presence of Amir Timur. This had been widely talked about the world over. That is the reason Jalaluddin Muhammad Akbar Badshah Ghazi, son of Humayun Badshah son of Babur Badshah son of Umar Sheikh Mirza son of Sultan Abu Sayeed son of Sultan Muhammad Mirza son of Miran Shah son of Amir Timur Sahib-i-Qiran, could not tolerate a slight from the Ottoman Sultan of Turkey.

Badshah Salamat was startled by the firman Sultan Murad III of Turkey sent to the Sharif of Mecca—

'The Emperor's relatives and other Hindustanis should return to their country. The authorities of Hejaz should not permit any activity contrary to the sharia near the Ka'ba. Do not allow the alms sent by the Emperor to be distributed among the people.'

It was clear that doubts were being raised about the faith of Badshah Salamat, and it was deemed improper to accept alms sent by him. Badshah Salamat did not send alms for the people of Mecca ever again and completely severed his links with them.

Now when Sheikh Abd-un-Nabi and Makhdum-ul-Mulk Abdullah Sultanpuri returned to India, they faced the full brunt of Badshah Salamat's anger.

Sheikh Abd-un-Nabi stood as a prisoner in the presence of an emperor who was more powerful and stable than ever before. Mullah Abdul Qadir Badayuni was watching Badshah Salamat's mood—

'Amongst the many wrong and anti-sharia measures he implemented, one was the prohibition to eat beef. The origin of this embargo was that from his tender years the Emperor had often been in company of orthodox Hindus, and thence a reverence for the cow became firmly fixed in his mind, which in their view is the cause of stability of the world. Moreover, there were a whole host of the daughters of eminent Hindu rajas in his harem, and they had influenced his mind against the eating of beef and garlic and onion, and association with people with beards—and such things he then avoided and still does avoid. And he introduced bad practices of Hindus into his assemblies, and still retains them. And in order to gain their love and goodwill and that of their castes, he abstained entirely from everything which was a natural abhorrence to these people. He looked on it as a mark of special devotion to himself if men shaved off their beards—so that this became common practice. And ulema who shaved their beard began to present arguments in favour of it.'

Badshah Salamat would say, 'Divine grace is shed upon all alike, but some from unpreparedness in due season and others from incapacity are unable to profit thereby; the handiwork of the potter evidences this truth.

'Formerly I persecuted men into conformity and my faith deemed it Islam. As I grew in knowledge, I was overwhelmed with shame. Not being a Muslim myself, it was excessive to force others to become thus. What constancy is to be expected from proselytes on compulsion?

'It is my duty to have good understanding with all men. If they walk in the way of God's will, interference with them would be in itself reprehensible; and if otherwise, they are under the malady of ignorance and deserve my compassion.'

When in Badshah Salamat's nocturnal gatherings, an issue of religion arose among the nobles, such was the mood that people would say, 'You had better ask the mullahs about it, as we only settle things which appeal to man's reason.'

Shortly after returning from Bhera in his twenty-third regnal year, in the October month of 1578 CE, Badshah Salamat had opened the doors of the Ibadat Khana to all faiths and Fatehpur Sikri was tense. Simmering with tension. On top of it, the entry of three people into the Ibadat Khana set it ablaze.

3

Badshah Salamat very well remembered the fire that had been lit in his presence. As it leapt, it could be seen dancing on the faces of the ulema and the priests who had come from Goa. Badshah Salamat had waited for the ulema of the court and the priests from Goa to enter the fire to prove whose faith and Book are the most truthful.

On the twenty-seventh day of September, 1540 CE—a short while before the birth of Badshah Salamat—the Society of Jesus was formed with the approval of Pope Paul III, with the goal of helping souls progress in Christian life and doctrine and the propagation of the faith in service of the Lord and pope.

In the twenty-fourth regnal year, in the month of February of 1580 CE, the priests of this very Society of Jesus, Rudolf Acquaviva, Francis Henriques and, after some time, Antonio Monserrate reached the court of Badshah Salamat at Fatehpur Sikri.

Badshah Salamat met the Portuguese from Goa the first time during the siege of Surat. Sporadic interactions began with the Christians soon after. One of those he met was Father Gil Eanes Pereira, who could not answer all of Badshah Salamat's queries but at his advice a message was sent to Goa. This letter was carried by Badshah Salamat's envoy Abdullah and the interpreter Dominic Pires—

'Jalaluddin Muhammad Akbar

'King by God appointed.

'Know O Chief Fathers of the Order of St Paul

'That we are very well disposed unto you.

'We are sending unto you Abdullah our envoy and Dominic Pires that they may communicate to you our desire that two learned priests should be sent unto us. They should bring with them the principal books of the law and the Gospel, in order that we may learn the law and its full meaning and perfect truths in every respect. It is our earnest request that the learned priests come as soon as our ambassadors reach there. Let the priests understand that we shall receive them with all possible kindness and honour. Their arrival shall be a great delight to us. When we have learnt what we long to know about the law and its perfection and the salvation it offers, they shall be allowed to return as soon as they like. They shall be sent back with honours and gifts. Let them have no fear in coming. For we take them under our own protection and guarantee.'

Shortly after getting Badshah Salamat's message, Father Rudolf Acquaviva and Father Francis Henriques reached Daman from Goa by the sea route, where Father Monserrate joined them. Then the three travelled overland through Surat, Mandu, Ujjain, Sarangpur, Sironj, Narwar, Gwalior, Dholpur and reached Fatehpur Sikri. They first sighted the lake on the banks of which Firdaus Makani Babur Badshah had once pitched his tent. The city of Fatehpur Sikri now stood by the side of this lake. Reaching Sikri, they were struck by Hiran Minar and then the huge gateway which had stone elephants on its sides. This was the gateway through which Badshah Salamat and his visitors passed.

Father Monserrate noted, 'The magnificent palaces are built from the foundation to cornice of hewn stone, and are decorated both with painting and carving. Unlike the palaces built by other Indian kings, they are lofty, for an Indian palace is generally as low and humble as an idol-temple. Their total circuit is so large that it easily embraces four great royal dwellings, of which the King's own palace is the largest and the finest. The second palace belongs to the queens, and the third to the royal princes, whilst the fourth is used as a storehouse and magazine. The roofs of these palaces are not tiled, but are dome-shaped, being protected from the weather on the outside by solid plaster covering the stone slabs. This forms a roof absolutely impervious to moisture.'

Father Francis Henriques was born in 1538 CE in Persia and had converted to Christianity from Islam. He was forty-two when he reached Badshah Salamat's court. Father Antonio Monserrate was born in Spain and was elder to Francis Henriques by two years. During the epidemic of 1569 CE in Lisbon, he served a large number of patients. Younger to both these priests was Father Rudolf Acquaviva, who was born in 1550 CE and was just thirty. He belonged to a high-ranking family of Naples. He was made the leader of this delegation.

Daulat Khana-i-Aam, where Badshah Salamat held his court, was reached after passing through the gate which had elephants on either side on the hills of Sikri. The building comprising one hundred and fourteen bays, had in the centre of its western side a raised pavilion. Badshah Salamat sat on his throne in this pavilion when he held court. The courtiers and petitioners standing below faced the direction of namaz.

From the height of his seat in Daulat Khana-i-Aam, Badshah Salamat observed the priests in black robe and black cap. Among the courtiers below stood an attendant with a saiban in his hands so long that it reached up to Badshah Salamat's head even from below. Badshah Salamat was seated on the flowery carpet, while the courtiers stood with their feet bare and hands respectfully folded.

This was a critical time in Badshah Salamat's life. The mansabdars in the east and Mirza Hakim in the west were in rebellion. A fatwa had been issued against him from Jaunpur. On top of it, the Portuguese had become a headache for the Haj pilgrims and traders of his kingdom. Ships going towards and coming from Jeddah had to take the permission of the Portuguese. About seven years ago an agreement had been reached with the Portuguese that the hajis would get free permit of passage, and no custom duty would be levied on the goods that would be brought back on their ships. But about two and a half years ago, the Portuguese confiscated one royal and five other ships that had returned from Jeddah. Badshah Salamat knew that Hindustan was under his control just as the Portuguese held sway over the seas.

The priests standing below in the court looked up to the Emperor, whose conversion was the aim of their visit. Jalaluddin Muhammad Akbar was one of the most powerful emperors of the world and a threat to Portuguese power. His victory over Gujarat had made them neighbours and at this moment both wanted to assess the other.

The Christian priests presented a map of the world to Badshah Salamat, which had been sent by the Archbishop of Goa for him. In the court, Badshah Salamat neither displayed any indifference, nor showed any warmth, but after the darbar ended he took them towards the Daulat Khana-i-Khas. When it began to rain suddenly, he wore the Portuguese cloak and cap and also made the princes don the same apparel to please the priests.

A few days after this, the priests presented the Bible in four languages, in seven volumes, to Badshah Salamat, who took each of the volumes in his hands and kissed it and placed it on his head with reverence. He then ordered that the Bible be kept in his own room.

For the people of Fatehpur Sikri, these priests in black robes appeared strange. People would often come up to them and yell—

'Black robed!'

'Kafir!'

'What a spectacle!'

The priests were first put up at a sarai, which was crowded and did not agree with them. They were then given a place towards the west of Diwan Khana-i-Aam, which was used to produce and store perfumes. This khushbu khana was cleared for them so that they be near Badshah Salamat and they could meet without too many knowing of it.

Jalaluddin Muhammad Akbar with his three princes—Salim, Murad and Daniyal—came to the priests' place of residence. Sheikh Abul Fazl and many others accompanied them. Badshah Salamat took off his shoes outside the place. Seeing this, the others followed suit. Badshah Salamat instructed the three princes to be respectful in the church. The picture of Virgin Mary brought from Rome mesmerized Badshah Salamat and others with him. The princes were so thrilled with the picture of baby Jesus in the arms of Virgin Mary that it seemed they would start playing with him.

After the Christian priests reached Fatehpur Sikri, Badshah Salamat bestowed a great honour on them one day.

The tablecloth had been spread and Badshah Salamat sat down for his meal. He usually ate only once in twenty-four hours. There was no fixed time for his meal but such were the arrangements that whenever he was hungry about a hundred dishes could be served within an hour. Neither did Badshah Salamat ever ask what had been cooked, nor did he ever completely satisfy his hunger.

Badshah Salamat had heard the story about a God-seeking man, who had a problem of overeating. When he sought advice, he was given a bowl made of dried pumpkin and told to have his meals in it, and also to stroke the rim of the bowl each time and apply what rubbed off on his hand as tilak. He was also taught a prayer. Very soon he was cured, the bowl getting smaller with every rub.

Like every day, food was prepared under the supervision of the Mir Bakawal. Rainwater and the waters of Yamuna and Chenab were used for cooking food. A little bit of water of the holy Ganga was also added. Badshah Salamat would always drink water from the Ganga. Trusted people would carefully draw water from the river and send it in sealed vessels. The space where food was cooked was cordoned off by an awning so that it was protected from the eyes of onlookers. The cooks tucked up their sleeves, and the hems of their garments, and held their hands before their noses and mouths when the food was taken out. In accordance with the routine, food was placed in utensils of gold, silver, copper and china after the cook, the Bakawal and the Mir Bakawal had tasted it. The utensils of gold and silver were tied up in red cloth and those of copper and china in white. The Mir Bakawal would put his seal on each dish and write on it the contents of the vessel. A list of all vessels and dishes was drawn up on a piece of paper and sent inside. Breads, curd, pickles, fresh ginger, lemon and green vegetables were also sent in a similar manner. With armed men preceding and following, the Bakawals, the cooks and servants carried the food inside. Before being laid for Badshah Salamat, the food was again tasted. The share of the dervishes was put aside before Badshah Salamat had his meal.

One day, while having his food, it suddenly occurred to Badshah Salamat, 'Probably the eyes of some hungry one had fallen upon the food. How, therefore, could we eat while the hungry were debarred from it?' Badshah Salamat then ordered that the hungry be fed with some of the food prepared for himself, and that he should be served afterwards.

That day, out of the food laid out for him, Badshah Salamat sent some for the Christian priests. He had it sent many times subsequently. It was so much food that the priests could eat it and distribute it as well. Badshah Salamat took special care of the priests and also began sending them food cooked in Portuguese style from his own kitchen.

As soon as the priests reached Fatehpur, Badshah Salamat made them part of the Ibadat Khana debates, which created a storm. After listening to these deliberations in the Ibadat Khana, Badshah Salamat said,

'We perceive that there are varying customs and beliefs

of varying religious paths. For the teachings of the Hindus, the Muslims, the Parsis, the Jews and the Christians are all different. But the followers of each religion regard the institutions of their own religion as better than those of any other. Not only so, but they strive to convert the rest to their own way of belief. If these refuse to be converted, they not only despise them, but also regard them for this very reason as their enemies. And this causes me to feel many serious doubts. Wherefore I desire that on appointed days the books of all the religious laws be brought forward, and that the doctors meet together and hold discussions, so that I may hear them, and that each one may determine which is the truest and the mightiest religion.'

Not long after their arrival at Fatehpur Sikri, the priests got into a dispute with the ulema on which was the true scripture.

The priest said, 'The Gospel could be proved and confirmed with the authoritative testimony of other sacred scriptures, whereas the Quran could not be proved and had not been testified to by anyone.'

The ulema were so displeased at this that Badshah Salamat took the priests aside after the debate ended and said, 'We are pleased with you and find your religion to be good, but since our people are bad it would be advisable for you to speak to and deal with them discreetly.'

The priests replied, 'As far as the mullahs are concerned, we would conduct ourselves cautiously with them, not because we are afraid, but only to fulfil the command of Your Highness.'

One day Badshah Salamat said, 'We wish to have Christians and churches in our land in the same manner as the Turks have. None could object to it, since Hindus also have their own temples and rituals.'

This pleased the priests. There was no opportunity to talk further on it that day. So after two to three days they had a private audience with Badshah Salamat, where they said, 'Your Highness sent a firman to our Father Provincial asking for Fathers who might explain to you God's law. We arrived here with such great happiness because God had brought us before a very noble and learned king who is so keen to learn about His holy law that we cannot thank him enough. We were overjoyed when Your Highness told us that your greatest wish was to find out which was the true religion and that you would submit to it if we could convince you about it. We thus consider it our duty to spare no effort to find the ways and means of achieving what we were called for by Your Highness, in order that everything turns out well, not only for the benefit of the souls, but also for Your Highness' life and status; and that this be without any disturbances and rebellions which usually happen when matters are not entrusted to God's care and are managed indiscreetly. That is why on the days when we are not here, we pray and entrust Your Highness and ourselves to the Lord's keeping, so that he may enlighten us.'

Although Father Francis Henriques was born in Persia he had almost forgotten the language of that land. Now after reaching Fatehpur Sikri, he had again begun to speak Persian. Father Rudolf Acquaviva was fast learning Persian from Sheikh Abul Fazl. Very soon people were to marvel at his Persian, in spite of his Portuguese accent, and wondered how a foreigner could speak it so well.

Father Henriques was telling Badshah Salamat, '... And having been reminded by God of the two parables in the Gospel of Christ, about the King going out to wage war and about man wanting to build, which Your Highness is already aware of, it should be settled between us and Your Highness how, in the event, as Your Highness has said, of your being convinced of God's law and wishing to submit to it, you will retain the throne and how, with the zeal to spread the faith, you will win over others. Unless Your Highness is fully involved in this without fear of consequences, and finding ways to overcome the consequences, then even though you may be convinced in your mind, your enthusiasm will cool down and you will cease wanting to be instructed in the law. If Your Highness desires we shall try to find the means to resolve the problems, but it will take time. Until then Your Highness must progressively distance himself from some of the practices which are repugnant to the Christian faith. If Your Highness takes up these means, then one can look forward to as many Fathers coming here as Your Majesty may wish but if there is no progress, asking for them would be pointless. For these reasons we felt that we should first settle this issue before proceeding further. However, we are subject to the will of Your Highness and are at your service.'

Silence descended when Father Henriques stopped speaking. There was no witness other than the priests to what Badshah Salamat said when he broke the silence. In a letter written to Father Rui Vicente in Goa, these priests wrote of this confidential conversation.

Father Provincial Rui Vicente was the Jesuit head in Goa. He had been posted here from Rome by the head of the Society of Jesus. Father Rui Vicente had chosen the three priests for this mission after considerable discussion and prayer. The priests would write to inform him of the progress they were making in converting Badshah Salamat to Christianity.

In a letter dated 13 July 1580 CE, the priests reported, 'His Highness replied that it is in the hands of God Almighty to provide the necessary means. He said that he does not have any worldly desire now. Wife, children and kingdom does not matter to him. If there is no other option, he would pretend that he is leaving for Mecca and then would go to Goa and become a Christian.'

One day Badshah Salamat came to the priests' oratory, took off his turban before the picture of Christ and of the Virgin Mary and prayed in the manner of Christians, Muslims and Hindus. Badshah Salamat said, 'God should be adored with every form of adoration.'

Then he sat on the ground with the priests and said, 'We well understand that the miracles of Christ are much greater than those of a mere man. Nonetheless, we have great doubt as to how God could have a son. While all the rest of your law satisfies us, if we could understand this we would become a Christian.'

The priests would at times become hopeful of Badshah Salamat's conversion while losing hope at other times. The reason for this was Badshah Salamat himself. He would sometimes express his inclination towards Christianity and would be silent for long spells on other occasions.

Wearying of this, the priests finally sought a private audience with Badshah Salamat.

As soon as they met, Badshah Salamat asked, 'Why are you not instructing us?'

The priests replied, 'Your Highness should not think that we have ceased explaining the matters relating to the faith because we are not willing to do so. We have done so because we do not observe in Your Highness the required preparation, that is, to withdraw from sin, to cohabit with the first wife only, and to listen with determination to things of God. There is far greater need for Your Highness to find the leisure to learn about things of God. We are ready to be here day and night if Your Highness can find time and is keen to listen without interrupting us. Your interruption is disrespect of God's law. If we still teach we shall thereby invite both on Your Highness and on ourselves the curse: "*Maledictus homo qui opus Dei facit negligenter*"—cursed be the man who does the work of the Lord carelessly.'

On the eighteenth of July 1580 CE, Rudolf Acquaviva wrote in a letter to Superior General of the Society of Jesus, Father Everard Mercurian, 'We are in great doubt about the conversion of this king. First, because he doubts everything and so it is not enough to prove to him the mysteries of the faith with scriptures; he desires to understand them with his reason.'

Two days later, in a letter to Father Rui Vicente, the Provincial—seniormost priest of the Society of Jesus in Goa—Father Rudolf Acquaviva expressed his disappointment more openly—

'In Father Monserrate's opinion and mine the King has a vocation from God, but weak, according to his capacity. We think so because he is neither happy with his religion nor with his mullahs, and feels rather that his religion is unsound. We have also perceived this from his searching inquiries about the various religions, whose only purpose seems to be to find out which is the true one. Secondly, the King is inclined more towards our religion than towards any other because it strikes him as good but he has serious doubts about the basic tenets of our faith, namely the Trinity, incarnation and passion and death of the Lord. To understand these tenets he has to overcome considerable obstacles. The first is that he does not pay adequate attention to the word of God. Second, he does not believe the sacred book of scripture and, even if he believes, he doubts the genuineness of the ones we have and hence he wants to understand the mysteries of faith and to attain that inaccessible light of God through his own wisdom. The third obstacle is that he is greatly occupied with his people, granting them audiences, and in watching the deer, pigeons, elephants and camels that are brought to him daily for inspection. Part of his time he spends with the numerous women he keeps in his house, so that he has no time available to care for what is of consequence to him; "*sed venit diabulus et rapit verbum de corde eius, quia semen cecidit secus viam*" [but the devil comes and takes away the word from his heart, because the seed fell by the wayside]. The fourth obstacle is that the King has every sort of recreation one can imagine, so that "*cum exortum fuerit verbum, simul exortae spinae suffocant illud*" [when the word has grown, the thorns that have grown at the same time choke it]. The fifth obstacle is the opposition of his own people. Believe me, Your Reverence, this is a great obstacle. On one side, he has his mother, wives, and friends to importune him, and on the other are those who wish him ill, like those of Bengal who frighten him with their uprising, so that "*in tempore tentationis*" [in time of temptation] as he now is, he is going back, "*et natum aruit quia non habet humorem*" [and what was born dried up, because it lacks humidity]. The sixth obstacle is that he has some defects both native and acquired. Native such as curiosity and inconsistency, acquired such as of drink and desire of personal glory, of which he is extremely fond.'

One day Badshah Salamat inquired, 'We wish Pahadi to learn to read and speak Portuguese. Is tomorrow a good day to begin?'

The priests said, 'Tomorrow is our Sunday.'

When a Hindu courtier of Badshah Salamat also said that it was a good day, Prince Murad's teaching began the next day. Badshah Salamat fondly called his second son Pahadi because he was born on the hills of Sikri.

Badshah Salamat asked, 'We teach "alif", "be", "te", "ce" first. How do you begin?'

The priests said, 'We start with A-B-C.'

Badshah Salamat said, 'When we wish to begin something, it is our custom to pray and you should also pray in your manner.'

Father Monserrate writes, 'He turned towards his captains and asked them to pray, and all did. Some prayed standing, some sitting. The palms of their hands were turned towards heaven, like someone who wishes to catch something that would fall from above. They then passed the palms over their beard.'

Badshah Salamat decided that instead of '*Bismillah al Rehman al Rahim*' at the head of the sheet on which Portuguese letters were written for Murad, the priest should write, '*Ai naam-i-tu Jesus-o-Kiristo*'—in the name of Jesus Christ.

Murad would begin his lessons by taking the name of Jesus Christ and Virgin Mary, and making the sign of the cross by touching his forehead, face and breast.

Jalaluddin Muhammad Akbar was strict with his children. He loved them, but would issue brusque orders when he wanted something done. He would even punish them with harsh words and blows. And this is the authority he gave to Father Monserrate, who was the prince's tutor. To allay Murad's fears, the priest told him, 'It is not the custom of the Portuguese to allow a prince to be beaten by anyone except their own parents and, in infancy, their nurses; and in addition to this, it is not fitting that a stranger should chastise the son of so great a ruler. The King in his great wisdom has not overlooked the fact that we would not avail of this privilege.'

When the prince saw that the priest did not punish him like other tutors, he became very close to him. Badshah Salamat would have the prince recite before him every day whatever he had learnt. In three months Prince Murad had learnt to read and write what would take other children a year. Father Monserrate remained Murad's tutor as long as he stayed in Fatehpur Sikri. This responsibility was taken up by Father Rudolf Acquaviva after his departure.

One Saturday, Father Rudolf presented Badshah Salamat a portion of the Gospel in Persian which contained the birth of Jesus Christ. Badshah Salamat listened to it very attentively, when Abul Fazl read it out, and asked many questions. After the paper had been fully read, the ulema questioned the Christian scriptures.

From his side, Sheikh Abul Fazl explained to the gathering how Jesus Christ is believed to be the Son of God. The priests greatly liked the manner in which Abul Fazl explained their stand.

The Christian priests had begun to develop a high degree of regard for Sheikh Abul Fazl. Father Monserrate writes, 'About the mullah Abul Fazl I was happy "*omni ex parte*" [on all sides] because in the explanation of the Gospel and in the defence of the truth and the fidelity of our scriptures he spoke as a Christian. This mullah is a companion of the King and a great favourite of his, and in matters of religion he is in the same state as the King. He is the liveliest and keenest mind which I have seen till now. The King said we should speak to him as if with His Highness. We came to understand the great prudence of the King, who in order not to excite his people to rebellion, shows himself to be on their side, and in order that we should not remain without favour, has given orders that this one should always be on ours. Thus he carries on being instructed and understanding the things of our faith with as little scandal of his own as possible.'

According to Father Monserrate, whenever Sheikh Abul Fazl entered the church, he would say, 'I am deeply moved in my mind, but the reverse is the case when I enter a mosque.'

When the priests said in Badshah Salamat's gathering that Christ is God, the ulema present said, '*Astaghfirullah!*'

Monserrate had been ill. This was thus the first occasion on which he attended a gathering of this nature. He wrote about this to the Provincial—the Jesuit head in Goa—Father Rui Vicente—

'I was happy about some things and unhappy about others. To begin with, the way the King conducted himself in that session. I understood that he was temporizing with his mullahs and he wished to give to understand that he was listening out of courtesy. While not a point escaped him and he asked some things in order to understand better what was being read, he was nodding, pretending to be asleep. On the other hand, he cast his very bright eyes all about the room taking stock of the persons with the dissimulation of a very prudent and wise man. Finally, when there was talk of Muhammad, he pretended to regret the offence to a person so honourable—in whom he believes as much as the Pope—saying "No, no", contorting his face and bending over. I believe he said that to satisfy the mullahs of the opposition. I was a bit unhappy and doubtful if His Highness had the same opinion about our scriptures, since due to some reasons which we brought forward he favoured the opposite side so forcefully that it seemed he actually believed in it. In general I was unhappy over our discord over the truth of the scriptures which is the first door in this matter. Since the dogma of our faith are based on what God has revealed in the sacred scriptures, and human reason does not attain to it, if these are not entirely believed, for the rest it is just discussing obstinately...'

There was such heated debate that the next day Badshah Salamat again sent word that the priests should mind their words. Replying through Sheikh Abul Fazl, the priests said, 'We could not refrain from telling the truth, even though they might cut off our heads. It is not reasonable that they should say our scriptures are false, thus insulting the Holy Spirit who inspired them, and the Saints who wrote them, and Holy Mother Church and the fellowship of Christians in which there were and are many saints and learned men who revere them, without us proclaiming the falsity of theirs and of the author who wrote them. And since we had patience when on our saying that Christ is God they say "*stafarla*" [astaghfirullah] they also should have it when we say what we feel about Muhammad. If His Highness wants to prevent this he should tell his people that they should not say the scriptures are false.'

Sheikh Abul Fazl described in these words the sharp debates of the Ibadat Khana:

'The wide capacity and the tolerance of the Shadow of God were unveiled. Sufi, philosopher, orator, jurist, Sunni, Shia, Brahman, Jati, Sevra, Charvaka, Nazarene, Jew, Christian, Zoroastrian and others enjoyed exquisite pleasure... The conferences were excellently arranged by the acuteness and keen quest of truth of the Lord of the World. Every time, eyes and heart gained fresh lustre, and the lamp of vigils acquired new glory... The Shahanshah's court became the home of the inquirers of the seven climes, and the assemblage of the wise of every religion and sect... Reason was exalted and the star of fortune shone for the acquirers of knowledge. The bigoted ulema and the routine lawyers, who reckoned themselves among the chiefs of philosophies and leaders of enlightenment, found their position difficult. The veil was removed from the face of many of them.'

Such was the mood that after a round of debate, Mullah Abdul Qadir Badayuni asked Sheikh Abul Fazl, 'For which of these notorious heresies have you yourself the greatest inclination?'

Sheikh Abul Fazl replied, 'I wish to wander for a few days in the vale of infidelity for sport.'

In these debates Abul Fazl humiliated the ulema to such an extent that they sent him a message, 'Why are you always falling foul of us?'

To this the Sheikh replied, 'The fact of the matter is I am the servant of a mere mortal.'

Badshah Salamat grew so fond of this debate on matters of faith that when he left on a campaign against Mirza Hakim, he took Father Monserrate along.

His Majesty's camp had been pitched on the banks of the river Indus. It was night and the akashdiya was burning bright in the centre of the encampment. Badshah Salamat was seated with Father Monserrate in his do-ashiyana manzil and looking at an atlas to see how far Portugal was from his own kingdom.

Suddenly Badshah Salamat lifted his head from the atlas and asked Father Monserrate, 'Why is a priest celibate? Is it not a divine command that all men should have wives? You appear either to condemn matrimony or to contradict yourself when you say that celibacy is good and matrimony is also good.'

Father Monserrate replied, 'Does not Your Highness know that, of two good things, one often happens to be better than the other? Thus silver is good, but gold is better; whilst wisdom is better than gold and virtue better than anything else. The moon is beautiful but the sun is more beautiful and superior to her.'

When Badshah Salamat agreed to this, Father Monserrate said, 'Priests remain celibate and unmarried that they may follow better things. That they may imitate Christ. And that, free from the cares of a wife, children and family, they may spend their time apart from all desire. For by the sixth commandment of God all luxury is forbidden to Christians, and indeed to all mankind.'

Badshah Salamat asked, 'You declare, do you not, that Christ is God. Do you not then act rashly and insolently in wishing to be like him?'

The priest replied, 'We do indeed believe and asseverate that Christ is God, but we declare at the same time that he is man. And, being man he practised chastity as an example to us, and also praised it highly very many times in the Gospel. As regards his being God, it would indeed be mark of a proud and insolent mind to wish to be like Christ. It is indeed an impossible ambition; and hence to entertain it shows the height of folly and madness. But on the other hand it shows piety and devotion to follow his footsteps in practising the virtues which he himself practised. For one of the many causes which led him to wish to become man was his desire that we might imitate him in the attributes and activities of his true manhood, such as his humility, self-sacrifice, chastity, poverty, obedience and other allied virtues. No painter or sculptor, however accurately and carefully he may paint his picture or carve his statue, endeavours actually to imitate nature. He would say rather that he desired to appropriate for himself the strength and virtue of nature. It has been found that, though we all struggle with our hearts to imitate Christ in those virtues which can be reproduced in a man, yet we are left far behind by him. Wherefore Christ greatly commends our endeavour to imitate himself, and is far from imputing it to pride or insolence or rashness.'

To this Badshah Salamat said, 'The descent from Adam thus perishes in you.'

Father Monserrate said, 'What if I had died when I was a boy eight-year-old or just at the time of marriage? What if my wife had been barren, or I myself, as many are? What if I had been born, or made a eunuch, like the many that are in your palace? Let not Your Highness mistakenly imagine that marriage is enjoined. God indeed allowed much stress to be laid on the value of matrimony under the law of nature, in order that the human race might be increased. And also, amongst the Jews, under the Law of Moses, in order that the religion and worship of true God may be extended. But under the law of the Gospel, which excels all other laws as the substance excels the shadow, the human race having been sufficiently increased, Christ laid down the principle in regard to marriage that each man may freely follow what course he chooses, and stop where he wishes.'

Interrupting him, Badshah Salamat asked, 'If God ordered anyone to cross a river, he would be a sinner if he disobeyed.'

The priest replied, 'That is true but I declared a few moments since that marriage is not enjoined. Nor must you imagine that celibates, though they have no wives, lack offspring. For there is a spiritual begetting. And those whom a man instructs in the faith and virtues of Christianity are in a manner called his sons; for those, whom he baptizes, and whose confessions he hears are no less his spiritual sons than if he had begotten them by his body. Permit me to declare to you, O King, that if you listen to the advice of Rudolf and myself, and believe in what we say, and are baptized by him, you will be more truly and spiritually the son of Rudolf than the son of King Humayun. It may of course happen that some are compelled and commanded to marry.'

'Who?' asked Badshah Salamat.

'A king who must have an heir for the sake of the peace and tranquillity of the state.'

The army camped by the Indus for fifty days. Badshah Salamat spent time hunting in the nearby forest. During this period, his meetings with Father Monserrate continued because Badshah Salamat had a long list of queries.

One night Badshah Salamat asked, 'When would the Last Judgment occur? Would Christ be the Judge?'

Father Monserrate said, 'God alone knows the time when the judgment will take place and in His unsearchable wisdom He has desired this to be hidden from us. Christ himself refused to make it known to his disciples. He did not wish either that we should become negligent through knowing it to be far distant, or that we should be saddened by knowing that it is near at hand. But he wished us to prepare ourselves for that day that we may make good use of the gifts which he has given us, and abstain from sin and from all that he has forbidden, being in fear of the Judgment, though we know not when it will come. Yet signs shall precede that day which will enable men to conclude with confidence that it is at hand.'

Badshah Salamat asked, 'What should these signs be?'

The priest replied, 'Christ mentioned especially wars and rebellions, the fall of kingdoms and nations, the invasion, devastation and conquest of nation by nation and kingdom by kingdom...and these things we see happening very frequently in our time.'

Time passed but the priests could not fully understand Badshah Salamat, nor could they make Badshah Salamat fully understand them.

Father Monserrate wrote in very clear terms—

'...the priests began to suspect that he was intending to found a new religion with matter taken from all the existing systems. And hence they also gradually withdrew themselves from the meetings. For at this time the King was daily showing increasing favours to the Hindus, at whose request he had forbidden the sale of cow in the meat market. Hence the priests did not feel it right to give him the pearls of the Gospel to tread and crush under his feet. Furthermore he had caused a wooden building of ingenious workmanship to be constructed, and had it placed on the very highest point of the palace-roof, and from this he watched the dawn and worshipped the rising sun.'

Father Monserrate went to the extent of saying, 'When Badshah Salamat is giving everybody a right to follow their faith, he is demeaning all faiths.'

Jalaluddin Muhammad Akbar had said many things that had shocked the priests but they had not expected that he would ask them to enter the fire.

After a sharp exchange, Sheikh Qutbuddin of Jalesar said, 'Let us make a pit fire. One of you come with the Gospel and one of us enter with the Quran. We pass through this fire in the presence of His Majesty. The Book and the faith of the one who emerges safe and alive would be believed to be the true one.'

Badshah Salamat did not have a good opinion of Sheikh Qutbuddin of Jalesar. When told that he had performed miracles, Badshah Salamat got the claims investigated and came to the conclusion that the miracles were actually tricks. It was learnt that Sheikh Qutbuddin was leading a life of comfort by deceiving the simple people of Jalesar.

The fire was made. Sheikh Qutbuddin pulled one of the Christian priests by the coat but the priests did not agree to the ordeal.

Flames could be seen on the face of the fair-skinned Monserrate and Rudolf Acquaviva, who were both in black cloak and cap. Father Rudolf Acquaviva had a light beard and was looking at the fire with anxiety. Father Monserrate, fourteen years elder to him, was seated just by his side. In comparison with Father Rudolf, he kept a thicker beard. Closest to Badshah Salamat was Sheikh Abul Fazl, who had a wheatish complexion. His moustache was black and long. Like Badshah Salamat, he too did not keep a beard.

Because Father Rudolf had spent the most time with Badshah Salamat, he was beginning to understand the Emperor's hidden agenda.

Father Rudolf Acquaviva wrote:

'I am afraid that he and some of his people may make use of me to disprove the Muhammadan religion and then avail of some matter out of the Holy Scripture, not for the benefit of our religion but for some other purpose, because there are those who feel that the King is bound to come out with something new one day.'

Father Rudolf did not like the idea of entering the fire but he thought this would be seen as cowardice. He told Badshah Salamat:

'Since, O King, you desire, with regard to the proposed ordeal, to put to the test the constancy of myself and my companions in the faith and religion of Jesus Christ, which we received from our ancestors and drank in with our mother's milk, in which we have been nurtured, and to which we are utterly devoted, we will, with a cheerful heart, and fortified by the help of God, most readily ascend not one but a thousand pyres. Nor do we hope or wish to be miraculously kept from harm... Trusting in divine aid, we have no fear of elephants, lions, panthers, leopards, precipices, crosses, stripes, and all manner of tortures. You can prove by immediate experiment, O King, if you so please, whether or not this is true... but if you propose this ordeal of fire in order that you may behold a miracle—as though any one of us were held so dear by God that He would not suffer the fire to do him any harm—we freely confess that, though our trust in God is unbounded, we have frequently fallen into wrongdoing in other respects, and still continue to so fall; for we are sinners, and hence are kept back by grave religious scruples from daring to expect for ourselves miracles, especially when we are ignorant whether God holds us dear or regards us as stumbling-blocks in His way. Moreover, to make trial by fire as to whether or not the Bible is from God, according as to whether or no its bearer are burnt, is at variance with teaching and example of Christ, whom you, O King, honour and esteem... When he was nailed on the Cross and the Jews were asking for a miracle and saying, "If thou art the son of God, come down from the Cross and we will believe in thee," even then he paid no attention. As regards ourselves, all those who have suffered torments on behalf of the Faith have been better men than we are. And yet many of them have been burnt. As regards our Book, many Churches and houses containing copies of the Gospels have been burnt by the enemies of our religion; and also many Musalman Mosques containing their sacred volumes have suffered a similar fate. And hence the proof by fire must need be doubtful and uncertain. Now, not to neglect the proposal of the Musalmans, if you definitely order us to undergo the ordeal, we demand that you should release them from their dangerous share in the compact, though indeed, we do not believe that a single one of them would be so faithful to his religion and his Prophet, or so utterly foolish, as to submit himself to such a risk. Indeed their nature is such that they demand miracles; but if a miracle were to be performed by some upright follower of our religion, they would say that it had been brought about by magic and sorcery.'

After attentively listening to this, Badshah Salamat said, 'God forbid that I should have summoned you hither in order that you may suffer any calamity. The Sheikh who wants trial by fire is a criminal and deserves death. We wish him to die in this manner in order not to arouse the people. You please help in this respect and say that you would follow him if he entered the fire first.'

When Badshah Salamat proposed his plan in the presence of Sheikh Qutbuddin, the priests stepped aside with the Emperor and said that they could not cooperate in anybody's death.

Badshah Salamat said, 'You don't have to undergo the ordeal. I only desire that you say that you would. And if this is not agreeable, you should at least make an affirmative sign with the head.'

To this the priests said, 'This is not possible.'

Badshah Salamat said again, 'We will say it in your presence and you could imply acquiescence by remaining silent.'

To this the priests said, 'We cannot do this either.'

Badshah Salamat said, 'We would say it in your absence that you wanted to do this.'

The priests replied, 'You should not do such a thing because, if we were asked, we would have to deny it. If you wish to test our fidelity to our religion you could have us thrown into the fire.'

Badshah Salamat replied, 'We would not do the least harm even to our slaves, much less to you.'

After this the Christian priests said in the presence of Sheikh Qutbuddin and others, 'If the Sheikh deserves to die because of his crimes, everyone should know it. What need is there of adopting this roundabout course in committing him to the flames? In the first place, your people should justify their religion, which they have not yet done. The question of trial by fire should arise only thereafter.'

Finally, neither the ulema entered the fire, nor did the priests. After that day Badshah Salamat too gave up the idea.

On the thirtieth of July 1581 CE, Father Acquaviva wrote a letter to Father Everard Mercurian, Superior General of the Society of Jesus, expressing his worry—

'This year I am writing to Your Paternity in greater detail than last year about affairs here, because we have learnt that much of what this King did last year and this year was dissembling. He knew that his brother was going to wage war against him. Since he had to personally march against the enemy, he wished to protect his back. This he did by making sure of the Portuguese by a show of attachment to our faith.

'People here have various views about the King. Some believe he is a Christian, others that he is a Hindu, and others a Muslim. Some other people with better judgment think he is neither a Christian, nor a Hindu, nor a Muslim. In my view this is true, or perhaps he is a Muslim, but conforms to all to win the goodwill of all. We have no idea whether he is a friend or an enemy of the King of Portugal but we have noticed some things we do not like. He has ambitions to be the greatest king of all, and apparently he cannot tolerate that the King of Portugal be the lord of the sea, and that his own ships have to pay taxes in the ports of the King of Portugal. Due to this, we fear an outbreak of war any day.'

It was around this time that heads of nine Portuguese soldiers were sent to Fatehpur Sikri from Surat and presented before Badshah Salamat. Initially Badshah Salamat and the priests both pretended they were unaware of the incident. But when it became widely known, the priests asked Badshah Salamat, 'Have you seen the heads of Portuguese soldiers?'

Badshah Salamat said, 'I have not seen. But I regret the fighting in Daman and Surat.'

Even the Pope wrote a letter to Badshah Salamat when the priests failed to convert him to Christianity. Badshah Salamat knew that there was a pope above the priests, who was obeyed by all. He could change any religious law and even kings bowed before his might.

Jalaluddin Muhammad Akbar also desired that a priest carry his message to the Pope—

'You must tell the Pope that I have learnt how great and august is his dignity, as being in the place of Christ on earth; and that I have heard that all kings fall at his feet. Say then that you have been sent by me to kiss his feet in my place, since I cannot be present publicly to kiss them myself. Ask him to order something to be written to me from which I may learn the way of God and the right manner of governing my dominions in fear and reverence towards God, so that when heaven and earth are consumed and I am brought to that fearful judgment before God, I may be able to render a good account of the brief career of my life.'

Pope Gregory XIII wrote a letter on the eighteenth of February 1582 CE, corresponding to the twenty-sixth regnal year:

'Gregory Bishop

'Servant of the Servants of God

'To Akbar

'Illustrious King of Mogor

May the Merciful God, who deigned to inspire you to listen to the teaching of the evangelical doctrine, transfer you as soon as possible from darkness to light. This we expect from the interest which, as it reached our ears, you have shown in the Christian religion. First of all, you summoned to your court our dear sons, priests of the Society of Jesus and ministers of true faith, you received them graciously and heard them discussing on the kingdom of God. All these are clear indications of your zeal and useful steps to receive the truth, but in such an important matter no delay should be admitted lest this movement of your spirit, which undoubtedly comes from God, be frustrated by tardiness in deliberation. Your Majesty should place, so to say, in one plate of the scales your kingdom, power, sons, the countless subjects, all riches and goods of the world; and in the other the dignity of your soul and the salvation promised by Christ to those who believe in him. If you weigh it alright, you will find in comparison with the latter that those are worth nothing. An everlasting kingdom compared with one of short duration, perishable and subject to many contingencies; transform your mortal power into undying bliss; prepare for yourself a new family and treasures in heaven. God will perhaps grant you that, if it be expedient for your salvation, you enjoy also this earthly kingdom. Life is short and human condition uncertain. See that you do not neglect your own salvation or appear to fail to the grace of God that calls you. Meanwhile do not brush aside this thought, and continue listening, as you did heretofore, to the aforesaid priests, by the help of whose prayers and labours both in the past and in the future you will be greatly helped in a matter of such moment, whom I recommend to you. Your personal interest and concern for them shall not go unrewarded by Him, who invites you to acknowledge the truth, the Lord God Almighty.'

Now the priests' time at Fatehpur Sikri was coming to an end. Antonio Monserrate left with the envoy whom Badshah Salamat had sent to Phillip II, the Emperor of Spain and Portugal. Badshah Salamat wanted to make a pact with the Emperor of Spain and Portugal against the Ottoman Turks but neither the envoy nor the letter reached the Emperor in which Jalaluddin Muhammad Akbar stated:

'It is not concealed and veiled from the minds of intelligent persons who have received the light of divine aid and are illuminated by the rays of wisdom and knowledge, that in this terrestrial world, which is the mirror of the celestial, there is nothing that excels love, and no propensity so worthy of cultivation as philanthropy, because the peace of the world and harmony of existence are based upon friendship and association; and in each heart illuminated by the rays of the sun of love the world of the soul or the faculties of the mind are by them purged of human darkness; and much more is this the case when they subsist between monarchs, peace among whom implies the peace of the world and of the denizens thereof. Considering these things we are with the whole power of our mind earnestly striving to establish and strengthen the bonds of love, harmony and union among the population, but above all with the exalted tribe of the princes who enjoy the noblest of distinctions in consequence of a greater share of divine favour, and especially with that illustrious representative of dominion, recipient of divine illumination, and propagator of the Christian religion, who needs not to be praised or made known; and this decision is on account of our propinquity, the claims whereof are well-established among mighty potentates and acknowledged to be the chief conditions of amicable relations. But as weighty obstacles and great hindrances have delayed personal intercourse, an exchange of messages and correspondence is the best substitute for it... We entertain hopes that the portals of correspondence will be continually kept open on both sides, whereby we may inform each other of various affairs and pleasant hopes. It will be known to your enlightened mind that by the unanimous consent of the adherents of all religions and governments, regarding the two states, namely, the religious and secular—the visible and the invisible world—it is believed and considered fully proved that in comparison to the next the present world is of no account. What laudable efforts the wisest men of the period, as well as the great princes of every country, are making to ameliorate the present perishable outward state! But they are nevertheless spending the essence of their lives, and the best of their time, in the acquisition of mundane objects, striving for and being fully absorbed in the enjoyment of pleasures, and the indulgence of appetites, which must soon vanish! Allah, the Most High, has, however, by His eternal favour and unceasing guidance—despite our multifarious occupations, drawbacks, connections and dependence on external circumstances—graciously inspired us with a longing after Him; but although we have brought the dominions of several great princes under subjection—the administration and amalgamation whereof engrosses our intellect, because we are bound to promote the happiness and welfare of all our subjects—nevertheless, Allah be praised, the purpose of all our activity, the head and the front of all we do, is a desire to meet with divine approbation and to discover that which is true.'

While Father Francis Henriques had already reached Goa in Badshah Salamat's twenty-sixth regnal year, corresponding to the year 1581 CE, in the month of November, Father Rudolf Acquaviva got ready to leave Fatehpur Sikri in Badshah Salamat's twenty-seventh regnal year, corresponding to February 1583 CE. When Father Rudolf Acquaviva got the order to return to Goa, he came to see Badshah Salamat with the letter of Father Provincial.

Father Rudolf Acquaviva had become a favourite of the Emperor. He spent much of his time in prayers at Fatehpur Sikri. He would even forget where he had placed his cap, spectacles and books. He would often sleep the whole night in his full attire or sometimes in a state of penance. He would often fast and led a frugal life. Once Prince Salim found a bloodstained whip in his room with which he flagellated himself. He was so shy that he would blush deeply while talking to Badshah Salamat.

Father Rudolf Acquaviva had such a longing for martyrdom that he would often say, 'Will these Muslims never martyr us?'

The other priests would reply, 'The King likes us very much. Nobody would dare touch us.'

This would sadden Father Rudolf.

He once wrote to the Superior General:

'At the end of this letter I shall convey to Your Paternity the greatest joy which I have here, which is to be very close to martyrdom, because we have confessed and not denied; we have confessed that Muhammad is not a prophet of God, and we have not denied that Christ is the son of God, of which things the second they cannot hear and they close their ears. The first, whoever should say it, has the death penalty. For the execution of the sentence already given, only the death of the King is awaited. To this is added that the Hindus too wish us evil, because we have publicly censured the custom that here exists of burning in the fire the living wives with the bodies of their husbands; and we have told the King that he was not doing right in countenancing such a thing.'

Badshah Salamat used to say, 'It is an ancient custom in Hindustan for a woman to burn herself however unwilling she may be, on her husband's funeral pyre and to give her priceless life with a cheerful countenance, conceiving it to be a means of her husband's salvation. It is a strange commentary on the magnanimity of men that they should seek their deliverance through the self-sacrifice of their wives.'

After Jaimal's death, his wife, the daughter of Mota Raja Udai Singh, refused to commit sati. When Badshah Salamat learnt that Mota Raja and Jaimal's son wanted to use force, he mounted the horse and rode rapidly to stop them.

After listening to Father Acquaviva's petition to leave, Badshah Salamat said, 'I love you, Father, and rejoice to have you near me. My disposition is such that I am ready to embrace the truth of the divine law if it is explained to me even by the humblest and the poorest, including a woman of the lowest rank. You have taught me many things which have pleased me more than all I have learnt from exponents of many religious beliefs. If you are bent on going, I shall not prevent you by force, but your departure is much against my will. If you forsake me in this state, the sin will be on your head.'

The priest replied, 'If one day God shows you the truth of our religion, it would be convenient that you have many Christians already with you. Therefore, it is good that I first leave the court.'

To this Badshah Salamat gave a cold reply, 'Do not say *your* religion. If God can show me the truth, he can also enlighten you, and when God shows me the truth, he will also help and strengthen me.'

The next day Father Rudolf tried pursuing the matter again and said, 'Very good and learned Fathers would come here in my place when you wish.'

Losing his cool, Jalaluddin Muhammad Akbar said, 'I want no more argument, for I will never willingly consent to your departure.'

Seeing his displeasure, Father Rudolf stayed back for some time. This made Badshah Salamat even more favourably disposed towards him, and more worried about his safety.

One day Badshah Salamat said, 'The mullahs are traitors and rogues. I am therefore going to appoint some of my own people to guard you and accompany you wherever you go, so that no evil may befall you.'

The priest replied, 'Your Majesty is aware that, when you summoned us to the court, the Viceroy had asked for hostages for our safety; but we had opposed it because it is our glory to die for the faith which we preach; and if Your Majesty were now to provide me with a guard, I should not be placing my sole reliance on God, which in all circumstances it is my duty to do.'

Badshah Salamat replied, 'Assuredly, there is reason in what you say; but I regard it as my duty to provide for your safety, since you are here under my protection and safeguard.'

Later Badshah Salamat told his courtiers, 'It is laudable that the Father is willing to shed his blood in defence of the law which he preaches. Our own mullahs have no desire to die in defence of their law.'

When Badshah Salamat did not convert to Christianity despite Father Rudolf staying on for some more time, he sought permission to leave once again. Upon his repeated and earnest requests, Badhshah Salamat agreed on the condition that he would obtain the consent of Father Provincial of the Society of Jesus in Goa and come back to the court.

The mission of the three Christian priests to Fatehpur Sikri was unsuccessful but Father Rudolf could see a way forward—

'...a seminary be started in Goa in the Persian language for the Muslims and in Hindustani for the Hindus, to cater for the children of both the Hindus and the Muslims that you will find over there, and those who may be sent from here. In my opinion, this method will be unique, since the King says openly that in his lands everyone is free to follow the religion of his choice.'

When the priests made a request for a hospital to be built where they could serve people, Badshah Salamat asked, 'Would you gain merit by doing good to persons who do not belong to your law?'

The priests said, 'Yes, because we are imitating God who does good to the good and the evil alike.'

Badshah Salamat said, 'God does many things that men cannot do.'

Badshah Salamat often tried to respond to religious matters by reason, which the priests found very odd.

In the twenty-seventh regnal year, corresponding to 1583 CE, by February all the Jesuits had departed Badshah Salamat's court. A major attempt to convert Badshah Salamat to Christianity had failed.

Some time after Father Rudolf left, Badshah Salamat learnt of an incident that deeply saddened him.

Father Rudolf was sent to Salsette after he returned to Goa. In the twenty-eighth regnal year, which was 1583 CE, on the fifteenth of July, he was killed by angry Hindu villagers when he broke their idols.

Badshah Salamat said, 'Alas, Father! Did I not tell you not to go? But you would not listen to me!'

4

A short while after the Christian priests left Fatehpur Sikri, Badshah Salamat came in touch with a new faith. The Christian fathers had created a storm among the ulema; the new set of guests created doubts in the minds of the Brahmins.

Badshah Salamat got mangoes from Una in Gujarat in the fortieth regnal year, which was 1595 CE. With these he learnt of the death of Hiravijaya Suri, who was the acharya of the Tapa Gachchha of the Shwetambar sect of the Jains.

Badshah Salamat had first heard of Hiravijaya Suri when there had been a procession in honour of the six-month fast of the Jain Sadhvi Champa. When Badshah Salamat inquired about the faith of Sadhvi Champa, he learnt that her guru was Hiravijaya Suri. He then sent a firman to Shahabuddin Khan, the governor of Gujarat, to invite Hiravijaya Suri to the court. Badshah Salamat also asked two prominent Jains of Agra, Bhanu Kalyan and Thansingh Ramji to invite Hiravijaya Suri to Fatehpur Sikri. In accordance with the royal orders, the governor proposed elephants, horses and a palanquin for the journey but Hiravijaya Suri declined the offer and set off on foot. In the twenty-eighth regnal year, in the month of June of 1583 CE, he reached Sikri from Gujarat. The Jain community of Fatehpur Sikri took Hiravijaya Suri and sixty-seven accompanying monks in a procession to the upashray. Although Hiravijaya Suri expressed a desire to have an immediate meeting with Badshah Salamat, it was Sheikh Abul Fazl who first made his acquaintance.

Impressed with Hiravijaya Suri, Badshah Salamat gave him the title of 'Jagatguru' and fulfilled many of his wishes.

On the sixteenth of November 1590 CE, in the thirty-fifth regnal year, Badshah Salamat wrote a firman to the governor of Gujarat, Mirza Aziz Koka—

'In view of the genuine yoga practices and search after God by Hiravijaya Suri Sevra and by the followers of his faith, who have received the honour of presenting themselves before us, it is ordered that no one should lodge in their temples or upashrayas or molest them. Moreover, if any charitable person wants to rebuild or repair these buildings, because they had fallen down or had become dilapidated, no one should put a restraint on such actions. Some persons, ignorant about the Godhead, accuse the Jain monks of preventing rainfall and doing similar acts which are in God's power, and harass them under the stupid idea that they exercise magical arts. It is ordered that no such ill-treatment be allowed. Hakims and mutasaddis should consider this order, which is equivalent to God's firman, as the means of bettering their condition, and they should not act contrary to the same. After keeping a copy, the firman should be handed over to the Jains in order that it may serve as a sanad to them for ever.'

About two years after this royal orders were issued to the governors, jagirdars and officials of the provinces of Malwa, Agra, Lahore, Multan, Ahmedabad, and the rest of the empire—

'Hiravijaya Suri, the acharya of the Jain Shwetambar religion had made a request that the heaven-reaching hills of Siddhachal, Girnar, Keshrinath and Abu, the five hills of Rajgir, the hills of Samet Shikhar or Parsvnath in Bengal, together with all the temples and kothis at the foot of these hills and likewise all other places of pilgrimage of the Jain Shwetambar community throughout the empire should be handed over to them, so that no one might kill any animal on these hills or near these temples... The Emperor, finding this request is just and reasonable and not contrary to the Islamic law, issues the order bestowing all these hills and temples on Hiravijaya Suri, as the representative of the Jain community, for whose benefit the order is issued.'

People say that on the night of the fourth of September 1595 CE, in the fortieth regnal year, a Brahmin who was sleeping near a mango orchard saw an otherworldly spectacle. Hiravijaya Suri had been cremated there that day. The Jain sanghas of Una and Div placed his body anointed with saffron and sandalwood on a pyre prepared with fifteen maunds of sandalwood, three maunds of aloe-wood, three sers each of camphor and saffron, and two sers of sweet musk and conducted the last rites in the mango orchard outside the town of Una.

It is said that when the Brahmin related to the people what he had seen, the thousands who flocked to the place were surprised to see that the mango trees had borne fruit despite it being the month of September, and that even a day earlier the trees had shown no sign of fruits or flowers. People say these mangoes were sent far and wide and also to Badshah Salamat. Jalaluddin Muhammad Akbar gifted the orchard and adjoining land measuring twenty-two bigha to the Jain community.

Hiravijaya Suri's paduka—wooden sandals—were consecrated at that very place, and the following was inscribed on them:

'These are the footmarks of holy Hiravijaya, the best of the Suris, on his monument—manifesting their spiritual eminence through the ringing of the bells of heavenly vehicles heard and lights seen every day. Holy Hiravijaya, the guru of the world, who had been on a pilgrimage to the sacred hill of Shatrunjaya with a caravan of pilgrims from all countries, and, attaining nirvana on the eleventh day of the bright half of Bhadrapada, had caused the mango trees in the vicinity of the place of his cremation to bear fruit. The mighty Emperor Akbar, king of kings, filled with admiration on hearing reports of his many good qualities, such as penance, asceticism and lovability, had invited him to the province of Delhi from Gujarat, had listened to his preaching, and had presented to him a library of manuscripts. At his instance, the Emperor had proscribed fishing in the big lake named Devara, prohibited the killing of animals for six months in the year, abolished for good the poll-tax on pilgrims visiting the sacred Mount Shatrunjaya, reduced the jizya tax, annulled escheatage throughout the land, disallowed taking of prisoners in battle, and promulgated such other acts of piety.'

Hiravijaya Suri and the monk Bhanuchandra, who came after him, were responsible for the increasing influence of the Jain religion at the court. Bhanuchandra explained to Badshah Salamat the significance of a thousand names of the sun and was thus called 'Patshah Akbar Jalaluddin Surya Sahasranamadhyapak'. In accordance with his advice, Badshah Salamat would every day turn his face towards the sun and recite the thousand names. When Prince Salim's daughter was born in a constellation that was deemed to be very inauspicious for the father, astrologers advised that the father should not see his daughter's face. It was Bhanuchandra who had suggested a remedy.

On shukl purnima of Chaitra, the idol of Jina was ritually bathed one hundred and eight times in the presence of Badshah Salamat and Prince Salim. A prayer was made to Adinath Jina and the Bhaktamar stotra was recited. Badshah Salamat very respectfully took the water and applied it to his eyes and sent it to the harem for the ladies.

Badshah Salamat had great regard for Bhanuchandra. In the August of 1592 CE, in the thirty-seventh regnal year, Bhanuchandra accompanied the Emperor's entourage on foot and walked up to Kashmir. When he suffered a foot injury in the Pir Panjal range, the Emperor waited three days for it to heal. In Kashmir, an antelope injured Badshah Salamat and he was confined to bed for fifty days. People say that only Sheikh Abul Fazl and Bhanuchandra were allowed to meet him during this period. As thanksgiving, Badshah Salamat sent five hundred cows that Bhanuchandra gifted to the Brahmins.

It is said that Badshah Salamat once had a severe headache that was proving to be incurable, and Bhanuchandra cured him by placing his hand on his forehead and praying to Chintamani Parsvnath. When the nobles wanted to celebrate the recovery, Badshah Salamat immediately restrained them from sacrificing animals.

With the increasing influence of Jainism at the court, Hiravijaya Suri's successor Vijayasena Suri narrowly escaped falling victim to a conspiracy hatched by the Brahmins.

Vijayasena Suri left Radhanpur in Gujarat on the twenty-seventh of November 1592 CE, in the thirty-seventh regnal year. He was received at Ludhiana by Sheikh Faizi. Then he reached Lahore, where Badshah Salamat was holding his court at the time.

The Brahmins began to poison Badshah Salamat's ears through Ram Das Kachhwaha. They said, 'Vijayasena Suri and his followers do not believe in Vedas or God. Not once do they do pranam to God.'

When Badshah Salamat sought an explanation, Vijayasena Suri replied, 'The Brahmins have hurled these charges out of jealousy. There is no such mandatory requirement.'

Jalaluddin Muhammad Akbar conveyed Vijayasena Suri's reply to Bhattacharya, a Brahmin, who said, 'They are just saying this, when in fact there is nothing of this kind in their texts.'

On the orders of Badshah Salamat, Sheikh Abul Fazl arranged a debate between Vijayasena Suri and the Brahmins.

Sheikh Abul Fazl told Vijayasena Suri, 'If you believe in Shiva then talk to the Brahmins.'

Then Bhattacharya said, 'We believe that Shiva is the creator or karta of the universe. But what is your logic behind the destruction of Shiva?'

To this Vijayasena replied, 'It does not seem correct for you to say that Shiva is the karta of the universe. This would need some thinking. Body is formed of dharma and adharma. There is no body part without dharma and adharma. There is no mouth if there are no body parts. There is no speech if there is no mouth. So how can somebody else be the controller of speech? How can one who does not have a body be the creator?'

Bhattacharya and many other Brahmins were listening to Vijayasena Suri in the presence of Sheikh Abul Fazl.

'One who gets engrossed in play gets joy like a child. One who has created the universe should get joy out of what he has created. What of the creator's graciousness is evidenced by the creation of a being that is troubled by birth, adverse circumstances and a sorrowful life?'

Vijayasena Suri did not mince words, 'If creation happens because of karma, what then is so special about a powerless Shiva? And if the nature of God is beyond logic, why are you people making this fuss of seeking replies from us? If we do not believe in the creator of the universe, we do not become an atheist? A believer cannot be slammed just because he does not believe in a particular dharma.'

Vijayasena Suri, the successor of Hiravijaya Suri, did not stop here. He asked how believers in Samkhya and Vaiseshika could be called theists. He then began to speak of the Vedanta.

Vijayasena Suri said, 'This universe is made of maya. Even God is not its creator. How can a Vedantist who believes in this be taken to be a believer in God?'

Bhanuchandra wrote that Vijayasena gave a fitting reply to Bhattacharya and other Brahmins, who had nothing more to say. Sheikh Abul Fazl reported to the Emperor that Vijayasena Suri's explanations were quite satisfactory.

Sheikh Abul Fazl wrote of the meeting between the Brahmins and the Jains in the court of Badshah Salamat, 'The Brahmins worship Krishna as a deity, while the Jains relegate him to service in hell. The Brahmins deem it better to face a raging elephant or ravening lion than to meet with one of this sect. Badshah Salamat, however, in his earnest search after truth, has particularly dispelled the darkness of the age by the light of universal toleration, and the numerous sectaries, relinquishing their mutual aversion, live in the happy accomplishment of a common harmony.'

Badshah Salamat had just about opened the doors of the Ibadat Khana for every faith when disturbing news was received from the town of Banaras.

The imam was delivering the khutba in the Jama Masjid of the town—

'All praise be to Allah. We all praise Him and seek His help. And we all have faith in Him and depend upon him. And we all seek from Allah forgiveness for the failings in our character and our wrong deeds. He whom Allah guides will never stray, and he whom He finds unworthy of this guidance is guided by none, and we hold witness that Allah is one, there is none else to be worshipped. None can share His place, and we hold witness that Muhammad, peace be upon him, is a man of God and Prophet. O people! You should strengthen your hearts by worship of Allah and offer durood to the compassionate Prophet for forgiveness of sins on the Day of Judgment. O Allah! Bestow as many blessings upon Muhammad, peace be upon him, and his children, as are the number of people observing namaz and fasting. O Allah! Bestow as many blessings upon Muhammad and his children as is the number of people standing or sitting in namaz! And upon all prophets and your own special angels, and upon all your obedient followers, bestow blessings! O Allah! Upon all your believing men and women and all Muslim men and women, whether alive or dead, grant deliverance. Indeed, you are the one who accepts prayers. And you are the one to grant status. With your compassion and mercy, O Allah! Upon the respected late emperors, great emperors who were leaders, who took righteous decisions, and they were people who did justice, be merciful. They are the people who follow the path shown by their Creator and they are successful. Especially on great leaders, resting in the garden of paradise, Amir Timur Sahib-i-Qiran, who laid down the traditions of rule and governance, and upon the great emperor Abu Sayeed Bahadur Khan, who lived in grandeur, who are aligned to mercy in the eyes of Allah. And those sultans, whose sins were forgiven by Allah and His compassion was bestowed upon them, who sit on the throne by His wish and compassion, which is upon Sultan Umar Sheikh Bahadur Khan, and upon the famed Sultan Miran Shah, who did complete justice and good deeds, and the emperor who performed numerous good deeds and acts of charity, so high was his stature that he carried out jihad and war in the path of Allah, which is upon Zahiruddin Muhammad Babur Badshah Ghazi, may Allah keep his grave luminous and spread fragrance upon it! O Allah! Upon the pious emperor, holy warrior and martyr, the God-knowing one, who performed jihad in accordance with the dictates of Allah, charitable person of a very high order, who is second to none in dispensing justice, one who raised the standard of war and jihad on the path of Allah, Nasiruddin Muhammad Humayun Badshah Ghazi, may Allah keep his grave clean and his residence a paradise.

'O Allah! One who stamped out oppression and disobedience, the one who is chief of the emperors of the Muslim countries, Arab and Ajam, Hindustan and Turkestan, patron to the emperors and rulers of the world, the one who sits on the throne by virtue of inheritance and ability, whose one moment of justice equals the justice of the ruler of human beings and angels, which is Abul Muzaffar Jalaluddin Muhammad Akbar Badshah Ghazi. May Allah preserve his rule and empire, and his magnanimity, for all times. And spread his good deeds all over the world.

'O followers of Allah! Indeed, Allah enjoins justice and good deeds and enjoins close people to obey orders and be merciful, and enjoins not to be disobedient, not to have unlawful relationships and not to indulge in wrong deeds. Enjoins you so that you take Allah's name, none being bigger than Him. He is and would always be. He too remembers you. You thank him and He shall give you even more. You seek deliverance from Him and He shall grant deliverance. Indeed, Allah's name is the highest, most respected, greatest and all encompassing.

'May the generosity and mercy of Allah always remain upon the father and grandfather of the Emperor of the World.

'Upon Amir Timur who had a high stature.

'And after him upon Emperor Miran Shah who had good qualities.

'And after him upon Emperor Abu Sayeed who had a high stature.

'And after him upon the famous and blessed Emperor Umar Sheikh Mirza.

'And after him upon Emperor Babur Ghazi, under whom the world took refuge, and Emperor Humayun who nurtured the faith.

'And after him upon Jalaluddin Muhammad Akbar Badshah Ghazi, who is the emperor of the whole world and in whom the world takes refuge.

'O Allah! May the highest level of paradise be his abode. O Allah! May the rule of the respected emperor and the chief of the emperors of Arab and Ajam last for ever.'

No sooner had he heard this than Shah Tayyab, a prominent name in the religious and worldly circles of Banaras, dragged the imam down from the pulpit and said, 'How can you take a kafir's name in the Friday khutba!'

Badshah Salamat's coronation had been proclaimed through a khutba from the mosque, and since then, every Friday a khutba in his name had been read from every mosque in his empire. Objecting to this khutba was an open challenge to Jalaluddin Muhammad Akbar.

Behind this clash lay an aspect of Badshah Salamat's thought that linked him to a personality that preceded him by many centuries. This person bequeathed a new way of thinking to the Islamic world.

Ibn-i-Arabi was born in Spain on the seventeenth of the month of Ramzan in the year 560 of the Hijri calendar, which was the twenty-eighth of July 1165 CE. He had faith in Islam but also believed that an inner light was his guide. He believed that all creation is a manifestation of the divine light and the different religions are thus equivalent. He would say—

My heart has become capable of every form.
It is a meadow for gazelles and monastery for Christian monks.
A temple for idols and the pilgrim's Ka'ba.
The table of the Law and the book of Quran.
I profess the religion of love, and whatever direction
Its steed may take, Love is my religion and my faith.

Ibn-i-Arabi said:

'The believer praises the God who is in his form of belief and with whom he has connected himself. He praises none but himself, for his God is made by himself, and to praise the work is to praise the maker of it: its excellence or imperfection belongs to its maker. For this reason, he blames the beliefs of others, which he would not do, if he were just. Beyond doubt, the worshipper of this particular God shows ignorance when he criticizes others on account of their beliefs. If he understands the saying of Junayd, "The colour of the water is the colour of the vessel containing it," he would not interfere with the beliefs of others and instead would perceive God in every form and in every belief. He has opinion, not knowledge: therefore God said, "I am in My servant's opinion of Me," that is, "I do not manifest Myself to him save in the form of his belief."'

This was the belief in the Unity of Being—'Wahdat-ul-Wajud'—of Ibn-i-Arabi that Badshah Salamat had internalized.

Some at the court believed that Badshah Salamat was the Perfect Man of the kind mentioned by Ibn-i-Arabi. Naturally, Abul Fazl's voice was loudest among them—

'Kingship is a gift of God and is not bestowed till many thousand grand requisites have been gathered together in one individual. Lineage and wealth and the backing of a mob are not enough for this great position. It is clear to the wise that a few of the holy qualities are magnanimity, lofty benevolence, wide capacity, abundant endurance, exalted understanding, innate graciousness, natural courage, justice, rectitude, strenuous labour, proper conduct. And with all those marks of perfection...so long as the subject of such encomium does not have wisdom sufficient to overpower improper desires and unbecoming anger, he cannot be fit for this lofty office.'

Ibn-i-Arabi used to say that the Perfect Man is closest to God—

'Just as one and the same light is variously coloured as it passes through pieces of glasses of various colours, the same Form of the Absolute is differently manifested in different men with different capacities.'

In the privacy of his home, Mullah Abdul Qadir Badayuni secretly wrote:

'... And since in Badshah Salamat's opinion, it was a settled fact that the thousand years since the time of the mission of the

Prophet, which was to be the period of the continuance of the faith of Islam, were now completed, no hindrance remained to the promulgation of those secret designs, which he nursed in his heart. And so, considering any further respect or regard for the sheikhs and the ulema—who were unbending and uncompromising—to be unnecessary, he felt at liberty to embark fearlessly on his design of annulling the statutes and ordinances of Islam and of establishing his own cherished pernicious belief.'

Those who were keeping an eye on the ever larger projection of Badshah Salamat's personality did not fail to see that a very big event had happened very silently. In 1580 CE, which was the twenty-fifth regnal year, Badshah Salamat did not visit the shrine of Muinuddin Chishti on the occasion of the urs. And never visited the shrine thereafter. It had been his wont until now to visit the shrine every year in the month of Rajab and distribute alms. Those expecting Badshah Salamat this year saw Prince Daniyal visit and fulfil their hopes instead.

A thought had begun to occur in Badshah Salamat's mind—

'If union with the spirit of the saint be the object, then proximity or remoteness does not matter. If the idea be to reverence worn-out dust then it is polytheism and idolatory.'

On the thirtieth of July 1585 CE, which was the thirtieth regnal year, Badshah Salamat's stepbrother, Mirza Hakim, the ruler of Kabul passed away, causing fear that an attempt may be made to raise one of his children to the throne and that the Uzbek ruler might make an intervention. Seeing the sensitivity of the situation, Badshah Salamat marched towards Punjab. But he did not return to Fatehpur Sikri even after the threat passed. He made Agra his base and abandoned the city he had built solely because his pir, Sheikh Salim Chishti, was present there. Now Badshah Salamat distanced his rule from the shrine of Sheikh Salim Chishti.

Sheikh Abul Fazl openly declared in the *Akbarnama* that now Badshah Salamat was himself the leader of the spiritual world—

'Whenever, from lucky circumstances, the time arrives that a nation learns to understand how to worship truth, the people will naturally look to their king, on account of the high position which he occupies and expect him to be their spiritual leader as well; for a king possesses, independent of men, the ray of divine wisdom, which banishes from his heart everything that is conflicting. A king will therefore sometimes observe the element of harmony in a multitude of things, or sometimes reversely, a multitude of things in that which is apparently one; for he sits on the throne of distinction, and is thus equally removed from joy or sorrow.

'Now this is the case with the monarch of the present age, and this book is a witness to it. Men versed in foretelling the future knew this when His Majesty was born, and together with all others that were cognizant of the secret, they have since been waiting in joyful expectation. His Majesty, however, wisely surrounded himself for a time with a veil, as if he were an outsider, or a stranger to their hopes. But can man counteract the will of God? His Majesty, at first, took all such by surprise as were wedded to the prejudices of the age; but he could not help revealing his intentions; they grew to maturity in spite of him, and are now fully known. He now is the spiritual guide of the nation, and sees in the performance of this duty a means of pleasing God.'

Claiming leadership in both the worldly and spiritual domains, Jalaluddin Muhammad Akbar took a major step. Replacing the calendar that had begun with the migration of Prophet Muhammad from Mecca to Medina, he started a new calendar. It started with a major event in Badshah Salamat's life.

The firman proclaiming the launch of the new Ilahi era was also drafted by Abul Fazl—

'God be praised! During this mighty sovereignty there have been in the visible world so many great events and shining actions, such as the subjugation of great cities, and the complete capture of impregnable forts and other victories, and divine aids, any one of which was fit to be made the foundation of an era. But if Your Majesty directs that the new era commence from the day of your seating yourself on the throne of sovereignty, which was one of God's great gifts and never-ending boons, and from which auspicious day this is the twenty-ninth solar, and the thirtieth lunar year, assuredly such a good deed will be at once a mark of thanksgiving and a fulfilment of the wishes of mankind. Moreover, there is not involved in this good deed any breach of the respect due to the glory of the Hijri era—which comes from the day when His Majesty, the best of men, migrated from Mecca to Medina on account of the predominance of foes. This is the supposition of worthless persons infirm in nature and of mean understanding.'

Mullah Abdul Qadir Badayuni could not speak his mind openly but he wrote down what he thought in his secret book—

'The Hijri era was now abolished, and a new era was introduced, of which the first year was the year of the Emperor's accession, viz. nine hundred and sixty-three Hijri. The months had the same names as at the time of the old Persian kings... Fourteen festivals also were introduced corresponding to the feasts of Zoroastrians; but the feasts of the Musalmans and their glory were trodden down, the Friday prayer alone being retained, because some old, decrepit, silly people used to go to it... On copper coins and gold mohurs, the era of the Millennium was used as indicating that the end of the religion of Muhammad, which was to last one thousand years, was drawing near. Reading and learning Arabic was looked on as a crime, and Muhammadan law, and the exegesis of the Quran, and the tradition, as also those who studied them, were considered bad and deserving of disapproval...'

Mullah Badayuni even heard people say that Badshah Salamat would perform a feat like Shah Ismail of Persia. After all, Shah Ismail was believed to be the Perfect pir. People say that soldiers would pray facing his tent.

Shah Ismail's diktat was, 'Whoever among our sincere soldiers and special servants love our imperial head should partake of the flesh of the enemy.'

It was known to Badshah Salamat that Shah Ismail's soldiers had eaten the corpse of the Uzbek ruler Shaibani Khan.

A very new spectacle was seen in Badshah Salamat's assembly on Sunday at Fatehpur Sikri. The ceremony of initiation into Din-i-Ilahi happened on Sunday because it was believed that the sun was strongest then. That Sunday, Raja Birbal took off his turban and, taking it in his hands, placed his head at the feet of Badshah Salamat. Then Badshah Salamat raised him from his sijda and, putting the turban back on his head, made him his murid—a disciple. To those who believed, the person placing his turban at the feet of Badshah Salamat had given up conceit and selfishness, and by raising the person, Badshah Salamat gave him a new life. His Majesty gave Raja Birbal a token of discipleship upon which was inscribed 'Allahu Akbar'.

Mullah Badayuni also saw people becoming disciples but he remembered the ceremony in these words:

'I who am so and so, son of so and so, do voluntarily, and with sincere predilection and inclination, utterly and entirely renounce and repudiate the religion of Islam, which I have seen and heard of my fathers, and do embrace the Din-i-Ilahi—the Divine Religion of Akbar Shah, and do accept the four grades of entire devotion, that is, sacrifice of property, life, honour, and religion.'

Badshah Salamat had wanted the entire court to prostrate before him but the ulema protested that prostration can only be to God. So Badshah Salamat decided that prostration would only be permitted in his private assemblies.

Sheikh Abul Fazl said, 'Many people wanted to perform the sijda for the blessings it would get them. Because some dark-hearted people viewed this a worship of a mortal, His Majesty, in view of practical wisdom, exempted everybody. Even his private attendants were not allowed to prostrate themselves in open court.'

These disciples of Jalaluddin Muhạmmad Akbar stood out by the way they greeted each other. When they met, one would say, 'Allahu Akbar!' The other disciple would respond, 'Jalla Jalaluhu!'

New practices came to be adopted by them. Instead of food being distributed after death, they would feed people in their lifetime. They would throw a lavish feast on their birthday. Badshah Salamat's disciples would try to abstain from meat and would not even look at it in the month of their birth. They would shun the vessels used by butchers, fishermen, and bird catchers and not have physical relations with women who were old, barren, minor, or pregnant.

Now Badshah Salamat's miracles began to be talked about. His disciple Sheikh Abul Fazl wrote:

'Many sincere inquirers, from the mere light of his wisdom, or his holy breath, obtain a degree of awakening which other spiritual doctors could not produce by repeated fasting and prayers for forty days. Numbers of those who have renounced the world, sanyasis, jogis, sevra, qalandars, hakims, and Sufis and thousands of such as follow the worldly pursuits as soldiers, tradespeople, mechanics, and husbandmen, have daily their eyes opened to insight, or have the light of their knowledge increased. Men of all nations, young and old, friends and strangers, the far and near, look upon offering a vow to His Majesty as the means of solving all their difficulties, and bend down in worship on obtaining their desire. Others again, from the distance of their homes, or to avoid the crowds gathering at the court, offer their vows in secret, and pass their lives in grateful praises. But when Badshah Salamat leaves court, in order to settle the affairs of a province, to conquer a kingdom, or to enjoy the pleasures of the chase, there is not a hamlet, a town, or a city that does not send forth crowds of men and women with vow-offerings in their hands, and prayer on their lips, touching ground with their foreheads, praising the efficacy of their vows, or proclaiming the accounts of the spiritual assistance received. Other multitudes ask for lasting bliss, for an upright heart, for advice how best to act, for strength of the body, for enlightenment, for the birth of son, the reunion of friends, a long life, increase of wealth, elevation in rank, and many other things. His Majesty, who knows what is really good, gives satisfactory answers to everyone, and applies remedies to their religious perplexities. Not a day passes but people bring cups of water to him, beseeching him to breathe upon it. He who reads the letters of the divine orders in the book of fate, on seeing the tidings of hope, takes the water with blessed hands, places it in the rays of the world-illuminating sun, and fulfils the desire of the supplicant. Many sick people of broken hopes, whose diseases the most eminent physicians pronounce incurable, have been restored to health by this divine means.'

Once some people told Badshah Salamat near Ajmer, 'A traveller was passing through a dreadful forest in the vicinity, and a tiger rose up to destroy his life, but a remedy was found by the man. He immediately drew a line round himself and called upon the name of the world's lord. On hearing the honoured name, the beast stood still, and the man escaped mortal danger.'

Badshah Salamat's disciple, a prominent poet of his time, Qasim-i-Kahi wrote:

The king of faith, Akbar Muhammad has such grandeur and majesty,
That if it were not infidelity I would have called him another God.

Another prominent poet of Badshah Salamat's time, Sheikh Rahai said:

My intelligence is puzzled by your being,
You are both an angel and a man.
No mine contains a gem,
Nor the sky a star like you.

Mullah Sheri, a poet known for his wit and repartee in the era of Jalaluddin Muhammad Akbar, went to the extent of saying:

This year the king has declared himself Prophet,
In the following year, if God so wills, he will become God.

No attempt was made to force anyone to become a disciple but there definitely was an attempt to persuade people. When Raja Bhagwant Das of Amber was asked to accept the discipleship of Badshah Salamat, he said, 'I would willingly believe that Hindus and Musalmans have each a bad religion, but only tell us what the new sect is, and what opinion they hold, so that I may believe.'

Badshah Salamat thought for a bit and then decided not to press the matter.

Badshah Salamat had a relationship with this family that spanned three generations. Such was their affiliation that in the book *Mancharit*, written in praise of Raja Man Singh, the poet Amrit Rai says:

One day Hazrat summoned the poets.
He asked about the noble Kachhwaha clan:
Who is its founder? What is the clan's extent? To which god do they owe their origin?
In which region did they establish themselves? Which village takes pride in their fame?
Keeping in mind the Emperor's command, I proceed to write the Mancharit.

After Raja Bharmal came close and became a loyalist, Badshah Salamat got married to his daughter, the sister of Bhagwant Das. By virtue of this marriage, Badshah Salamat was Kunwar Man Singh's phoopha—uncle. Badshah Salamat was so fond of Kunwar Man Singh that he would call him farzand—son. According to

Mancharitra Raso written by the poet Narottam in praise of Man Singh,

Akbar's rule is not the rule of Turks, it is the rule of Hindus,
Always in service of God, he bathes in the Ganga's water every day.
He does not kill animals.
It is Arjun who is born in this lifetime as Akbar,
Who respects the Vedas and Puranas, and abolished the pilgrim tax.
He loves Hindus and keeps distance from Turks.
He killed his family in the previous birth,
Thus born an asur in this lifetime, Man Singh his Bheem.

The *Mancharit* says:

Born in the Timur clan, Humayun's son is worshipped by heroes of the three worlds,
He is an avtar who has come to remove sorrow from people's lives.
He is an all-powerful emperor of the Chaghatai clan, nourishing humanity,
May the jewel of the world Shah Jalal live for ever.

Raja Man Singh built the grand Govinddev Temple on the lines of the buildings created by Badshah Salamat. Man Singh got the following inscribed in the temple:

Honourable Akbar in a natural manner nourished the entire earth
So that all were happily following their faiths
Deeming Lord Govind's feet a fit place to reside
The exalted Vaishnavites bless him eternally.

Despite such respect and honour bestowed by Badshah Salamat, Kunwar Man Singh gave him a blunt reply, 'If discipleship means willingness to sacrifice one's life, I already carry my life in my hand: what need is there of further proof? If, however, the term has another meaning and refers to faith, I certainly am a Hindu. If you order me to do so, I will become a Musalman, but I know not of the existence of any other religion than these two.'

Badshah Salamat gave no answer that day and the matter ended. But there was an uproar when a move was made to turn Qutbuddin Muhammad Khan and Shahbaz Khan into Badshah Salamat's disciples.

Qutbuddin Muhammad Khan enjoyed a high status in the empire. He was the brother of Shamsuddin Muhammad Atka Khan. He was granted the jagir of Bharuch and a mansab of five thousand after the victory over Gujarat. Around the year 1579–80 CE, in the twenty-fourth regnal year, he was appointed guardian to Prince Salim and he organized a lavish banquet for Badshah Salamat. Badshah Salamat enhanced his glory when he placed the prince on his shoulders.

Qutbuddin Muhammad Khan said, 'What would the kings of the West say, such as the Sultan of Constantinople, if they heard this? For they all hold the same faith be it a travesty or not.'

Badshah Salamat said, 'Are you in India on a secret mission from Constantinople that you show such opposition? If you wish to keep a small place warm for yourself, you should go away from India and become an honoured subject there. Leave at once.'

On this occasion, an argument broke out between Shahbaz Khan and Birbal.

Both were close to Badshah Salamat and enjoyed a mansab of two thousand each. Raja Birbal was the lone Hindu who had become Badshah Salamat's disciple. Shahbaz Khan had served the empire well in Jodhpur, Mewar and Bihar. He meticulously followed the sharia. He never drank, nor did he shave his beard or become a disciple of Badshah Salamat. He always had the rosary in his hand and never missed a namaz.

It is said that Shahbaz Khan was a man of many qualities and could have risen higher if he had learnt to use discretion.

One day towards the evening, Badshah Salamat was talking to Shahbaz Khan while enjoying the fresh air on the banks of the Fatehpur tank. Shahbaz Khan was looking at the sun lest he miss the namaz. But Badshah Salamat had him by his arms.

Standing some distance away, Hakim Abul Fath said, 'If this man does not miss his evening prayers today, we will know that he is really pious.'

As soon as it was time for prayer, Shahbaz Khan sought permission from Badshah Salamat, who said, 'You can miss it. Surely you are not going to leave me alone.'

Shahbaz Khan withdrew his arm and spreading his shawl on the ground sat down to offer namaz. Badshah Salamat kept striking him on the head every now and then, asking him to get up. This moved Hakim Abul Fath to remark, 'Let not all favours be exhausted on just this one person; there are others too who yearn for your grace.'

Badshah Salamat obliged Hakim Abul Fath. He left Shahbaz Khan and went over to him.

In course of the debate that began with Din-i-Ilahi, an agitated Shahbaz Khan told Raja Birbal in Badshah Salamat's assembly, 'You cursed infidel, will you go on talking in this manner until I am able to pay you out!'

Badshah Salamat looked angrily at Shahbaz Khan and addressed all those present, 'Would that a shoeful of excrement were thrown into your faces.'

5

When Badshah Salamat felt the fingers of Hakim Gilani on his pulse, he was reminded of the riddle Raja Birbal had posed—

Hand speaks and only hand listens, not the ear,
Listen Emperor Akbar to Birbal's riddle.

To this Badshah Salamat had replied, 'Pulse.'

When Raja Birbal lost his life in the campaign against the Yusufzai tribe, Badshah Salamat was plunged into sorrow. He said:

Birbal had always kept sorrow for himself and given away the rest,
But now we say, he has even given sorrow, keeping nothing for himself.

Badshah Salamat asked Birbal's son, 'How many queens committed sati with Birbal?'

Birbal's son replied, 'Bravery, Benevolence, Wisdom. Fame is left behind.'

Raja Birbal was a slim man. Like all Hindus his jama was tied towards the left, which was the custom at the court. Stuck in the sash at his waist was a dagger and he held a long staff. He wore an

Akbarite turban. Since he was a disciple and had been initiated into the Din-i-Ilahi faith, he kept a small image of Badshah Salamat wrapped in a jewel-studded cloth in his turban. A special painting depicts Jalaluddin Muhammad Akbar seated on a throne of gold with eight legs, falcon in his one hand and sword in the other, a pearl-studded sceptre over him and Raja Birbal standing behind with a mace in his hand.

Raja Birbal was born in a Brahmin family at Tikwapur in Kalpi. After serving at the court of Raja Bhagwant Das of Amber and Raja Ramchandra of Rewa, he reached Badshah Salamat and was his courtier for thirty years. He was born Mahesh Das but he was given the title of 'Birbar'—the brave one—which became popular as Birbal. He earned fame for his poetry and wit. Raja Birbal wrote poetry under the pen name Brahma and was bestowed the title 'Kavirai' by Badshah Salamat.

Badshah Salamat had a house built for Raja Birbal near his own palace in Fatehpur Sikri. When Raja Birbal's palace was ready, Badshah Salamat honoured him with a visit.

Once when Badshah Salamat was enjoying an elephant fight, one of the beasts suddenly turned towards Raja Birbal. His life was saved by Badshah Salamat who sped on his horse to obstruct the elephant's path to Raja Birbal.

Badshah Salamat considered him so dear that never ever in three decades did he display any displeasure towards him. Stories were told of their close bonding and witty conversations. It is said that Badshah Salamat, Prince Salim and Birbal were out hunting once. Because of the heat Badshah Salamat and Prince Salim took off their shirt and shawl and gave them to Birbal.

Badshah Salamat joked, 'It is a donkey's load.'

To which Raja Birbal replied, 'Two donkeys.'

Once Badshah Salamat asked Birbal,

Who wants it to rain, who wants sunshine?
Who is for speech, who is for silence?

Raja Birbal replied,

The gardener wants rain, washerman sunshine,
The emperor is for speech, the thief for silence.

Badshah Salamat had had the courtesans of Fatehpur Sikri settle outside the city in an area called 'Shaitanpura'—the abode of the devil—and by his orders, whoever wished to take them home or associate with them had to have his name and condition registered. When Badshah Salamat summoned the courtesans and inquired privately, he learnt that many nobles were associating with them without permission. Raja Birbal was at his jagir when he learnt that the list His Majesty had contained his name as well. Many among the nobles were reprimanded, punished and even imprisoned. Raja Birbal decided to become a mendicant but Badshah Salamat reassured him and called him back to the court. No punishment was awarded to him.

It is said that Emperor Akbar, once when he heard of the qualities of Praveen Rai, the mistress of the Prince of Orchha, Inderjit Singh, summoned her, to which she replied that only dogs and crows would eat from a plate from which food has already been had. When Badshah Salamat's orders were not complied with, a fine of one crore was imposed. The poet Keshavdas was a friend of Prince Inderjit as also Raja Birbal's.

In a secret meeting with Raja Birbal he said:

The creator of fire, animal, bird, stone, serpent, river, the world
and ten directions has created a unique one,
O Keshav, it is not possible to praise the creations of the one
who has created gods and un-gods.
Even God must feel blessed after creating the exalted soul, Birbal,
By bestowing divinity upon him, He has created another god.

A flattered Raja Birbal gave six lakh rupees and got Inderjit Singh's fine waived.

Some people in the court could not abide the status Raja Birbal enjoyed. Mullah Abdul Qadir Badayuni wrote in his secret book:

'The Emperor right from his youth had shown a special predilection and inclination for the society of various religious sects, such as Brahmins, and musicians, and other sections of Hindus. Accordingly, at the beginning of his reign, a certain Brahmin musician, Gadai Brahmadas by name, from the district of Kalpi, whose entire business was perpetually to praise the Hindus, and who was possessed of a considerable amount of capacity and genius, came to the court. By means of conversing with the Emperor and taking advantage of the idiosyncrasies of his disposition, he crept day by day into favour, until he attained to high rank, and was honoured with the distinction of becoming the Emperor's confidant, and it became a case of "Thy flesh is my flesh, and thy blood my blood".'

The region where Raja Birbal died was often a source of trouble for the Timuri kingdom. When the Rajputs had at first resisted crossing Attock for fear of pollution, Badshah Salamat wrote this couplet and sent it to them:

All world is God's, wherein is Attock,
Only the one who has a block—atak—inside will be stuck.

Badshah Salamat was related to the Yusufzais. His grandfather Babur Badshah had married Bibi Mubarka of the Yusufzai tribe.

This is spoken of a time when Babur Badshah ruled over Kabul. Despite a campaign against the Yusufzais, the fort at the Mahura Hills could not be taken. To judge the Yusufzais' strength, Firdaus Makani Babur Badshah disguised himself and went to their stronghold. There the granddaughter of the chief of the Yusufzai tribe, Bibi Mubarka's eyes fell upon him, and taking him to be a qalandar—mendicant—she sent a servant to him with some cooked meat folded between two loaves.

Babur Badshah asked the servant, 'Who has sent this?'

When the servant told him, Firdaus Makani asked, 'Where is she?'

'That is she, sitting in front of you in the tent.'

Emperor Babur was at once captivated by her beauty. Before leaving the place, he hid between two stones the food that had been sent for him.

After returning, when he sent a message seeking Bibi Mubarka's hand, many excuses were made from the girl's side. They even claimed that they did not have any girl of marriageable age. Babur Badshah then wrote in a letter, 'I have seen Bibi Mubarka myself. If you seek evidence for my truth, find the food I have hidden near your house.'

Although Bibi Mubarka's family was not willing, the tribesmen felt that by giving a daughter, the Yusufzai tribe could be saved from the wrath of Babur.

After the marriage, when Babur Badshah came to Bibi Mubarka for the first time, she was standing in her tent with folded hands. She bowed to Emperor Babur but her face remained covered. After seating himself on the divan, Firdaus Makani twice asked Bibi Mubarka to sit close to him. She just bowed and came and stood a bit nearer.

Losing patience, when Firdaus Makani removed the veil from her face and asked her again to sit, she said, 'I have a petition. If you permit, I will make it.'

After receiving permission, Bibi Mubarka took one end of her dress in her hands and said, 'Imagine that the entire Yusufzai tribe is enfolded in this skirt and pardon their offences for my sake.'

Emperor Babur replied, 'I forgive the Yusufzais all their offences in your presence and cast them all in your skirt. Hereafter, I shall have no ill-feeling to the Yusufzai.'

Bibi Mubarka lived to see the reign of Babur Badshah, Humayun Badshah and the early years of Badshah Salamat.

Despite this family relationship, insubordination could not be forgiven.

In 1586 CE, which was the thirtieth regnal year of Badshah Salamat, Zain Khan Koka was deputed to defeat the Yusufzai tribe. His army was tired by the time he reached Swat after bringing Bajaur under control. When he requisitioned reinforcements, Badshah Salamat decided upon Birbal's name after casting a die. As a precautionary measure, he also sent Hakim Abul Fath after some time.

Raja Birbal was not on good terms with Hakim Abul Fath or Zain Khan Koka. Travelling through the hills, Raja Birbal told his people, 'It looks as if my fortune has been inverted that I should traverse with the Hakim to support the Koka.'

When Raja Birbal and Abul Fath arrived, Zain Khan Koka arranged a feast for them which Birbal refused to attend. He said that all should come to him and decide the future course. Zain Khan Koka held back his anger and came to Raja Birbal. In the meeting there was a harsh exchange between Raja Birbal and Hakim Abul Fath.

Zain Khan Koka said, 'The work in the hills is nearly over, and the rebels of Karakar and Buner have come forward in a submissive manner. But they have not advanced from words to deeds. I have thus asked for reinforcements in order that a body of men remain in the fort, and the rest march to punish the malcontents. The reinforcements should undertake this task. I and the old army will remain in the centre of the country on guard. Or the reinforcements might elect to remain at Chakdara and I would go and punish the hillmen.'

Raja Birbal and Hakim Abul Fath said, 'Neither proposition is acceptable to us. The orders were to attack the country, not to guard it. We should all combine to chastise the enemy and then hasten by that road together to the court.'

Zain Khan Koka replied, 'Why should we leave disorganized a country which has come into our hands after so much fighting?'

Zain Khan Koka told Raja Birbal that it was not advisable to take the route he proposed to take.

Zain Khan Koka said, 'If you don't accept my suggestion and are resolved to march, it is far better to go back the way we came. On that side there are troops stationed, and the enemy will have no power to interfere with us.'

When Raja Birbal and Hakim Abul Fath refused to heed his advice, Zain Khan Koka did not insist. Since he thought that these two could poison Badshah Salamat's ears, it was better to agree.

Raja Birbal and Hakim Abul Fath had their way and decided to embark in the wrong direction. The apprehensions proved well-founded.

There was a fierce clash between the royal forces and the Afghan rebels. When the army halted at Khanpur, it had suffered heavily as a result of attacks and plunder but thousands of Afghans had been taken prisoner and a lot of booty obtained.

When Zain Khan Koka went to the tent of Raja Birbal and pointed out to him the poor consequences that had resulted from haste, he was told, 'Little of the road remains to be traversed. The proper course would be to get through the defile and then halt for some days and to then renew the punishment of the rebels.'

Zain Khan Koka said, 'The defiles in front of us are the worst of all, and to go by such a route would be to cast away our honour.

The proper course is to build a wall at the station where we are, for it is fairly spacious. There is no danger of being attacked from the heights, and there is abundance of water and grass, and plenty of food. Here we should stand firm and afterward inflict punishment on the presumptuous rebels who have taken possession of all the heights. Another course is that as we have in our hands the enemy's families and much of their property, we may write soothingly to them, and take from them promises of obedience. We may return the prisoners, keeping some as hostages. If this proposition is also not approved, we could halt for a time and send news to court. An army would come from there and guard the top of the pass.'

Zain Khan Koka's proposals were rejected and a decision taken to press forward. Raja Birbal, Hakim Abul Fath, Zain Khan Koka and the army moved ahead through the defiles and there was a fight fiercer than before. The Afghans attacked them with arms and stones from all sides with such ferocity that one could not tell the horses from the elephants or the men. Raja Birbal was besieged in such a manner that even his body could not be recovered. Badshah Salamat had not grieved over the death of any noble the way he grieved now.

Mancharitra Raso written in praise of Raja Man Singh says:

The world knows Brahmadas has merged into the Brahma,
Maya could not control him, so why would he stay here?
Brahmadas strived, so did nobles with a mansab of thousands.
Many fled from the battle, defiled their name and honour.
The Emperor was not at peace, no sleep in his eyes.
He said that his army never lost, never heard wails of sorrow.
The Emperor called Raja Man and asked,
I am in deep pain, I do not feel like eating.
O King, come what may, do not grieve.
I would set out for the difficult valley tomorrow.
Would shove them or tie them and bring them here.
Would raze their fort and burn the city.
A happy Emperor said, our honour is in your hands now.
He dined and bade goodbye to Man Singh.
After a peaceful night, drums were sounded in the morning.
There was commotion as Man Singh's army marched.
Then the Emperor said to Raja Man,

He was my Brahmin friend and my honour.
When you reach there, do remember.
Find his body and carefully consign it to the Ganga.
Man Singh said, I am a Hindu, he a Brahmin.
I would immerse his remains and that of others in the Ganga.

That Raja Birbal's body could not be found remained a cause for deep sorrow to Badshah Salamat. He lamented, 'Alas, that they could not bring his body out of that defile, that it might have been consigned to the flames.'

The nobles told him, 'Since he is freed and delivered from all the bonds of mortality, the light of the sun is sufficient purifier for him, although indeed he did not require any purification.'

When he heard a rumour that Raja Birbal had been sighted in Nagarkot in the company of mendicants and monks, he thought that Birbal had detached himself from the world and become a faqir. When Badshah Salamat sent somebody to Nagarkot to investigate, this report was found to be false.

Then it was heard that Raja Birbal had been seen in his fief at Kalinjar. It was reported that he was being anointed with oil, when a confidant of his, a barber, recognized him by certain marks on his body. Thereafter he vanished. When Badshah Salamat sought a report, the official took hold of a man who had been condemned to death, kept him concealed as Birbal and had him killed not long after. The official then reported that Birbal died before he could reach the court.

Badshah Salamat mourned for Birbal a second time.

A letter condoling the death reached Gujarat also. People saw the governor come out himself and, after bending in a taslim, receive the royal communication, placing it on his head in accordance with protocol. The person holding the letter on his head was not just the governor, he was also a high-ranking mansabdar of five thousand. A short while ago he had been bestowed the highest title of Khan-i-Khanan. Badshah Salamat expressed his sorrow at losing Raja Birbal in the letter to Abdur Rahim Khan-i-Khanan—

'In these joyful times when there is ample cause for celebration and news of victory pours in from all sides, the imperial forces sent to conquer Swat and Bajaur met with a misfortune of incalculable proportions. Though the Afghans were defeated, and Swat and

Bajaur came under imperial sway, the wicked Afghans who were lying in ambush in the interior of the hills were not chased with sufficient prudence. Although some of them were killed, the wise men holding charge of the imperial forces lost control and began to traverse through a difficult terrain with a large load of goods at a time that was not appropriate. The onslaught of the short-sighted Afghans from the sides of the hills caused such chaos that the royal army lost its way and some people even fell down the hill. In this disorderly situation Raja Birbal lost his life.

'Raja Birbal was among the closest of the close—a faithful, sincere, wise and knowledgeable courtier, a companion of pleasant gatherings, a loyalist, a well-wisher, a person who shone in the gathering of fluent orators, one who had an insight into human associations, a relentless seeker of truth, a person with firm belief in discharging obligations, a good-natured son, truly a devoted person, and a jewel of the sacred abode of sovereignty. Despite being in the worldly state of bondage, he had been free. Having now sacrificed his life for the Emperor, he has departed from this ephemeral world and taken a path which all must take. Even the obligation of surrendering life for the master was fulfilled while discharging his imperial duties.

'We deeply regret not attending the funeral due to late arrival of messengers. We could not see our friend for one last time and display our affection to a person deeply devoted to our aims. Although our feelings for him are known to those close to us, we wish to express it fully so that everybody realizes how the Emperor values the devoted ones.

'We live in a transient world, which is like a ravine through which flows blood. The departure of the person from this world to the next does not affect us, as the qualities and appearance of the person who has travelled to the other world are etched in our mind. However, even this temporary separation from a person of unparalleled qualities has created a void and caused pain which is beyond words. Anybody who has come into being from nothingness would ultimately lapse into nothingness. Khan-i-Khanan should accept the will of God with fortitude, and instead of grieving, should now spend his life seeking divine truth and in expressing gratitude to Him.'

Abdur Rahim was very close to Badshah Salamat. As he grew up, Badshah Salamat kept entrusting higher responsibilities to him. When he attained the age of majority, he was awarded the title of Mirza Khan and married to Mah Bano, the daughter of Shamsuddin Muhammad Atka Khan and sister of Mirza Aziz Koka.

In the twenty-fifth regnal year, Badshah Salamat felt the need of a person who would make no distinction between acquaintance and stranger, friend and foe, but lay before the Emperor all proper requests, and at an appropriate time receive the replies to them, and who should not be disheartened upon not getting a gracious reply, but should have the courage to repeat the request at another time. For this he appointed Mirza Khan to the high office of Mir Arz—the chief of petitions.

In 1575 CE, in the twentieth regnal year of Badshah Salamat, Mirza Aziz Koka gave up the office of the governor of Gujarat in protest; Mirza Abdur Rahim got this significant responsibility at an early age. After about nine years when Muzaffar Hussain Mirza reared his head, Gujarat again slipped from the hands of Badshah Salamat. Badshah Salamat had then given the governorship of Gujarat to Mirza Abdur Rahim for a second time. When he broke the back of Muzaffar Hussain Mirza, he got the highest title which once belonged to his father Bairam Khan.

Once the poet Naziri Nishapuri told the Khan-i-Khanan, 'I have never seen one lakh rupees.'

When Abdur Rahim Khan-i-Khanan made a pile of one lakh, Naziri thanked God. At this the Khan-i-Khanan said, 'Why thank God for such a small matter?'

He gifted the entire amount to Naziri Nishapuri and said, 'Now it would be appropriate to thank God.'

The poet Sant wrote of the Khan-i-Khanan:

As upright and proper as the lion, as patient as the mountain,
He is beautiful and famous.
As rich as Kuber, did wonders in Kaliyuga,
Saviour to those in prison or in distress.
For meeting the dervishes and giving them alms,
His deeds are talked about the world over.
For the seeker of high qualities and seeker of happiness,
O poet Sant, Khan-i-Khanan is a treasury of wealth.

Impressed with the benevolence of Abdur Rahim Khan-i-Khanan, the poet Gang asked,

> *O nobleman, wherefrom did you learn this manner of giving,*
> *You lower your eyes as you raise your hands to give?*

To this the Khan-i-Khanan replied:

> *The Giver is someone else, who sends day and night,*
> *People think it's me, thus, I lower my eyes.*

Once Miyan Tansen recited Surdas's poetry about Lord Krishna's mother Yashoda in the court—

> *Jasoda baar baar yon bhakhe,*
> *Hai kaun Braj mein hitu, hamaro chalat Gopal hi rakhe.*

When Badshah Salamat asked what it meant, Miyan Tansen replied, 'Jasoda says, who is such a benefactor of ours, who may prevent Gopal from going so often—"baar baar"—to Mathura.'

Sheikh Faizi said, '"Baar baar" means weeping. So it means Jasoda is weeping and saying...'

Raja Birbal said, '"Baar baar" means door to door. So it means Jasoda moves from door to door saying...'

An astrologer present in the assembly said, '"Baar" means day. So it means, Jasoda says every day...'

Finally Abdur Rahim Khan-i-Khanan said, '"Baar baar" means "baal baal", that is, every hair. So it means, every hair of Jasoda speaks...'

Having heard everyone, Badshah Salamat said, 'Each one of you gave a different meaning of "baar baar". How come?'

The Khan-i-Khanan replied, 'Poetic skill lies in the use of a word that has multiple meanings. Every listener would have his own interpretation. But the meaning which I gave is accurate. Tansen just writes songs. His duty is to sing often—'baar baar'—the Darbari Raga at Your Majesty's court. Thus his interpretation. Faizi is just a poet. What does he know except weeping and wailing? Birbal is a Brahmin who goes from door to door. So he gave the meaning accordingly. And what would an astrologer know except days, nights, stars, planets and constellations?'

In his sleeping apartment at the Agra Fort, Badshah Salamat remembered the poet Holrai who had said:

There is no throne like Delhi's, no age like the Mughal's,
There is no city like Agra.
None as talented as Gang, none as musical as Tansen,
No ruler like Man and none generous as Birbal.
No human as Khan-i-Khanan,
There is no revenue minister as Todar Mal.
In nine continents, seven islands and the seven seas,
There is none like Jalaluddin Shah Akbar.

Now the assemblies had long since ended and there was nothing but the silence and loneliness of a sinking life.

6

Badshah Salamat heard pigeons flutter their wings outside. He owned twenty thousand pigeons. He called pigeon-flying 'ishqbazi'—love affair. Badshah Salamat believed that the joy one derives from the flying and tumbling of the pigeons was like the ecstasy of the dervishes. When young, Badshah Salamat was fond of pigeon-flying but when he grew older, he gave it up. Thereafter, on mature consideration, he took to pigeon-flying again. Badshah Salamat was fond of a pigeon named Mohana. This well-trained pigeon of bluish colour was a gift from Mirza Aziz Koka. Badshah Salamat made Mohana the chief of imperial pigeons. Many excellent pigeons like Ashki, Parizad, Almas and Shah Udi had descended from Mohana. When Badshah Salamat inspected the pigeons he would first look at Mohana's stock and then to the rest of the pigeons. Badshah Salamat enjoyed the skills the pigeons displayed. He particularly liked the trick called charkh, in which the pigeon threw itself over in a full circle, and bazi, in which the pigeon would have its feet up and quickly turn around.

In a letter to Abdur Rahim Khan-i-Khanan, Badshah Salamat expressed his joy at receiving pigeons from Abdullah Khan Uzbek—

'In the way they soar skyward and perform their acrobatics, they are incomparable to any species of pigeons known from earliest times till now. Even when a loyal friend like Khan-i-Khanan is absent from our assemblies, he would always be remembered at such joyful times.

'Various groups of pigeons have silently conveyed their greetings to Khan-i-Khanan. Some of the pigeons are old but perform like young, as the skilful Purnigar. They say that their prayers were answered when they got the opportunity to come under the patronage of the Emperor; they were filled with a vigour and found a new life. Now they wish to make up for lost years and perform for the Emperor and do not want to be dispersed. They have thus requested the Khan-i-Khanan—who is devoted to the Emperor—and other well-meaning courtiers to not ask for the pigeons in a veiled manner. Another pigeon Sabzgahi, the daughter of Sarsabz, of high breed, desires that it should be allowed to stay here along with her progeny and relatives, to serve the Emperor in the best possible manner. Although the pigeons have spent a lifetime attracting others, they are now attracted to their beloved Emperor. The desires of the courtiers, especially the Khan-i-Khanan, should not be an impediment to the joys of the Emperor. They should desist asking for the pigeons. Separation is better than union.

'The pigeon called Kuttapar is of Khurasan stock, although the name comes from Transoxiana. It is the leader of the trustworthy pigeons, somewhat shorn of their plumage, and soars high in the sky.

'One who is light in weight flies conveniently,
A light bird flies higher and quicker.

'There's another known as Masha'al-i-kalan which rises high like a torch in the air. Its black tail is like the smoke rising from the burning heart of the lovers of pigeons. The pigeon named Purnigar reminds one of the legendary figure Laila the movement of whose feet would mesmerize people. All the pigeons are of a high stock and are good looking—a few like Purnigar, most like Sabzgahi. Since all the pigeons had come to display their skills and please the Emperor and others at the court, they would not want their group to be dispersed. So much so that they want to send a message to the pigeons of Mecca, who were flying round the holy Ka'ba, that they should pray for the realization of this goal.'

The ruler who sent the pigeons was one whose power had caused unease to Badshah Salamat. Abdullah Khan Uzbek drew his lineage to Changez Khan's eldest son Jochi, through Shaibani Khan. Jalaluddin Muhammad Akbar's grandfather Babur Badshah had been forced to flee Samarqand by this Uzbek power and he had to thus come to Kabul, and then Hindustan. After the death of Shah Tahmasp of Persia, Abdullah Khan Uzbek had attacked Khurasan and the Ottoman ruler had invaded northern Persia. Badshah Salamat refused to be part of a campaign against Persia. He did not want to see Ottoman Turks or the Uzbek power become stronger. When Abdullah Khan Uzbek captured Balkh and Badakhshan, and Badshah Salamat annexed Kabul after the death of Mirza Hakim, the two empires became immediate neighbours. Now Badshah Salamat moved to Lahore to keep a watch on the situation.

On the third of September 1586 CE, in the thirty-first regnal year, a firman was written on behalf of Badshah Salamat for Abdullah Khan Uzbek, one draft of which was prepared by Hakim Abul Fath and another by Sheikh Abul Fazl.

Badshah Salamat would often get two people to write a draft firman. He once asked Sheikh Abul Fazl and Hakim Abul Fath to prepare drafts while on the move near Sirhind. When Hakim Abul Fath came to him the next day, Badshah Salamat asked, 'It rained so much last night. More than it would in the rainy season. You wrote the firman or went to sleep?'

Hakim Abul Fath took the firman from his pocket and read it out. Badshah Salamat listened to it very attentively from beginning to the end and said, 'It is very well written.'

When Sheikh Abul Fazl presented his draft, Badshah Salamat said, 'Hakim Abul Fath has written a very good draft. Tell us if something is left out so that it can be included.'

In a similar manner, Hakim Abul Fath read out to Badshah Salamat his draft of the firman for Abdullah Khan Uzbek—

'We have always sought divine approval for our deeds. But there being serious differences in matters of religion, we have been asking for proof for every argument that is presented. To fully understand the subtleties of religion, we are looking into interpretations of the jurists, objectives of theologians, sources of arguments that are presented, beliefs old and new, and multiple views that have arisen in the past one thousand years. As a result, many regarded as learned faced a devaluation. On the other hand, it brought to the fore some competent people who had been forced into a life of anonymity by the theologians. Mistakenly regarded as wise, these theologians even misguided some rebellious nobles of Bengal. They would sometimes say that the Emperor claims to be God, and at other times Prophet. They brought about their own downfall. Divinity cannot be associated with worldly deeds, nor can prophethood be reached by those who are tied to worldly desires.

'It is surprising that a divinely assisted individual like Abdullah Khan has lent credence to even an iota of this gossip. We do not resent this slander because of our faith in the will of God. Why should ordinary human beings worry about slander when even God and the Prophet have not been spared? Our lofty fortunes stand testimony to the fact that we live by the commands of God and the Prophet.

'Emperors seek peace for the people and wish to save them from exploitation, so that they can pray to God and earn their livelihood. As custodian of our subjects, we have subjugated recalcitrant rulers and brought together a heterogeneous group of people. The places of worship of the infidels and the heretics have turned into the abodes of God-fearing dervishes. With divine grace we have renewed our efforts to deliver justice to the people.'

The draft that Abul Fazl prepared on the instructions of Badshah Salamat did not contain any criticism of the ulema or any reference to the sharp reactions that his religious views had evoked. After referring to his exploits in Hindustan, Badshah Salamat said that his attention was now outwards—

'I have kept before my mind the idea that when I should be entirely at liberty from these tasks, I should, under the guidance of God's favour, undertake the destruction of the Firangi infidels who have come up to the islands of the ocean, and have lifted up the head of turbulence, and stretched out the hand of oppression upon the pilgrims to the holy places. They have become great in number and are stumbling blocks to the pilgrims and traders. We thought of going in person and cleansing that road of thorns and weeds. But as we heard that some of the officers of Persia had proved disloyal to their sovereign, and had cast away the firm handle of fidelity—which had been the means of their exaltation—and had committed various improprieties, it passed into our mind that we should appoint to that region one of our sons—from whose forehead there streamed the rays of auspiciousness, and in whose horoscope were the lights of justice—and not undertake any other work until that was disposed of. At present when the Sultan of Turkey, regarding the treaties and agreements made by his father and grandfather as non-existent, has looked to the ostensibly feeble condition of Persia and has, several times, sent his troops there, we shall, passing over the circumstance of the deviation from the highway of Sunnism and looking only to the relationship with the family of the Prophet, proceed thither and help them. Assuredly, ancient things should be borne in mind, especially at this time when, as we hear, the ruler of Persia has dispatched able men of that country with presents, and with a prayer for help. It befits our sublime spirit that we should fling out the reins of interest towards Iraq and Khurasan and Abdullah Khan meet us in Khurasan...'

A few years after this Badshah Salamat wrote to Abdullah Khan Uzbek:

'... Our stay in Punjab had been wrongly interpreted. Things have been mentioned that are far from our mind. Though we are fond of hunting, and the climate of Punjab suited us, we have decided to return to Agra, so that liars are silenced.'

Despite writing this, Badshah Salamat did not leave Punjab while Abdullah Khan Uzbek was alive. On the banks of the Ravi, a dervish disallowed anybody from entering his cell. He said, 'I am engaged in special devotion. Until the death of Abdullah Khan, the governor of Turan, I will not leave this place, nor allow anyone access.'

At this Badshah Salamat said, 'If his are the prayers that are heard, then let him gird up his loins for my welfare, and refrain from this foolish prayer.'

On the first day of the forty-third regnal year of Badshah Salamat, news was received that Abdullah Khan Uzbek, the king of Turan, had passed away. When some rejoiced, Badshah Salamat restrained them and said, 'Farsighted people would not do this.'

Badshah Salamat also rejected the suggestion that an expedition be sent against Turan. He said, 'Now that Turan is a seat of turmoil, how does an expedition there agree with our humanity? It is far better that an able ambassador be sent to offer condolences, and to speak words of counsel.'

One day Badshah Salamat got a piece of bad news from Persia. With his own hands Shah Abbas had cut the Nuqtawi and a disciple of Badshah Salamat in two.

Like Turan, Badshah Salamat's religious views had rattled the Persian court as well.

Iskander Beg Munshi, the chronicler of Shah Abbas's reign, wrote in the *Tarikh-i-Alam Ara-i-Abbasi*:

'Sheikh Abul Fazl, a learned man in the service of the Mughal emperor Jalaluddin Muhammad Akbar had converted the Emperor to latitudinarian ideas and seduced him from the path of the sharia. A document which had been signed by Sheikh Abul Fazl and sent to Mir Sayyid Ahmed Kashi and had been found among his papers, corroborated this.'

'Firman of Hazrat Jalaluddin Akbar Padshah for Mir Ahmed Kashi...'

The firman that Badshah Salamat sent in 1584 CE was the kind that is sent to disciples—

'...work in Persia as our representative and guide the people of Persia. Keep us informed of your spiritual experiences and seek our advice in every matter. Geographical distance does not matter when there is spiritual affinity.'

The Nuqtawi believed that human life arises from a point—a nuqta—of earth. They presupposed transmigration of souls. They performed certain prayers with their faces turned towards the sun and believed in the Mahdi—the promised guide.

The Nuqtawis believed that in the year 990 of the Hijri calendar, which was 1582 CE, there would be a conjunction of planets and the age of Islam would end and under their messiah the Nuqtawi movement would be at the pinnacle. The Nuqtawis believed that Safavid rule would end and its place would be taken by a new king and messiah.

And the day did come when a Nuqtawi sat on the throne of Persia. But under strange circumstances. In 1587 CE Shah Abbas became the king after deposing his father Muhammad Khudabanda and an era of powerful rule began in Persia. Around 1590 CE, astrologers found that a conjunction of inauspicious planets would claim the life of a ruler and that too probably in Persia. Upon examination of Shah Abbas's horoscope, it was ascertained that he was extremely vulnerable on certain two to three specific days. A plan was devised to avert the evil influence. A Nuqtawi was placed on the throne of Persia. Shah Abbas himself prostrated before him and stood in his presence like a courtier. The nobles of the realm attended the court of the new emperor. As soon as the three days of kingship were over, the Nuqtawi was killed and his body hung for public display.

After proving the Nuqtawi prophesy of the end of Safavid rule wrong, Shah Abbas returned to his throne and killed every Nuqtawi who could be found. Only those who escaped to Hindustan or melted into a life of anonymity could save their lives.

In December of 1594 CE, which was the thirty-ninth regnal year, Badshah Salamat wrote to Shah Abbas:

'Allahu Akbar! Praise and supplication of the sublime threshold of Unity are such that if all the niceties of reason and all the categories of intellect and the host of sciences were gathered together, that would not amount to one ray of that sun, though, in the eyes of truth, all the modes of existence are a fountainhead of divine praise. Since one cannot adequately express one's gratitude to God, it is better to apply oneself to the laudation of the glorious company of the prophets and apostles. Let us proclaim their glorious conditions and their beautiful gifts whereby they have led mankind from the defiles of error into the highway of favour and guidance, and let us tell of the bounties and noble qualities of the family of Prophet Muhammad, who are the confidants of the great secrets and unveilers of the mysteries of the prophets, and let us implore mercy through them. The greatness of the congregation of spiritual persons who have laid down their lives for truth are a reflection of His qualities.

'The beholding of the honoured letter exuding goodwill sent along with Yadgar Sultan Shamlu in the midst of spring and at the time of equability of night and day made our loving soul to exult. What you have written about the delay in writing letters of affection is very appropriate. In truth, spiritual relationships require that there should not be such delays. But you must have learnt from comers and goers about important affairs and continued wars against the princes of India, which has been reckoned by geometricians as four-sixths of the seven climes. During this long period, this vast country with numerous chiefs and rulers has by divine aid been conquered. From the mountains of the Hindukush to the shores of the ocean all the arrogant rajas, short-sighted Afghan tribesmen, desert-dwelling Baluchi tribesmen, forest-dwellers and zamindars have come under the shade of obedience, and the tribes of mankind have enjoyed equability in concord.

'When Punjab had become the seat of sovereignty it was our intention to send an able ambassador but some urgent expeditions delayed this. The chief of these was the deliverance of the inhabitants of Kashmir from the hands of villainous tyrants. In spite of the strength of the country, and the long marches, the dense forests, the numerous ravines—which can with difficulty be crossed by the forces of imagination—were, by divine aid and blessings of the Imams, traversed by the sublime army in an excellent manner. Several thousand stone-cutters went on, stage by stage, in advance to make the roads, enabling the conquest in a short time. When that splendid country—which is lauded by all who approve of beauty—was granted to us by divine favour, we ourselves went there and offered thanksgiving. We travelled to the hill country of Tibet and then proceeded by the difficult route of Pakli and Damtaur to Kabul and Ghazni. We punished the Afghan plunderers of Swat, Bajaur, Tirah and Bangash, who are a threat to travellers to Turan, and punished the wicked Baluchis and other desert dwellers who are an obstacle in the path of travellers to Persia.

'However, the root of the delay was the confusion in Persia and the distracted state of the country after the death of His Majesty the Shah. When the ambassador arrived with an auspicious message, it became known that the confusion is diminishing.

'In the rules of humanity as also sovereignty, concord is preferable to opposition and peace better than war. It has been our disposition not to pay attention to differences of religion and to regard the tribes of mankind as servants of God. The blessings of this lofty principle—which is in accord with magnanimity—have once again shown themselves. At this time when Punjab was the seat of our government, our intention was to move towards Transoxiana, which was the country of our ancestors, so that it might come under our possession, and also that the family of the Prophet might be assisted in a suitable manner. Meanwhile, Abdullah Khan, the ruler of Turan, sent loving letters referring to ancient relationships. Since going to war with one who is disposed to peace is contrary to divine decrees, our head turned away from this project.

'We hope that knowing that our loving heart is disposed towards every kind of subject and enterprise, the Shah will tread the beautiful path of correspondence and diurnal reports.

'In every undertaking it is advisable to have regard for caution and a thought for the final result. Let not your heart be perplexed by the fictions of interested people. Bear with the mistakes of hereditary servants and new employees and exercise supreme caution before putting anyone to death and destroying what is an edifice of God. Many lifelong friends have lost their lives due to the craft of the enemies and seeming friends. Many enemies and seeming friends have donned the garb of loyalty and engaged in destroying the foundations of dominion. It must be considered that divine mercy extends to every creed and there should be sulh-i-kul—peace with all. The increase of one's good fortune must always be kept in view, for the eternal God is bounteous to all souls. Hence it is fitting that kings, who are a shadow of God, should not cast away this principle. The Creator has decreed that the kings are the guardians of all mankind. Men do not intentionally make mistakes. Why would they be negligent in the affairs of faith and religion, which are permanent and everlasting? The position of every sect comes under one of the two categories. Either it is in possession of truth, and in that case one should seek directions from it and accept its views. Or it is in the wrong, and then it is unfortunate and suffering from ignorance, and is a subject of pitying kindness, not harshness and reproach. One must exercise wide toleration so that friends are not destroyed under the idea that they are enemies, and enemies masquerading as friends will not have an opportunity for deceit. One must strenuously adhere to one's word, for this is a pillar of rule. Patience and endurance must ever be one's companions, for the maintenance of permanent dominion depends thereon.'

There was unease over Badshah Salamat's religious views not just in the royal courts of other countries but inside Badshah Salamat's family also.

In 1601 CE, a firman of the rebel Prince Salim reached Badshah Salamat—

'At the instigation of some mischievous persons, my father has abolished the arrangements for the maintenance of the khatib, muezzin and imam in the mosques and has prohibited the performance of namaz in congregation. He has converted many of the mosques into storehouses and stables. It was improper on his part to have acted in this manner. Stipends for the maintenance of the mosques, the khatib, the muezzin and the imam should be resumed and people should be induced to offer prayers. Anyone showing slackness in this respect would be duly punished.'

Badshah Salamat used to say, 'The object of outward worship which they affect to call a new divine institute, is for the awakening of slumberers, otherwise the praise of God comes from the heart not the body… That which is without form cannot be seen whether in sleeping or waking, but it is apprehensible by force of imagination.'

Once Prince Murad asked Badshah Salamat, 'Worship should be truly spiritual and is done from the heart but if someone in my camp is found performing in the manner of imitating theologians those physical movements that are called namaz and not eating from morning till night which is called roza…when real prayer to God does not include the body and physical movements, is he to be forbidden or left in his ways?'

Badshah Salamat replied, 'The presence of people of various kinds is divine strength. You should remain firm on sulh-i-kul with the entire world. To have noble intentions and to give advice is proper for every person. Every person treading the path of reason is fortunate and one who is stuck in the barren land of tradition is helpless. To know and worship God through any path is good. To stop an ignorant from considering physical movements as worship is just like stopping somebody from remembering God.'

Badshah Salamat told Murad, 'The worship of one who is matchless is beyond the boundary of words…the worship of the matchless would be matchless. God willing, you will understand this divine secret. For now, as an auspicious beginning, all that can be said is that you should have thoughts of honesty and praiseworthy deeds in your mind and keep us pleased so that with our blessings another door may open for the worship of God.'

Murad asked, 'If I get to know of any dervish, yogi, monk or faqir, what are the instructions about meeting him?'

Badshah Salamat replied, 'Meeting them is an indicator of the quest for God. Do meet them but care should be exercised in meeting those who have given up worldly affairs. Don't meet them if you learn that more of the things they say create a scare and do meet them if you learn that there is more of good in what they say.'

The prince asked, 'Can I get a book or two that will elevate my mind and remove old thinking to guide me?'

Badshah Salamat said, 'There is unlikely to be such a book in the quagmire of tradition but thinking of you I am sending a translation of *Mahabharata* which is a strange story.'

On the first day of the first month of Farwardin of the fortieth regnal year, which was the ninth of the month of Rajab of 1003 of the Hijri calendar, indicating towards Mullah Badayuni, Badshah Salamat said, 'We thought that he is an unworldly individual of Sufi tendencies, but he appears to be such a bigoted lawyer that no sword can sever the jugular vein of his bigotry.'

Abul Fazl asked, 'In what book has the author written thus?'

'In *Razmnama*,' replied Badshah Salamat.

When the translation of *Mahabharata* was completed under the name *Razmnama*, Badshah Salamat was so pleased that he asked the nobles to have copies made.

Mullah Abdul Qadir Badayuni said, 'The following considerations disposed the Emperor to the work. When he had had the *Shahnama* and *The Story of Amir Hamza* in seventeen volumes transcribed in fifteen years, and had spent much gold in illuminating it...it suddenly came into his mind that most of these books were nothing but poetry and fiction; but that, since they were first related in a lucky hour, and when their star was in the act of passing over the sky, they obtained great fame. But now he ordered those Hindu books, which holy sages had written, and were all clear and convincing proofs, and which were the very pivot on which all their religion, and faith, and holiness turned, to be translated from the Indian to the Persian language, and thought to himself, "Why should I not have them done in my name, for they are by no means trite, but quite fresh, and they will produce all kind of fruits of felicity both temporal and spiritual, and will be the cause of circumstance and pomp, and will ensure an abundance of children and wealth, as is written in the preface of these books." Accordingly, he became much interested in the work.'

In *Tarikh-i-Alfi*, Asaf Khan Jafar Beg wrote about Badshah Salamat: 'His heart is inclined to justice, desiring that the followers of different faiths, each having become acquainted with the truth and reality of others' religion, should act with restraint and abandon bigotry. He has accordingly ordered that the rational contents of different religions and faiths should be translated in the language of each, and that the rose garden of traditional aspects of each religion should, as far as possible, be cleared of the thorns of bigotry.'

At night, Badshah Salamat would study the meaning of the text of the *Mahabharata* himself through Devi Mishra, Madhusudan Mishra, Rudra Bhattacharya and Sheikh Bhawan, and then explain it to Naqib Khan, Sultan Haji Thanesari, Mullah Sheri and Mullah Abdul Qadir Badayuni so that they could translate.

Now it transpired that in Mullah Abdul Qadir Badayuni's translation into Persian, a saint says before death, 'It is right that a man should step out of the limits of ignorance and negligence, and should first of all become acquainted with the peerless Creator, and should pursue the path of knowledge; and not be satisfied with mere knowledge without practice, for that yields no fruit, but should choose the path of virtue, and as far as in him lies, withdraw his hand from evil actions, and should know for a certainty that every action will be inquired into.'

Badshah Salamat felt that instead of translating the *Mahabharata* into Persian, Mullah Badayuni had interpolated some issues regarding the Day of Judgment.

'Useless, greedy fellow, *shalghamkhor*!' Badshah Salamat said in anger.

Mullah Abdul Qadir explained, 'The people of India speak of reward and punishment of good and bad actions. Their beliefs are as follows: when a person dies, the scribe, who writes the chronicle of the deeds of mankind throughout the course of their lives, takes it before the angel, who is the Seizer of Souls, and is called the King of Justice. After he has examined into their good and bad actions, and has seen which has the preponderance, he says, "This person has his choice." Then he asks him, "Shall I first for thy good actions take thee to paradise, that thou mayest there enjoy to the full delights in proportion to thy good actions, and after that send thee to Hell to expiate thy sins; or vice versa?" When that period comes to an end, then he gives orders that the person should return to the Earth, and entering a form suitable to his actions should pass a certain period. And so on ad infinitum, until the time when he attains absolute release, and is freed from coming into and leaving the world.'

The entire court was all ears to what Mullah Abdul Qadir Badayuni was saying. He said, 'I am a translator. Nothing more. Whatever the sages of India had represented therein, I had translated without alteration, but that if I had written it myself, I should have been to blame, and should have acted wrongly.'

Sheikh Abul Fazl realized what had happened and saved Mullah Abdul Qadir by preventing the matter from taking an ugly turn that day.

7

A naubat was playing at the royal fort of Agra. It was dawn. One ghari before sunrise, the musicians had commenced blowing the surna. Once the sun rose, the kuvarga sounded and after that the karna, nafir, and then the rest of the instruments of the ensemble. After a little pause the surna and nafir were again played. An hour after this early morning naubat, the naqqara was played and then all musicians played the auspicious strain.

It was time for Badshah Salamat to appear on the jharokha but he was in no state. In his entire life after accession, only on very few occasions did he fail to appear for the jharokha to enable the subjects to view him. When Birbal had died in the thirtieth regnal year, when he fell from the elephant in the thirty-fourth year, when he was injured by an antelope in the forty-first year, when Abul Fazl died in the forty-seventh year and now in the last four days of his life. When it would be time for him to appear on the jharokha after his prayers, a large gathering present would claim that let alone eating and drinking, they would not even rinse their mouth without seeing the Emperor.

Badshah Salamat had been read out from his favourite book *Akhlaq-i-Nasiri*—

'The ruler is like a gracious, compassionate and sympathetic father to his subjects. The subject should be like the intelligent son and offer his father obedience and respect. And the subjects should behave like brothers among themselves.'

Before appearing on the balcony for his subjects, Badshah Salamat would wake up every day and pray for five ghari, three ghari devoted to paying attention to clothing and to his toilet. He would hold an open court for a pahar and a half where he would dispense justice and listen to the common man. Every afternoon was spent in the female apartments where he heard petitions. In the Diwan-i-Khas-o-Aam in the afternoon he inspected the animals, took decisions to grant offices or increase mansabs. Special guests and ambassadors presented themselves here. So were the prisoners of war. Usually he spent four ghari here but if the workload demanded, he remained here till sunset. At nighttime, there were assemblies with learned men. When matters of governance demanded more of his time, each day of the week was assigned to a particular activity. Sundays were fixed for the inspection of horses, Mondays for the inspection of camels, mules and bullocks, Tuesdays for inspecting soldiers, Wednesdays for the business of viziership, Thursdays for dispensing justice, Fridays for receiving people and Saturdays for inspecting the elephant stables. To record each utterance and action of Badshah Salamat, two waqianawis—record keepers—were deployed every day.

Now Badshah Salamat was bedridden and the record keepers were idle. They had nothing to record.

A passage from *Bawariq al-ilma*, a book on music, had been read out to Badshah Salamat: 'The tambourine is a reference to the cycle of existing things; the skin which is fitted onto it is a reference to general existence...the striking that takes place on the tambourine is a reference to the descent of the divine visitations...from the innermost arcana...upon general existence to bring forth the things pertaining to the essence from the interior to the exterior.'

Badshah Salamat could recognize each of the instruments of the naubat sounding from the naqqar khana. There were deep and heavy sounds emanating from eighteen damamas, twenty naqqaras, four duhuls, four karnas, nine surnas, two seengs, three sanjs and some nafirs.

The *Bawariq al-ilma* says of a flute-like instrument, 'The nine holes are a reference to the openings in the outer frame, which are nine, viz. the ears, the nostrils, the eyes, the mouth, and the private parts. Nine other holes are inverted from the exterior to the interior, viz. the armpits, the inner part of the elbows, under the knees, the inner part of the wrists and the navel.'

Badshah Salamat himself played the naqqara—the kettledrum—very well. Once in Kashmir, hearing somebody sing, he said, 'The singer is above twenty but below thirty years of age.'

It was found that the singer was twenty-five years old.

The ensemble performed at least two hundred tunes that had been composed by Badshah Salamat himself. A dhrupad sung in the court went:

More endowed with qualities than Lord Indra,
Badshah Salamat has a unique knowledge of raga and sur.
He composes ragas and plays instruments,
The gods and the gandharvas are all enthralled in your assembly,
O master of the masters, Jalaluddin Muhammad,
People find solace when they catch a glimpse of you.

Badshah Salamat had felt very happy to have invited the greatest musician of his time, Tansen, and very sad to bid farewell to him.

'With Pithal departed the assemblies, with Tansen the ragas…' Badshah Salamat thought.

When Miyan Tansen passed away twenty-seven years after coming to the court, all the musicians were ordered to accompany the funeral procession and perform all the way to the graveyard. Badshah Salamat had then remarked that music had died with Tansen. From the royal court to the Vaishnavite circles, Tansen was a popular figure. A popular anecdote was told about him in the Vaishnav sect—

'Tansen was a high-caste man. He had a very good command over the art of singing. He lived in Delhi with Prithvipati—lord of the earth. Tansen was the chief among all the singers. He would sing for all the kings and influential people of the world. He would get hundreds of thousands of rupees in gifts. All were afraid of him since he sang for Prithvipati.

'One day Tansen came to sing for Shri Gosainji, who gave him ten thousand rupees and a small coin of a cawrie. At this Tansen asked, "This ten thousand is fine but what for is this cawrie?"

'Shri Gosainji said, "You are an artiste of the Emperor. So ten thousand for that. And your singing is worth a cawrie in comparison with our singers."

'Tansen said, "How do I believe this?"

'Shri Gosainji summoned Govindswami and asked him to sing. Govindswami sang this line in Raga Sarang—

> *How do I describe the unique personality of the son of*
> *Shri Vallabhacharya.*

'Tansen was mesmerized by this. He thought, "My singing is really no match for his. The reward of a cawrie is appropriate."

'Then, Tansen told Govindswami, "Sir, teach me how to sing."

'Govindswami replied, "We don't even talk to those of other sects."

'Tansen thereafter became a disciple of Shri Gosainji, presented twenty-five thousand rupees and learnt the art of singing from Govindswami. He began to sing for Lord Krishna. Once a month Tansen would go to the Emperor when he mostly stayed at the Mahavan.'

It is said that Badshah Salamat once asked Tansen, 'Who has taught you? Does anyone sing better than you?'

Tansen said, 'Who am I! There is Haridasji Vaishnav in Vrindavan. I am his disciple.'

Tansen then accompanied Badshah Salamat to Vrindavan. After singing himself, Tansen requested Haridas, 'Maharaj, please do sing a bit.'

When Haridasji sang the Raga Megh Malhar, it began raining even in the summer month of Chaitra–Vaishakh.

Tansen was born to a Brahmin, Makrand Pande, in Behat near Gwalior. When they lost many children after birth, Makrand Pande and his wife went to see the Sufi Hazrat Muhammad Ghaus at the insistence of their neighbours. Hazrat Muhammad Ghaus gave an amulet to the wife of Makrand Pande. After some time, they were blessed with a son who later became known as Tansen. When Zain Khan, a singer of the Panna court, reached the court of Jalaluddin Muhammad Akbar and spoke in praise of Tansen, Badshah Salamat dispatched a commander to fetch him.

It is said that Raja Ramchandra of Panna gave a diamond bracelet to Tansen, who promised, 'The right hand that wears this will not rise to accept a gift from anybody else.'

When Tansen stopped on the way to have water, he was shocked to find Raja Ramchandra shouldering the palanquin he was travelling in. Raja Ramchandra said, 'It is our tradition to offer our shoulder to the dead. The Emperor has ensured that you are dead to us.'

Badshah Salamat's own spiritual guide Sheikh Salim Chishti was fond of Tansen. Miyan Tansen had recited to him the poetry he had composed in praise of the Prophet—

Prophet Muhammad is the light of Allah,
Praise be to God, who is a forgiver of sins.
You are present everywhere.
You are matchless,
You are the beginning, the end, the near, the far.
Wherever I see, on land or in the water, I find You,
O Tansen, from earth to the skies, You are present.

Badshah Salamat asked Sheikh Salim Chishti, 'When will you depart from the ephemeral world to the abiding world?'

Placing his hand on the head of Prince Salim, Sheikh Salim Chishti said, 'When the prince, by the instruction of a teacher or in any other way, shall commit something to memory and shall recite it, this will be a sign of my union with God.'

People say that Badshah Salamat gave strict orders that the prince be taught nothing. But after two years and seven months, the unthinkable happened.

An old woman was in attendance on the prince to constantly burn rue to avert the evil eye. On purpose or by mistake, she made Prince Salim memorize the couplet:

O God, open the rosebud of hope,
Display a flower from the everlasting garden.

The prince went to Sheikh Salim Chishti and recited the couplet, who immediately informed Badshah Salamat. That night he caught fever. The next morning, he called Tansen and listened to his singing. He then called for Badshah Salamat and said, 'The promised time of union has come, and I must take leave of you.'

Now Badshah Salamat's own life was waning.

Mullah Abdul Qadir wrote in his secret history:

'On a fixed night, which comes once a year, a great meeting was held of jogis from all parts. This night they called sivrat. The Emperor ate and drank with the principal jogis, who promised him that he should live three of four times as long as ordinary men. His Majesty fully believed it and...it became impressed on his mind as indelibly as though it were engraved on a rock. Fawning court doctors, wisely enough, found proofs for the longevity of the Emperor and said that the cycle of the moon, during which the lives of men are short, was drawing to its close, and that the cycle of Saturn was at hand, with which a new cycle of ages, and consequently the original longevity of mankind, would again commence. Thus they said, it was mentioned in some holy books that men used to live up to the age of one thousand years while in some of their own Sanskrit books the age of men was described as ten thousand years; and in Tibet there was even now a class of lamas or devotees, and recluses, and hermits of China, who live two hundred years, and more. For this reason, His Majesty, in imitation of the usages of these lamas, limited the time he spent in the harem, curtailed his food and drink, but especially abstained from meat. He also shaved the hair of the crown of his head, and let the hair at the sides grow, because he believed that the soul of perfect beings, at the time of death, passes out by the crown—which is the tenth opening of the human body—with a noise resembling thunder, which the dying man may look upon as a proof of his happiness and salvation from sin, and as a sign that his soul by metempsychosis will pass into the body of some grand and mighty king.'

Badshah Salamat failed in his desire to live a thousand years. His condition was now worsening and he even lost his voice.

Many years ago, near the Sutlej river he set out on foot to hunt wild asses with three or four close huntsmen. He kept hunting with his gun and the herd of wild asses led him further on. When Badshah Salamat felt thirsty, he realized that he had come too far away from his entourage. People with him looked around for the water-carrier but could not find him. Badshah Salamat felt such weakness from thirst that he lost his voice. Finally, when the water-carrier was found everybody felt relieved.

Sheikh Abul Fazl said of this, 'A divine message impressed itself by a mystic tongue on the heart of His Majesty that he should consider his own holy person and be more careful in guarding it, for in reality it was watching over mankind at large, or rather it was returning of thanks for divine favours, and the preserving of divine gifts.'

The royal doctor's treatment was not showing any result now.

'If in the ailments of the body which are visible, its physicians have made and do make such errors of treatment, in the disorders of the soul, which is invisible and its remedies scarce attainable, what medicine will avail?' Badshah Salamat thought.

Badshah Salamat was looking at the painting made by the artist Madhu of his atelier. In this painting made in the last regnal year of Badshah Salamat, a bareheaded king stood with folded hands in the presence of Sheikh Najmuddin. A vessel of gold, a sword and a shroud presented by the king lay in front of the Sheikh. The vessel of gold was given as blood money for a murder for which the king was responsible.

Badshah Salamat was being read a book on the miracles in the lives of saints, *Nafahat al-Uns*, written by the Persian poet Jami—

'When Sheikh Najmuddin learnt through his mystical powers that his disciple had spoken disrespectfully of him, he cursed the young man to die. The terrified disciple sought forgiveness. Even though Sheikh Najmuddin forgave him, he could not take back his curse. Soon the Sultan was misled that there is a liaison between Sheikh Najmuddin's disciple and the Sultan's mother. The Sultan got the disciple killed. Hearing this, Sheikh Najmuddin prayed that the kingdom be taken as blood money.'

Jalaluddin Muhammad Akbar looked closely at the sword, the shroud and the vessel of gold.

'Sheikh Najmuddin prophesied that the Sultan would lose his life and property. Soon Changez Khan took over the kingdom.'

Nafahat al-Uns was copied by the excellent calligrapher of the age Ambarin Qalam. The library that Badshah Salamat was leaving behind in this world had twenty-four thousand books that he had commissioned, got calligraphed or acquired.

Badshah Salamat remembered the moment when Jannat Ashiyani Humayun Badshah had returned from Persia and embraced him. Two camels loaded with precious books that had been lost in the battlefield were just then recovered, which doubled the happiness of the occasion for Jannat Ashiyani. Emperor Humayun was fond of taking books—which had to be loaded on camels—into the battlefield. He had lost the *Zafarnama,* the book on the life of Amir Timur, in the Gujarat campaign. This book came into Badshah Salamat's possession three decades later. It was one of those few books which had Badshah Salamat's amateurish writing.

Badshah Salamat was not adept as far as reading and writing were concerned. Sheikh Abul Fazl used to say, 'It is a sign of God that he is so gifted that he did not need to read or write.'

When Badshah Salamat attained the age of four years, four months and four days, Humayun Badshah consulted astrologers for an auspicious time to begin his education. The astrologers came up with a time that they said comes once in many a lifetime. The auspicious time arrived and passed but Mirza Akbar had disappeared and could not be found despite a frantic search.

8

Badshah Salamat's eyes were open yet and were seeking Sheikhu. He also longed for Princes Murad and Daniyal but they were no longer alive.

A short while ago, heart-wrenching news had been received from the Deccan.

When Badshah Salamat learned of the drunkenness of the youngest prince Daniyal, he gave orders for strict vigilance so that he couldn't get wine. In that state Prince Daniyal wept and said to his attendant, 'Put wine in Yaka-u-janaza and bring it to me.'

'Yaka-u-janaza'—that which is like a funeral—was the name Prince Daniyal had given to his favourite gun because he believed that one shot from it could dispatch people to the other world.

When the attendant complied out of greed and brought wine filled in the barrel of the gun, the rust acted as poison. The prince took to bed as soon as he drank from Yaka-u-janaza. His body began to weaken. After an illness of forty days, he departed from the world at the age of thirty-three on the eleventh of March 1605 CE in Badshah Salamat's fiftieth, that is, the last regnal year.

He wrote excellent poetry in Hindi and was a good-looking man. He was born at the residence of a khadim to the dargah of Sheikh Muinuddin Chishti, whose name was Daniyal. Thus the prince was named Daniyal. Before sending the prince to the Deccan, Badshah Salamat married him to Abdur Rahim Khan-i-Khanan's daughter Jana Begum. After becoming a widow, Jana Begum wore white all her life and never used coloured clothing even to cover her head or to dry herself.

The elder brother of Daniyal, Shah Murad died at the age of thirty. Shah Murad had an innocent, chubby face. He had a light moustache and did not keep a beard.

Badshah Salamat had patronized Prince Murad with many advisories. It seemed like yesterday that Badshah Salamat had dispatched him to Malwa and told him:

'The first step is to inquire into what is God's will, in order that right actions may be performed. After that, outward purification is to be pursued. Food and clothing are not to be made ends. Profundity of view is to be exercised. Tyrannical actions are to be abstained from. The rules of moderation and of fitting season are not to be departed from. Every member of the body is to be kept to its proper office. Much speaking and laughing are to be avoided. Sleep is not to exceed one-third part of the day and night. There must be an endeavour to improve the army, and the country, to provide for the safety of the roads, and the obedience of the refractory; and thieves and robbers must be put down. Then attention is to be paid to internal improvement. Lust and wrath must be subjected to the commands of wisdom, for the Creator has placed two sentinels in the palace of the body. The one sees that proper things are done; the other that evil things are abstained from. Out of somnolent intellect human beings have given these two a loose rein, and have made what should be the adornment of life the supplier of death. Do not neglect the knowledge of what is right, and support the power of reason. Preserve the equability of the four humours, and keep far from excess and effect which constitute evil. Use justice and discretion in this daily market of hypocrisy and double-facedness. Study the action of everyone and be not disturbed by seeing improprieties. Let not love or hate, or threats or encouragements, transgress bounds. A frown will affect with many what in other men require sword and dagger. Let not difference of religion interfere with policy, and be not violent in inflicting retribution. Adorn the confidential council with men who know their work. If apologies be made, accept them. Be not stiff in your own opinions. Do not consider anyone suitable for employment as advisor except a far-seeing, right-thinking and disinterested person. Do not make ease your rule and do not reject help in times of distress. Do not be dismayed by repeated failures. Choose the observance of your promises above all advantage to yourself and live so that the crowd of foreigners be not distressed. Especially see to it that merchants have a good opinion of you for their report carries far. Expect from everyone service in proportion to their ability. Be not deceived in your inquiries by eulogizing words. Love is produced by one of four things. First, the idea of worldly advantage. This is slow to come and soon goes. Second, spiritual advantage. This is the opposite of the first. Third, goodness of disposition. This lasts throughout life. Its permanency or its non-existence depends upon wisdom. Fourth, loyalty. One must by the route of this fourfold stream look narrowly into the condition of followers and regulate his actions according to such knowledge. You must study instructive books, and apply your knowledge to practice. Secure the affection of contented hermits and of the matted-haired and barefooted. Be not uplifted by beholding doors who have been robbed of splendour. Apply yourself to sympathizing with the soldier, and give him his pay in due season. Demand from everyone suitable horses, arms and tents for him. Reward good service. Do not lose sight of an old servant. Fail not to encourage husbandmen. For every employment secure truthful and active-minded men so that they may do good work without desire of money, or of greatness or praise. Do not withhold your own supervision from them. Exalt the right-thinking, and admonish and punish the foolish. Be not satisfied in the administration of justice with oaths and witnesses. Make various inquiries and study physiognomy. Do not introduce new customs which yield little advantage and much evil. Make over the passes to brave and experienced men and neglect not the security of the roads. In prosperity remember adversity and prepare remedies for everything. Choose a good companion, and be not offended at his truthful speech. Obey wisdom and refrain from ebullitions of temper.'

After this advice, Badshah Salamat sent Sheikh Abul Fazl to the prince with this message, 'There was spiritual union between father and son though there was physical separation.'

Badshah Salamat did not have Murad and Daniyal in his life any more. Prince Salim was the only son alive. The prince had not yet come to see him. Many moments of joy and sorrow were flashing in the mind of Jalaluddin Muhammad Akbar.

In 1582 CE, in the twenty-seventh regnal year, flowers of gold and silver had been showered from the royal fort to the residence of Abdur Rahim Mirza Khan. Badshah Salamat had appointed Abdur Rahim Mirza Khan the tutor of Prince Salim. For the celebrations, Abdur Rahim Mirza Khan had a dais made for Badshah Salamat that was worth a lakh and a quarter rupees. After Badshah Salamat left the gathering, Abdur Rahim Mirza Khan gave permission for this dais to be plundered by those present. Many nobles carried off precious things from this dais.

In the thirtieth regnal year of Badshah Salamat, a spectacle was seen that was the first of its kind in Hindustan. A prince of the Timuri dynasty rode to the bride's house on horseback. In the time of Babur Badshah and Humayun Badshah, marriages were solemnized in the homes of the groom. During the reign of Jalaluddin Muhammad Akbar the marriage processions of bridegrooms had begun to go to the bride's place. At the age of sixteen, Prince Salim's first matrimonial alliance was made with the family of Raja Bhagwant Das. The rituals of both sides were performed in this wedding. A mahr of two crore tankas was settled on and the qazi performed the nikah. Prince Salim and the daughter of Raja Bhagwant Das circumambulated seven times the sacred fire. On the orders of Badshah Salamat, gold was showered on the palanquin of the bride all along the path from her parent's place to her in-laws' place. Raja Bhagwant Das gave horses, elephants, servants and utensils of gold and silver in dowry.

When Prince Khusrau was born of this wedlock, Prince Salim gave his wife the title of Shah Begum.

Sheikh Abul Fazl wrote, 'The Almighty Creator has adorned the honoured personality of Badshah Salamat with thousands of praiseworthy qualities, and his fortune is daily increasing. But the arrival of everything depends on the movements of the heavens and is associated with a particular time. At this time which was the beginning of the springtime of dominion, with the appearance of a grandson—which is one of the great gifts of God, and the most excellent fruit of age—the universe had new expansion, and mankind had new strength. After the lapse of ten hours and thirty-six minutes, on the twenty-fourth day of the Amurdad month of the Ilahi calendar, the auspicious pearl displayed itself in the city of Lahore, in the bedchamber of Prince Sultan Salim, from the chaste womb of the daughter of Raja Bhagwant Das. The news brought joy, and the age set itself to rejoice.'

Sadly, Khusrau was a source of trouble for Prince Salim. Being the son-in-law of Mirza Aziz Koka and nephew of Raja Man Singh, he had the support of two powerful nobles of the empire. People say that Shah Begum was deeply disillusioned when her son Khusrau showed signs of rebellion, and committed suicide by taking opium. The death of Shah Begum affected Prince Salim so deeply that he did not take food or water for four days. Badshah Salamat sent a firman to offer solace and sent a khilat and a turban taken off his own head, which calmed Prince Salim.

Badshah Salamat was pleased to marry Prince Salim to Mani Bai, the daughter of Mota Raja Udai Singh of Jodhpur. Because she was from Jodhpur, she was called Jodhbai. When Jalaluddin Muhammad Akbar took the marriage party to Jodhpur the grandeur of the wedding became a talking point far and wide and songs were sung about it—

O my father, get fresh bamboo
For the wedding tent.
O my father, get the bamboo from the hills
For the wedding tent
Get the Astrologers,
In midst of everyone.
O my father, as dear is the daughter,
So grand should be the occasion.
There is a pinnacle above the wedding tent,
The kings and nobles gape at it.
Give me an elephant,
O father, you have a large heart.
Give gold and rupees,
And also studded jewellery.
I did not get a comb,
For which my mother-in-law and sister-in-law taunted me.
I was kept in the womb for nine months,
Today I can't be kept any more.
My brother was given a lofty palace,
For me a foreign place.
O father, you keep this place,
I am going to my lover's country.
Our daughter is a slave girl of your palace,
We are your slaves.
Your daughter is the queen of our palace,
And you a noble.

In Jodhpur, Prince Salim's wedding party was received with celebratory songs. The members of the party were garlanded and saffron water sprinkled over them. When the barber lowered the toran—the decorative door hanging—the prince touched it with his sword from his elephant back and completed the ritual. He was permitted to pass from under the toran only after he did so. Due to the rules of seclusion, the arti—welcoming ritual—was performed on behalf of the would-be mother-in-law by the priestess. A garland of turmeric was put four times around the prince, who stood on a silver stool. The woman garlanding the prince then put it around her own neck to signify that the place of the son-in-law is in the heart. After this, at the doorway of the female apartment, the mother-in-law applied curd on the forehead of the prince and tried to catch hold of his nose and pull it. It is said that the bridegroom takes the side of his in-laws for all times to come if the mother-in-law manages to catch the nose. To ward off the evil eye, an arti was then performed, four times from right to left, for the bridegroom.

The priest made a swastika on the bride's hand with vermilion, and placing a silver rupee in henna, joined her hand with that of the bridegroom. Their hands were tied with a colourful thread and a saffron cloth was wrapped around them. After this the bride and the bridegroom paid obeisance to Lord Vinayak. They were then escorted to the chanvari—the enclosure specially made by erecting bamboo on four sides—for the ritual circumambulation of the sacred fire.

The enclosure created by erecting sixteen bamboos was decorated with banana leaves and flowers. Above it were ropes coming in from four directions and tied in the middle. There was a brocade cloth in the centre. Beautiful earthen lamps hung from a rope. In the centre of the enclosure was a big vessel filled with millet, on top of which were eleven vessels. There were two low seats for the bride and the groom. The bride was seated to the right of the groom. A piece of cloth was tied to join the lower end of the embroidered shawl the bride wore over her bridal dress to the shoulder of the bridegroom. The bride's brother took the groom's sword before the circumambulation of the sacred fire began. It was returned once the brother received a gift for it after the fourth round, thus completing the ritual of sala-katari. After the first and second circumambulation of the fire, the bride's maternal uncle performed the sevra—taking one end of the turban clothing in his hand and giving his blessings. In subsequent rounds around the fire, the sevra was performed by the bride's brother. After the third round, the bridegroom took the lead for the fourth. The bride and the bridegroom then, after the fourth round, stood in front of the low seats and the priest gave them a sermon on their duties towards each other. Thereafter the seats of the bride and the groom were interchanged. The bride tipped seven small mounds of rice over with the first finger of her right foot and broke an overturned diya—earthen lamp—by stepping on it. After this, Prince Salim too walked over a stone that was kept next to the earthen lamp. The prince then filled the bride's hair parting with vermilion, a symbol of marital status. At the time of kanyadan—ritual handing over of the daughter—the father of the bride took water in his hand and ceremonially gifted a cow. The hennaed hands of the bride and the groom were then washed in a vessel.

The girl's side sang a song for Jalaluddin Muhammad Akbar—

We have come to inspect the dwelling of Jalla,
Jalal of our couple, Jalal of the doe-eyed
We are here to inspect your dwelling,
Among the kings Rathores are the best,
Among the queens Rani Bhatiyani the best,
Among the cities Jodhpur the best,
Its water bodies have the sweetest water,
What do you have in your place?

The bride was shown the Pole Star so that the marriage be as everlasting as the star. After this the bride and the bridegroom worshipped Lord Vinayak. It was now the turn of the mother-in-law to perform another arti of Prince Salim. In accordance with the tradition, the groom took hold of one end of the mother-in-law's dress. He was given a gift to let go of it. The bride then performed the dyorhi puja, betokening she had always respected the boundary of the house and was now crossing the door—dyorhi—with her husband. Mota Raja Udai Singh and the queen blessed the bride to remain in eternal wedlock. The palanquin was lifted, accompanied by songs of farewell. The palanquin with a golden spire had four extended sticks to carry it with four palanquin-bearers for each of them. But that day, no palanquin-bearer got a chance. Jalaluddin Muhammad Akbar from one side and Prince Salim from the other side took the palanquin on their shoulders. Seeing this the nobles jostled for an opportunity to carry the palanquin of the new bride of the Timuri family to the royal enclosure. Badshah Salamat gave Mani Bai alias Jodhbai the title of Taj Bibi.

In January 1592 CE, in the thirty-sixth regnal year, Taj Bibi gave birth to a son. When Badshah Salamat saw the child on the third day, he was so pleased that he named him Khurram—the happy one. This grandson was so dear to Badshah Salamat that he would seat him on his lap on elephant back and take him hunting.

9

The *Tutinama* was being read out to Badshah Salamat in the royal fort of Agra. Badshah Salamat was fond of this book. It had been written by Ziauddin Naqshabi two centuries ago and had been illustrated in the royal atelier. This was the tale of a young trader who went on a tour, telling his wife Khojasta not to take a step without the permission of his myna and parrot. The myna lost its life when it stopped Khojasta from going to her lover. Now when permission was sought from the parrot, it related a story every night to her so that she stayed home. Of the fifty-two stories of fifty-two nights, people loved listening to the story of the third night the most—

'Two close friends—a goldsmith and a carpenter—find themselves destitute in a foreign place. Pretending to be pious worshippers they steal the temple gold. Once they are back home, the goldsmith hides the entire treasure for himself. The carpenter retaliates by carving a wooden statue of the goldsmith; he then trains two bear cubs to run to the dummy when they see it and rewards them with food every time they do so. Kidnapping the goldsmith's two sons the carpenter pretends they have been turned into bear cubs.'

Badshah Salamat saw in the illustration that under the sharp gaze of the judge, the bear cubs are reaching out to the goldsmith, who is trying to get away.

The storyteller completed the story of the third night—

'The judge finds the carpenter's claim to be valid because he sees the bear cubs greet the goldsmith eagerly. The goldsmith returns two-thirds of the money back to the carpenter and gets his sons back.'

All his life, Badshah Salamat had toiled like labourers. He would quarry stones with the workers and get busy practising crafts with artisans. He even had a small workshop made near his palace in Fatehpur Sikri for making paintings, jewellery, garments, carpets, curtains and even weapons. Badshah Salamat observed it all and even tried his hand to relax himself.

Now confined to bed, Badshah Salamat could only listen to stories. He could not spend time in his workshop, nor go to play polo. Badshah Salamat had set up a city called Nagarchain near Agra for rest and recreation. He loved playing polo here so much that he even played at night. For this, he invented a unique method of setting the wooden ball on fire and turning it into a ball of ember. In the dark, this ball emitted sparks as it was hit.

Sheikh Abul Fazl would say, 'Superficial observers look upon this game as a mere amusement, and consider it mere play; but men of more exalted views see in it a means of learning promptitude and decision. It tests the value of a man, and strengthens the bond of friendship. Strong men learn in playing this game the art of riding; and the animals learn to perform feats of agility and to obey the reins. Hence Badshah Salamat is very fond of this game. Externally, the game adds to the splendour of the court; but viewed from a higher point, it reveals concealed talents.'

Now in this illness, Badshah Salamat expressed a desire to watch an elephant fight. For his amusement a fight was arranged between Prince Salim's elephant Giranbar and his son Prince Khusrau's elephant Aprup.

Badshah Salamat used to say, 'When I came to India I was much attracted by the elephants, and I thought that the use of their extraordinary strength was a prognostication of my universal ascendancy.'

This happened a few years after Badshah Salamat's accession, outside the fort at Agra. Badshah Salamat mounted the ferocious, powerful and ill-tempered elephant Hawai when it was mast. Not just this, he got Hawai to fight another elephant Ranbhaga, which was akin to Hawai in strength. Seeing this the nobles lost their nerve. People called Atka Khan in the hope that Badshah Salamat would pay heed to him. When Atka Khan saw what was happening, he began wailing. Raising his hands, he prayed for the life of Badshah Salamat.

Badshah Salamat said, 'Stop crying. I will drop myself from the elephant if you do not stop.'

Atka Khan's fears were not allayed but there was little he could do.

Beaten by Badshah Salamat's elephant Hawai, Ranbhaga fled. When it mounted the boat-bridge built over Yamuna, Badshah Salamat went in hot pursuit on Hawai. This was too much of a weight for the boat-bridge, which became unstable. The boats were overturned at many points. Attendants jumped into the river so that they could save Badshah Salamat's life. There was chaos all around. Attendants stood holding the insignia of royalty, the saiban and tumantogh on the riverbank as Badshah Salamat sped ahead on the elephant. The Emperor finally stopped only after driving Ranbhaga across the bridge.

Badshah Salamat was only fourteen when he had first mounted an elephant that was mast. After that, in the course of his life, he mounted more than one hundred such elephants, who had killed their mahout, could ruin a city and pose a challenge to an army. He had such a command over an elephant in heat that he could put his foot on its tusk and mount it. Badshah Salamat had a hundred elephants for his personal use.

Now in the last stage of his life, Jalaluddin Muhammad Akbar did not possess enough strength to mount an elephant. He and Prince Khurram sat on the jharokha. Prince Salim and his son Khusrau were on horseback so that they could watch the fight up close. On the orders of Badshah Salamat, Giranbar and Aprup stood facing each other. Giranbar was perhaps more powerful than any other elephant of the royal stable. Aprup too was a mighty beast.

The elephant drivers sat with their feet on the kalava—the rope tied around the elephant. Another tougher rope—dulthi—was bound to the kalava to give it strength. There was a rope that was tied between the neck and the tail, so that when needed it could be pulled to bring the elephant under control. There was a brass chain near the tail and also a bell that dangled from the elephant's behind. Under the dulthi was a cushion to give relief to the elephant. Bound from both sides by a chain, a bell called pitkachchh dangled below the belly. In addition to this, there were six chains each on either side. Three chains were bound to the kalava. Elegant bells were tied to the cloth that was spread on the elephant's back. To add to the grandeur, there was the tail of a Tibetan yak on the tusk, forehead and the neck. For defence and offence, there was armour, over which was spread three-layered clothing. There were rings to strengthen and beautify the tusk. Drivers of both the elephants had an ankush—a small crook—to guide the elephant and also to stop it. Badshah Salamat had devised a method to control the elephant in case one overpowered another and could not be controlled by the mahout. A third elephant was kept ready to separate the two. That day it was the royal elephant Ranmathan which was kept in readiness for this purpose.

Badshah Salamat had also invented many devices to control elephants. The loh langar was a chain that was tied to the elephant's right foot on one end and to a yard-long log, kept near the driver, on the other. This log was dropped when the need arose to control the elephant. In addition, there was a piece of canvas one and a half yards square. Badshah Salamat changed its name from andhiyari—darkness—to ujiyali—light. It was dropped down over the eyes of the elephant to block its vision. Badshah Salamat got three bells attached to this cloth to keep it down.

Badshah Salamat began the use of fire crackers to control a rutting elephant. To make the fire cracker called charkhi, a hollow bamboo stick was filled with gunpowder at both ends. A stick was put into a hole made in the middle of this bamboo at a right angle, which served as a handle. When fire was put to both ends, it would start turning round allowing the elephant to be reined back in.

The fight began and after many rounds of attack, it seemed that Prince Salim's elephant Giranbar had an upper hand. When the royal elephant Ranmathan was brought in to stop the fight, Prince Salim's attendants threw stones and mud at the elephant driver to stop him. Prince Khusrau ran and complained to Badshah Salamat, who asked Prince Khurram, presently seated beside him, to go to Prince Salim.

With utmost politeness, Prince Khurram told his father Prince Salim, 'Shah Baba is saying that you have won this elephant fight. Then why this attack and inappropriate behaviour?'

At this Prince Salim replied, 'We are not aware of this. Neither did we order an attack on the elephant or its driver, nor do we approve of it.'

Prince Khurram replied, 'If it is so, please allow us to separate the elephants with fire crackers and other means.'

Bans—firework rockets—and charkhi were fired, after Prince Salim authorized it, to little effect. Ranmathan and Giranbar jumped into the river fighting. Giranbar was not ready to give up the fight. But a large boat drifted up suddenly between the two elephants, making Giranbar unable to launch any more attacks.

Prince Khurram went back and clarified to Badshah Salamat, 'It was a wrong report. He did not approve or order this.'

Badshah Salamat was, however, left perturbed by this rivalry between his son and grandson. People say his health deteriorated further after this.

Once Badshah Salamat had said, 'We do not agree with what people from olden times say that the prophets are put to greatest trial, followed by saints and then good people. Why would God punish His chosen people?'

Some thinkers present said that God does this to test His people. Expressing surprise at it, Jalaluddin Muhammad Akbar said, 'How far is it correct for Him to test when He knows all that is seen and unseen?'

The person who gave voice to the thoughts of Jalaluddin Muhammad Akbar was not around any more. His voice had been silenced for ever by the heir apparent to the throne.

Some years ago, people at the court were horrified and Badshah Salamat was beside himself when Abul Fazl's representative presented himself with a blue handkerchief round his wrist. In the Timuri tradition, this was an announcement of death.

Before this Badshah Salamat had lost Abul Fazl's brother and a close courtier, Abul Faiz Faizi.

On the midnight of the fifth of October 1595 CE, in the fortieth regnal year, Badshah Salamat had reached the house of Abul Faiz Faizi.

Faizi too had given expression to the thoughts of Badshah Salamat, and had been bestowed the title of 'Malik-us-Shora'—poet laureate—but was now in no state to express himself. Badshah Salamat gently lifted Faizi's head and said, 'Sheikh ji, I have come with Hakim Ali. Will you not speak to me?'

Faizi was just fifty and had been ill for six months. He was unconscious and did not respond to Badshah Salamat.

Now Badshah Salamat threw his turban off and wept and wailed. Then offering words of consolation to Abul Fazl, he left the place.

This was the last time Badshah Salamat saw Faizi. A short while after Badshah Salamat left, Faizi passed away. He had already told his friends in his lifetime:

Do not sprinkle Zam Zam water on the grave of Faizi,
This intoxicated one, who is polluted by all debaucheries, will be purified by fire alone.

On the orders of Badshah Salamat, Faizi had translated *Nal Damyanti, Bhagwad Gita* and Bhaskaracharya's work on arithmetic, *Lilawati*. He wrote a hundred books. He wrote a commentary on the Quran which did not have a single dot.

The learned men said, 'Howsoever learned, nobody has written a commentary without dots.'

Faizi replied, 'Kalma-i-Tayyaba, which is the basis of faith does not have any dot. What more evidence do you need?'

In addition to Arabic and Persian, Faizi was such a great expert of Hindi that his listeners would be left mesmerized. In a poem addressed to Raja Birbal, he says:

At some places a few leaves fall off the tree,
At some places there is a yellowness in the leaves.
At some places all leaves turn yellow,
At some places they fall in a torrent.
At some places the trees shed their clothes,
At some places the shoots turn green.
O Faiz, this gives joy to life,
O Bir, what is the season that has come.

A few years before this when the mother of Sheikh Abul Fazl had passed away, Badshah Salamat had visited his residence and consoled him, 'If people of this world lived for ever and did not only once die, kind friends would not be required to direct their hearts to trust in God and resignation to His will; but no one lives long in the caravanserai of the world, and hence the afflicted do well to accept consolation.'

But Badshah Salamat was not able to come to terms with the death of Abul Fazl. People say Badshah Salamat felt more grief at Abul Fazl's death than at the death of his son.

Badshah Salamat said, 'O Sheikhu ji, you should have killed me if you needed kingship. Why did you kill the Sheikh?'

It is said that if ever there arose any misunderstanding between Badshah Salamat and Sheikh Abul Fazl, the cause was Prince Salim.

One day, Prince Salim saw forty calligraphers copying the Quran and its commentary for divine favour at the residence of Sheikh Abul Fazl. He took all the books and presented them before Badshah Salamat.

Badshah Salamat said, 'He incites me for one thing and does something else when he goes home.'

In 1598 CE in the forty-third regnal year, a distance developed between Sheikh Abul Fazl and Badshah Salamat for some time.

Sheikh Abul Fazl said, 'I withdrew my hand from everything and tucked my foot into my shirt. I shut my door in the face of both stranger and acquaintance. What the ancients used to say, viz. that "Service quickly leads to high dignity, but owing to the triumph of envy even friends rise up as antagonists", and what has not been said, becomes credited. Whenever Badshah Salamat summoned me to the court, and endeavoured to make me carry on my previous duties, I replied, "Since by the wondrous working of fortune, his mystery-knowing heart has become somewhat loaded by the speeches of my old enemies, it is fitting that he leave me to myself, so that I may be lightened of the weight of life. If he held me captive, willing or unwilling, he will obtain only formal service. From the beginning of my years of discretion my mind was not turned to the world; it was princely kindness which bound me to it, whether I wished or not. If he looked for the old zeal, let the Lord of the World sit in judgment. Let him make a thorough inquiry so that my honesty may be made manifest, and the envious be put to shame..."'

When Badshah Salamat's misunderstanding was removed, Abul Fazl thought, 'Do not suspect the farsighted sovereign of shortness of view. Your acuteness and steadiness have been impressed on his mind. Win over the hearts of ill-wishers. What are you thinking of that you should go headlong, and trouble yourself unnecessarily?'

In 1602 CE, in the forty-seventh regnal year of Badshah Salamat, Prince Salim was ordered to crush the rebellion in the east along with Raja Man Singh. Prince Salim did not comply with the order and kept hunting in the vicinity of Allahabad. When he did move towards Agra to present himself before Badshah Salamat, he was misled into stopping at Itawa.

Badshah Salamat wrote from Agra, 'If he is in earnest in his wish to pay his respects, he ought to display his confidence by doing so alone, and dismiss his attendants to their jagirs; if on the contrary, suspicion withheld him, he had better retire to Allahabad, there to re-assure his heart, and repair to court when he was able to do so with full trust and confidence.'

Alarmed at this, Prince Salim sent Mir Sadr-i-Jahan to Badshah Salamat with a message of apology.

Mir Sadr-i-Jahan was an Indian Muslim and belonged to Pihani in Hardoi. Some years ago he had attained the office once held by Sheikh Abd-un-Nabi. Badshah Salamat held him in high esteem. He had become Badshah Salamat's disciple by joining the Din-i-Ilahi. After becoming a disciple, he had taken Badshah Salamat's permission to grow a beard. When it was reported that the ulema were being forcibly sent to Mecca, Sadr-i-Jahan said, 'We fear that our name might be in the list.'

The person making the list replied, 'When did you take God's name that you should be forcibly sent to Mecca?'

When the king of Turan Abdullah Khan Uzbek accused Badshah Salamat of heresy, Mir Sadr-i-Jahan too was sent along with Hakim Humam to dispel this impression. Mir Sadr-i-Jahan also wrote poetry but gave it up after becoming a mufti. Even as a mufti, he had drunk wine in the presence of Badshah Salamat. Along with Sheikh Abd-un-Nabi, he had imparted religious instruction to Prince Salim and the prince was fond of him.

At this moment Mir Sadr-i-Jahan was Badshah Salamat's agent with the prince. Prince Salim sent a message that Sadr-i-Jahan would himself give testimony to his sense of duty and allegiance. After this Prince Salim turned towards Allahabad.

When Badshah Salamat recalled Sheikh Abul Fazl from the Deccan front, Prince Salim felt that Abul Fazl would poison Badshah Salamat's ears if he reached Agra.

Prince Salim sent a message to Bir Singh Bundela of Orchha, 'You would get a handsome reward if you kill Abul Fazl.'

Bir Singh Bundela had already rebelled against Badshah Salamat. He got ready to kill Sheikh Abul Fazl as soon as he got Prince Salim's message. His men waited in ambush at Narwar. When Sheikh Abul Fazl reached Ujjain, he was cautioned to change his route but he did not agree.

On Friday, the twelfth of August 1602 CE, in the forty-seventh regnal year, six miles from Narwar, at Sarai Barar, Bir Singh Bundela's men came forward. The few men who were with Sheikh Abul Fazl recommended to him that it would be better to go back two kos where more troops were present.

Sheikh Abul Fazl said, 'The fear of death is vain, for its period cannot be deferred. I have been raised by my gallantry from the position of the son of a dervish to the rank of nobility. How then shall I basely seek shelter from another?'

His special attendant Gadai Khan Afghan said, 'Soldiers often do this. When the situation is not appropriate to take on the enemy, it is not cowardice to leave the scene and seek revenge at another occasion. We have time. Please leave this dangerous place.'

Sheikh Abul Fazl said, 'I will not run away from this robber.'

According to the poet Keshavdas, who was an advisor and guru to the king of Orchha, and had a high station in the court of Orchha, Gadai Khan Afghan said:

O noble, this is not the place to fight,
Not even by mistake should you face the enemy.
If there is any way possible, you should leave,
Because the Emperor would be happy to see you.
Then with a fresh resolve in your mind,
March against Salim Shah.

To this Sheikh Abul Fazl replied:

Would run if I could,
And how would the enemy allow that.
Look, in my feet are fetters of honour,
And on my head the weight of the Emperor's kindness.
Honour envelops my whole body,
How can one run away.
Hearing this, the pathan let go of the reins,
And the Sheikh unsheathed his sword and charged.

Sheikh Abul Fazl fought gallantly but was besieged. A Rajput soldier of Bir Singh Bundela struck him with a spear in the back with such force that it came out through his breast. The Sheikh tried to leap over a stream on horseback but fell. His attendant Habshi

Jabbar drew him from under his horse and carried him a little off the road. But having located Sheikh Abul Fazl's horse and with further information from the driver of his she-elephant, Bir Singh Bundela reached the spot. Sitting down, he placed Abul Fazl's head on his lap and wiped his face with his cloth.

When the Sheikh opened his eyes a bit, Bir Singh Bundela saluted him while remaining seated and said to his people, 'Get the firman.'

Then Bir Singh Bundela told Sheikh Abul Fazl, 'The all-conquering lord has sent for you courteously.'

When the Sheikh looked at him angrily, Bir Singh replied that he would be carried to safety. But Bir Singh's men informed him that the wounds were so serious that it would not be possible to take him anywhere.

Even in this state Sheikh Abul Fazl took Bir Singh Bundela to task and abused him angrily. Just then Jabbar emerged from behind the trees and launching an attack on Bir Singh Bundela's soldiers killed a few of them. He was about to get to Bir Singh when he was killed. Letting go of Sheikh Abul Fazl's head Bir Singh Bundela rose, and his men cut off the Sheikh's head. Bir Singh Bundela sent this head to Prince Salim in Allahabad.

When Badshah Salamat saw the headless body of the Sheikh, he said,

My Sheikh in his zeal was coming to us
To kiss our feet, but he came without head and feet.

When Prince Salim got the head of Sheikh Abul Fazl, according to the poet Keshav,

Prince Salim said to all,
This is like the killing of a member of the ruling family,
Bir Singh's strong resolve,
Has given us the kingship.
We are indebted to Bir Singh,
He has made our rule strong and stable,
As if the rule of Kabul has been established again,
He has done a deed for the whole world.

Sheikh Abul Fazl departed from the world without completing the history of his 'Insan-i-Kamil'—the Perfect Man.

When Badshah Salamat had commissioned him to write the *Akbarnama*, the Sheikh had said, 'Wings came to my soul, and strength to my tongue, and in an admirable manner I brought the hidden things of the heart from the soul's ocean to the shore of paper.'

Badshah Salamat had instated the Qanoon-i-Waqianawis—record keepers' office—which would record his life in great detail. To write the *Akbarnama*, Abul Fazl read the whole record. In addition, he took testimony of more than twenty intelligent people for each event he wanted to write about. He was amazed that people had a different recollection even of recent happenings. In such cases, he would take Badshah Salamat's view to be the correct one.

Sheikh Abul Fazl placed Jalaluddin Muhammad Akbar on a high spiritual pedestal through the *Akbarnama*. He believed that there was a divine light in Badshah Salamat. That is why the writing of *Akbarnama* was a landmark for Badshah Salamat. On his orders, Govardhan captured the moment when Sheikh Abul Fazl presented the *Akbarnama* to him.

Govardhan had begun his work from the atelier of Badshah Salamat and had then joined the atelier of Prince Salim. By the last days of Badshah Salamat, he came back. He was known for his keen eye and use of light colours.

In the painting made by Govardhan, Badshah Salamat was shown seated on a low golden throne with a red pillow behind him and Abul Fazl, seated a little below, had the second part of *Akbarnama* in his hands. The first part lay on the carpet in front of them. Everybody in the court was looking at Badshah Salamat and Sheikh Abul Fazl. Badshah Salamat wore a red headgear which had a string of white pearls and a sarpech on it. Under a transparent light-coloured jama can be seen a yellow yar-i-pairhan. He wore gems and pearls around his neck and had a dagger with a red sheath and golden hilt in the sash. Sheikh Abul Fazl wore a green shawl over a jama of light colour.

Sheikh Abul Fazl earned great fame in his time and even the poet Keshav, who was close to Bir Singh Bundela, had to say:

He was a firm believer in the dharma, a protector of Brahmins and faiths,
He fought the battle and gave his life for the honour of the Emperor.

Sheikh Abul Fazl was known for his generosity. He was extremely kind. He never withheld anybody's wages, nor did he reduce them, impose a fine or remove anyone. He said, 'People would say Abul Fazl had employed a wrong person and he does not have the capability to estimate people.'

When he was in the Deccan, every day one thousand plates of food were laid for the nobles in a big tent, and in another tent khichdi would be cooked all day for all persons, high and low. Sheikh Abul Fazl was fond of food. It is said that he ate twenty-two ser of food every day but if he found something distasteful in the meal, he would not mention it. He just passed that dish on to his son.

The scale of Prince Salim's rebellion was evident from a painting of Ustad Mansur of the royal atelier. Ustad Mansur had made paintings for *Akbarnama* and *Baburnama* and earned a name for his paintings of birds and animals. When he joined Prince Salim's atelier after working in Badshah Salamat's for many years, something startling happened. In a painting made with Manohar, Prince Salim is shown seated on an elegant throne just like emperors. Prince Salim wore a blue jama with golden work. He had a string of pearls around his neck, a dagger at the waist and a saffron turban. Mansur had made the throne in this painting. On the margin was written: 'Manohar made a likeness of Jamshed upon which Mansur's pen worked. Now without error tell me the year that emerges from these words—"surat badshah"—image of the Emperor.'

This was a phase of rebellion. Master Mansur had likened the prince's image to that of the Emperor and used words the letters of which would numerically yield the current year. Very clearly, Master Mansur was not just favouring the prince's claim to kingship, he was also announcing it.

Jannat Ashiyani Humayun Badshah's sister Gulbadan Begum and Badshah Salamat's mother Maryam Makani Hamida Banu Begum tried hard to get a pardon for Prince Salim. The prince's defiance of royal authority was of a very serious nature but it was not easy for Badshah Salamat to ignore the elderly ladies' request.

Once in the absence of Firdaus Makani Babur Badshah, a cousin of his staged a coup and took over Kabul. This had happened at the instance of Firdaus Makani's step-grandmother Shah Begum.

Despite this, the moment Kabul was reclaimed, Babur Badshah went to Shah Begum and bowing with respect, said, 'If a mother has special affection for one son, why should she denigrate the other son?'

Babur Badshah then said, 'I have come from far and have been awake for long.'

Saying this, he placed his head in the lap of his step-grandmother and went to sleep.

The Timuri dynasty had a long tradition of respecting the elderly ladies of the house. The Emperor bowed to his mother the way all, high and low, bowed to him.

Badshah Salamat forgave the prince for his defiance. Badshah Salamat's wife Salima Sultan Begum was sent with the elephant Fateh Lashkar, a special horse and a robe to fetch the prince. At the request of the prince, Maryam Makani took him by his hand and brought him to Badshah Salamat's feet. When the prince expressed contrition, Badshah Salamat embraced him and ostensibly forgave him. Inwardly Badshah Salamat was still not satisfied with his conduct. Despite this, he took off his own turban and placed it on the head of the prince to allay his fears. When Badshah Salamat counselled the prince and sent him off on a campaign against Rana Pratap, the prince began making excuses as soon as he had travelled ten kos.

Badshah Salamat sent a message: 'It would not be proper to return at a time deemed unfavourable by the astrologers. As you had taken leave at a favourable time, it was better that you should go to Allahabad...'

Now Badshah Salamat began getting disturbing reports from Allahabad. The prince had become excessively addicted to wine. When wine did not suffice to induce intoxication, he added opium to wine. Badshah Salamat learnt that this double intoxication made him ill-tempered. He began awarding severe punishments for minor offences. When it was learnt that the prince had got his waqianawis flayed alive, had a servant beaten so much that he died and castrated one of his pages, Badshah Salamat said, 'Through the course of our rule, we have endeavoured to not hurt even an ant, and are not willing that a sheep should be flayed—though that may appear to be no offence. How has our honoured son the courage to do such things? And how has he ventured to spoil what has been built up by God?'

To bring the prince back on the right path, Badshah Salamat set out through the river route for Allahabad at an auspicious time on the twenty-first of August 1604 CE, in the forty-ninth regnal year. He had travelled a very short distance when the boat got stuck in sand and did not budge for all their effort. So much so that Badshah Salamat was forced to spend the night in the boat. The next day he came to his camp but there was such rain and high wind for three days that save himself and a few intimate servants no one was left with a tent. Badshah Salamat was wondering what to do next when a report was received that his mother Maryam Makani was unwell. But Badshah Salamat decided not to return because he felt Maryam Makani was feigning illness so that no action be taken against her grandson. So he sent his grandson Khurram to find out the truth. Only when Khurram returned and informed him that Maryam Makani was indeed in a serious condition did Badshah Salamat agree to call off his trip to Allahabad and return to Agra.

Badshah Salamat got to see his mother for one last time but could not hear her voice. He called many times but no reply came from Maryam Makani.

Badshah Salamat became lost in his childhood memories. Jannat Ashiyani had returned from Persia and after conquering Kabul had planned a celebration on the occasion of the circumcision of his son Mirza Akbar. When Jannat Ashiyani Humayun Badshah and Maryam Makani Hamida Banu Begum had fled to Persia, Mirza Akbar was about a year old. Now the mother was to meet her son for the first time after her return from Persia. To see whether the son would recognize her or not, Hamida Banu Begum went and sat in the midst of a group of women.

A spectacle of galloping horses was depicted on the wall of the elegant portico. Below the red awning stretched over the portico and outside, guests were enjoying the party. Many women in Chaghatai headgear were dancing to the beat of the daira. There were two people on the nai, one on the surna and three on the naqqara outside the door. One man performed acrobatics with a sword.

The moment finally arrived when a three-and-a-half-year-old

Mirza Akbar entered the assembly. Everybody was wonderstruck when he was able to single out and recognize his mother in the multitude. He went straight and sat in the lap of his mother Hamida Banu Begum.

But now Hamida Banu Begum was going far away from her son. When she did not respond to anything that the son spoke, Jalaluddin Muhammad Akbar stood up from her side. A few days later, on the twenty-ninth of August 1604 CE, in the forty-ninth regnal year, she breathed her last. Badshah Salamat shaved his head, moustache and even the eyebrows. He was the first one to bear the body of Hamida Banu Begum on his shoulder. Nobles followed him. The funeral procession then left for Delhi where she was buried near her husband Jannat Ashiyani Humayun Badshah. Among those who had breastfed Badshah Salamat, Bibi Rupa had passed away fourteen years ago. Her death had deeply saddened Badshah Salamat. Bhawal Anga too had died some years ago. The death of Jiji Anga after her came as yet another terrible shock to Badshah Salamat. He shaved his moustache and head and bore the body on his shoulder.

When Prince Salim heard that Badshah Salamat had gone back, he came to Agra on the pretext of condoling the death. Casting his head at the feet of Badshah Salamat, he presented diamonds worth one lakh, two hundred and nine mohurs weighing a hundred tola each, two hundred mohurs of fifty tola each, three mohurs of twenty tola each and two hundred elephants. Jalaluddin Muhammad Akbar embraced his son but imprisoned him for his defiance. The prince could scarcely muster the courage to meet Badshah Salamat's gaze when the latter rebuked him sharply. In custody, he was deprived of wine. But Badshah Salamat's heart melted after a full ten days of confinement and Prince Salim was released.

10

Badshah Salamat heard a faint noise and saw Khan-i-Azam Mirza Aziz Koka kissing his feet.

Badshah Salamat would often say that Mirza Aziz Koka and he were joined by a stream of milk. After all, his mother Jiji Anga had breastfed Badshah Salamat.

Mirza Aziz Koka understood well the world and its people. He once said, 'A man said something, and I thought it was true. He was vehement about it, and I began to doubt it. When he swore to it, I knew it was a lie.'

Despite such practical wisdom, Mirza Aziz Koka took a startling step.

The problem began when Mirza Aziz Koka came to the court uttering such strong words about Badshah Salamat's religious inclinations that it became a cause célèbre. He then left the court on the pretext that he had vowed to keep a beard and would return only after it grew.

When he did not return for some time, Badshah Salamat wrote to him, 'Has your beard not yet grown that you did not come?'

At this Mirza Aziz Koka replied so insolently that he was dismissed from his office.

One day in the year 1593 CE, in the thirty-ninth regnal year, Mirza Aziz Koka's mother Jiji Anga suddenly came and circled a cup of water over Badshah Salamat's head and then drank it.

Jiji Anga said, 'I dreamt at night that something untoward happened to the Emperor. Now I have taken it upon myself.'

Badshah Salamat said, 'She sees her son in me.'

Mirza Aziz Koka unexpectedly left for Mecca after this with his six sons, six daughters, and their mothers.

Badshah Salamat got Mirza Aziz Koka's message—

'There have been powerful emperors before but nobody has thought of claiming prophethood. Until one has a revealed Book, chosen companions, and miracles, people would never accept it. I can get the title of Azam Khan in the court of the Ottoman sultan for the battles I have fought against the infidels. But I have decided to run a madrasa in His Majesty's name in Mecca. The Emperor may bestow the title of Azam Khan on anybody he wishes.'

Badshah Salamat immediately replied to the letter of Mirza Aziz Koka—

'When we were expecting Aziz Koka to come to the court to pay respects to us, and earn favours, we learnt that he has left for pilgrimage along with his family and attendants without permission. We are surprised that a sincere companion like him has disregarded the rights of the Emperor. It is also surprising that he had left without his mother's permission since divine worship would yield rewards only with her blessings. What caused Mirza Koka to take such a step?

'Aziz Koka's mind is gripped by false fears to such an extent that he has lost his farsightedness. This has led him in a direction that runs contrary to the religious path as also prudence. If he were apprehensive of missing the right season for departure in case of delay in our permission, and his love of God were overwhelming, he could have gone alone. Explaining his reasons, he could then have left his family under our patronage. We would have consented to his request and given his jagirs to his capable sons. Even if Aziz Koka were unmindful of our deep affection for him and consequently did not think of doing this, he could still have sent his family to the Emperor and requested that they be suitably looked after, or he could just have left them under our protection and patronage and left the question of their future to our discretion and they would have been well looked after. Why has he been led to give up the right path?

'We are deeply mindful of the services rendered by Aziz Koka's family, especially by his mother Jiji. Instead of anger, we feel pain at Aziz Koka's folly. However, we would not be affected for long. We would not want him to give up the right path or face annihilation in a foreign land. If only Aziz Koka were aware of one-thousandth part of the affection we have for him, he would not have had needless fears. Do not feel encumbered. To please us and for the sake of your deeply distressed mother you can come back even now. This will save you from grief in this world as also the next one.

'For long we have wanted to send a distinguished ambassador to the Ottoman Sultan to deepen the bonds of love. After this letter we shall write to the Ottoman Sultan. We hope you would return to the court even before the letter reaches him.'

Mullah Abdul Qadir Badayuni said, '... Azam Khan returned from Mecca, where he had suffered much harm at the hands of the sharifs, and throwing away the blessing which he had derived from the pilgrimage, joined immediately on his return, the divine faith, performing the sijda, and following all other rules of discipleship; he cut off his beard... He learnt the rules of the new faith from his reverend Abul Fazl, and received Ghazipur and Hajipur as jagir.'

11

Prince Salim feared a conspiracy by Khusrau's father-in-law Mirza Aziz Koka and maternal uncle Raja Man Singh. So he chose not to alight from his boat at the last moment when he came with the intention of seeing Badshah Salamat. He went back.

Badshah Salamat was still breathing but the nobles knew that the end was near.

Calling all the nobles together, Raja Man Singh and Mirza Aziz Koka said, 'The character of the high and mighty Prince Sultan Salim is well known, and the Emperor's feelings towards him are notorious; for he by no means wishes him to be his successor. We must all agree to put Sultan Khusrau on the throne.'

As soon as this was said, a prominent noble of the empire, Sayyid Khan said, 'Of what do you speak, that in the existence of a prince like Salim Shah, we should place his son upon the throne! This is contrary to the laws and customs of the Chaghatais, and shall never be.'

Prince Salim had returned to his palace but the tide had begun to turn against Khusrau in the fort at Agra. One after another, the nobles began deserting Raja Man Singh and Mirza Aziz Koka.

Oblivious of this, Prince Salim was contemplating fleeing by boat. His close ones had filled him with worry—'Why does Your Highness sit careless here? Your enemies have completed their work, and placed Sultan Khusrau on the throne, and declared that they will point the guns of the fort against this house.'

Just then the nobles began making a beeline for Prince Salim. Now Prince Salim decided to go and see Badshah Salamat along with the prominent nobles.

Badshah Salamat was now nearing the end of his life. Hakim Ali Gilani had given up.

Badshah Salamat had always heeded to the advice of Hakim Ali Gilani. Once when Mirza Asad Beg had presented a huqqa after returning from the Deccan, Badshah Salamat asked the experts of medicine about it.

The experts replied, 'This is not mentioned in our books but this is a new invention and its shoots are brought from China. The doctors of Firang have praised it in their writings.'

Until then Badshah Salamat had neither seen, nor puffed at a huqqa.

When asked, Mirza Aziz Koka said, 'This is tobacco, which is very well known to people in Mecca and Medina. It has been brought as a medicine for Your Majesty.'

When Badshah Salamat began pulling at it, Hakim Ali Gilani tried to dissuade him. Badshah Salamat said, 'Let me have some to please Asad Beg.'

Mirza Asad Beg had spent seventeen years of his life in the service of Sheikh Abul Fazl. After the murder of Sheikh Abul Fazl, he found a place in the court of Badshah Salamat and was sent on many crucial assignments. He had just returned from the Deccan with gifts for Badshah Salamat.

When Badshah Salamat pulled at the huqqa two or three times, Hakim Ali became extremely perturbed. When he tried to stop him again, Badshah Salamat handed the huqqa to Khan-i-Azam Mirza Aziz Koka.

Hakim Ali Gilani said to Badshah Salamat, 'This medicine has not been used before. The hakims have not written about it. What can we tell Badshah Salamat about such unknown things? It is not appropriate for Badshah Salamat to have it.'

Mirza Asad Beg told the Hakim, 'The Firangis are not such fools that they would not know about it. There are such wise people among them who never make mistakes. Without knowing a thing completely how can you arrive at a conclusion that the hakims, the Emperor, important people and the nobles can believe in? Things should be evaluated on the basis of their good and bad qualities.'

Hakim Ali Gilani said, 'We will not follow the Firangis without experiencing it ourselves and take a path our wise people do not agree with.'

Mirza Asad Beg said, 'What a strange thing to say! Every tradition in this world is a new practice some time or the other. From Adam till now, traditions have been built gradually. When a new practice emerges and the people of the world become acquainted with it, it comes to be accepted by everyone. Hakims and the wise men should assess a thing in accordance with its merits and demerits. It is possible that the merit is not visible immediately. In the same manner, this thing grown in China was not found in earlier times. This has been found now and is beneficial in ailments.'

When Asad Beg had spoken, Badshah Salamat said, 'Well said. We should not reject things from wise people of other nations just because they are not in our books. How would we progress if we do this?'

Hakim Gilani would have said more but Badshah Salamat cut him short and called in the Christian priest. The priest praised the tobacco but even he could not convince Hakim Ali. Badshah Salamat, however, did not use the huqqa ever again after that day.

Now every treatment that Hakim Gilani tried had failed. For the first eight days he did not administer any medicine. He did give medicines when the weakness and illness increased, but every medicine had an effect opposite to what was intended. Badshah Salamat longed for Hakim Abul Fath Gilani and Vaidya Narayan Mishra who were not alive. Well-wishers had thought that the death of these physicians meant Badshah Salamat would never again need treatment.

In that state of illness, Badshah Salamat said to Hakim Ali Gilani, 'We raise you from the position of a dervish to lofty rank though you had not performed any service, with the idea that one day you would be of use to us. In the end the opposite appears to be the case.'

When Hakim Ali Gilani gave a most powerful astringent to stop diarrhoea, it caused constipation. To cure constipation, he gave purgatives which again caused diarrhoea. This proved fatal.

Finally, on the twenty-ninth day of the illness, Hakim Ali Gilani stopped treating Badshah Salamat.

On the twenty-fifth of October 1605 CE, the last evening of the last regnal year, time had come for the recitation of the Sura-i-Yaseen—the verse of the Quran that was customarily read to people in their last moments—by his bedside.

The Christian priests waited outside and tried many times to meet Badshah Salamat but this time there was nobody to call them in.

A few days before this when the priests got to know that Badshah Salamat's condition was serious, they came to try one last time to convert him.

Father Jerome Xavier, present at the court of Jalaluddin Muhammad Akbar, wrote what he saw that night—

'After a time, he rose up to go into the mahal, the place of the women, and he went there as if he were in sound health, and with even less signs of weakness than when he was well. He having retired, we remained there awaiting the time when he would return, and when it was midnight, he passed through there again in order to go to the place where he used to pray. We saw him coming without anyone's support and as talkative and smiling as ever, all of which we noted. In the end, we decided that it was not the right moment to talk to him, as he showed no signs of illness, and he retired thereafter in order to pray. At midnight, we came away being persuaded that he was well. The next day in the morning, he showed himself at the window to the people with a very good appearance. What I have described was Saturday night, on Sunday he was well; but on Monday, it began to be said that the King was dying.'

This was the last meeting the Christian priests had with Badshah Salamat.

The priests could not convert Badshah Salamat to Christianity but were successful in extracting many significant concessions.

'Firman of Jalaluddin Muhammad Akbar Badshah Ghazi...'

Badshah Salamat's firman permitting the construction of a church in Khambhat had the names of all emperors from Amir Timur to Jalaluddin Muhammad Akbar on the round seal. Badshah Salamat's name was in the centre. Amir Timur's just above him. In addition to them, the names of Jannat Ashiyani Humayun Badshah, Firdaus Makani Babur Badshah, Umar Sheikh Mirza, Sultan Abu Sayeed Mirza, Sultan Muhammad Mirza, and the third son of Amir Timur, Jalaluddin Miran Shah were inscribed on the seal—

'Whereas it has reached our eminent and holy notice that the Padres of the Holy Society of Jesus wish to build a house of prayer in the city of Khambhat; thereafter an exalted royal mandate proper to be submitted to, has received the dignity and honour of being issued, to the effect that the dignitaries of the city of Khambhat should in no case stand in their way, but should allow them to build a church so that they may engage themselves in their own worship. It is necessary that the order of the Emperor should be obeyed in every way. Written on the twenty-fifth of the month of Farwardin in the forty-second year of the Ilahi era.'

On the fifth of May 1595 CE, in the fortieth regnal year, the Jesuit priests presented themselves at the court for the third time at the invitation of Badshah Salamat. As on the previous two occasions, this time too Badshah Salamat sent a firman to Goa expressing a desire to learn about Christianity. A few years after the departure of Father Antonio Monserrate, Father Rudolf Acquaviva and Father Francis Henriques, priests from Goa reached Lahore, where Badshah Salamat was holding his court at the time. Like the previous mission, they returned empty-handed after spending some time there. Among the priests that came with the third mission from Goa was Father Jerome Xavier, who was related to the first prominent missionary of the Society of Jesus, Father Francis Xavier. Father Jerome Xavier had been in the Society of Jesus for twenty-six years and had spent most of his time at Bassein, Kochi and Goa. Along with Father Jerome Xavier was Benoist de Gois who was born in 1562 CE and was younger than Father Jerome. He stayed at Lahore for eight years and died on the China border. Also among the priests was Emmanuel Pinheiro who was born in 1556 CE. In all he stayed in India for twenty-three years. He was a pastor with a sizable congregation in Lahore. He was involved in religious as also temporal matters. He continued to make efforts to lower the prestige and status of English traders.

Two powerful emperors of the age were watching the activities of the priests for their own reasons. In 1596 CE, Philip II of Spain wrote a letter to Viceroy Matias de Albuquerque—

'Thank the Provincial in Goa for sending men of religion to the Mughal court... Request that our Viceroy may favour such things... Keep me informed about the progress of the mission.'

On the other side, Jalaluddin Muhammad Akbar was so keen to meet the priests that they were asked to present themselves the very next night to their arrival. The three priests, when presented before Badshah Salamat and Prince Salim, felt that Father Rudolf Acquaviva's memory was alive in Badshah Salamat's heart. Badshah Salamat showed them the books that Father Rudolf had presented to him. He also showed them the images of Virgin Mary and Jesus

Christ which had been gifted by Father Rudolf Acquaviva. Seeing the images both the priests folded their hands and fell upon their knees. Seeing them, Prince Salim's son Prince Khusrau also did likewise.

Badshah Salamat smiled and told Prince Salim, 'Look at your son!'

The priests found Badshah Salamat's court much the same as was found by the priests who first arrived there.

Badshah Salamat asked, 'Why did the Turks capture Father Monserrate and treat him so badly?'

Father Xavier said, 'The Saracens and the Turks were sworn enemies of the Christians, especially of the Fathers of the Order, whom they ill-treated in every way possible because of their opposition to the law of Muhammad. Although they ought to love the Fathers because of their desire to show them the true road to salvation.'

Many in the court took offence at this. One of them was a friend of Father Xavier. He said, 'Be more guarded in your language, for there are none but Muhammadans present. When you speak evil of their law, they thirst for your blood. And even I, who am your sincere and firm friend, when I hear you speak ill of our Prophet, am so angered that I could plunge my dagger into your body.'

On the first Christmas after their arrival, Father Benoist de Gois adorned the altar of the new church with such a beautiful crèche representing the birth of Jesus Christ that Hindus and Muslims flocked to see it. A pastorale was played in Persian, in which Hindustani words were used. This gave to many a new idea of the Christians and their law. Many people prostrated themselves before the image of Jesus Christ. Some had come with offerings. One woman said, 'I besought Bibi Maryam to grant me a son; having obtained my desire, I bring this as a thank-offering to her for her goodness.'

It was the Christmas of 1601 CE, which was the forty-sixth regnal year, when Badshah Salamat learnt in Agra that a huge crowd had assembled to see a picture of Virgin Mary. Commoners to nobles, all were going there.

The priests had got this image from Portugal, which was a copy of a picture in Rome. Pope Gregory IX had brought it to Rome when it was affected with plague. It was believed that this picture could cause miracles. The priests had hidden this picture from Badshah Salamat, lest he ask for it.

This picture of the Holy Virgin was placed in the chapel on Christmas. Candles were lit on two sides of it and it was covered with two curtains, one thin and transparent and the other a silk taffeta. A soon as the church was full of people, the curtains were lifted. People were told that Virgin Mary and Jesus Christ had come to show the right path to the world. Such was the impact of this picture that ten thousand people flocked to see it in a day. On the first two days, it was people from the lower strata that came, but after this, the ulema and the nobles did too.

When Badshah Salamat asked for the picture to be brought to him, the priests replied that it would be best to see it in the church. Badshah Salamat agreed but the nobles said that it would be inappropriate for him to go that far. Finally, the picture was brought to Badshah Salamat the next night. The moment the picture was uncovered, Badshah Salamat descended from his throne out of reverence and said, 'Had our father Jannat Ashiyani been presented this picture, he would have granted the giver the highest favour the person could ask for.'

That night Virgin Mary's picture was kept in Badshah Salamat's sleeping apartment so that his wives and daughters may also see it. The next morning the picture was sent back to the church but was brought again at the insistence of Maryam Makani Hamida Banu Begum. It was brought a third time so that artists of Badshah Salamat's atelier could make a copy of it.

Sheikh Abul Fazl said, 'The painters of Firang succeed in drawing figures expressive of the conceptions which the artist has of the mental states, taking one to the place of inner meaning.'

Efforts continued to convert Badshah Salamat to Christianity. In reply Badshah Salamat told Father Xavier that he had tried to find the real divine language but had failed. He told the Father about an experiment conducted two decades ago—

'We caused thirty little infants to be shut up before they had learnt to talk, and had them strictly watched, to prevent the nurses who fed them from teaching them the language of the country, desiring to know by this experiment what language they would speak when they grow up; for we had intended to follow the law of that nation whose language they speak. But when released, it was found that none of the children could utter distinctly or intelligibly a single word; and on this account we decided not to change our faith.'

During this time the rebel Prince Salim wrote in his own hand a letter to Father Xavier. The prince complained that Father Xavier did not send any news about himself. Along with the letter he also sent a black robe. Since the prince was a rebel at the time, as a precaution the priests showed the letter and the robe to Badshah Salamat, who took the robe in his hands and returned it after looking at it.

Prince Salim had an old link to the Christian priests. He had childhood memories of his meetings with Father Monserrate, Father Rudolf and Father Henriques. There was an Italian in the employment of Prince Salim, through whom he assured Father Xavier that he was much like before and had not changed.

Prince Salim told Father Xavier, 'We greatly desire one of you to be with us. If you do not dare come without the permission of Badshah Salamat, we would obtain it for you.'

The Fathers replied, 'This would be the best way for us to come. There is no other way.'

It was the sixteenth day of the month of July 1598 CE, in the forty-fourth regnal year. It was summer. Badshah Salamat's court had shifted from Lahore to Agra and father Xavier had also shifted with him.

Father Xavier had received this letter from the Provincial—

'Since you have now been five years with the King, and have acquired the language of the country, I have no doubt that he is now able to understand you well. Therefore you will humbly beg him, since he has called you to hear the declaration of the Gospel, now to say what he requires of you, so that I may decide how I ought to employ you.'

Finding Badshah Salamat in a favourable mood, Father Xavier said, 'I desire to communicate to you privately.'

When Badshah Salamat took him aside, Father Xavier read out the letter to him and said, 'It is a great trial and grief to us to remain at your court without being able to accomplish anything. We therefore beg Your Majesty to be pleased to listen to us, in accordance with the promise made to us on the day that we arrived at your court, so that you may hear what concerns your salvation, and that you may discover the truth, which you had assured us it is your desire to know.'

After listening to Father Xavier, Badshah Salamat said, 'We acknowledge that we have summoned you in order to understand and know the truth, so that we may embrace and follow the law which we find most in conformity with reason. But now we are proceeding to the Deccan, where we shall halt very close to Goa. We shall then be less occupied with other affairs and shall have leisure to attend to you. It is because of our special desire to speak with and listen to you that you have been sent to me. But how can you say that the time you have spent with us has been profitless, seeing that formerly the Muslims had so much credit in my land that if any had dared to say that Jesus Christ was the true God, he would straightway have been put to death; whereas you are now able to say this, and to preach the same in all security?'

Forced to flee from place to place because of his religious orientation, when Sharif Amuli of Persia finally found refuge in the court of Badshah Salamat, Mullah Abdul Qadir Badayuni said, 'Hindustan is a wide place, where there is an open field for all licentiousness, and no one interferes with another's business so that everyone can do just as he pleases.'

In his letter, Father Xavier wrote of the last years of Badshah Salamat's rule—

'Although the work of spreading Christianity seems to make little progress in this land of the Mogor, where Mahometanism and paganism are so strongly established, nevertheless, through the few Christians dwelling there, our Saviour is often glorified, both by the constancy with which they hold to their faith and by their earnest devotion, which is seen not only among the older Christians at Lahore but among those more recently converted at Agra; for in both these places there are churches and a good number of Christians whose devotion is being stimulated by every means possible. Moreover, the infidels are often deeply impressed when they see the adornment of our churches and the vestments which are used at the divine services; for, by these outward demonstrations, our faith gains much credit among people, who, notwithstanding that they are infidels, frequently, and of their own accord, come to the church, bringing with them offerings, sometimes for our Saviour, and sometimes for his glorious Mother, to whom, in their need, they have recourse as their advocate with God, that, through their intercession, their prayers may be heard.'

The Hindus and Muslims of Lahore posed various kinds of queries to Father Emmanuel Pinheiro.

They would ask, 'We can neither understand nor believe that God could have a son.'

The Father asked, 'Can God hear and see?'

People would say, 'Yes.'

The Father then asked, 'If God has neither eyes nor ears, how is it possible for him to see and hear?'

People would say, 'It is by some means which none could understand.'

Father Emmanuel Pinheiro replied, 'Likewise, in some wonderful manner which none can understand, God has a son.'

It was around this time that the Fathers' relationship with the governor of Lahore, Qulij Khan, and the Hindus of the city became strained.

Qulij Khan's family had served the Chaghatai dynasty over generations. For this reason, Badshah Salamat had high regard for him. His daughter was married to Prince Daniyal.

Khwaja Abul Hasan, the diwan of Deccan and a mansabdar associated with Prince Daniyal, had once remarked, 'Badshah Salamat's skirt is of double wool, while mine is only single, and how wide and large the former is.'

At this Qulij Khan replied, 'Khwaja, beneath your skirt are some hamlets and wasteland, while beneath Badshah Salamat's is a universe; that is why the Emperor has so loose a skirt.'

After reducing the fort of Surat, Badshah Salamat gave Qulij Khan its charge. Thereafter he became a vizier. Sometime after the death of Raja Todar Mal, he became the Diwan. In the forty-fourth regnal year, when Badshah Salamat went to Khandesh, Qulij Khan was left in charge of Agra. He was posted to Punjab in the forty-sixth regnal year.

Qulij Khan was believed to be so pious that a strange tale is heard from a relative of his—

'In the year 1000 of the Hijri calendar, when Jaunpur was assigned to Qulij Khan in fief, he started to lay the foundation for a building. In digging for the foundation a dome came into view. In my presence Qulij Khan spent ten days from morning to evening, in company of a number of noblemen and officers of that city, till the dome was fully visible. Qulij Khan broke the lock weighing a maund which was set on its iron door, and entered the dome along with a huge crowd. A man with a grizzled beard and a wheaty complexion was found seated opposite the qibla in the fashion of the jogis. At the noise of the opening of the door, and of men entering the dome, he raised his head, and asked in Hindi, "Has the incarnation of Raja Ram Chandra taken place?"

'They answered, "It has."

'He asked, "Has Sita, whom Ravan had carried off, returned to Raja Ram Chandra?"

'They replied, "She did."

"Has Krishna avtar appeared in Mathura?"

'They replied, "It was four thousand years ago that he came and departed."

'He asked, "Has Muhammad, the real of the prophets, appeared in Arabia?"

'They replied, "It was a thousand years ago that he departed from the world, and his faith has rendered vain all other faiths."

'He asked, "Is the river Ganga still flowing?"

'They replied, "It is the glory of the world."

'The man then asked them to carry him outside. Qulij Khan set up seven tents close together, and every day the jogi changed from one to the other. On the eighth day he came out, and said his prayers according to the rites of Islam. With sleep and food, he became a different man. He lived for six months. He spoke to no one.'

Qulij Khan was a staunch Sunni. Even as the governor of Lahore, he would take time out every day to spend in a madrasa reading theology. In fact, those in Lahore who wanted to get close to him would diligently study theology.

One day Qulij Khan asked the Fathers, 'How do you regard Jesus Christ?'

The Fathers replied, 'We believe him to be, beyond all question of doubt, the true Son of God.'

Hearing this, Qulij Khan tried to change the topic and began discussing other issues but the priests continued to reiterate their statement by offering arguments.

Qulij Khan said, 'If you do not desist, we would have your heads cut off.'

The Fathers replied, 'If such is your will, we would gladly offer our heads; for it is our intention to confess our faith not only before you, but before the whole world. If we had a thousand lives, we would be ready to sacrifice them all in doing so.'

The matter went out of hand and a furious Qulij Khan said, 'You are vagabonds and you roam the world to cheat mankind. Now you keep to your house, where you are welcome to expound your doctrine to anyone who is sufficiently depraved to seek you out. Never speak ill of Muhammad in our presence.'

The Fathers answered, 'Not only in our house with its doors closed, but in the centre of the city, in its street and open places, nay, on every side, far and near, would we preach the truth of Christian law, for it is for this purpose that we have been sent here.'

Qulij Khan now received complaints from some Hindus of the city. These Hindus wished the Fathers to leave the country and that those who had been converted renounce their faith.

The list of allegations that the Hindus submitted to Qulij Khan is mentioned in a letter written by the Christian priests—

'They placed in his hands a scandalous indictment of the Fathers, in which some of the least crimes imputed to them were that they ate human flesh, stole children and sent them to be sold in Portuguese countries, committed murders, and used spells to make people abandon their law and embrace Christianity... They begged him to sell them a large house which the King had given to the Fathers, and in which a number of Christians were lodged.'

The governor got the Fathers to vacate the house but before any other action could be taken Qulij Khan fell on bad times. His son failed in an important campaign and Qulij Khan became too occupied with this to worry about the Fathers. Upon the recommendation of the Fathers in Agra, the Fathers in Lahore were soon restored their house by a royal firman and the crisis passed.

It was the summer of 1602 CE, in the forty-seventh regnal year. The priests of Agra petitioned Badshah Salamat, 'To ensure that nobody should harass us in future, give us a firman which should proclaim your goodwill towards the Christians, so that all in the empire know that you regard us as your own.'

The Fathers submitted a draft to the person entrusted with the responsibility of drawing up the firman. The draft clearly said, 'All the subjects of His Majesty should know that they are free to become Christians if they so wished, without any person being able to hinder them.'

This draft created commotion in the court.

One courtier said, 'This clause should be deleted from the firman.'

Another courtier said, 'The Fathers have no business to demand such an edict. It was sufficient for them to be able to make converts in the manner they had done hitherto.'

Mirza Aziz Koka himself tried to defer the firman. He had just been conferred the office of the Vakil of the empire and it was his responsibility to prepare the firman and present it to Badshah Salamat for approval. Despite his dilly-dallying, the firman was finally issued because Badshah Salamat had given his word.

Mullah Abdul Qadir Badayuni especially mentioned in his book, 'If a Hindu, child or otherwise, had been made a Musalman against his will, he was to be allowed, if he pleased, to go back to the religion of his fathers. No man should be interfered with on account of his religion, and any one was allowed to go over to any religion he pleased... If any of the infidels chose to build a church, or a synagogue, or idol-temple, or a Parsi "tower of silence", no one was to hinder him.'

A major wish granted, the Fathers thanked God and then Badshah Salamat.

Upon the orders of Badshah Salamat, Father Jerome Xavier wrote a book on the life of Jesus Christ. Father Jerome Xavier began the book with these words:

'Praise be to God, Lord of the universe, Lord of the final reward of the pious, and salutations to Prophet Muhammad and his family and companions.'

Badshah Salamat keenly listened to the book written by Father Jerome Xavier—

'This marvellous and rare book has been written on the qualities of Lord Jesus, the Spirit of God, peace be upon him, son of Lady Mary, may God be content with her. It is called *Mirat al-quds*—the Mirror of Holiness. It is in four parts. The entire life of Lord Jesus, peace be upon him, can be known by reading it, Insha'Allah Ta'la.

'When the miracles of Jesus became known the world over, King Abgar of Edessa had the good fortune to desire an audience with him. So he sent an envoy with this message: "If he comes to my country, I shall present half my kingdom to him." He also sent an expert artist with the envoy so that if the holy person does not wish to come, at least an image could be made of the unique one, which he can see. Otherwise, he would not be able to fulfil his desire to see him. Fortunately, the envoy could meet and convey his master's message. When the envoy learnt that the great one would not be able to go there, the master artist used all skills at his command to create an image as best he could, and felt happy. The next day when he matched the image, he felt embarrassed. He overcame his embarrassment by correcting the mistakes and praised God. When he matched the image on the second and third day he felt even more embarrassed and made the image again. In all, he did this thrice. But the work that would seem complete to him would seem incomplete and full of errors the next day. He felt disheartened. Jesus took mercy upon him and asked him for a piece of cloth when he sought leave. Lord Jesus passed the cloth over his blessed face and returned it to him. The precious image of Jesus got perfectly imprinted on it. The artist happily took the image to his master who accepted it with humility, respect and happiness. Due to this, he gained many victories.'

Hearing the story of King Abgar, it struck Badshah Salamat that it was a name similar to his own.

'I have related this story because when the Emperor, in whom the world finds refuge, heard of miraculous stories of Lord Jesus, he desired to hear them as they were. As a seeker of truth and lover of knowledge, His Majesty asked this most humble self, Father Jeronimo Xavier, who has had the privilege to present himself at the royal threshold, to commit to Persian all that is there in our books about the sayings and actions of Jesus. Believing that I have done this for forty years and have been learning Persian for seven to eight years, I thought I could render this service. I wholeheartedly devoted myself to this work. Ignoring basic necessities of life and without rest, I got down to fulfilling the command of Zill-i-Ilahi—the shadow of God—because anything less than this will not suffice to carry out the royal command, especially in matters the hiding of which from people would be unjust and conveying an act of worship. As the Angel Raphael said to Prophet Tobias, "It is good to keep the secrets of the kings but laudable to clearly tell to all the secrets of God, which would please all." If I took a long time in writing and copying this book, it really was because, many a time, I would give it a shape and think that the book is complete but when I would match the Persian with Latin books, I would be disheartened and find the work incomplete. With great effort, with the blessings of the Lord and good fortune of His Majesty, the Shadow of God, I finally succeeded and felt satisfied, and had the courage to place it before the true ones. May it be the will of Lord Jesus that His Majesty and others who listen to it feel happy with it.

'I can say that of all works that have been translated into Persian in His Majesty's time, this one is notable. I would not know whether something of this nature has been done before this. Those who knew Persian were ignorant of Latin, or those who knew Latin were ignorant of Persian. And mother earth did not give birth to an emperor of lofty fortune as His Majesty, who would know and patronize knowledge so much. I hope His Majesty would approve of this work that this servant has created with hard work, deep devotion and complete submission but also believe that Blessed Jesus said and did these things.

'Let it not be hidden that the book has four parts. The first part relates the life of Lord Jesus from his birth to the beginning of his education. The second part has his miracles and some of his teachings. The third has his death, his sorrows for the salvation of mankind, and his love for human beings. The fourth part has the rising and his ascension to heaven. I have not written all that I could have. I have written just that which His Majesty can know of Lord Jesus. I think this is sufficient because an elephant is known by its footprints and a lion by the prints of its claw.

'Now this humble self submits that my desire to serve be assessed on the basis of my effort. Secondly, it is requested that an order be given for its reading in pious gatherings because it is the foundation of learning goodness, solace to hearts and cure for the souls. If someone has said that books are a medicine for the soul, then this is all the more true for His Majesty's precious soul because Lord Jesus would say, "My words are a medicine for the soul and also for eternal life." So that people have faith in these things, it is necessary for me to say that most of what is written here has been taken from the Gospels, and I have ignored what has been written by others. For better verification, I have written on the margins the source of every quotation so that it can be easily found. A summary is also written on the margins. Some of the sayings of Lord Jesus are so deep that the mind is unable to comprehend them and one gets lost, but this and similar matters are dealt with in another book, *Aina-i-Haqnuma*, much of which is complete, Insha'Allah!

'May Lord Jesus protect His Majesty and give him knowledge of his self which is necessary for his salvation. This is what his servant desires.

'Completed in the sixteen hundred and second year of the Lord, on the fifteenth of Urdibihisht, in the capital city of Agra.'

Mullah Abdul Qadir Badayuni had seen Badshah Salamat at close quarters. He secretly wrote:

'From childhood to manhood, and from manhood to his declining years, the Emperor had combined in himself various phases from various religions and opposite sectarian beliefs, and had made his own all that can be seen and read in books. Thus a faith of a materialistic character became painted on the mirror of his mind and the storehouse of his imagination, and from the general impression this conviction took form, like an engraving upon a stone, that there are wise men to be found and ready at hand in all religions, and men of asceticism, and recipients of revelation and workers of miracles among all nations, and that the Truth is an inhabitant of every place, and that consequently, how could it be right to consider it as confined to one religion or creed and one which had only recently made its appearance and had not endured a thousand years, And why assert one thing and deny another, and claim pre-eminence for that which is not essentially pre-eminent?'

Badshah Salamat clearly wrote to Philip II of Spain, 'As most men are fettered by bonds of tradition, and by imitating the ways followed by their fathers, ancestors, relatives, and acquaintances, everyone continues, without investigating the arguments and reasons to follow the religion in which he was born and educated, thus excluding himself from the possibility of ascertaining the truth, which is the noblest aim of the human intellect. Therefore, we associate at convenient seasons with learned men of all religions, thus deriving profit from their exquisite discourses and exalted aspirations.'

It did not escape people's attention that Badshah Salamat had got the scene of the coronation of Abaqa Khan painted for *Changeznama*. The great-grandson of Changez Khan, Abaqa Khan, ruled Persia and was a Buddhist with close links to Christians. His brother had accepted Islam but his son Arghun Khan was a Buddhist and had a Jewish vizier.

12

An ebbing life was going back to an incident from the past.

As was the practice, the damama was being beaten on the hills of Sikri to call the courtiers to assemble. After doing kornish, the nobles took their place with folded arms.

When Badshah Salamat sat on the throne, it was custom for all to take their place, allocated according to one's status, after performing kornish. Prince Salim stood between one to four yards from Badshah Salamat, and Prince Murad and Prince Daniyal at a distance of one and one-half to six yards, but sometimes Badshah Salamat would out of affection call the youngest prince closer. Beyond this, at a distance of three to fifteen yards, stood those courtiers whom Badshah Salamat thought fit to be given spiritual guidance. Beyond them stood the rest of the nobles and courtiers. The waqianawis would be in attendance to record the proceedings of the court in minute detail. Not just this, those nobles who were not physically present had their representatives in court. Nobles stationed in far-flung places got to know of the proceedings of the darbar through the akhbarat—the dispatches sent by these representatives.

Sheikh Abd-un-Nabi stood before Badshah Salamat like a criminal.

Jalaluddin Muhammad Akbar had borne insults for too long a time. Once Sheikh Abd-un-Nabi had even thrown his staff at him. As Sadr-us-Sudur, he had caused severe resentment in the court and the harem by ordering the death of a Brahmin. He had misguided Badshah Salamat about the number of wives that were allowed to him and created misgivings about him in Mecca. He had openly challenged Badshah Salamat's supremacy in matters of faith. Now Badshah Salamat was convinced that, when it came to scholarship, Sheikh Abd-un-Nabi was an empty vessel.

People would tremble in fear when faced with the anger of Jalaluddin Muhammad Akbar because he could be very severe in his punishments. But quickly forgiving people was also a part of his temperament. Once Badshah Salamat asked a mansabdar to look for a specific place on the Indus where the river could be forded. The mansabdar went upstream twenty-five miles. He asked the people there but could not find a place and thought it pointless to proceed further. He returned and said, 'Your Majesty there is no place where the army could ford the river. A bridge would have to be built.'

Badshah Salamat asked, 'Did you go up to the place I had told you to?'

When Badshah Salamat learnt that the mansabdar had not gone to that spot, he was dragged to that place, bound on an inflated bag of ox-hide and thrown into the river. The entire army saw how he begged Badshah Salamat for his life. When he was carried past the royal pavilion, Badshah Salamat pardoned him and got him auctioned as a slave. A friend of the mansabdar bought him by depositing money in the royal treasury. Later, Badshah Salamat forgave him.

A long time ago Hamid Bakri, the yasawul—officer in charge of arrangements at the court—had fired an arrow at an attendant of the court. When Badshah Salamat learnt of this, a death sentence was pronounced on him. Badshah Salamat gave his own sword to Qulij Khan to execute the sentence. Qulij Khan struck him twice but could not cause any injury. Badshah Salamat accepted that he was destined to live and spared his life. However, as a warning, he was mounted on an ass and paraded.

Many years ago, the rebel Masud Hussain Mirza, along with

about three hundred people, was brought to the court in a strange state. The hides of freshly-slaughtered animals, along with their heads, were sewed onto the naked bodies of the captives. There were so many heads of animals in this gathering that when Badshah Salamat got a painting made of this scene, the line drawing was made by Basawan but colours were filled in by Master Mansur, who was an expert in painting animals. The prisoners were enveloped in the hides of buffalo, deer, blackbuck, camel, bear, monkey, wild goat, cheetah, dog, and horse in such a manner that the heads of the animals were above their heads and the animal skins wrapped around them. Flies buzzed around them as they begged for their lives. It caused much amusement among the courtiers. But Badshah Salamat had ordered that they be freed of the animal hides immediately.

There was to be no forgiveness at the court of Fatehpur Sikri today. Badshah Salamat's anger erupted and he struck a powerful blow on Sheikh Abd-un-Nabi's face.

The Sheikh said, 'Why don't you just strike me with a dagger?'

Sheikh Abd-un-Nabi was handed over to Raja Todar Mal—as if he were a petty employee of the state—so that the money Badshah Salamat had given him when he was leaving for Mecca be investigated and accounted for. After this, he was sent into the custody of Sheikh Abul Fazl—the very man who had once come to him with a petition.

One day in 1584 CE, in the twenty-ninth regnal year, Badshah Salamat learnt that, on the preceding night, someone had strangled Sheikh Abd-un-Nabi to death while he was in the custody of Sheikh Abul Fazl. Nobody had noticed until afternoon that he was dead.

When Sheikh Abd-un-Nabi died, Mullah Abdul Qadir Badayuni said:

Whoever this world fosters,
At last it spills his blood.
What can be the condition of the child,
Whose own mother is its enemy!

When Makhdum-ul-Mulk Abdullah Sultanpuri, who had returned from Mecca with Sheikh Abd-un-Nabi, died at Ahmedabad, his huge wealth was discovered. There was a large quantity of gold buried in the mausoleum he had built for himself. All his gold was deposited in the official treasury, and his family fell on hard times.

Mullah Badayuni had seen Abdullah Sultanpuri's better days and his bad days as well. He said after his death:

'He left behind children who were vagabond and forgettable. And let me say here that this entire generation is born to give cause of complaint to those who have brought them into the world. Indeed, such are the times, what else can you expect. I see no good in the world; this seems to be the age of impotence.'

Badshah Salamat believed that there were three kinds of caravans in this short life. The first was the one that proceeded from fathers to the wombs of mothers. The second was the becoming of a celestial soul and a body descending into clay. The third was the strange condition of the beings who in this variegated abode partook of joy and sorrow, in which the enlightened heart moved on with firm foot, and he who did not understand stayed confused and bewildered.

On the eastern side of the Buland Darwaza of Fatehpur Sikri, Badshah Salamat had inscribed, 'Jesus, peace be upon him, has said, "The World is a bridge; pass over it and do not inhabit it."'

Many years ago, while on a hunt, Badshah Salamat had fallen off the saddle with such force that his face had hit the stones. As soon as he recovered, he said in the court, 'It seems we are about to embark on the last journey but empty-handed.'

Badshah Salamat remembered Raja Birbal's poem—

One begins by rising in the womb,
Ascends the cradle, then gets the lap of the beloved.
Then rides horses and elephants
Draws admiration from friends, envy of enemies,
But is carried on shoulders for the last rites.

13

Sensing movement, Badshah Salamat opened his eyes and saw Prince Salim in front of him. About fifteen years ago, when Badshah Salamat had an ailment of the stomach, his unconscious mumblings had created a suspicion that Prince Salim had tried to poison him—

'Sheikhu ji! The whole empire is yours. Then why have you made this attack on me? To take away my life there was no need of injustice; I would have given it to you, if you had asked me.'

At that time, Prince Salim had deputed some of his own confidants to watch the movements of Prince Murad. The ladies of the harem and Prince Murad told Badshah Salamat about it when he recovered.

Badshah Salamat's life had been spent in the shadow of conspiracies. In childhood there was a fear that he could be poisoned. He had related to Sheikh Abul Fazl an incident about his stepmother Haji Begum—

'The kindness and affection which she showed to me, and my love for her are beyond expression. Every one who did not know the real facts thought that she was my own mother. In my sixth year I was distracted by toothache. She said she had a medicine which she had tested and went off to get it. My mother being a world of vigilance and caution was in agony lest she should give me the medicine, and yet she did not venture to say anything out of respect to His Majesty Jannat Ashiyani. So she tried to take me away to her own house, but I would not leave Haji Begum. Just then she brought the medicine, and as she knew what the state of feeling was, she, in her love to me swallowed some of it without there being any order to that effect, and then rubbed the medicine on my teeth. The minds of the superficial were set at rest, and also my pain was soothed.'

Badshah Salamat did not have strength to punish Prince Salim or even to show affection. On his indication, the crown was placed on Sheikhu's head. The crown of Babur Badshah, Humayun Badshah and of Badshah Jalaluddin Muhammad Akbar now passed on to Salim. Badshah Jalaluddin Muhammad Akbar then pointed to Amir Timur's sword, which Salim presently girded to his waist.

Finally, when Salim prostrated himself before him for the last time, Badshah Salamat gestured weakly, permitting him to leave.

The grandson of Jalaluddin Muhammad Akbar, Prince Khurram, was constantly in attendance, looking after him. Prince Khurram's mother Taj Bibi sent a message repeatedly: 'It is not appropriate to be there in this chaotic atmosphere.'

Prince Khurram sent the message: 'While Shah Baba breathes, the question of leaving him does not arise.'

When Prince Salim came out after seeing Badshah Salamat for the last time, he did not let Khurram stay there any longer. He brought him to his palace.

In his last painting Badshah Salamat is shown in a light-coloured jama. He has an expression of weakness and despair. In the painting made by Manohar, there are no strings of precious stones around his neck, nor any jewels on him. The sash holds no dagger. Behind Jalaluddin Muhammad Akbar stand his two anxious grandsons Khusrau and Khurram.

By now Prince Salim's loyalist Ram Das Kachhwaha had placed his men in the fort and the magazines. Ram Das Kachhwaha came from a humble background. Through his hard work and service, he had come close to Badshah Salamat and become a loyalist. He was always in attendance at the guard room with two hundred Rajputs, because Badshah Salamat had no fixed time for entering or leaving the zenana. Ram Das Kachhwaha was so generous that whatever he gave once as present to any musician or charan was gifted every year. He was so fond of playing the chaupar that he could keep playing for two days at a stretch but would get angry if he lost. When his son Naman Das left the court for his native place without permission, an effort was made to bring him back at the request of Ram Das. But Naman Das resisted coming back and was killed. Ram Das was plunged into grief. Badshah Salamat had himself come to the guard room to console Ram Das. Today, at this crucial juncture, from among the Kachhwahas, Raja Man Singh sided with Prince Khusrau and Ram Das with Prince Salim.

The naubat had just finished sounding from the naqqar khana. This was the last time Badshah Salamat heard the naubat. Despite this proclamation of the stability of the empire and of Badshah Salamat, it was clear that he was not long for this world. The body that was weighed in gold and eleven precious things on his solar birthday and silver and seven kinds of precious things on his lunar birthday, was giving up now.

On the twenty-fifth of October 1605 CE, in the fiftieth regnal year, on the last night of his life, only close relatives and the Sadr-us-Sudur were with Badshah Salamat. People saw that Badshah Salamat was silent. None knew whether he heard or understood the Sura-i-Yaseen—

Does not man see
That it is We Who
Created him from sperm?
Yet behold! he (stands forth)
As an open adversary!

And he makes comparisons
For Us, and forgets his own
(Origin and) Creation:
He says, 'Who can give
Life to (dry) bones
And decomposed ones (at that)?'

Say 'He will give them
Life Who created them
For the first time!
For He fully knows
All creation.

'The same Who produces
For you fire out of
The green tree, when behold!
Ye kindle therewith
(Your own fires)!

'Is not He Who created
The heavens and the earth
Able to create the like
Thereof?'—Yea, indeed!
For He is the Creator Supreme,
Of skill and knowledge (infinite)!

Verily, when He intends
A thing, His Command is,
'Be', and it is!

So glory to Him
In Whose Hands is

The dominion of all things:
And to Him will ye
Be all brought back.

A tear filled his eye and he left this ephemeral world after a rule of fifty years.

The Christian priests' efforts of a quarter of a century bore no fruit. With a heavy heart they said, 'He died as he lived. No one knew in what faith he lived. No one knew in what faith he died.'

On Wednesday morning, the people of Agra saw a strange sight. The wall of Agra Fort was broken and a small gate was created from which the funeral procession of Jalaluddin Muhammad Akbar emerged. For the first time in fifty years, Jalaluddin Muhammad Akbar did not come out of the Shahi Darwaza—the royal gate. The new Emperor of Hindustan, Salim carried his father's bier on his shoulder for some distance and then came back. Bareheaded and barefoot nobles accompanied the funeral procession. On their shoulders Arsh Ashiyani—dweller of the skies—Jalaluddin Muhammad Akbar reached his final destination.

Far away in Jaunpur, Banarsidas was sitting on the stairs of his house when he received the news of Badshah Salamat's death. He said:

In the month of Kartik, Samvat 1662, at the end of the
rainy season,
The great Emperor Akbar passed away at Agra.
At Jaunpur, people felt orphaned when they heard this news.
Scared and distressed, their faces became pale.
Banarsi had been sitting on the stairs when he suddenly learnt
of Akbar's death.
Shocked, he lost control of himself and fainted and fell.
He injured his head and bled, the word 'God' on his lips.
His head hit the stone floor of the courtyard, which turned red.
A cry rose from everybody there; his mother and father were
distressed.
His mother held him in her arms, applied a piece of burnt cloth
to his wound.
Then laying a cot, she put her son on it and wept incessantly.

On the eighth day after the death of Badshah Salamat, the news reached Abdur Rahim Khan-i-Khanan at midnight at Daulatabad in the Deccan. He had been made the governor of Deccan after the death of his son-in-law Prince Daniyal. As soon as he learnt of Badshah Salamat's death, he donned black clothes, called the mansabdars and expressed his condolences. Immediately after this he changed his dress and had the khutba recited in the name of Jahangir Badshah and dispatched his representative to the court with a petition and gifts. Accepting the offering, Emperor Jahangir confirmed him in the viceroyalty of the Deccan and sent him a jewelled sword as a gift.

After some time when a firman was sent to summon him to the court, Abdur Rahim Khan-i-Khanan came out and, after doing taslim, reverentially placed the firman on his head and took it inside.

Jahangir Badshah has himself described what happened when Khan-i-Khanan arrived at the court—

'Delight and happiness had so overpowered him that he did not know whether he came on his head or foot. He threw himself bewildered at my feet. By way of favour and kindness, I lifted up his head and held him in an embrace of kindliness and affection, and kissed his face. He brought me as offerings two strings of pearls and some rubies and emeralds. The value of the jewels was three lakh rupees. Besides these he laid before me many valuable things.'

When Jahangir Badshah learnt that Raja Man Singh was contemplating fleeing to Bengal with his nephew Khusrau, he sent his brother Madhav Singh to him. Madhav Singh asked Man Singh, 'What is the point of such acts against the Emperor!'

Raja Man Singh said, 'What can I do? The prince is young and does not understand these things. I am having to do all this for his satisfaction. I shall bring him if the Emperor promises that no harm will come to him.'

Once the Emperor made this promise, Raja Man Singh reached the court with Prince Khusrau. Emperor Jahangir embraced and kissed Khusrau.

After a few days of mourning, the new emperor left his palace and entered the fort at the head of a procession. The sages of Hindustan had once told him that a person by the name of Nuruddin would become the ruler after the death of Emperor Jalaluddin Muhammad

Akbar. He held his first court and took the name Nuruddin Jahangir Badshah.

Sitting in Jaunpur, Banarsidas said:

Akbar kau nandan baro Sahib Sahi Salem,
Nagar Agre mein takhat baitho Akbar jem.
Naon dharaiyon Noordin Jahangir Sultan,
Phiri duhai muluk mein, bartein jahan tahan aan.

[Akbar's eldest son, Saheb Shah Salim,
Has, in the city of Agra, ascended the throne in Akbar's place,
As Nuruddin Jahangir Sultan.
People are informed all over the kingdom, wherever the
Emperor's writ runs.]

Thus ends the story.

Glossary and Explanations

Adinath Jina: The first Tirthankar according to Jain belief.

Ain-i-Akbari: 'Regulations of Akbar'.

Ajam: Term used to denote *non*-Arab lands and languages.

akashdiya: A lamp that was lit at a tall height in the royal camp.

Akbarnama: 'Book of Akbar'.

alam: A processional standard.

Allahu Akbar: A phrase that means 'God is great'.

Amir: A noble of high rank. Its plural is umra.

Amir-ul-Momineen: The chief of the Muslim community across national boundaries.

Anga: Foster mother who had breastfed the Emperor.

astaghfirullah: 'May Allah forgive'; mentioned as '*stafarla*' by Jesuits. Is uttered to disassociate from blasphemy or other shocking statement/s made in one's presence.

Atka: Foster father; husband of Anga.

Ayat al-Kursi: The 'Throne Verse' of the Quran.

Badshah Salamat: It was the phrase by which the Mughal emperor was addressed. It means the same as 'God Save the King'.

Bakhshi: A military administrative officer.

been: A stringed instrument.

Beg: A title of minor nobility; commander.

Begum: A title of respect for all royal wives and daughters.

bhang: An intoxicant.

bida'at: Innovation; some view, thing or mode of action the like of which did not exist in the Prophet's time.

bigha: A measure of land area.

buyutat: Workshops and stores.

Chaghatai: The Mughals were also called Chaghatai because they traced their lineage to Changez Khan's son Chaghatai.

charan: Bard.

Charvaka: A sect following materialist philosophy.

chaupar: A board game.

Chintamani Parsvnath: Twenty-third Jain Tirthankar who is believed to eliminate pain.

daira: Single-headed frame drum with jingling disks.

dam: One-fortieth of a rupee.

damama: Large bowl-shaped drum.

darbar: Royal court.

Daulat Khana-i-Aam: Hall of public audience.

dharma and *adharma* (in Jainism): Two of the six constituents the universe is composed of, dharma being the medium through which movement is possible and adharma the medium that makes rest and immobility possible.

dharma (in Hinduism): Right behaviour; law; virtue.

Diwan: The minister in charge of the administration of finance.

do-ashiyana manzil: The two-storey tent that the Emperor used when travelling.

duhul: Double-headed cylindrical or barrel-shaped drum.

durood: Prayer in praise of Prophet Muhammad.

faqir: Mendicant.

Farrash Khana: The textile storage department.

farsakh: A distance of about two miles and a quarter.

farzand: Son.

Fatehnama: Edict issued after a victory.

Fatiha: Those ayats (verses) of the Quran which are read for somebody's well-being, on the occasion of beginning a mission or upon the death of a person.

fatwa: It is a formal legal opinion given by a mufti in answer to a question.

fiqh: Islamic jurisprudence.

Firangi: Frenchman; European.

Firdaus Makani: One whose place is in paradise.

firman: Written edict of the Emperor.

ghari: A period of twenty-four minutes.

ghazi: A warrior for faith.

ghichak: Bowed, spiked lute-type stringed instrument.

Govind: Lord Krishna.

guna: Virtue.

Hadith: The record of actions or sayings of Prophet Muhammad and his companions.

hakim: Physician.

Hazrat: An honorific.

huruk: Hourglass-shaped drum with two heads laced together.

Ibadat Khana: House of worship or devotion.

Imam: A preacher; one who leads the congregation in prayer.

Imam-i-Adil: The just leader.

Insha'Allah: 'God willing'.

jagirdar: A person holding an administrative grant of land from which an income is obtained.

Jalla Jalaluhu: 'Exalted be His glory'.

jama: A robe worn by men with a tie fastened under one shoulder.

Jannat Ashiyani: One who is nested in paradise.

jati: Same as yati, a Jain devotee.

jauhar: Rajput custom of women killing themselves when defeat is imminent.

jharokha darshan: The practice that Mughal emperors followed of showing themselves at the window of their balcony early in the morning every day.

jharokha: Balcony.

jizya: A tax imposed on non-Muslims in an Islamic regime.

jogi: Mendicant.

kabaddi: An outdoor game.

kafir: Unbeliever.

Kahaf-ul-Anam: One who gives refuge to the world.

kalawant: A class of musicians.

Kaliyuga: Believed to be one of the four cosmic ages in Hindu belief.

Kalma-i-Tayyaba: The first kalma, belief in which is obligatory on all Muslims.

karna: Horn-type instrument.

karori: Revenue collector.

karta: Doer; creator.

khadim: Literally, attendant. In the context of this novel, those who served the shrines of Sufi saints.

Khair baqa: It means 'the best place'. It is a tradition in Arabic, Persian, and Urdu languages to write words or phrases that total up—each letter having a pre-defined numeral—to yield a figure that stands for a year that is to be commemorated, e.g. birth, death, or date of construction. 'Khair baqa' totalled up yields the figure of 983, which is the year of construction of the mosque built by Sheikh Abd-un-Nabi according to the Hijri calendar. The same logic is applicable to the phrase 'surat badshah' in Mansur's painting which totals to the year in which the painting was made.

Khan-i-Khanan: The highest title a Mughal noble could achieve.

khanqah: A Sufi hospice.

khatib: One who delivers the khutba—sermon—in the mosque.

khilat: Robe of honour.

Khilat-i-Fattahi: Robe given as a reward for victory.

Khurasan: Today's Iran and its neighbouring area was called Khurasan.

khushbu khana: Perfumery.

khutba: Friday sermon at the mosque which mentioned the ruler's name.

koka/kokaltash: Foster brother.

kornish: A formal salute to the emperor.

kufr: Heresy.

Kunwar: Rajput title for prince, heir apparent.

kuvarga: Bowl-shaped drum.

mahabali: Extremely powerful.

mahram: As per sharia, one in whose presence a woman can be without a veil.

mahzarnama: A memorandum.

Malpura: A suburb of Amber.

mansabdar: Mughal civil servant.

Maryam Makani: One who is equivalent in station to Mary.

Maryam Zamani: Mary of the age.

mast: An elephant in heat.

maya: Illusion.

mahr: The gift that the bridegroom gives to the bride at the time of marriage.

Mir Arz: Chief of petitions.

Mir Bakawal: Superintendent of the royal kitchen.

Mir-i-Haj: Leader of the Haj contingent.

Mirza: A princely title given to all Timuri males. Used for Akbar in this work before he became the emperor.

mithqal: A unit of weight equivalent to 4.6 grams.

mlechchha: Non-Aryan.

mridang: Double-headed, barrel-shaped drum.

muezzin: One who gives the azan—call to prayer.

mufti: A canon lawyer of standing who is authorized to issue a fatwa.

mujtahid: One who interprets the Quran and Hadith in accordance with the needs of the times.

mullah: Person leading Muslim prayers.

murid: Disciple; follower.

mushrik: One who worships another besides God.

mut'a: Temporary marrriage.

mutasaddi: General designation for an official.

nafir: Trumpet or horn-like instrument.

nai: Long, vertical, flute-like instrument.

na-mahram: As per sharia, one in whose presence a woman cannot be unless veiled.

naqqar khana: The imperial ensemble; also the place where it is housed.

naqqara: Kettledrum; bowl-shaped drum.

naubat: Imperial ensemble of wind and percussion instruments that performed at particular times of the day.

Nazarene: In the context of this book, a Christian.

neem-qalam: Technique of finishing a painting, usually in fine black and white shading.

nuhbahr: It is the ninth division of a sign, with a planet assigned to each division.

pahar: A watch; a period of three hours.

pargana: District.

parvanchas: Written orders.

pir: Spiritual guide.

Provincial: The leading father in a province who oversaw spiritual and practical matters of fellow Jesuits in that province. He was appointed by the head of the Society of Jesus.

qamargah: A way of hunting in which a large area is surrounded and beaters progressively shrink the circle until the game is trapped in a relatively small area.

qanoongo: Hereditary keeper of revenue records.

qazi: A person who dispenses justice in accordance with Islamic law.

qizilbash: Safavid soldiers.

rabab: Plucked lute, believed to be the precursor of the sarod.

sabat: A path with a protective covering, used during a siege.

sadhvi: Female hermit.

sadra: A Parsi garment believed to protect the wearer from evil.

Sadr-us-Sudur: Chief of all clerics; highest authority in the empire on matters of Islamic faith. Also responsible for land grants to religious persons.

Sahib-i-Qiran: One who is born under a conjunction of the two auspicious planets, Jupiter and Venus. A title of Amir Timur.

saiban/chhatr: Parasol, symbolically held over the Emperor as protection for the subjects.

Samkhya: One of the six major systems of Hindu philosophy, based on a dualism of matter and soul. Samkhya was essentially atheistic.

sanj: Cymbal.

sanyasi: A Hindu ascetic who has abandoned all worldly possessions.

saropa: Headgear and robe.

sarpech: A turban ornament.

seeng: C-shaped, horn-like wind instrument.

sevra: A Jain monk.

Shab-i-barat: The night intervening the 14th and 15th of the Shaban month of the Hijri calendar. It is believed that prayer on this night causes sins to be forgiven and gives manifold rewards.

sheikh: A title of religious dignity; religious divine; complimentary epithet for Indian Muslims.

Sheikh-ul-Islam: A prominent scholar of Islam; one who shows people the path of true faith.

shalghamkhor: Greedy.

Sharif: Title of the ruler of Mecca.

sijda: Prostration.

Subadar: Governor of a province.

sulh-i-kul: A policy of amity for all.

Sultan-i-Adil: The just ruler.

Sultan-ul-Islam: Sultan of Islam.

sunnat: Prophet Muhammad's sayings and his actions.

sura: A chapter of the Quran is called sura. Sections of a sura are called ayats.

Sura-i-Yaseen: Quranic verses that are recited to a person who is on his/her deathbed.

surna: Shawm-like, double-reed, wind instrument.

sayyid: A person who claims descent from Prophet Muhammad through his daughter.

tabaqchi: Person in charge of plates and dishes.

tanka: A coin.

taslim: Formal kowtow before the Emperor.

tasvir khana: Atelier.

tola: Unit of weight often used to measure gold; about ten grams.

Tora: Changez Khan's regulations which the Timuris followed.

toshakchi: Person in charge of the linen.

tuman: Unit of currency of Iran.

tumantogh: Insignia of royalty; emblem of high office.

Turan: Can be equated with Transoxiana.

Twelve Imams: Most Shiite Muslims believe in the Twelve Imams. Hazrat Ali, the fourth caliph, is believed to be the first Imam. They are believed to be the carriers of divine light. Humayun had circumambulated the shrine of Imam Riza, who is the eighth Imam.

ulema: Muslim clerics.

upashray: Resting place.

ustad: Master.

Vaiseshika: One of the six major systems of Hindu philosophy. According to this school, the universe was created from a number of atoms, but these were distinct from the soul.

Vakil: Highest minister at the imperial court.

Vedanta: One of the six major systems of Hindu philosophy, based on the Upanishads.

vilayat: Province.

Vinayak: Lord Ganesha.

waqf: Property earmarked for utilization for religious or charitable purposes.

Waqianama: One of the names by which *Baburnama* is known because we do not know what name Babur gave to it.

waqianawis: Record keeper.

wuzu: Obligatory ablutions before prayer.

yar-i-pairhan: The lower pyjama-like garment worn with the jama.

Yasawul: Officer in charge of the arrangements at the court.

zamindar: Local notable responsible for collecting land revenue from cultivators in an area.

Zam Zam: A sacred wellspring of Mecca.

zenana: Women's quarters in the royal palace.

Zill-i-Ilahi: Shadow of God.

Timeline

1483: Birth of Zahiruddin Muhammad Babur.

1498: Death of Babur's father Umar Sheikh Mirza. Babur's coronation.

1508: Birth of Nasiruddin Muhammad Humayun.

1524: Persian King Shah Tahmasp's coronation.

1526: Ibrahim Lodhi's defeat in the First Battle of Panipat by Babur.

1530: Death of Babur. Coronation of Nasiruddin Muhammad Humayun.

1539: Sher Shah defeats Humayun in the Battle of Chausa.

1540: Sher Shah again defeats Humayun in the Battle of Kannauj.

1541: Humayun's marriage to Hamida Banu Begum.

1542: Birth of Jalaluddin Muhammad Akbar.

1543: Humayun and Hamid Banu Begum leave for Persia. Young Akbar falls into the captivity of his uncles.

1544: Humayun's meeting with Shah Tahmasp, the King of Persia.

1545: Humayun returns. Sher Shah's death.

1553: Kamran Mirza is blinded.

1555: Sikandar Sur is defeated by Humayun at Sirhind.

1556: Death of Humayun. Coronation of Jalaluddin Muhammad Akbar. Hemu seizes Delhi. Hemu's defeat in the Second Battle of Panipat. Coronation of Spain's (and later Portugal's) Emperor Philip II.

1557: Death of Mirza Kamran.

1558: Death of Mirza Askari.

1560: Bairam Khan is relieved of his post.

1561: Bairam Khan is killed. Akbar's victory over Malwa.

1562: Akbar's first visit to Ajmer. Marriage to the daughter of Amber's Raja Bharmal. Death of Adham Khan.

1563: Tax on pilgrimage is abolished.

1564: Assassination attempt on Akbar. Uzbek revolt. Death of twin sons Hasan and Hussain. Construction of Agra Fort begins.

1566: Mirza revolt.

1568: Faizi reaches the court. Chittor victory.

1569: Ranthambhor victory. Birth of Salim.

1570: Murad is born.

1571: Construction of a new city in Sikri begins.

1572: Gujarat victory. Daniyal is born.

1573: A lightning march of nine days from Sikri to Ahmedabad. Ahmedabad victory.

1574: Sheikh Abul Fazl and Mullah Abdul Qadir Badayuni arrive at the court. Attack on Patna. Victory over parts of Bihar and Bengal. To log all the activities of the Emperor a new office of records is established. Coronation of Ottoman emperor Sultan Murad III.

1575: Gulbadan Begum and Salima Sultan Begum leave for Haj. Ibadat Khana built. Weekly debates on religion begin. Navsari's Dastur Mehrji Rana arrives at the court.

1576: Battle of Haldighati. Bengal victory. Persian emperor Shah Tahmasp's death.

1577: A Brahmin from Mathura is given death sentence. A comet is sighted.

1578: A big hunt is organized in Bhera. Akbar's state of trance. Death of Sheikh Mustafa Gujarati.

1579: Akbar attempts to read khutba. Mahzarnama signed. Sheikh Abd-un-Nabi and Abdullah Sultanpuri leave for Mecca. Akbar's last visit to Ajmer.

1580: Mirza Hakim's revolt. Fatwa against Akbar from Jaunpur. First group of Christian missionaries reaches the court.

1581: Mirza Hakim is defeated.

1582: Pope Gregory XIII writes letter to Akbar. Din-i-Ilahi is founded. Persian translation of *Mahabharata* begins. Jain saint Hiravijaya Suri is invited to Fatehpur Sikri.

1583: Victory of Abdullah Khan Uzbek over Balkh region.

1584: Beginning of Ilahi calendar. Assassination of Sheikh Abd-un-Nabi.

1585: Victory of Abdullah Khan Uzbek over Badakhshan. Akbar leaves Sikri. Kabul is annexed after the death of Mirza Hakim.

1586: Abul Fazl is directed to write *Akbarnama*. Victory over Kashmir. Akbar makes Lahore his capital. Raja Birbal is killed.

1587: Birth of Khusrau. Persian translation of *Ramayana*. Coronation of Persia's Shah Abbas.

1589: Death of Raja Todar Mal. Death of Raja Bhagwant Das. Miyan Tansen's death. Victory over Sindh. Translation of *Tuzuk-i-Baburi*.

1591: Second Jesuit mission reaches Lahore.

1592: Qandhar victory. Orissa victory. Birth of Khurram—the future Shah Jahan.

1593: Death of Sheikh Mubarak.

1595: Third Jesuit mission reaches Lahore. Faizi dies. Ottoman emperor Murad III dies.

1598: Abdullah Khan Uzbek's death. Akbar leaves Lahore. Emperor Philip II dies.

1599: Death of Prince Murad.

1600: Ahmednagar is won. Salim revolts.

1601: Akbar returns to Agra.

1602: Sheikh Abul Fazl is assassinated. On Akbar's order, a book is written in Persian on Jesus Christ.

1604: Hamida Banu Begum dies.

1605: Death of Prince Daniyal. Death of Jalaluddin Muhammad Akbar. Coronation of Nuruddin Muhammad Jahangir.

Across the Various Eras: A Converter

Ilahi and Corresponding Hijri, CE and Vikram Dates

Ilahi	*Hijri*	*Common Era*	*Vikram Samvat*
1 Farwardin 1	28 Rabi us-Sani 963	11 March 1556	30 Chaitra 1612
1 Farwardin 2	9 Jamadi ul-Awwal 964	11 March 1557	11 Chaitra 1614
1 Farwardin 3	19 Jamadi ul-Awwal 965	11 March 1558	7 Chaitra 1614
1 Farwardin 4	2 Jamadi us-Sani 966	12 March 1559	3 Chaitra 1616
1 Farwardin 5	13 Jamadi us-Sani 967	11 March 1560	14 Phalgun 1616
1 Farwardin 6	24 Jamadi us-Sani 968	11 March 1561	11 Chaitra 1617
1 Farwardin 7	5 Rajab 969	11 March 1562	6 Chaitra 1619
1 Farwardin 8	16 Rajab 970	11 March 1563	1 Chaitra 1619
1 Farwardin 9	27 Rajab 971	11 March 1564	13/14 Chaitra 1616
1 Farwardin 10	7 Shaban 972	11 March 1565	10 Chaitra 1622
1 Farwardin 11	18 Shaban 973	11 March 1566	5 Chaitra 1622
1 Farwardin 12	30 Shaban 974	11 March 1567	2 Chaitra 1624
1 Farwardin 13	11 Ramzan, 975	11 March 1568	13 Chaitra 1625
1 Farwardin 14	2 Ramzan 976	11 March 1569	9 Chaitra 1625
1 Farwardin 15	3 Shawwal 977	11 March 1570	5 Chaitra 1627
1 Farwardin 16	15 Shawwal 978	12 March 1571	1 Chaitra 1627
1 Farwardin 17	25 Shawwal 979	11 March 1572	12 Chaitra 1628
1 Farwardin 18	6 Ziqad 980	11 March 1573	8 Chaitra 1630
1 Farwardin 19	17 Ziqad 981	11 March 1574	4 Chaitra 1630
1 Farwardin 20	27 Ziqad 982	11 March 1575	14 Chaitra 1631
1 Farwardin 21	9 Zil Hijj 983	11 March 1576	11 Chaitra 1633
1 Farwardin 22	20 Zil Hijj 984	11 March 1577	8 Chaitra 1634
1 Farwardin 23	1 Muharram 986	11 March 1578	3 Chaitra 1635
1 Farwardin 24	13 Muharram 987	11 March 1579	14 Phalgun 1635
1 Farwardin 25	24 Muharram 988	12 March 1580	11 Chaitra 1636
1 Farwardin 26	5 Safar 989	11 March 1581	7 Chaitra 1638
1 Farwardin 27	15 Safar 990	11 March 1582	2 Chaitra 1638
1 Farwardin 28	15 Safar 991	12 March 1583	14 Chaitra 1639
1 Farwardin 29	9 Rabi ul-Awwal 992	11 March 1584	10 Chaitra 1641
1 Farwardin 30	18 Rabi ul-Awwal 993	11 March 1585	6 Chaitra 1641
1 Farwardin 31	29 Rabi ul-Awwal 994	11 March 1586	1 Chaitra 1643
1 Farwardin 32	11 Rabi us-Sani 995	11 March 1587	12 Chaitra 1644
1 Farwardin 33	22 Rabi us-Sani 996	11 March 1588	8 Chaitra 1644

1 Farwardin 34	4 Jamadi ul-Awwal 997	11 March 1589	5 Chaitra 1646
1 Farwardin 35	14 Jamadi ul-Awwal 998	11 March 1590	15 Phalgun 1646
1 Farwardin 36	24 Jamadi ul-Awwal 999	11 March 1591	11 Chaitra 1647
1 Farwardin 37	6 Jamadi us-Sani 1000	11 March 1592	8/9 Chaitra 1649
1 Farwardin 38	4 Jamadi us-Sani 1001	11 March 1593	4 Chaitra 1649
1 Farwardin 39	28 Jamadi us-Sani 1002	11 March 1594	30 Chaitra 1650
1 Farwardin 40	9 Rajab 1003	11 March 1595	10 Chaitra 1652
1 Farwardin 41	21 Rajab 1004	11 March 1596	8 Chaitra 1652
1 Farwardin 42	2 Shaban 1005	11 March 1597	4 Chaitra 1654
1 Farwardin 43	13 Shaban 1006	11 March 1598	14 Phalgun 1654
1 Farwardin 44	23 Shaban 1007	11 March 1599	9/10 Chaitra 1655
1 Farwardin 45	5 Ramzan 1008	11 March 1600	7 Chaitra 1657
1 Farwardin 46	15 Ramzan 1009	11 March 1601	3 Chaitra 1657
1 Farwardin 47	26 Ramzan 1010	11 March 1602	13 Chaitra 1658
1 Farwardin 48	7 Shawwal 1011	11 March 1603	9 Chaitra 1660
1 Farwardin 49	19 Shawwal 1012	11 March 1604	6 Chaitra 1660
1 Farwardin 50	30 Shawwal 1013	11 March 1605	2 Chaitra 1662

Source: Raghubir Sinh, *The Julusi Sanehs of the Mughal Emperors of India, 1556–1857 A.D.*, Sitamau: Shri Natnagar Shodh-Samsthan, 1984.

Note on Sources

This novel has been the product of years of bibliographic and creative engagement with Jalaluddin Muhammad Akbar. My affair with Akbar started early in life. It received an impetus as an undergraduate student of history at St. Stephen's College under the tutelage of the great Amin Saheb (Mohammad Amin). My reading up on Akbar was, therefore, not the 'due diligence' of a novelist to get the historical context right. Akbar to me is as much a product of the imagination of the creative writer as a culled out 'version' from scholarly writings of not only historiographers of medieval India but also of chroniclers contemporary to the life and times of the son of Humayun Badshah.

Since the reading was not confined to the period immediately preceding writing of the novel, it is not possible to recall all the authorities who contributed to my understanding of the person and events around which my creative narrative is woven. I would content myself, therefore, to recalling authorities, scholars, and sources that come to mind and those that figure in my preparatory notes. So the list that follows is detailed but lays no claim to being exhaustive. My deep gratitude to the scholars who have contributed to my quest.

Quotes and information from the *Akbarnama* are primarily derived from the following translations: Henry Beveridge's translation of *The Akbarnama of Abul Fazl*, 3 volumes (Kolkata, 2010); Heinrich Blochmann's translation of *Ain-i-Akbari*, Volume 1 (Kolkata, 2010); Henry Sullivan Jarrett's translation of *Ain-i-Akbari*, Volumes 2 and 3 (Kolkata, 2010). I have also benefited from the *Akbarnama*'s latest translation by Wheeler M. Thackston (and the accompanying Persian text) as published by Harvard University Press, brought out by the Murthy Classical Library of India, Volumes 1, 2, 3, and 4 (London, 2015, 2016, 2017, and 2018 respectively). Unfortunately, its volumes are still coming out as my translation nears completion. I have also consulted the Persian edition of *Ain-i-Akbari* (Aligarh, 2005) by Syed Ahmed Khan. Quotes and information from Mullah Abdul Qadir Badayuni's *Muntakhab-ut-Tawarikh* are mostly derived from George S.A. Ranking's translation (New Delhi, 1990).

For Humayun's life I have relied upon Annette Susannah Beveridge's translation (Delhi, 2011) of *The History of Humayun* by Gulbadan

Begum. I have also benefited from W.M. Thackston's *Three Memoirs of Humayun: Gulbadan Begum's Humayunnama; Jawhar Aftabachi's Tadhkiratul-waqiat; Bayazid Bayat's Tarikh-i Humayun* (California, 2009). I have relied upon A.S. Beveridge's translation of the *Baburnama* (Delhi, 2012) as well as that of W.M. Thackston (New York, 2002). I also consulted Yugjeet Navalpuri's Hindi translation of *Baburnama* (New Delhi, 1991). For the life of Jahangir, I have relied upon Alexander Rogers's translation of *The Tuzuk-i-Jahangiri* (Delhi, 2006). I have also benefited from W.M. Thackston's translation of the *Jahangirnama* (New York, 1999).

Other primary sources that I consulted in the writing as well as translation of this book were Rawat Saraswat's translation of *Dalpat Vilas* (Bikaner, 1960); H. Beveridge's translation of *The Maathir-ul-Umara*, Volumes 1 and 2 (Kolkata, 2003); Tasneem Ahmad's translation of *Tarikh-i-Akbari* (Delhi, 1993); the original Persian text of *Tarikh-i-Akbari* edited by Haji Muinuddin Nadwi, Azhar Ali Dihlawi and Imtiaz Ali Arshi (Rampur, 1962); Brajendranath De's translation, *The Tabaqat-i-Akbari of Khwajah Nizamuddin Ahmad*, Volumes 1, 2 and 3 (Kolkata, 2015); G.M. Wickens's translation of *Akhlaq-i-Nasiri* (New York, 2011); for the original Persian text of the *Akhlaq-i-Nasiri*, the Lucknow edition (1964); H.M. Elliot and John Dowson's translation of *Tarikh-i-Sher Shahi* (Lahore, 2006), and Volumes 5 and 6 of their *History of India, as Told by Its Own Historians* (Delhi, 2014); Rohini Chowdhury's translation of *Ardhkathanak* by Banarsidas (New Delhi, 2009); Baini Prashad's translation of *Qanun-i-Humayuni* (Kolkata, 2011); *Mirat-ul Istelah* edited by Chander Shekhar, Hamidreza Ghelichkani and Houman Yousefdahi (New Delhi, 2013); Gopal Narayan Bahura's *Mancharitavali* (Jaipur, 1990); and Kishori Lal's translation of *Virsinghdev Charit* (Allahabad, 1997).

I found Mansura Haidar's *Mukatabat-i-Allami* (New Delhi, 1998) useful for details of Akbar's diplomatic correspondence with various contemporary rulers. Ishtiaq Ahmad Zilli's *The Mughal State and Culture, 1556–1598* (New Delhi, 2007) is a compilation of select documents of *Munshat-i-Namakin*. I have accessed the Persian original of the Fatehnama-i-Chittor, the fatehnama issued after Ali Quli Khan's defeat, and text of the khutba from this book. John Seyller's *The Adventures of Hamza* (Washington, 2002) has been useful for the tales that were read out to Emperor Akbar, for the passages from *Hamzanama* translated by W.M. Thackston and Akbar's letter to Phillip II in the chapter written by Ebba Koch.

For Akbar's interactions with various religious groups I consulted the following books: for the Jesuits' impression of Akbar, J.S. Hoyland and S.N. Banerjee's *The Commentary of Father Monserrate* (New Delhi, 2003) has been very useful. So was *Akbar and Jesuits* (Delhi, 2008) of Father Pierre Du Jarric. I also found John Correia-Afonso's *Letters from the Mughal Court* (Anand, 1980) useful for the letters of the Jesuit priests at Akbar's court; Pope Gregory XIII's letter to Emperor Akbar has been taken from this book. From Pedro Moura Carvalho's *Mirat al-quds (Mirror of Holiness): A Life of Christ for Emperor Akbar* (Leiden, 2012), I have consulted the Persian original and the English translation by W.M. Thackston. For the Vaishnavite perspective, I have consulted *Chaurasi Vaishnavan Ki Varta* (Mumbai, 2010), as well as its 2008 Lucknow edition which was edited by Kamla Shankar Tripathi, and *Do Sau Baavan Vaishnav ki Varta* (Mumbai, 1996). For the debate between Mahdawi Mustafa Gujarati and the ulema in Akbar's court, I have relied and drawn upon Sheikh Mustafa Gujarati's Persian text *Majalis-i-Khamsa* and its Urdu version (Hyderabad, 1389 Hijri), and its English translation *Five Sessions of Emperor Akbar's Court* by Syed Ziaullah (Hyderabad, 1997). For the Jain perspective on Akbar, I consulted *Bhanuchandra-charita* edited by Mohanlal D. Desai (1941).

Iqtidar Alam Khan's paper 'Akbar's Personality Traits and World Outlook—A Critical Appraisal' in *Akbar and His India* (New Delhi, 2010), edited by Irfan Habib, has been especially useful for getting into the Emperor's mind and for the translation of Salim's firman. Athar Ali's 'The Vision in the Salt Range, 1578: An Interpretation' in his book *Mughal India* (New Delhi, 2006) has also been highly instructive for an understanding of Akbar's state of mind. S.A.A. Rizvi's *Religious and Intellectual History of the Muslims in Akbar's Reign* (New Delhi, 1975) and his *A History of Sufism in India* (New Delhi, 2009) and *Muslim Revivalist Movements in Northern India* (New Delhi, 2014) have been particularly useful for their detail and translated passages from primary sources regarding issues of faith during Akbar's reign. Iqtidar Alam Khan's works, *The Political Biography of a Mughal Noble: Munim Khan Khan-i Khanan* (New Delhi, 1991), *India's Polity in the Age of Akbar* (Ranikhet, 2016), and *The Mughal Nobility* (Ranikhet, 2016), in addition to details, have also been useful for translated passages from primary sources. A. Azfar Moin's *The Millennial Sovereign* (Delhi, 2017) was particularly useful in clarifying issues around the Islamic millennium, for details of Humayun's time in Persia and also translations of primary source material. Khaliq Ahmad Nizami's *Akbar and Religion* (Delhi,

1989) was instructive for translated passages of primary works. Naimur Rehman Farooqi's *Mughal–Ottoman Relations* (Delhi, 1989) has been useful for its translation of primary sources as well.

Other works that I consulted for insight into the political and administrative, as well as economic and cultural aspects of Akbar's world are Jivanji Jamshedji Modi's *The Parsees at the Court of Akbar and Dastur Meherjee Rana* (Mumbai, 1903); Hariharniwas Dwivedi's *Tansen* (Gwalior, 1986); Chhotubhai Ranchhodji Naik's *Abdur-Rahim Khan-i-Khanan and His Literary Circle* (Ahmedabad,1966); Parmeshwar Prasad Sinha's *Raja Birbal* (Patna, 1980); Rajiv Nain Prasad's *Raja Man Singh of Amber* (Kolkata, 1966); Derryl N. MacLean's 'Real Men and False Men at the Court of Akbar' in *Beyond Turk and Hindu* (Florida, 2000), edited by David Gilmartin and Bruce B. Lawrence; Sukumar Ray's *Humayun in Persia* (Kolkata, 2002); Shireen Moosvi's *Episodes in the Life of Akbar* (New Delhi, 2010); Ellen Smart's 'Akbar, Illiterate Genius' in *Kaladarsana* (New Delhi, 1981), edited by Joanna C. Williams; Jyotiprasad Jain's *Pramukh Etihasik Jain Purush aur Mahilayein* (Delhi, 2000); Ishtiaq Husain Qureshi's *The Administration of the Mughal Empire* (Delhi, 2010); Ibn Hasan's *The Central Structure of the Mughal Empire* (New Delhi, 2001); Abdul Aziz's *The Mughal Court and Its Institutions* (Lahore, 2002); Mubarak Ali's *The Court of the Great Mughals* (Lahore, 2014); William Irvine's *The Army of the Indian Mughals* (Delhi, 2012); Jos Gommans's *Mughal Warfare* (London, 2002); Irfan Habib's *The Agrarian System of Mughal India* (New Delhi, 2010); Mahendra Singh Nagar's *Marwar ke Rajvansh ki Sanskritik Paramaparayein* (Jodhpur, 2011); Ramnarayan Dugar's translation of *Munhnot Nainsi Ki Khyat* (Jodhpur, 2010); Rajendra Shankar Bhatt's *Mewar ke Maharana aur Shahanshah Akbar* (Jaipur, 2002); and Madhukanta Sharma's 'Akbar–Rajput Sambandh (Samsamayik Granth *Dalpat Vilas* Ke Vishesh Sandarbh Mein)' in *Akbar-kaleen Bharat* (Jaipur, 2007), edited by Ramnath Pandey; Kishori Lal's translation of *Virsinghdev Charit* (Allahabad, 1997); Shyamaldas's *Veer Vinod* (Udaipur, 2007); James Tod's *Annals and Antiquities of Rajasthan* (New Delhi, 2011); Azra Alavi's *Socio-Religious Outlook of Abul Fazl* (Delhi, 1983); Sri Ram Sharma's *The Religious Policy of the Mughal Emperors* (New Delhi, 1988); Afzal Husain's *The Nobility under Akbar and Jahangir* (New Delhi, 1999); Allison Busch's *Poetry of Kings* (New York, 2011); Ramchandra Shukla's *Hindi Sahitya ka Itihas* (New Delhi, 2009); Satyaprakash Mishra's *Rahim Rachnavali* (Allahabad, 2004); Shailesh Zaidi's *Hindi ke Katipay Musalman Kavi* (Aligarh, 1977); S.M. Ikram's

Rud-i-Kausar (Delhi, 2004); I.H. Qureshi's *Akbar* (Delhi, 1987); Satish Chandra's *Essays on Medieval Indian History* (New Delhi, 2005); Sanjay Subrahmanyam's *Explorations in Connected History* (New Delhi, 2011); Pius Malekandathil's *The Mughals, The Portuguese and the Indian Ocean* (Delhi, 2013); Satish Chandra's *Medieval India* (New Delhi, 2014); Raghubir Sinh's *The Julusi Sanehs of the Mughal Emperors of India* (Sitamau, 1984); *Princely Historian* (Jaipur, 1994), edited by Manohar Sinh Ranawat; C.M. Naim's 'Popular Jokes and Political History—The Case of Akbar, Birbal and Mulla Do-Piyaza' in *Economic and Political Weekly*, vol. 30, no. 24 (17 June 1995); Muhammad Hussain Azad's *Darbar-i-Akbari* (New Delhi, 2010); Bashiruddin Ahmed's *Waqiat-i-Darul Hukumat Dehli* (Delhi, 2001); S.A.A. Rizvi's *Mughalkaleen Bharat—Babur* (New Delhi 2010); Harbans Mukhia's *The Mughals of India* (New Delhi, 2009); Gian Carlo Calza's *Akbar* (Milano, 2012); Athar Ali's *The Apparatus of Empire* (Delhi, 1985); Irfan Habib's *Atlas of Mughal Empire* (New Delhi, 1986); Ziauddin Sardar's *Mecca* (New Delhi, 2014); Linda Woodhead's *Christianity: A Very Short Introduction* (Oxford, 2014). S.H. Prater's *The Book of Indian Animals* (Mumbai, 2005) helped me fill the gaps in zoological detail required particularly for the hunting scenes in the novel.

For the history of Akbar's ancestors I consulted the following: Jack Weatherford's *Genghis Khan and the Making of the Modern World* (New York, 2004); David Morgan's *The Mongols* (Victoria, 2007); Justin Marozzi's *Tamerlane* (London, 2005); and Beatrice Forbes Manz's *The Rise and Rule of Tamerlane* (Cambridge, 1999).

Michael Brand and Glenn D. Lowry's *Akbar's India: Art from the Mughal City of Victory* (New York, 1985) was useful for its translations from primary works and detailed descriptions. *Fatehpur Sikri* (Massachusetts, 1985) by the same authors, in addition to architectural details, was useful for translated passages from primary works including Arif Qandhari's *Tarikh-i-Akbari*. For further information on the built heritage, particularly the imperial capital Fatehpur Sikri, I consulted Syed Ali Nadeem Rezavi's *Fatehpur Sikri Revisited* (New Delhi, 2013); in addition to architectural details, it was also useful for the translated passages from primary works. I must also mention here Centre for Cultural Resources and Training's *Fatehpur Sikri* (New Delhi, 2012) and Lucy Peck's *Fatehpur Sikri* (New Delhi, 2014). Catherine B. Asher's *The New Cambridge History of India*, Volume 1, Part 4 (New Delhi, 1995) and Ebba Koch's *Mughal Architecture* (New Delhi, 2002) were also useful for the architectural details they provide. For the monuments of Delhi in particular, I consulted *Delhi: The Built Heritage—A Listing* (New Delhi, 1999) and Maulvi Zafar Hasan's *Monuments of Delhi*, 3 volumes (New Delhi, 2008).

In addition to details on music, Bonnie C. Wade's *Imaging Sound* (Chicago, 1998) was also useful for its translated passages, including those from the *Bawariq al-ilma*, glossary and the Mughal miniatures. I also consulted, for Mughal art and information on it, Susan Strong's *Painting for the Mughal Emperor* (London, 2002); B.N. Goswamy's *Painted Visions* (New Delhi, 1999); John Guy and Deborah Swallow's *Arts of India* (London, 2004); Rosemary Crill and Kapil Jariwala's *The Indian Portrait* (Ahmedabad, 2010); *The Art of Play* (Mumbai, 2006) edited by Andrew Topsfield; Milo Cleveland Beach's *The Imperial Image* (Ahmedabad, 2012); *Masters of Indian Painting* (2011), edited by Milo C. Beach, Eberhard Fischer and B.N. Goswamy; Som Pal Verma's *Painting the Mughal Experience* (New Delhi, 2005) and *Mughal Painters and their Work* (Delhi, 1994); Linda York Leach's *Mughal and Other Indian Paintings* (London, 1995), which has been useful for the text of *Nafahat al-Uns* and the *Tutinama* story as read out to the Emperor in this novel, in addition to Mughal miniatures and their details; K.K. Aziz's *The Meaning of Islamic Art* (Lahore, 2004); Kalpana Desai's *Jewels on the Crescent* (Mumbai, 2002); Andrew Topsfield's *Indian Paintings* (Oxford, 1994), which has been useful for the story *Husn-o-Dil* as read out to the Emperor in the novel; Nasser D. Khalili's *The Timeline History of Islamic Art and Architecture* (2005); Toby Falk and Mildred Archer's *Indian Miniatures in the India Office Library* (London, 1981); Barbara Schmitz and Ziaud-Din Desai's *Mughal and Persian Paintings and Illustrated Manuscripts in The Raza Library, Rampur* (New Delhi, 2006); B.N. Goswamy's *The Spirit of Indian Painting* (New Delhi, 2014) and *Indian Costumes in the Collection of the Calico Museum of Textiles* (Ahmedabad, 2010); Asok Kumar Das's *Wonders of Nature: Ustad Mansur at the Mughal Court* (Mumbai, 2012); B.N. Goswamy's *Patkas in the collection of the Calico Museum of Textiles* (Ahmedabad, 2008); Usha R. Bala Krishnan and Meera Sushil Kumar's *Dance of the Peacock* (Mumbai, 1999); Daniel Walker's *Flowers Underfoot* (London, 1998); Amina Okada's *Indian Miniatures of the Mughal Court* (New York); Amin Jaffer's *Beyond Extravagance* (New York, 2013); and Eleanor Sims's *Peerless Images* (Ahmedabad, 2002).

Gratitude

A large number of friends, colleagues and patrons helped me in every possible manner. I am deeply grateful to Dr Amit Gupta and his colleagues at Oxford for estimating for me Akbar's height on the basis of the specifications of his armour; Sajid Shapoo (New York City) for throwing light on Islamic issues and being with me in this exploratory journey; Naved Masood (Delhi) for simplifying for me the complexities of history and language and opening the doors of knowledge; Madhuker Upadhyay (Delhi) for throwing light on the intricacies of language and literature; Prof Harbans Mukhia (Gurgaon) for explaining the court protocol; Dr Vishwanath Tripathi, Kumar Anupam, Ravikant and Vijay Vidrohi (Delhi) for helping translate documents in Braj and Awadhi languages; Manish Sharma and Bhanwardan Ratnu (Jaipur) and Dr Mahendra Singh Tanvar and Karni Singh Jassol (Jodhpur) for explaining the meaning of documents from Rajasthan; Brajesh Kumar Singh for explaining the meaning of documents from Gujarat; Pavan Sinha (Delhi) for explaining Akbar's horoscope; Dr Abdus Salam Jeelani (Aligarh) for translation of original Persian documents; Prof Iqtidar Alam Khan for explaining the intricacies of Akbar's period; Pankaj Rag (Delhi), Deepika Pokharna (Rampur Raza Library), and Jayanta Sengupta (Indian Museum, Kolkata) for help in procuring images; Prof S.P. Verma (Aligarh) for helping understand the paintings of that period; Divyabhanusinh Chavda (Jaipur), Dr Mahesh Rangarajan and Nitya Ramakrishnan (Delhi) for helping identify the animals struck in the hunters' siege; Dr Feroz Ahmed (Istanbul) for throwing light on Turkish and Mongol antecedents of the Mughals; Father Francis Dibrito (Mumbai) for explaining the meaning of Christian terms; Professor Bhagirathi Nand (Delhi) for translating Sanskrit documents; Dr Ali Nadeem Rezavi for answering queries related to Fatehpur Sikri; Dr Muhammad Mudassir (Goa), Kishore Ajwani, and Radhika Bordia (Delhi) for clarification on European names; and for finding solutions to the various issues that came up while writing this book, Deepak Sareen (Jaipur), Khalid bin Umar (Dubai), Danish Khan (Oxford), Ejazurrehman, Prof Najaf Haider (Delhi), Dr Muhammad Sajjad (Aligarh), Abhijit Das, Rajiv Khandekar (Mumbai), Suman De (Kolkata), Pankaj Jha (Lucknow), Prakash Kumar (Patna), Jagwinder Patial (Chandigarh), Abhilash Kumar, Anirudh Sarkar, Abhishek Upadhyay, Rishi Sinha, Yasser Usman, Ravi Goel, Rajnish Ahuja, and Milind Khandekar (Delhi).